THEY KNOW
IF YOU'VE BEEN BAD OR GOOD

Also by Alta Hensley

NAUGHTY OR NICE
He Sees You When You're Sleeping
He Knows When You're Awake

Songbird in the Gallows
Heathens
Villains Are Made
Sucker Punch

THEY KNOW IF YOU'VE BEEN BAD OR GOOD

A Naughty or Nice Novel

ALTA HENSLEY

An Imprint of HarperCollins*Publishers*

HarperCollins books may be purchased for educational, business, or sales promotional use. For information, please email the Special Markets Department at SPsales@harpercollins.com.

hc.com

FIRST EDITION

Interior text design by Diahann Sturge-Campbell

Fir branch illustration © Andrei/Stock.Adobe.com
Christmas lights illustration © Galih/Stock.Adobe.com
Candy cane illustration © Marina/Stock.Adobe.com

Library of Congress Cataloging-in-Publication Data

Names: Hensley, Alta author
Title: They know if you've been bad or good : a novel / Alta Hensley.
Other titles: They know if you have been bad or good
Description: First edition. | New York, NY : Avon a, 2026. | Series: Naughty or nice ; book 3
Identifiers: LCCN 2026013647 | ISBN 9780063569621 trade paperback | ISBN 9780063578814 trade paperback | ISBN 9780063569638 ebook
Subjects: LCGFT: Romance fiction | Thrillers (Fiction) | Christmas fiction | Novels
Classification: LCC PS3608.E58626 T47 2026
LC record available at https://lccn.loc.gov/2026013647

ISBN 978-0-06-356962-1

Printed in the United States of America

26 27 28 29 30 LBC 5 4 3 2 1

To Laura and Katie.

Two women who made my dreams of seeing

New York Times *bestselling author happen. Thank you.*

Content Warning

Stalking (now a group activity)
Candy cane used as a weapon of seduction
Googly-eyed Santa sweater that honks when you press its nose (the real horror of this book)
Nonconsensual Canadian vacation
MMF so hot it could melt any snowstorm
Swords crossing
Possessive love, multiplied
One cabin, three people, not enough beds
Graphic gunfight at a ranger station (shoutout to Michelle, the real MVP)
Aggressive Christmas cheer

THEY KNOW

IF YOU'VE BEEN BAD OR GOOD

Chapter One

HAILEY

Silver bells, city sidewalks, and a stalker who thinks I don't notice him. He's following me again, like he has been for the past three months, and he's still convinced I'm oblivious.

I spot him half a block behind me on Fifth Avenue, his silver-blond head visible above the evening crowd even with his collar turned up against the December wind. He's trying to blend in with the after-work rush, but that rigid spine gives him away every time. Arrow-straight, scanning everything, moving like a man on a mission instead of someone heading home after a long day. Even from here, I can see the way his suit jacket stretches across shoulders broad enough to block out the Christmas lights behind him. Knox Bishop is built like a weapon someone forgot to put away. Tension held in every muscle, intensity that could snap at any moment. One look at him and you feel hunted.

I've been tailed by professionals who could ghost a target for weeks without detection. Knox Bishop, former Marine turned head of security for billionaire Cole Asher, is good at what he does. Really good.

And Jesus, the man is sexy. Shadow Daddy sexy.

But I spent five years looking over my shoulder, and you don't survive that long without learning to spot a tail.

I slow my pace as I turn into Bryant Park, letting the winter magic wash over me. The park is transformed this time of year, and tonight it's gorgeous. Fairy lights strung overhead cast everything in soft gold, turning the vendor stalls into a scene from a snow globe.

The massive Christmas tree dominates the center of the park, its lights twinkling against the darkening sky. Around me, the crowd is thick with tourists and locals alike, all bundled in wool coats and scarves, breath misting in cold air that smells like roasted chestnuts and cinnamon.

My Doc Martens crunch through the slush as I weave between stalls. The vendor booths are packed shoulder-to-shoulder, selling everything from handblown glass ornaments to artisanal hot chocolate topped with homemade marshmallows. Holiday music drifts from speakers hidden in the trees, something classic and sentimental that has everyone grinning like they're extras in a rom-com.

I should probably be more freaked out about the stalking situation. Normal people would be. But Knox doesn't feel threatening. He feels . . . intense. Electric. Like standing too close to a live wire.

I stop at a stall displaying glass baubles, each one catching the light differently. The vendor launches into his sales pitch but I'm not listening. I'm tracking Knox's position by instinct more than anything else. That prickle at the back of my neck that tells me I'm being watched. The way the crowd seems to part in my peripheral vision. He's good, but I'm better at this game than he realizes.

I pick up a crimson ornament, turn it over in my hands, watch the light refract through the glass. Set it down and move to the next booth.

This vendor sells candy canes in flavors that should probably be illegal. Pickle. Wasabi. Bacon. Egg . . . yes, egg! I select a traditional peppermint and unwrap it slowly, taking my time with the cellophane. The night air is biting enough that my fingers ache, but I don't rush.

I let my tongue trace the curve of the candy cane before sliding it between my lips. Slow. Deliberate. Is he watching right now? Is he imagining what else my mouth could do? What my tongue could trace? Warmth spreads through me despite the December cold.

I pull the candy from my lips with an audible pop and let it rest against my bottom lip for a moment before taking it back into my mouth.

Your move, Knox Bishop.

I don't look in his direction. That would break the spell.

A group of tourists jostles past me, speaking rapid French and laughing at something on someone's phone. The Rink is packed with skaters doing wobbly circles under the lights, their laughter mixing with the scrape of blades on ice.

I drift toward the book stall, running my fingers along paperback spines. Behind me, Knox maintains his distance. Three stalls back, pretending to examine a display of leather gloves. When he reaches for a pair, his sleeve rides up to reveal the edge of dark ink wrapping around his wrist. Tattoos he keeps hidden under those perfectly tailored suits. I've caught glimpses before. Enough to know there's more underneath. Enough to wonder what stories they tell and where else they might go. He thinks he's being subtle. It's adorable.

We've been doing this dance for months now. He watches, I pretend not to see him, we both act like this is totally normal behavior. But last month, the dynamic shifted. He started showing up at Sloane's studio more often, the jewelry studio where I work as her assistant. Security checks, he'd call them. But the way his eyes found me every time told a different story. Lingering longer. Finding excuses to talk to me. Last week, he'd asked me about the book I was reading, and even started asking me about the jewelry I was working on.

Tonight isn't the first time I've taken the scenic route home. I do this at least once a week now—walk through Bryant Park, past the holiday windows, down streets lit up with Christmas decorations. It's like the world's most romantic date, except we never acknowledge we're on one.

Hallmark Meets Stalker: A Love Story.

It's fucked up and addictive, and I can't get enough of it.

The temperature has dropped in the last hour, that particular brand of cold that happens only in New York in December. The bitter air cuts through my coat and makes my teeth ache. Around me, people are bundled in layers, scarves wrapped to their noses, hands shoved deep in pockets. Steam rises from grates in the sidewalk, and the windows of surrounding buildings glow warm against the dark sky.

Behind me, Knox's footsteps match my pace. We're in sync now, this weird choreography we've developed over months of surveillance and countersurveillance. I know exactly where he is without looking. Third position, right side, maintaining civilian spacing but ready to close the distance if needed.

Does he know I've clocked him? Sometimes I wonder. He's too smart not to pick up on the fact that I never startle, never look nervous, never do any of the things someone being stalked should do. Maybe he thinks I'm oblivious. Or maybe he thinks I'm playing along.

If only he knew how right that second guess is.

I head east toward the library with its stone lions wearing Christmas wreaths, past the holiday window displays that draw crowds three-deep on the sidewalk. Macy's has outdone themselves this year with animated scenes of winter landscapes and dancing snowflakes. The light from the windows spills onto the sidewalk, turning the slush into something that almost looks magical.

New York in December is chaos wrapped in tinsel and fairy lights. I love it.

The crowds thin as I make my way toward the subway at Grand Central. I descend into the station, hit immediately by the change in temperature. It's warmer down here, that particular subway warmth that comes from too many bodies and the heat of trains rushing through tunnels. A busker plays saxophone near the entrance, the music echoing off the tile walls.

I lose sight of Knox in the crowd but I know he's there. Probably near the stairs, keeping the exit in view. Watching. Protecting. Always protecting.

The F train pulls in with a screech of brakes and a rush of stale air. I squeeze on with everyone else, grabbing a pole near the door. Through the window, I catch a glimpse of Knox on the platform, watching my car disappear into the tunnel. Those battle-hardened eyes tracking me until the darkness swallows the train whole. He won't get on the train. Too confined, too easy for me to spot him.

But he'll be there when I get off. He always is.

Predictable. But also sweet in a deeply disturbed way.

I pull out my phone and scroll through messages. There's one from Sloane.

SOS. Need you early tomorrow. Cole set up a client meeting and these pieces are NOT cooperating. They're staging a rebellion.

I grin and type back.

How early are we talking?

Like before I've had coffee early. Which means 8am. I know. I'm a monster.

I'll bring the coffee.

Fair warning: I might cry on you. These earrings are personally attacking me.

Your earrings can't hurt you. They're earrings.

YOU DON'T KNOW THAT.

I laugh and pocket my phone.

Working for Sloane and Cole has been good for me. Legitimate work, legitimate income. A life I'm actually proud of.

The train takes me into Brooklyn and I emerge at Bergen Street into the cold night air. Cobble Hill is quieter, residential streets lined with brownstones decorated for Christmas.

A guy outside a bar on Smith Street whistles as I pass. I flip him off without breaking stride.

"Yo, fuck you too!" he yells after me, but his friends are already pulling him back inside.

New York. Gotta love it.

I wonder if Knox saw that. If he's filing away the guy's face, running threat assessments in his head.

Obsessive stalking has its perks.

I spot the rose before I even reach my building. A single red bloom, placed carefully on my doorstep like an offering. The petals are perfect despite the cold, closed tight against the winter air.

My heart beats faster. No note. Never a note. Just a perfect red rose that Knox leaves like a breadcrumb marking his obsession.

A single rose: It means something different than a bouquet. Anyone can throw money at a dozen long-stems and call it romance. That's easy. Expected. But a single rose? That's intentional. That's someone saying *you're the only thing I'm thinking about*. One flower, one focus, one obsession. It's not trying to impress with quantity. It's confident enough to stand alone.

I've never told anyone that. Never mentioned it to friends, never written it down. But Knox figured it out anyway.

That's either incredibly romantic or deeply unsettling. Possibly both.

I haven't figured out how he beats me here. He can't get here faster, I'd swear to it. But the rose is always waiting. Maybe he leaves it before the stalking. Maybe he's that good. Either way, it's impressive.

When did this start being romantic instead of concerning? When did I start looking forward to finding each rose?

I pick it up and unlock my door, carrying it inside like a trophy.

I add the rose to my collection near the kitchen window. Four stems now, hanging upside down, drying into something permanent. Outside the window, Brooklyn stretches out in a patchwork of lit windows and dark rooftops, the Manhattan skyline glittering in the distance.

I walk to the window and look down at the street. There, on the corner across from my building, Knox stands under a streetlight. He's not even trying to hide now. His hands are shoved in his coat pockets, his breath misting in the cold air. Standing there. Watching my window like it's the most natural thing in the world.

Should I wave? Let him know I see him? No. Not yet.

The game isn't over yet.

But our silent date has come to an end, so I close the curtains but leave them slightly parted. Not quite an invitation, but not a rejection either.

I see you, Knox Bishop. I see you.

Chapter Two

KNOX

She knows.

I'm standing under the streetlight like a fucking amateur, watching her window, and the worst part is I don't even care. Let her see me. Let her know I'm here. At this point, I'm past pretending this is about security protocols or threat assessment or any of the other bullshit I tell myself in the dark hours when I can't sleep.

Her curtains are pulled shut now, but she left a gap. Enough light spilling through to cast a stripe of gold across the snow-dusted sidewalk. An invitation? A taunt? With Hailey, I never know.

I check my watch: 10:47. She won't go to bed for hours. I know her patterns better than my own at this point. She'll change into sweats, pour herself a glass of wine, curl up with whatever book she's reading this week. Around midnight she'll start sketching, designs that never make it past her notebook. I've seen her through the apartment windows, the way her silver rings catch the light as she moves her pencil across the page. Her lamp will stay on until 2 a.m., sometimes later.

I know all of this because I've been watching her for three months.

Before that, I watched her differently. From a distance. Professional observation only. Another person in Cole's orbit who needed to be protected. But somewhere along the way, professional became personal, and I stopped pretending otherwise.

The cold bites through my coat and I welcome it. It reminds me I'm alive. Reminds me I'm real, standing on this street corner in Brooklyn like some lovesick psychopath. A dog barks somewhere down the block. A window slams shut three stories up. The neighborhood settling into sleep while I stand here like a ghost who doesn't know he's dead.

Hailey doesn't need me. I've read her file, what little of it exists. Enough gaps to tell me someone didn't want her past found. No employment history before Sloane. No social media footprint older than two years. A previous address in Chicago that leads to a building that burned down, all records lost. Enough fragments to know she survived things that would break most people.

She doesn't need to be protected.

I need to protect her anyway.

A taxi honks somewhere down the block and I shift my weight, eyes fixed on that gap in her curtains. I lost her for almost half an hour tonight. Twenty-five minutes between Grand Central and Bergen Street where she was underground, out of reach. I'd left my car near Bryant Park and pushed through traffic, running every yellow light between Midtown and the bridge, but I couldn't close the gap fast enough.

By the time I made it to her block, she was already inside. Door closed, lights on, safe.

Twenty-five minutes. Anything could happen in twenty-five minutes.

My phone buzzes. Cole.

Update on the Hartwell situation?

I type back without looking away from her building.

Handled. Meeting rescheduled for next week. Full briefing tomorrow.

His response is instant.

You okay? You seem distracted lately.

I almost laugh. Cole Asher, billionaire tech mogul, asking if his head of security is okay. A year ago, he was the one spiraling, obsessed with a woman he thought he'd lost. Now he's settled, happy, playing domestic bliss with Sloane. He'd recognize what I'm doing if he knew. He'd probably understand it better than anyone.

Fine, I type. Just finishing up some recon.

The lie sits heavy in my chest. But admitting this out loud would make it real in a way I'm not ready for.

Real means consequences. Real means doing something about it. Real means risking the rejection that would gut me.

I pocket my phone and check the time again. 11:23. Her light is still on. The temperature has dropped at least ten degrees since I got here, and I can't feel my fingers anymore. I shove my hands deeper into my pockets and stay planted.

Tonight at Bryant Park, she was different. Slower. Intentional. That candy cane performance wasn't accidental. She unwrapped it like she had all the time in the world, like she knew exactly where I was standing, like she wanted me to watch her mouth work that peppermint into something obscene.

My teeth grind together at the memory. My cock twitches, straining against my zipper like it has any say in this situation.

I can see her perfectly. Black hair cut in blunt bangs that frame her face, the rest falling past her shoulders in waves that catch the light. Those dark eyes, always lined blacker, like she's daring you to look closer. Lips painted deep red tonight to match the season. She's got this edge to her, halfway between goth and glam that shouldn't work for me but does. The way she dresses in all black like she's perpetually attending a funeral she finds vaguely amusing. That tiny stud in her nose that catches the light when she laughs.

Gorgeous doesn't cover it. She's a mystery wrapped in makeup and combat boots, and I've spent a year trying to solve her.

If she knows I'm following her, why hasn't she confronted me? Why hasn't she called the cops, or told Sloane, or done any of the things a normal person would do when they realize they have a shadow?

Because she's not normal. And neither am I.

We're both fucked up in ways that maybe fit together. Or maybe I'm telling myself that because the alternative is admitting I've become the thing I used to hunt.

Before Cole, I worked private security for high-profile clients. Politicians, executives, people who made enemies without trying. Part of the job was identifying threats. Stalkers, obsessives, the ones who convinced themselves their attention was wanted. I'd seen the letters they wrote, the rationalizations they made, the way they confused surveillance with love.

I know what I look like from the outside.

The leather notebook in my inside pocket presses against my ribs. Pages filled with observations that read like confessions. Her coffee order. The knot in the silver lace of her left boot. The way she hums while she works, melodies I can never quite place. I've written it all down, recorded her life in neat handwriting that would horrify a therapist.

A couple walks past, arm in arm, laughing at something on one of their phones. They don't notice me. Most people don't. It's a skill, making yourself invisible. I learned it in the Marines, perfected it in the years since. Blend with the shadows, move like you belong, never make eye contact unless you want to be remembered.

Tonight I'm not trying to be invisible. I'm standing under a streetlight, for fuck's sake. But Hailey's curtain stays closed and I stay rooted to the spot like the pathetic bastard I've become.

At 12:30, her light shines. She's moved to the back of the apartment, probably the bedroom area. Winding down, or pretending to. The wind picks up, cutting through my coat like it's made of paper. My ears burn. I don't move.

I should go home. Get some sleep before the briefing tomorrow. But I stay another hour, watching her window, watching the shadows move behind her curtains.

At 1:47, her light goes out.

Only then do I walk back to where I parked, hands shoved in my pockets, breath clouding in the frozen air. Tomorrow she'll go to work early, coffee in hand, tired but pretending otherwise. I'll be there too, watching from a distance. Making sure she's safe.

Making sure she's mine.

A year ago, that thought would have disturbed me. Now it feels like the truth.

The drive back to Manhattan is quiet this time of night, me and the occasional cab racing down empty streets. I find a spot near my building and kill the engine but don't get out. Sit there in the dark, hands on the wheel.

Behind my closed eyes, I see her. That black hair. That red mouth. The way she moves through crowds like water, aware of everything, afraid of nothing.

Tomorrow I'll watch for any shift in her pattern. If she acts different around me, if anything changes. Every twitch, every glance—I overanalyze all of it.

And if she keeps playing along? If she keeps taking the long way home and leaving gaps in her curtains?

Then maybe this isn't just my obsession.

Maybe it's ours.

Maybe it's time to do something about this . . . maybe tomorrow, I decide. Tomorrow I stop watching from the shadows. I'll find a reason to talk to her. A real conversation, not just security check-ins and small talk about jewelry designs. A conversation that lets me see if this tension between us is real or a fever dream I've been nursing for twelve months.

And if she shuts me down? If she looks at me like I'm exactly what I am—an obsessive stalker.

Then I'll know. And I'll figure out how to live with that.

But if she doesn't. If those dark eyes spark the way I think they will . . .

Chapter Three

HAILEY

I spend the entire morning waiting for Knox to show up. It's pathetic, really. Sloane's bent over her workbench, wrestling with a clasp that refuses to cooperate, muttering threats under her breath that would make a sailor blush. Cole's upstairs in his glass tower doing whatever billionaires do before noon. And I'm sitting here, supposedly sorting through gemstone samples, but actually watching the elevator like it might dispense a six-foot-three Christmas present at any moment.

He stops by at least twice a week. Always has some excuse. Checking on the new vault. Updating Cole on building access. Dropping off paperwork that could absolutely be emailed. The reasons don't matter. What matters is that his eyes find me every single time, and lately, they've been finding me more often.

Today, I dressed for combat.

Fitted black jeans that make my ass look phenomenal. A deep burgundy sweater that's just tight enough to be interesting without crossing into desperate territory. The color does something to my skin, makes it glow in a way that even I had to appreciate this morning. And my Doc Martens, obviously. The black ones with silver laces. My armor.

I even put on lipstick. Dark red, because I'm not subtle and I refuse to start now.

"You're staring at the elevator again."

I snap my attention to Sloane, who hasn't looked up from her work but is clearly psychic.

"I'm not staring. I'm . . . observing."

"You've been 'observing' for forty-five minutes." She glances up, her eyes caught somewhere between amusement and concern. "Is there something you want to tell me?"

"Nope."

"Because if there's anything going on I should know about—"

"There's nothing going on. I just like elevators. They're fascinating. All that vertical movement."

Sloane sets down her pliers and gives me the look. The one she's perfected over the year I've worked for her, the one that says *I'm not buying your bullshit but I'll let you keep shoveling.*

"Uh-huh."

Before she can interrogate me further, the elevator chimes.

My heart is out of control. I force myself not to turn around immediately, to keep my eyes on the gemstones spread across my workspace like I'm actually fascinated by the difference between sapphire and tanzanite. Which I am. Professionally. But right now, they could be pebbles for all I care.

"Knox." Sloane's voice is warm. "What brings you by?"

"Cole wanted me to go over the updated access codes for the vault." His voice rolls through the studio like distant thunder. "Shouldn't take long."

"Of course he did." Sloane's tone suggests she's as convinced by this excuse as I am. "Help yourself. You know where everything is."

My skin prickles with awareness as he moves through the studio, checking panels and keypads that definitely don't need checking. But his mission is unmistakable.

He's circling. Getting closer.

I pick up a piece of citrine and hold it to the light like it's the most captivating thing I've ever seen. My pulse is doing something ridiculous.

"Hailey."

God, the way he says my name. Like it's a word he's been practicing in private.

I turn slowly, letting my eyes travel up. Past the perfectly tailored charcoal suit. The broad chest. The strong jaw, a face that would look at home on a recruitment poster. Finally landing on those silver-blue eyes that never seem to know where to look when they're looking at me.

"Knox." I match his tone exactly, because I'm nothing if not petty.

His gaze drops to my sweater. Just for a second. But I catch it. The way his hands flex at his sides like he's resisting the urge to reach out.

I let my lips curve into the smallest smile. Hold his stare. Count the seconds.

One. Two. Three.

He looks away first.

Point to me.

"The vault codes," he says, clearing his throat. "They updated properly?"

"Seems like it." I wave vaguely toward Sloane's workspace. "Everything's very . . . vaulted."

There's amusement before he schools it back to neutral. "Good. That's . . . good."

We stand there for a moment, neither of us moving. The air between us tightens, energized with something that has no business existing in a jewelry studio at ten in the morning.

"Was there something else?" I ask innocently.

He swallows. "No."

"Then I guess you should probably get back to doing security stuff." I turn back to my gemstones. "Lots of things to verify, I'm sure."

He stands there for another five seconds before he moves away. When the elevator chimes his departure, I let out a breath I was holding.

From across the studio, Sloane catches my eye and raises one perfectly arched eyebrow.

"Fascinating," she says.

"Elevators usually are."

❄

THE AFTERNOON DRAGS.

I actually get work done, which feels like a minor miracle given my state of distraction. Sloane and I fall into our rhythm, sorting gemstones, discussing settings, debating whether a particular sapphire is more midnight blue or navy. Working with her has sharpened my eye in ways I didn't expect. My own designs used to lean toward bold statement pieces, dark metals, and unconventional stones. Sloane's taught me the elegance of restraint, the power of negative space. I'm a better designer now than I was a year ago, and I have her to thank for it.

Around 4:30, Sloane stretches her neck and groans. "I think these earrings are trying to kill me."

"You've been fighting with that clasp for two hours. Maybe it's time to call it."

"I don't lose to jewelry, Hailey. It's a matter of principle." She glares at the offending piece like it personally insulted her mother. "This clasp will bend to my will or I'll melt it down and start over."

"That seems healthy."

"It's called determination."

"It's called a grudge match with an inanimate object."

She throws a wadded-up piece of polishing cloth at me. I catch it without looking, which earns me an impressed eyebrow raise.

Before she can comment, the elevator chimes again.

This time it's not Knox.

Chloe Hallman bursts through the doors like she's announcing a royal arrival, arms full of shopping bags and energy that could power a small city. "Ladies! We're leaving!"

Sloane blinks. "We are?"

"Yes. Now. Immediately." Chloe crosses the studio in record time, depositing her bags on my workspace with zero regard for the carefully sorted gemstones I've been organizing for the past hour. "It's after four. That's basically the end of the day. And we have traditions to uphold."

"What traditions?" I ask, already suspicious.

"Ugly sweater and martini night at Tonic." Chloe's grin is wide and dangerous. "Annual event. Nonnegotiable. And this year, you're coming."

"I'm not—"

"You are." She pulls something out of one of the bags, and I immediately want to leave the country.

It's a sweater. I think. It might also be a cry for help rendered in knitwear.

The base is bright red, which is already a crime against my personal aesthetic. But the real horror is the design: a large felt Santa face covers the entire front, complete with a fluffy white beard made of actual cotton balls, googly eyes that move when you breathe, and a nose that honks when you press it. HONKS. There are also tiny jingle bells sewn along the hem, because apparently visual assault wasn't enough. Auditory assault was also required.

"Absolutely not."

"Absolutely yes." Chloe shakes the sweater at me, and the bells jingle merrily, mocking my pain. "I picked this one specifically for you. It matches your holiday spirit."

"I don't have holiday spirit."

"Hence the honking nose. It'll help you find some."

Sloane's already digging in another bag, pulling out her own monstrosity. Hers is green with a massive gingerbread man whose limbs are positioned to make him look like he's running for his life. One arm is detachable with Velcro, and there's a bite mark on his head with the words "OH SNAP" bedazzled underneath. The whole thing is trimmed with rickrack that looks like frosting.

"This is incredible," Sloane says, genuinely delighted. "The existential horror of being a cookie. I love it."

"Right? I found it at that vintage shop in Chelsea." Chloe pulls out her own selection. Hers features a knitted scene of cats tangled in Christmas lights, their eyes made of actual tiny LED bulbs that blink in an erratic pattern. The words "MEOWY CHRISTMAS" arc across the top in fuzzy letters, and there's a small speaker somewhere that plays a tinny version of "Jingle Bells" when you press a hidden button.

"You're all insane," I say.

"We're festive," Chloe corrects. "There's a difference."

"The difference is medication."

"Come on, Hails." Sloane's already holding her gingerbread sweater up to her chest, checking the fit. "It's tradition. Chloe and I have been doing this for years. Last year you had 'plans.'" She makes air quotes. "This year, you're not escaping."

"I have plans this year too."

"What plans?"

I open my mouth. Close it. The truth is, my plans involved walking home the long way, seeing if Knox would follow, maybe stopping at the Strand to browse. Our weird little shadow date that he doesn't know I know about.

"Private plans."

Chloe and Sloane exchange a look. The conspiratorial kind that says they've discussed this.

"Hailey." Sloane sets down the sweater and gives me her serious face. "You've been working here for over a year. You've become one of my closest friends. And in all that time, I've never once seen you do anything social that wasn't work-related."

"I'm an introvert."

"You're a hermit."

"Same thing."

"It's not." Chloe jumps in. "Introverts recharge alone. Hermits are hiding from something."

That hits a little too close to home, and something must show on my face because Sloane softens.

"One night," she says. "A few martinis. Some questionable fashion choices. You might actually have fun."

"I have fun."

"Walking around the city by yourself doesn't count."

"It does if you're doing it right."

Chloe picks up the Santa sweater and holds it against me. The googly eyes wobble accusingly. "Look. The red brings out your inner rage, and the honking nose represents your suppressed emotions trying to escape."

Despite myself, I snort. "That's the worst sales pitch I've ever heard."

"Is it working?"

I look at the sweater. At my two friends, who apparently coordinated this ambush. At the way Sloane's eyes are practically pleading.

I like them. I do. And I've spent so long keeping everyone at arm's length that I've almost forgotten how to let people in. This new life in New York was supposed to be different. Real job, real friends, a real existence. But old habits die hard, and pushing people away is the oldest habit I have.

"Fine."

Chloe actually squeals. "Really?"

"One condition." I take the sweater from her. "If anyone honks my nose without permission, I'm committing a felony."

"Deal." Sloane's already texting, probably letting Cole know she's cutting out early. "This is going to be amazing."

"This is going to be humiliating."

"Same thing," Chloe says cheerfully. "Now put on the sweater. We need pictures."

"You said no pictures."

"I said no such thing."

"Sloane, tell her I get no pictures."

Sloane's face is buried in her phone, conveniently deaf to my protests.

I look at the Santa sweater in my hands. The googly eyes stare back, unblinking and chaotic.

What have I agreed to?

Chapter Four

HAILEY

Tonic is packed. The bar is dressed for the season, strands of white lights wrapped around exposed brick columns and hanging in swoops from the ceiling. The crowd is the usual mix of Manhattan professionals and tourists, most of them in actual cocktail attire because this is still Midtown and people have standards.

People who are not us.

We walk in like we own the place, three women in spectacularly ugly sweaters. Sloane's gingerbread man bounces with each step, his detachable arm threatening to Velcro itself to passing strangers. Chloe's cat eyes blink erratically, casting tiny spots of light across nearby faces. And I jingle with every movement, Santa's googly eyes wobbling in opposite directions like he's having a seizure.

"Table's ready!" Chloe calls over the noise, leading us through the crowd. People part for us, probably out of concern that our holiday disasters are contagious.

We settle into a corner booth, red vinyl seats that have probably heard a thousand drunk confessions. A waitress appears almost immediately, and Chloe orders a round of peppermint martinis before I can suggest literally anything else.

"I hate peppermint," I say.

"You'll learn to love it. It's tradition."

"Your tradition sounds terrible."

"And yet, here you are."

She's got me there.

The martinis arrive, pink and frothy and topped with crushed candy canes that I immediately push aside. Sloane raises her glass.

"To friendship. And to finally getting Hailey to participate in a social activity."

"To peer pressure," I counter, but I clink my glass against theirs anyway.

The first sip is actually decent. Sweet enough to mask the alcohol, minty enough to feel like the holidays, strong enough that I'll need to pace myself if I want to walk home in a straight line later.

"So." Chloe leans forward, elbows on the table, clearly hungry for gossip. "Sloane says there've been developments. With a certain tall, brooding individual."

I shoot Sloane a betrayed look. She shrugs, unrepentant. "I said there's been tension. I didn't say there were developments."

"Tension IS a development." Chloe's practically bouncing. "What kind of tension? Sexual tension? Angry tension? Sexual-angry tension?"

"There's no tension."

"Your eye twitched."

"It did not."

"It definitely did." Sloane sips her martini. "The same way it twitches every time Knox walks into the studio. Which has been happening for a year now. A year of eye-twitching, Hailey."

"Maybe I have a condition."

"You have a condition, all right." Chloe wiggles her eyebrows. "It's called wanting to climb Knox Bishop like a tree."

I choke on my martini. "I do not—"

"Come on, Hails. We've seen the way you two look at each other. Since day one. Remember when Sloane introduced you? You shook his hand and turned bright red."

"I was cold. It was December."

"You were blushing."

"I don't blush."

"You're blushing right now," Chloe points out.

"That's the martini."

"You run avoiding-the-question." Chloe grins. "So what's the deal? A whole year of eye-fucking across crowded rooms and nothing's happened?"

"We don't eye-fuck."

"You absolutely eye-fuck. It's intense. People have noticed."

"What people?"

"Me. Sloane. Cole, probably. The barista at that coffee shop you both happen to frequent. Should I continue?"

I take a longer drink of my martini than is probably advisable. "Knox Bishop is not my type."

"And what's your type?" Sloane asks innocently.

"Not him."

"Be more specific."

I set down my glass. "He's too . . . uptight. All that military discipline and structure. He probably irons his underwear. Makes his bed with hospital corners. Has a spreadsheet for his feelings."

"So you've thought about his underwear," Chloe notes. "Interesting."

"That's not—" I stop, realizing I've been outmaneuvered. "You know what I mean. He's serious all the time. Controlled. I like men with edge."

"He has tattoos," Sloane offers. "Hidden ones. I've seen glimpses."

"Tattoos don't make someone edgy."

"He was in the Marines. Special operations. I'm pretty sure that qualifies."

"That's not—" I'm floundering and we all know it. "He follows rules. I don't follow rules. We're fundamentally incompatible."

Chloe exchanges another look with Sloane. The kind that says they're about to tag-team me.

"You know what I think?" Chloe says. "I think you like him more than you're comfortable with. And instead of dealing with that, you're finding reasons why it won't work."

"That's amateur psychology."

"It's accurate psychology."

"It's—"

I stop. Because I've spotted something through the window that makes my heart stutter.

Knox.

He's standing across the street, partially obscured by a group of people leaving a restaurant. But I'd recognize that silhouette anywhere. The way he holds himself. The broad shoulders visible even from here. He's pretending to look at his phone, but I know better.

He followed us.

He followed me.

"Hailey? You okay?" Sloane's voice cuts through my thoughts. "You went quiet."

I force my attention back to the table. "I'm fine. Just zoned out for a second."

But Sloane's already turning to look, and I watch her expression shift as she notices Knox's presence.

"Is that—" She squints through the window. "Is that Knox out there?"

Chloe cranes her neck. "Where? Oh! Yep, that's definitely him. What's he doing standing there?"

"Cole probably asked him to keep an eye on things." Sloane sighs, but there's affection in it. "He's always been protective. It's sweet, in an overbearing, slightly paranoid way."

She thinks Knox is here for her. Following Cole's orders. Doing his job.

She's wrong.

I watch him through the window, watch the way his eyes scan the bar until they land on our booth. On me. Even from this distance, through glass and Christmas lights and strangers, our gazes connect. He holds it for a moment before looking away.

But I saw. I know.

He's not here for Sloane.

I don't correct her assumption. Some truths are mine to keep.

"Let him lurk," I say, turning back to my martini. "It's cold out there. Serves him right."

"For what?" Chloe asks.

"For being so . . . him."

Chloe and Sloane exchange another look, but this one is different. Speculative. Like they're filing this moment away for future interrogation.

"We could invite him in," Chloe suggests.

"No."

"Why not? He could join us. Make it a double date."

"That math doesn't work. There's three of us."

"Sloane and I are clearly together." Chloe loops her arm through Sloane's. "We're the love story here. You and Knox are the side plot."

"Please don't drag me into this," Sloane says, but she doesn't pull her arm away.

"There is no side plot. And also, he's not my date."

"But you want him to be."

"I want to finish my drink without being psychoanalyzed, actually."

Chloe holds up her hands in surrender, but she's grinning. "Fine. I'll drop it. For now."

"That's ominous."

"It's holiday spirit. Everything's holiday spirit during December, including my interrogation techniques."

The rest of the night passes in a blur of laughter and terrible jokes and more martinis than I should probably be consuming on a Wednesday. Sloane tells stories about her first Christmas with Cole, which involved a ruined sweater and the most aggressive meet-cute in romantic history. This very bar, actually. Apparently Cole orchestrated a collision that ended with scotch all over Sloane's light-up reindeer. Romantic or psychotic, depending on your perspective.

I'm starting to think there's something in the water with these men.

Chloe talks about her plans with Jack, something about spending Christmas at the fire station since he's working the holiday shift.

I contribute less, mostly listening, but I relax as the evening goes on. This is nice. Being out. Having friends. Letting myself be part of something instead of always hovering at the edges.

Every few minutes, I catch myself glancing toward the window. Knox is still there. Different position now, leaning against a building across the street like he's just a guy enjoying the night air. But I feel his attention like heat against my skin.

He's watching over me.

It should be creepy. I know that. Objectively, rationally, a man standing outside a bar watching through the window is red flag behavior. But nothing about Knox feels threatening. Just . . . intense. Protective. Like he can't help himself any more than I can help looking for him.

We're both a little broken, I think. Maybe that's why this works.

Around seven, Sloane stifles a yawn and Chloe declares the evening a success. We pay our tab and bundle into our coats, sweaters still jingling and blinking underneath.

Outside, the cold hits like a slap. My breath fogs in the air and I pull my coat tighter, scanning the street automatically. Knox has repositioned again, farther down the block now, turned away like he's checking something on his phone.

Sloane doesn't notice. She's hugging Chloe goodbye, making plans for the next time, extracting promises about Christmas gatherings.

I hang back slightly, watching Knox not watch me.

I see you, I think. *I always see you.*

When it's my turn to say goodbye, Sloane pulls me into a hug that's warmer than I expected.

"This was fun," she says against my ear. "We should do it more often."

"Maybe." But I'm smiling when I say it, and I think she can tell.

They head toward the subway together, Chloe still chattering about something while Sloane laughs. I watch them go, then turn in the opposite direction.

Time to see if Knox will follow.

So . . . I take the long way.

Down Fifth Avenue, past the holiday windows that draw tourists even at this hour. Through the streams of people bundled in wool coats and scarves, their breath clouding under the glow of streetlights. The city is beautiful tonight, harsh and dramatic edges softened by fairy lights and the promise of snow.

I don't look behind me. I don't need to.

That prickle at the back of my neck tells me everything I need to know. Knox is there, keeping his distance, maintaining that careful spacing that lets him pretend this is surveillance instead of obsession. Two can play that game.

I stop at the Strand.

The bookstore is one of my favorite places in the city. Three floors of books, most of them used, all of them waiting to be discovered. At night, it's quieter than the daytime chaos, just a handful of serious browsers and students cramming for exams they definitely should have started studying for earlier.

I push through the doors and breathe in that particular Strand smell. Paper and dust and the accumulated wisdom of a million stories. The warmth hits my cheeks, still stinging from the cold.

For a few minutes, I actually browse. Run my fingers along spines in the fiction section, pull out paperbacks with interesting covers, read first paragraphs to see if they hook me. This is genuine. I love books. I love getting lost in other people's stories, lives more interesting than my own.

But I'm also waiting.

I move through the stacks toward the crime section, which feels appropriate given my history. The shelves here are packed tight, narrow aisles barely wide enough for two people to pass.

I drift deeper into the stacks, toward the back corner where the lighting is dimmer and the foot traffic is sparse.

There. Military history. Three aisles over.

I catch a glimpse of him through the gaps between books. That perfect posture, the expensive suit jacket that fits him like a second skin. He's pretending to examine a book on World War II tactics, and it might be convincing if I didn't know better.

Time for some fun.

I make a show of browsing, letting my fingers trail along book spines until I find what I'm looking for. A hardcover with a glossy dust jacket, the title visible even from a distance.

The Art of the Heist: A History of Legendary Jewel Thefts

I pull it from the shelf and turn it so the cover faces the aisle. Flip to a random page, pretend to read. Really, I'm giving him time to see what I've chosen.

It's a little on the nose. Okay, it's extremely on the nose, given that my past includes several notable jewelry acquisitions that were never recovered. But Knox doesn't know that. As far as he knows, I'm Hailey Parker, reformed party girl with a mysterious background, currently employed as a jewelry assistant. My interest in heist books could be nothing more than professional curiosity.

I flip another page. Hold the book a little higher.

From the corner of my eye, I see Knox shift position. He's definitely noticed the cover. I can practically feel his curiosity from here, that analytical brain cataloging this detail, filing it away with all the other pieces of my puzzle he's been collecting.

That's right, I think. *Wonder about me. Try to figure me out. I dare you.*

I browse for another fifteen minutes, selecting two more books that I actually want to read. Then I head toward the registers, timing my path to pass within a few feet of where Knox is standing.

He's still in military history, now holding something about Special Forces operations. Probably more comfortable territory for him.

As I walk past, I let my credit card slip from my fingers.

It clatters against the hardwood floor, landing between us.

For a moment, neither of us moves. The store hums with the quiet sounds of other browsers, the distant murmur of a cashier helping someone, the creak of old wooden floors.

Then Knox bends to pick it up.

When he straightens, he's closer than I expected. Close enough that I catch his scent. Something woody and warm underneath the cold night air clinging to his coat. Close enough that when he holds out the card, I have to tilt my chin up to meet his eyes.

"You dropped this."

His voice hits somewhere below my sternum. Those pale eyes meet mine, and for once, he doesn't look away.

"Thank you."

I reach for the card, and our fingers brush. Just a touch. Brief. But heat blooms from the point of contact, spreading up my arm, deep in my stomach. My breath catches, and I see his eyes darken as he notices.

Neither of us lets go.

"You're welcome." His thumb shifts, almost imperceptibly, grazing against my knuckle. The touch is so light it could be accidental. We both know it isn't.

My pulse throbs in my throat. In other places too, places that have no business responding to a man in a bookstore over something as innocent as a dropped credit card. But there's nothing innocent about the way Knox is looking at me. Like he wants to devour me right here between Military History and True Crime.

"Nice sweater," he says. There's almost a smile. Almost.

I look down at the honking Santa I wear, googly eyes wobbling from the movement. The bells along the hem jingle softly.

"Wasn't my choice."

"Looks good on you."

My skin flushes hot. "Does it?"

"Everything does." He says it like it costs him something. Like the words escaped before he could stop them. His voice drops even lower. "But you already know that."

Heat crawls up my neck. I don't know what to do with a compliment that direct, delivered in that voice, with those eyes pinning me in place. So I deflect.

"The sweater's doing a lot of heavy lifting."

He doesn't smile, but there's a change in his face. Warmer. "It's not the sweater."

My thighs clench. I hope he doesn't notice. I hope he does.

We stand there, frozen in this pocket of tension that feels like it might combust at any second. His fingers are still touching mine. The card hangs between us, forgotten. I'm acutely aware of how close he is, how easy it would be to lean forward and close the distance. To find out if his mouth is as demanding as his eyes.

A browser shuffles past at the end of the aisle, breaking the spell.

Knox releases the card. Steps back. But his eyes stay locked on mine, and I can see the war happening behind them. The restraint coiled in every muscle.

"Good night, Hailey." My name sounds different in his mouth. Rougher. Hungrier.

I tuck the card into my pocket with fingers that aren't quite steady. "Good night, Knox."

I step around him and walk toward the registers, hyper-aware of his gaze tracking my every movement. My skin feels too tight. My body hums with thwarted want.

At the counter, I fumble through the transaction, barely registering what the cashier says. Outside, the cold air hits me like a slap, but it does nothing to cool the heat simmering under my skin.

I start walking toward the subway, toward Brooklyn, toward home.

Behind me, I hear the bookstore door open and close.

He's following. Of course he is.

And tomorrow, we'll pretend this never happened. Pretend we're colleagues who happened to run into each other at a bookstore. Pretend my body didn't light up like a fuse at the brush of his fingers.

But we both know the truth.

This game we're playing? It's only getting more dangerous.

And I'm not sure either of us wants to stop.

Chapter Five

KNOX

Three hours since the Strand, and I'm sitting in my apartment replaying five seconds of contact like a man possessed. Which I suppose I am.

The leather notebook lies open on my kitchen table, but I can't make myself pick up the pen. I should document everything. Her face when our fingers touched. The catch in her breath. The way her pupils dilated, just slightly, when I told her everything looks good on her. That's what I do. That's what I've been doing for months. Studying her. Writing down observations that read like confessions.

But tonight was different.

Tonight wasn't data.

It's not the sweater.

I said that. Out loud. To her face. And she looked at me with those dark eyes and her cheeks flushed and for one perfect, terrifying moment, I thought she might close the distance between us.

She didn't.

Now the ghost of her fingers against mine is the only thing I can think about. The way the touch rewired something fundamental in my nervous system.

I scrub a hand over my face and check the time: 2:47 a.m. Her light went out an hour ago. I know because I drove past her building on the way home, just to make sure she got there safely. Just to see her window one more time.

I'm so far gone it's almost funny.

I close the notebook without writing anything. There are no words for what happened tonight. No clinical observations that capture the way my chest cavity cracked open when she looked at me.

Tomorrow.

The word echoes in my head, hollow and familiar. I've been telling myself tomorrow for months now. Tomorrow I'll stop watching from the shadows. Tomorrow I'll talk to her properly. Tomorrow I'll be brave enough to do something about this thing that's consuming me.

Tomorrow has become a lie I tell myself so I can sleep at night.

But tonight was different. Tonight she looked at me like she saw something worth seeing. Tonight her fingers brushed mine and neither of us pulled away.

Maybe tomorrow can finally mean something.

I've spent two winters in the Hindu Kush. I've walked into firefights where the odds were against me. I survived things that should have killed me, and I did it without flinching.

But the thought of asking Hailey Parker to have dinner with me makes my palms sweat like I'm seventeen again, working up the nerve to ask Jenny Morrison to junior prom.

I was braver then. Or maybe just dumber.

Same difference.

Morning comes too fast and not fast enough.

I'm at Cole's office by seven, running through the day's schedule with the focus of a man desperately trying not to think about anything else. Security protocols for the upcoming gala. Background checks on the new catering staff. A conference call with the team handling the London office transition.

Cole watches me through most of it, and I can feel him reading my behavior the same way I read everyone else's.

"You seem distracted," he says when the briefing is done.

"I'm fine."

"That's not what I asked."

I meet his eyes. Cole Asher built a tech empire by reading people, by seeing through the masks they wear. He's one of the few people I've never been able to fool.

"There's something I need to handle," I say carefully. "Personal."

Cole leans back in his chair, and I see . . . understanding.

"This is about Hailey."

"Cole—"

"Knox, I'm not blind. Neither is Sloane." He almost smiles. "You've been finding excuses to come down to the studio for months. Invented problems that don't exist. And every single time, you end up hovering near her workstation looking like you're trying to solve a puzzle you can't quite crack."

I don't say anything. There's nothing to say.

"Sloane thinks it's sweet," he continues. "She also thinks you're both idiots for not doing anything about it."

"It's not that simple."

"It's exactly that simple." He stands, gathering the files from our meeting. "You like her. She likes you. The only complicated part is the story you're telling yourself about why it won't work."

"You don't know that she—"

"I know exactly what I see. And what I see is two people who light up every time they're in the same room and then spend all their energy pretending they don't." He pauses at the door. "Just ask her, Knox. Whatever happens, it's better than this limbo you've been living in."

He shrugs. "And for what it's worth? Sloane's pretty sure she'll say yes."

He's gone before I can respond.

But his words echo in my head as I step back into the elevator and press the button for Sloane's floor. A year of watching. Months of following. And what has it gotten me? A notebook full of observations and a permanent ache in my core.

No more excuses. No more pretending. No more slow spirals through the studio acting like I'm there for any reason other than her. After last night, after the bookstore, the pretense feels pointless.

The doors open into Sloane's studio, and I walk straight toward Hailey's workstation.

Sloane looks up as I pass, eyebrows rising. I catch the question in her eyes, the curiosity, but I don't stop to explain. Let her wonder. Let her suspect. I'm past caring what anyone thinks.

Hailey's bent over something delicate, silver wire catching the light as she twists it into shape. But she must sense me approaching because her hands go still before I reach her. When she lifts her head, there's color already rising in her cheeks.

She felt it too. Last night. She's been thinking about it the same way I have.

"Knox."

"Hailey."

We stare at each other. The air between us feels different today. Charged with the memory of last night, with everything we didn't say at the Strand. Her fingers fidget with the wire in her hands, the only sign that she's not as composed as she's pretending to be.

"You're not checking anything," she observes. Her voice comes out slightly uneven. "No clipboard. No security panels."

"No."

"So this is . . ."

"Me asking you something."

Her breath catches, just barely. "Okay."

I clear my throat. "There's a holiday market. At Union Square."

She waits. Her eyes don't leave mine.

"I thought you might want to go." The words come out rougher than intended. "With me."

Silence.

Across the studio, I'm acutely aware of Sloane pretending not to listen. The soft clink of her tools, the careful way she's not looking in our direction.

Hailey stares at me. I've spent months studying her, learning every micro-expression, every tell. But right now, I can't tell if she's going to say yes or laugh in my face.

"You're asking me out," she says. Slowly. Like she's testing the words.

"Yes."

"On a date."

"Yes."

"To a holiday market."

"Yes." I'm starting to feel like a broken record, but I don't know what else to say.

She tilts her head, and I catch something. Not skepticism. Something softer. Almost hopeful.

"Why?"

The question catches me off guard. "Why?"

"Why me? Why now? We've worked in the same orbit for a year and you've never . . ." She trails off, gestures vaguely. "This."

I should have a careful answer. Something that doesn't reveal too much. Something that keeps the stalking and the obsession safely hidden.

Instead, what comes out is "Because I can't stop thinking about you."

Her breath catches. This time it's obvious. Her cheeks flush darker and she looks down at the wire in her hands like she's forgotten it was there.

"I don't . . ." She starts, then stops. Tries again. "This is unexpected."

"I know."

"I'm not . . ." Another pause. "I'm not good at this."

"Neither am I."

She laughs, short and surprised. Looks back up at me. "You seem pretty good at it. The whole tall, mysterious, appearing-out-of-nowhere thing. Very dramatic."

"I rehearsed this conversation for three hours last night."

The admission surprises us both. Hailey's eyes widen slightly, and I feel heat crawl up the back of my neck. I haven't blushed since I was a teenager. Apparently, she brings that out in me too.

"Three hours," she repeats.

"It went better in my head."

"What happened in your head?"

"You said yes immediately. We skipped all the awkward parts."

"This is the awkward part?"

"This is the awkward part."

Something softens. The coolness she usually keeps so carefully in place seems to blur, just for a moment.

"Tonight," she says. "Pick me up at six. You know where I live."

I do. Of course I do. I've stood outside her building a hundred times, watching her window, memorizing the pattern of her lights.

But I don't say that.

"Six," I confirm.

"Don't be late."

"I won't."

She holds my gaze for another long moment. Then she picks up her pendant, turns back to her work, and I'm dismissed.

I walk back to the elevator on legs that don't feel stable. When the doors close, I lean against the wall and exhale slowly.

She said yes . . . and Jesus Christ I'm a sweaty mess.

Chapter Six

KNOX

I'm at her building at 5:47 because I'm pathologically early and because waiting in my apartment was making me lose my mind. I've changed clothes three times, eventually settling on dark jeans and a charcoal sweater under my black coat. Casual, but not too casual. Trying to look like I'm not trying.

I'm definitely trying.

The neighborhood is quiet this time of evening, the brownstones lit from within, the sidewalks mostly empty. It's cold enough that my breath fogs, but not bitter, and I find myself thinking it's good weather for walking.

At exactly 5:59, I climb the steps to her building and press her buzzer.

"You're early," her voice crackles through the speaker.

"One minute."

"That's early."

"Would you prefer I wait outside until exactly six?"

A pause. Then the door buzzes open. "Get up here before you freeze."

I take the stairs two at a time, and her door is cracked when I reach her floor. I push it open slowly, unsure of the etiquette. Am I supposed to wait in the hall? Come inside? Normal people probably know these things, but I haven't been normal in a very long time.

Her apartment is small but intentional, dark colors and clean lines. Bookshelves overflow with paperbacks, and near the window, a collection of dried roses hangs upside down, red petals preserved, stems bound with twine.

Something possessive flares in my soul. Who gave her roses?

But I push it down. Maybe she bought them herself. Maybe she just likes roses. Not everything is a sign.

"Give me two minutes," Hailey calls from somewhere deeper in the apartment. "I'm almost ready."

"Take your time."

I don't move from the doorway because it feels wrong to intrude further without invitation, but I let my eyes wander, taking in details I couldn't see from the street. The art on her walls is mostly black and white prints of cities I don't recognize, and a stack of books sits on her coffee table, their spines worn soft from reading. The blanket thrown over her couch looks like something you'd wrap around yourself on cold nights, and I find myself imagining her here, curled up with a book, the city lights glittering outside her window.

I imagine myself beside her.

"Okay." Her voice is closer now, and I turn to find her emerging from what must be the bedroom. "Ready."

She's wearing black, because she's always wearing black, but it's different tonight. A fitted coat nips at her waist, a scarf wraps loosely around her neck, and she's got on those same boots with the silver laces. Her hair falls past her shoulders in waves, and she's done something with her eyes that makes them look bigger, smokier. The silver rings are back on her fingers.

She looks like trouble, and she looks like everything I want.

"You're staring," she says.

"Yes."

A beat of silence stretches between us, and she seems to be waiting for something more. An apology, maybe. An excuse.

I don't offer one.

"Well." She pulls on her gloves, breaking eye contact first. "At least you're honest about it."

"Would you prefer I pretend?"

"I'd prefer you have some chill."

"Fresh out."

She huffs in what might be a laugh and pushes past me into the hallway. I catch that scent again, dark flowers and midnight gardens.

"Come on," she says without looking back. "Let's see if you're as interesting in public as you are lurking around jewelry studios."

The F train is crowded this time of evening, packed with commuters and people rushing to early dinner reservations and others heading into Manhattan for the holiday lights. We stand near the doors, pressed closer than strictly necessary by the bodies around us, and when Hailey grips the overhead bar, I position myself between her and the rest of the car, blocking strangers from pressing too close.

She notices. I can see it in the slight tilt of her lips.

"You're doing that thing," she says, voice low enough that only I can hear.

"What thing?"

"The protective thing. Standing between me and everyone else."

"Force of habit."

"Is it?"

I don't answer. The train lurches, and I brace a hand against the pole above her head, leaning in to keep her from stumbling. For a moment, we're close enough that I can see the flecks of gold in her eyes, the slight part of her lips.

"Thank you," she says quietly.

"You're welcome."

We don't talk for the rest of the ride, but she doesn't move away, either. She just stands there in the circle of my arms, close enough that I can feel the warmth radiating from her body, and something deep within me unknots slightly. This is real. This is happening. I haven't ruined it yet.

Union Square is sensory overload. The holiday market sprawls across the park in rows of white tents glowing under strings of lights, and the smell hits first: roasted chestnuts and mulled wine, fresh pine and something sweet that might be caramelized apples. Music drifts from somewhere, holiday standards played on what sounds like an accordion.

People are everywhere. Couples and families and groups of friends wrapped in scarves and good cheer, moving between stalls selling jewelry and candles and soap and ornaments.

I hate crowds. Always have. Too many variables, too many sight lines to cover, too many places for threats to emerge.

But Hailey is already moving into the fray, her dark coat a beacon in the sea of red and green, and I follow without hesitation.

"I've never actually been here with anyone," she says, pausing at a stall selling hand-poured candles. "Always meant to, but . . ."

"But?"

She shrugs and picks up a candle, sniffing it before setting it back down. "I tend to do things solo. I don't really do people."

"You're here now."

"I'm here now." She glances at me sideways. "Jury's out on whether that was a good decision."

"I'll try not to disappoint."

"That's a lot of pressure."

"I work well under pressure."

Something flashes across her face. Not quite a smile, but close to one. "Military training?"

"Something like that."

We drift through the market, stopping at booths that catch her attention. She lingers over old jewelry, turning pieces over in her fingers with an expert eye, then pauses at a display of antique books and runs her fingers along the worn covers. At a chocolate stall, she samples three different truffles and pronounces them "acceptable," which I'm learning is high praise from Hailey.

I find myself watching her more than I watch the vendors. The way her face changes when she finds something interesting. The dry comments she makes about the more absurd offerings. The way she moves through crowds like water, always aware, always observing.

She catches me staring more than once but doesn't call me out on it.

At a booth selling metalwork, I find them: silver earrings, delicate spirals that catch the light, simple but distinctive. They're the kind of piece she'd choose for herself.

"These," I tell the vendor before I can talk myself out of it.

Hailey appears at my elbow, eyes narrowing when she sees what I'm buying. "What are you doing?"

"Buying you something."

"You can't just buy me jewelry."

"Why not?"

"Because . . ." She pauses, clearly searching for a reason. "It's too much. We're on a first date."

"Is that a rule?"

"It's common sense."

"I'm not particularly common, and I've never been accused of having much sense." I hand over my card before she can protest further.

The vendor, wisely, stays out of it and hands me the earrings in a small velvet pouch, wishing us a happy holiday.

I turn to Hailey, who looks like she can't decide whether to be annoyed or touched. "These are yours."

"Knox."

"Hailey."

"You can't just . . ." She takes a breath. "Why?"

"Because they reminded me of you."

"You've known me for an hour."

"I've known you for a year."

The words settle between us, and I watch something swirl behind her eyes. A softening. A crack in the wall she keeps so carefully maintained.

"We've worked in the same orbit for a year," she says carefully. "That's not the same as knowing someone."

"Isn't it?"

She doesn't answer. She just takes the velvet pouch from my hand, and when her fingers graze mine, neither of us pulls away.

"They're beautiful," she says quietly as she opens the pouch. She removes her current earrings, simple silver studs, and replaces them with the spirals. They catch the fairy lights, glinting against her hair. "How do they look?"

"Perfect."

She rolls her eyes, but she's fighting a smile. "You'd say that no matter what."

"Probably, but that doesn't make it less true."

For a moment, we just stand there while the market swirls around us. Lights and music and laughter that somehow doesn't reach us. We're in our own pocket of stillness, and I don't want to leave it.

Then she shakes her head slightly, breaking the spell.

"I need hot cider," she announces. "And you need to tell me about your taste in Christmas movies."

"*Die Hard*."

She stops mid-step and turns to stare at me. "That's your answer?"

"It's a perfectly valid answer."

"It's a cop-out. And cliche. I'm having to work hard not to roll my eyes."

"*Die Hard* takes place during Christmas. There's a Christmas party. There's decorations. There's holiday music."

"There's explosions and machine guns."

"Those are incompatible with Christmas?"

She laughs, and the sound does something to my entire being. Something warm and bright that I want to hold on to. "Fine. I'll allow *Die Hard*. But you have to give me something else. Something sincere."

We find a cider vendor and I buy two cups, passing one to her. The warmth seeps through my gloves as we start walking south, drifting away from the main market toward quieter streets.

"*Scrooged*," I say. "Bill Murray version."

"That's a comedy."

"It's a dark comedy. There's a difference."

"Mmm." She sips her cider, considering. "What about the classics? *Miracle on 34th Street*? *White Christmas*?"

"Haven't seen them."

"*It's a Wonderful Life*?"

"Never."

She stops walking. Actually stops, right there on the sidewalk, and stares at me.

"You've never seen *It's a Wonderful Life*."

"No."

"How is that possible? It's on every channel from Thanksgiving through New Year's."

"I don't watch much TV."

"It's a cultural institution, Knox. Jimmy Stewart. Zuzu's petals. Every time a bell rings, an angel gets its wings."

"I have no idea what any of that means."

"That's a crime."

"Arrest me."

The words drop an octave without my permission, and Hailey's gaze drops to my mouth for just a second before snapping back up. I watch her throat move as she swallows.

"Maybe I will," she says. "Handcuffs and everything."

Heat coils low in my stomach. "Is that a promise?"

"It's a threat."

"I don't feel threatened."

"You should." But she's almost smiling, and we've started walking again, close enough that I'm aware of every inch of space between us. Washington Square isn't far now, and the arch is visible ahead, lit with thousands of white lights against the darkening sky.

The park is magic. There's no other word for it. The Christmas tree in the center is massive, towering over the fountain, decorated with ornaments that catch and scatter the light like stars. The arch glows behind us, and everywhere I look, people are smiling and pointing at decorations and taking photos.

And as we stand there, taking it in, the first snowflakes begin to fall.

They drift down slowly, fat and lazy, catching the light as they spiral through the air. Within moments, the world transforms into something softened and hushed.

Hailey turns her face up to the sky with her eyes closed, snowflakes landing on her lashes and melting against her cheeks. She's smiling, really smiling, and my heart expands until I can barely breathe.

I want to tell her everything. The months of watching. The observations I've written down like love letters. I want to lay myself bare and let her see exactly how deep this obsession goes.

But I'm terrified that the truth will break whatever this is. That she'll look at me with horror instead of warmth. That I'll lose her before I ever really had her.

"Knox."

Her voice pulls me back. She's watching me now, snowflakes caught in her hair, her expression curious.

"You went somewhere," she says. "Just now. Where did you go?"

I take a breath. In my career, I've faced down armed combatants and walked into situations where the odds of walking out were slim, but none of that compares to what I'm about to do.

"There's something I need to tell you."

She waits. Patient. Watchful.

I step closer. Close enough to touch her. Close enough that the snow falls between us like a curtain closing out the rest of the world.

"I've been watching you." The words come out rough. Fractured. "For months. Following you, learning your patterns, your routines. Where you go, what you do, who you talk to. I know it's not normal, and I know what it makes me." My jaw locks. "But I can't stop."

Silence.

The snow keeps falling and the lights keep glowing. Somewhere nearby, a child laughs at something.

Hailey doesn't move. Doesn't speak. She watches me, and I can't read what's behind her eyes.

I've destroyed everything.

Then, slowly, she says, "I know."

My entire body goes rigid. "You know?"

"I've known for weeks, maybe longer." Her lips curve into something that's not quite a smile. "I let you follow me, Knox. I wanted you to."

I stare at her. The snow falls around us, and the words don't make sense. Can't make sense. I've confessed to stalking her, and she's looking at me like I've given her a gift.

"Why?" The word is hardly a sound.

She reaches up, and her fingers brush my jaw. I stop breathing.

"Because I like it," she says softly. "Because you make me feel protected and exposed at once. Because I've never felt more seen." Her eyes hold mine. "You look at me like I'm the only thing in the world worth watching. Do you have any idea what that feels like?"

"Yes." My voice cracks on the word. "I know exactly what that feels like."

Because she's looking at me the same way right now. Standing in the snow beneath Christmas lights, looking at me like I matter. Like I'm real.

I kiss her.

There's no decision to it, no conscious choice. One moment we're standing apart and the next my mouth is on hers, one hand in her hair, the other pressed against the small of her back. She tastes like apples and cinnamon, and when she makes a small sound against my lips, I pull her closer.

She kisses me back hard, her fingers gripping the front of my coat and pulling me in, and there's nothing gentle about it. This is months of want made physical. Every look across crowded rooms. Every accidental touch. Every night I spent watching her window and wishing I was brave enough to do exactly this.

Her mouth opens under mine and I deepen the kiss, my tongue sliding against hers, and the sound she makes shoots straight to my cock. I'm hardening in my jeans and I don't care, can't care, because she's pressing herself against me like she wants to crawl inside my skin. My hand fists in her hair and she gasps into my mouth, and the small, desperate noise undoes something in me.

I back her up until she's pressed against one of the stone pillars near the arch, my body covering hers, shielding her from the cold and from anyone who might be watching. She hooks her fingers through my belt loops and pulls my hips flush against hers, and when she feels how hard I am, she doesn't pull away. She rolls her hips against me, just slightly, and I groan against her mouth.

"Hailey." Her name comes out like a warning.

"Knox." Mine comes out like a dare.

I kiss her deeper, one hand braced against the stone beside her head, the other sliding down to grip her hip. She's making these small, breathy sounds that I want to memorize and replay for the rest of my life. The snow is falling around us and we're in public and I don't give a damn about any of it.

When we finally break apart, we're both breathing hard. Her lipstick is smeared, her cheeks flushed, her eyes bright with something that makes my dick ache.

"Well," she manages.

"Yeah."

"That was . . ."

"Yeah."

She laughs, breathless. "We should probably do that again."

"Definitely."

I kiss her again. Slower this time. Softer. Taking my time with her mouth and learning the shape of her, the way she sighs against my lips. Around us, the snow keeps falling and the city keeps moving, but none of it matters.

There's only her.

When we pull apart again, I notice she's shivering. The snow has been falling steadily, and her coat, while stylish, isn't exactly built for standing outside in a snowstorm.

"You're cold," I say.

"I'm fine."

"You're shivering."

"That's not completely from the cold." She smirks, but her teeth are chattering slightly, and something protective twists inside me.

I step back and scan the street until I spot a cab idling at the corner. I raise my hand and it pulls toward us, and I open the back door for her. She slides into the backseat without protest, and I follow her in, giving the driver her address.

The cab pulls into traffic, and Hailey is still shivering beside me, her teeth chattering despite the heat blasting from the vents. I shrug off my coat and drape it over her like a blanket, then pull her in close, my arm around her shoulders as I rub her arm through the fabric, trying to generate some warmth.

She goes tense for a moment, her body rigid against mine. I wait, not pushing, holding her and watching the city slide past the windows, everything muted by snow.

Slowly, degree by degree, she relaxes. Her weight settles against my side, and I feel some of the chill leave her body.

We don't talk. We don't need to.

The cab stops outside her building, and she stirs, pulling back to look at me. My coat is still draped around her shoulders, and she looks smaller wrapped in it, more vulnerable somehow.

"I had a good time tonight," she says. "In case that wasn't obvious."

"It was a little obvious."

"Shut up." But she's smiling. "So what happens now?"

"Now I take you out again. Tomorrow night."

She raises an eyebrow. "You're not even going to ask?"

"Would you say no?"

A pause. Then her lips curve. "Seven o'clock. Don't keep me waiting."

She leans in and presses a kiss to my cheek, brief and warm and over too quickly, then shrugs off my coat and hands it back to me.

"Keep it," I say. "You're still cold."

She blinks a few times as if she's not understanding my words. "Then what will you wear?"

"I'll survive."

She considers me for a moment, then pulls the coat back around her shoulders. "Fine. But I'm only taking it because it smells like you."

Before I can respond to that, she's opening the cab door. She steps out and walks toward her building, and halfway up the steps she pauses and bends down to pick something up. When she straightens, she's holding a single red rose, its petals dusted with snow. She turns back toward the cab, and even from here I can see her smile as she lifts the flower to her nose.

She thinks it's from me.

What the fuck?

She waves at me with the rose still in her hand, then disappears inside.

I didn't leave that rose. I've never left her anything.

The dried roses in her apartment flash through my mind. I'd assumed she bought them herself, but now I'm realizing I was wrong. Someone has been leaving her roses. Not only tonight, but for weeks. Maybe months.

And it isn't me.

I tell the driver to wait.

Her window lights up, and my stomach turns to ice.

That's when I notice him.

A figure stands across the street, half-hidden beneath an awning, nearly invisible in the falling snow. Dark coat, hood pulled up, face completely obscured. He's not moving, not fidgeting, just watching her building with a stillness that comes from training.

He's been here a while. Long before our cab pulled up.

I open the cab door and step out into the snow. His head turns at the movement, and for a long moment we stare at each other.

His hood is pulled too low and the distance is too great for me to make out any of his features, but I can see enough. The way he holds himself, the restraint in his posture. Former military. Someone who knows how to disappear when he wants to.

Someone who fucked up tonight by not noticing me first.

I take a step toward him. Before I can take another, he's turning away, walking down the sidewalk without hurry. He rounds the corner and disappears like he was never there.

I memorize everything I can. Height, approximately six feet. Build, lean but strong. The direction he went, the timing of his retreat. It's not much, but it's a start.

Hailey has a stalker. And it isn't me.

My jaw sets and my hands curl into fists inside my gloves.

I've spent months following this woman, learning her patterns, watching from a distance. But I've never left her anything. I've never made my presence known. This man has been leaving gifts, inserting himself into her life, and Hailey has no idea that the roses she's been drying and displaying aren't from some secret admirer with good intentions.

They're from someone who watches her window in the middle of the night.

Someone like me, but without my restraint.

If this stranger thinks he can get between me and Hailey, he's about to learn exactly what happens when you threaten what belongs to me.

Chapter Seven

HAILEY

You're glowing." Sloane says this from my bathroom doorway, wine glass in hand, watching me attempt to apply eyeliner without stabbing myself in the cornea. Chloe is sprawled across my bed, scrolling through her phone while simultaneously offering unsolicited fashion advice.

"I'm not glowing. I'm sweating."

"You're definitely glowing," Chloe confirms without looking up. "It's disgusting, actually. Very rom-com heroine energy."

I set down the eyeliner and examine myself in the mirror. The black dress hugs my waist and hits just above the knee. The neckline does its job without trying too hard. I touch the silver earrings Knox bought me at the market last night, still getting used to the unfamiliar weight of them.

"It's just dinner."

"It's your second date in two days." Sloane sips her wine. "That's not 'just dinner.' That's trajectory."

"Trajectory toward what?"

"Toward you finally getting laid," Chloe supplies helpfully. "Which, let's be honest, is long overdue."

I grab a lipstick and pretend to be very focused on application. "My sex life is not up for discussion."

"What sex life?" Chloe looks up, grinning. "Hails, I've known you for over two years. You haven't dated anyone. Not a single person. Not even a bad Tinder match for entertainment purposes."

"Maybe I'm selective."

"Maybe you're hiding."

I watch my reflection in the mirror, keeping it carefully neutral even as something twists inside. Chloe doesn't know how close to the mark she's hit.

"Okay, that came out harsher than I meant," she says quickly, sitting up. "I just mean . . . you never talk about your past. Like, at all. Not even embarrassing ex-boyfriend stories. Everyone has embarrassing ex-boyfriend stories."

Sloane shoots her a look. "Chloe."

"What? I'm just saying. We're her friends. We tell her everything. But Hailey's got this whole mysterious backstory thing going on, and now suddenly she's dating Knox Bishop, and I feel like we're missing important context."

I cap the lipstick and turn around, leaning against the bathroom counter. They're both watching me now, Sloane with gentle concern and Chloe with naked curiosity. I could deflect. I'm good at deflecting, have had years of practice building walls and changing subjects and steering conversations away from anything that matters. But these are my friends. Real friends, maybe the first ones I've had in a long time. And maybe I'm tired of carrying this alone.

"His name was Liam Calloway."

Chloe goes very still. Sloane sets down her wine.

"We were together for three years, and I loved him so much it scared me sometimes." I hear my own voice like it belongs to someone else, distant and too careful. "He was charming and brilliant and when he looked at me, I felt like I was the most interesting person in any room. Like nothing else existed except the two of us and whatever trouble we were about to get in to."

"What happened?" Sloane asks softly.

I look at the ceiling, at the cracks in the old plaster, at anything that isn't their faces. "I wanted more. He didn't. I wanted a future, a real one, something solid and permanent. And he wanted to keep living like tomorrow was optional, like making plans meant giving something up." My shoulders rise and fall. "So I walked away. Five years ago. Haven't dated anyone since."

No one says a word. I can practically hear them deciding how to respond.

"Five years," Chloe repeats. "Hailey, that's . . ."

"A long time to be alone. I know." I meet their eyes. "But when you love someone that completely, when you pour yourself into another person and they can't give you what you need . . . it takes a while to want to try again. You start to wonder if maybe the problem was you. If you wanted too much, asked for too much. If you're just not built for the kind of love that actually lasts."

Sloane crosses to me and pulls me into a hug that I didn't realize I needed. She smells like expensive perfume and friendship, and I let myself lean into it for a moment before the vulnerability gets to be too much.

"Knox is different," she says against my hair. "I can tell."

"He is." I pull back, surprised to find I'm smiling. "That's what terrifies me."

"Good terror or bad terror?" Chloe asks.

"I haven't decided yet." I check my reflection one more time, smoothing down a strand of hair that doesn't need smoothing. "He looks at me like I'm something worth figuring out. Like I'm a puzzle he actually wants to solve, not just a problem to fix or a girl to chase until he gets bored. Nobody's looked at me like that in a long time."

"Not even Liam?"

I pause, really considering the question. "Liam looked at me like I was a partner in crime. Someone to run with, to scheme with, to burn bright with until we both flamed out." I think about last night, Knox's face when he handed me the velvet pouch, how nervous he'd seemed despite all that military composure. "Knox looks at me like he wants to stay."

Chloe makes a sound that might be a squeal, quickly suppressed. "Okay, I take back every joke I made about your sex life. This is disgustingly romantic and I'm here for it."

"Nothing's happened yet."

"Hailey." Sloane gives me a knowing look. "I heard about what happened in Washington Square Park."

Heat rises to my cheeks. "How did you—"

"Knox told Cole. Cole told me." She smirks. "Apparently Knox showed up to work this morning looking like he hadn't slept and couldn't stop smiling. Cole said it was unsettling."

"We just kissed."

"You 'just kissed' for how long?"

I don't answer.

"Hailey." Chloe's voice drops into her interrogation register. "Spill. Now. You've given us nothing for years. No dating stories, no hook-up confessions, nothing. You owe us this."

"She's right," Sloane adds. "Consider it payment for all the times we've overshared about our love lives."

I think about deflecting, but the truth is, I want to tell someone. I've been carrying last night around like a lit match, and if I don't let some of it out, I might combust.

"It was . . . a lot." I sit on the edge of the bed, and Chloe immediately scoots closer like she's afraid she'll miss a word. "We were at Washington Square Park, and it was snowing, and he told me he'd been watching me for months. Following me. Learning my patterns."

Chloe and Sloane exchange a look that I can't quite read.

"What?" I ask.

"Nothing," Sloane says, pressing her lips together like she's trying not to laugh. "It's just . . . that sounds familiar."

"Very familiar," Chloe adds. "Cole literally moved Sloane into his penthouse and cataloged her sock drawer before their first official date."

"These men have a type," Sloane says. "And apparently that type is 'women worth stalking.'"

"It's practically a rite of passage at this point," Chloe agrees. "Welcome to the club."

I blink at them. "You're both disturbingly okay with this."

"We've made our peace." Sloane shrugs. "Now keep going. What happened after he confessed?"

"He kissed me, and I just . . . I stopped thinking. About anything. He backed me up against the arch and his hands were in my hair and I could feel how much he wanted me, and I wanted him right back. I would have let him do anything to me right there in the middle of the park. I didn't care who was watching."

Sloane's eyebrows have climbed toward her hairline. "That doesn't sound like 'just kissing.'"

"It wasn't. I mean, technically it was, but . . ." I blow out a breath. "When we finally stopped, I was shaking. Not from the cold. From wanting more. He put me in a cab and rode back to Brooklyn with me, and the whole time I was trying to figure out how to ask him upstairs."

"And?" Chloe is practically vibrating. "Did you?"

"No."

"Why the hell not?"

I hesitate. This is the part I haven't let myself examine too closely, the doubt that crept in somewhere between his mouth on mine and the cab pulling up to my building.

"Because as sexy as Knox is, I'm not sure he's my type. In bed, I mean." I glance between them, trying to gauge their reactions. "He's so controlled all the time. So buttoned up. And I need someone who can . . ." I trail off, not sure how to finish.

"Someone who can what?" Sloane prompts.

"Take control. Really take it. Someone with a darker side." I feel my cheeks flush. "I like things a certain way, and I don't know if Knox has that in him. He seems too . . . proper. Too careful."

Chloe bursts out laughing. "Oh honey. You might be surprised."

"What do you mean?"

"I mean, I thought the same thing about Jack when we first got together." She grins at the memory. "He's a firefighter. Boy Scout energy for days. Opens doors, calls older women *ma'am*, volunteers at the community center on weekends. I figured he'd be the same way in the bedroom. Sweet and gentle and . . . vanilla."

"And?"

"And I was very, very wrong." Her grin turns wicked. "Let's just say the man has depths. Plural. I made a comment once about liking it a little rough, and he just looked at me with these eyes and said, 'How rough?' I about died."

Sloane nods. "Cole's the same. That cold exterior, those perfect suits, and underneath . . ." She fans herself. "The controlled ones are always hiding something. It's like the discipline they show the world is just compression. Pressure building. And when they finally let it out . . ."

"Boom," Chloe finishes. "Knox might be exactly what you're looking for. You just have to crack through that military shell."

I think about Knox standing under the streetlamp outside my building. About the leather notebook I once glimpsed in his pocket, filled with God knows what observations about me. About the way he admitted to following me for months without a shred of shame.

He's a stalker, I remind myself. He's not as squeaky clean as he comes across.

Maybe they're right. Maybe there's more to Knox Bishop than pressed suits and rigid discipline. Maybe that careful composure is just a lid on something darker, something that would match me perfectly.

The thought sends heat pooling between my thighs.

"Where's he taking you tonight?" Chloe asks.

"Some Italian place in the West Village. He was annoyingly vague about the details."

"The man's a secret-keeper." Chloe grabs her phone and starts typing. "I'm going to look up West Village Italian restaurants and make predictions about which one."

"Please don't."

"Too late. Already committed." She scrolls, nodding to herself. "Ooh, there's one with a secret back garden. Very Knox energy. Very 'I surveilled this location before bringing my date here.'"

Despite myself, I laugh. "You're impossible."

"It's part of my charm." She looks up. "For real though, Hails. I'm happy for you. You deserve someone who looks at you like you're worth figuring out."

My phone buzzes. A text from Knox: I'm outside whenever you're ready. No rush.

"He's here." I grab my coat, check my reflection one last time. The woman looking back at me seems brighter than usual, more present, like someone who actually believes good things might happen to her. Maybe that's what hope looks like.

"Don't do anything I wouldn't do!" Chloe calls as I head for the door.

"That's a very short list."

"Exactly."

Chapter Eight

HAILEY

I'm still laughing when I hit the stairs, taking them two at a time, and when I push through the front door of my building, Knox is waiting on the sidewalk in a charcoal coat that makes his shoulders look impossibly broad. He watches me descend the steps with a look I'm still learning to read, something between hunger and reverence that makes my stomach flip.

"Hi," I say, because apparently I've forgotten how to form complex sentences.

"Hi." He offers his hand, and when I take it, his fingers close around mine like he's been waiting to touch me all day. "You look beautiful."

"You clean up okay yourself."

Understatement of the century. The man is lickable. His jaw is freshly shaved, and I want to drag my teeth across it just to hear what sound he'd make. A black sweater peeks out from under the coat, fitted enough that I can see the outline of muscle underneath, and suddenly I'm thinking about what it would feel like to slide my hands beneath that wool and find warm skin.

Down, girl.

But it's hard to behave when Knox Bishop is standing there looking like every dirty fantasy I've ever had, watching me with those gray eyes that seem to be calculating exactly how long it would take to get me out of this dress.

The restaurant is called Osteria del Cuore, and it's tucked behind an unmarked door between a dry cleaner and a boutique selling overpriced candles. Easy to miss unless you know what you're looking for. Knox leads me down a short flight of stairs into a candlelit cellar where exposed brick walls are hung with old photographs and dried herbs. The ceiling is low enough that he has to duck slightly, and there can't be more than ten tables, all of them tucked into intimate alcoves that feel like secrets.

"How did you find this place?" I ask as a hostess leads us to a corner booth hidden from the rest of the restaurant by a half-wall of wine bottles.

"I did recon."

"You scouted restaurants for our date?"

"I scouted several restaurants." He pulls out my chair, and when I sit, his hand brushes my shoulder in a way that sends heat racing down my spine. "I wanted to find somewhere we wouldn't be interrupted."

The table is small enough that our knees brush underneath, and neither of us moves away. I look around, taking in the flickering candles, the quiet murmur of other couples, the way the light catches the wine bottles like captured sunsets, and the tightness inside me loosens. This isn't a place for small talk or surface-level conversation. This is a place for telling truths.

Wine arrives without us ordering, something red and Italian that Knox apparently selected in advance. When he pours for me, his fingers brush mine on the stem of the glass, and I have to remind myself to breathe.

"So." He leans back, but his eyes never leave my face. "Tell me something I don't know about you."

"You probably already know everything, given your research methods."

"I know your patterns. Your routines. What coffee you order, what books you buy, how you walk when you think no one's watching." His voice drops lower. "I don't know what's underneath all that. The things you hide. The things that keep you up at night."

"Maybe there's nothing underneath. Maybe I'm exactly as shallow as I appear."

"There's always something underneath." He reaches across the table, and his fingers find mine, just resting there, warm and steady. "Tell me what you're afraid of."

Umm . . . I expected flirtation, banter, the usual dance of a second date. Not this. Not directness that cuts straight to bone.

"Wanting something I can't have," I hear myself say. "Getting close enough to taste it and then watching it disappear. I've done that before, wanted someone so badly I could hardly breathe, and when it fell apart . . ." I trail off, then force myself to continue. "I'm afraid of feeling that again. I'm afraid of not feeling it again. Both options terrify me."

His thumb traces a slow circle on my palm. "What do you want?"

"Right now?" I meet his eyes. "This. You. Whatever this is turning into."

"It's turning into something." His grip on my hand tightens slightly. "I've never been good at halfway, Hailey. When I want something, I want all of it. Every piece, every corner, every shadow. That can be a lot for some people."

"Is that a warning?"

"It's information. You should know what you're getting into."

Our first course arrives, a shared plate of burrata that's so creamy it practically melts on the tongue. Knox watches me take the first bite, and his mouth quirks when I close my eyes and make an involuntary sound of pleasure.

"Good?" he asks, his voice lower than before.

"Criminal." I open my eyes and catch him staring at my mouth. "You should try some before I finish it."

We eat in comfortable silence for a few minutes, trading bites of the burrata, and then the pasta arrives—fresh tagliatelle with truffle that fills the small alcove with an earthy, intoxicating scent. Somewhere between the first glass of wine and the second, the conversation drifts into different territory.

"I need to tell you something," Knox says, setting down his fork.

I tense, because nothing good ever follows those words. "Okay."

"I've noticed some things that concern me. Nothing I can put my finger on exactly, but my instincts are rarely wrong."

"Things like what?"

"Like someone standing outside your apartment last night. Watching." He takes a sip of wine, casual, but I can see the tension in his shoulders. "After I left. He was across the street, just standing there. I don't think that's a coincidence."

I raise an eyebrow. "You mean besides you?"

He doesn't flinch. "Besides me."

"Knox." I lean back in my chair, fighting a smile. "You just confessed to following me for months. Forgive me if I'm not panicking over a hunch."

"It's more than a hunch."

"Is it? Or is this your way of justifying why you need to keep stalking me?" I take a sip of wine, watching him over the rim of my glass. "Because if you need an excuse, you don't. I already told you I don't mind."

I can see him wrestling with how to respond. Part of me knows I should take this more seriously. But the other part—the louder part—is too amused by the irony. Yes, I have a stalker. I'm looking right at him. If Knox Bishop wants to use some phantom threat as an excuse to stay close, to keep watching, to continue this delicious game we've been playing? I'll humor him. There are worse fates than being obsessively protected by a man who looks like that.

"I'm not using it as an excuse," he says. "I'm telling you because you deserve to know. And because I plan on staying very close until I figure out what's going on."

"How close are we talking?"

"Close enough that if someone's watching you, they'll know they're not the only one." His eyes meet mine across the table. "Close enough that if anyone tries anything, I'll be there before they can blink."

"And what if I don't want you that close?"

"Then you'd tell me, and I'd back off." He reaches across the table, his fingers finding mine. "But something tells me that's not what you're going to say."

He's right. God help me, he's right.

"I don't mind," I admit quietly. "The watching. Knowing you're there." I turn my hand over so our palms press together. "Most people would probably run screaming from a man who just admitted to surveilling them."

"You're not most people."

"No. I'm not."

Something passes between us, an understanding that goes deeper than words. He knows what he is. I know what I am. And somehow, impossibly, those broken pieces fit together.

Somewhere between the main course and dessert, I set down my fork and decide to push.

"You said you like control. What does that mean, for you?"

"It means I like to know exactly what's happening. Where. When. How." His voice drops. "It means when I'm with someone, I want to be the only thing they're thinking about. I want to know I have their complete attention, and I want them to know they have mine."

"That sounds intense."

"It is."

"What if the other person likes giving up control?"

The air between us thickens. I watch him swallow, his throat working.

"Then we'd be very compatible."

I lean forward, closing the distance between us over the small table. "I'm not good at rules. Never have been. I like pushing, testing, seeing what I can get away with. Seeing how far I can go before someone stops me."

"I've noticed."

"Does that bother you?"

"It makes me want to push back."

My thighs clench under the table. I don't think he misses it. "And what about being watched? You seem to like that."

"I like watching," he corrects. "But I've been known to appreciate an audience, under the right circumstances."

"What circumstances?"

"The ones where I'm in charge of who sees what. Where I decide what gets revealed and what stays hidden. Where the person I'm with trusts me enough to let me make those calls."

His hand slides higher on my arm, fingers trailing up past my wrist, and I feel the touch everywhere. In my pulse, my spine, places much lower. Every nerve ending in my body is suddenly, painfully awake.

"I don't mind being seen," I say quietly. "When it's someone I want seeing me."

Knox's eyes are almost black in the candlelight, his pupils blown so wide there's barely any gray left. His breathing has changed, gone slower and more measured, and when he speaks, his voice has dropped to a rasp that scrapes over my skin.

"You're making it very hard to be a gentleman."

"Good."

He flags down the server without looking away from me. "Check, please."

The temperature has dropped by the time we step outside, and snow is drifting down in lazy spirals that catch the light from shop windows and streetlamps. Knox takes my hand as we walk, our breath fogging in the cold air, and for a while we don't speak. We don't need to. The West Village is beautiful at night, brownstones and bare trees and holiday decorations glowing in windows, our footsteps crunching on freshly fallen snow. Every few minutes Knox pulls me closer, his arm around my shoulders, his warmth bleeding into me through layers of wool and cotton.

The snow falls around us, and I find myself thinking about last night. The confession. The kiss. The way everything shifted between us in the space of a heartbeat.

"What are you thinking about?" he asks.

I stop walking and turn to face him. We're standing under a streetlamp, snow falling around us like the universe is trying too hard to be romantic, and I reach up to brush a snowflake from his jaw.

"Last night."

"What about it?"

"The part where you stopped being careful."

His hands find my waist, pulling me closer. Not kissing me yet. Just holding me there, our bodies pressed together through layers of winter clothing.

"I'm always careful."

"Not with me."

"No." His forehead drops to rest against mine. "Not with you."

When he kisses me, it feels different from last night. Slower. Like he's proving something, making a point about patience and control even as his tongue traces my lower lip before sliding inside. I make a sound that gets lost between our mouths, my fingers fisting in the front of his coat, pulling him closer even though there's no space left between us.

He walks me backward until my shoulders hit a building, and pins me there with his body. The stone is cold through my coat, but everywhere Knox touches burns. His hand slides up my side, fingers finding the curve of my waist, the edge of my ribs, higher. He stops just below my breast, not quite touching, and I arch into him, desperate to close the distance.

"Patience," he murmurs against my lips.

"I don't have any."

"I know." He kisses me again, harder this time, and I can feel his restraint starting to fray at the edges. "I've been watching you for months, Hailey. I know exactly how impatient you are. How you fidget when you're bored, how you tap your fingers when you're waiting for something, how you speed up when you're close to getting what you want."

"Then stop making me wait."

He pulls back just enough to meet my eyes. In the lamplight, with snow caught in his hair and want written across every line of his face, he's the most beautiful thing I've ever seen.

"Not yet," he says. "Not here."

"Then take me home."

Something flares in his eyes, hot and possessive, and for a moment I think he's going to kiss me again. Instead, he takes my hand and starts walking, his pace faster than before, his grip tight enough that I feel claimed.

Neither of us speaks. We don't need to. The tension between us is a living thing, coiling tighter with every step, every brush of our bodies as we navigate the snowy way home. By the time we reach my building, I'm practically vibrating with want.

At the front steps, I turn to face him. His breathing is ragged, his jaw tight, his eyes burning into mine with an intensity that makes my knees weak.

"Come upstairs," I say.

His whole body goes still. "Hailey."

"I mean it." I reach for the lapel of his coat, curling my fingers into the wool. "Come upstairs, Knox."

He catches my wrist, his thumb pressing against my pulse point where my heart is hammering out a frantic rhythm. "If I come up tonight, I'm not leaving."

The words hang between us, heavy with promise. Heavy with warning.

"That's the point," I whisper.

"No." He steps closer, backing me against the railing, his free hand coming up to grip my hip. "I don't think you do. I'm not talking about spending the night. I'm talking about more than that. Once I'm in, Hailey, I'm in. All the way. And I need you to be sure that's what you want before we cross that line."

My breath catches. He's not just talking about sex. He's talking about everything. The watching, the wanting, the obsession that runs both ways. He's asking if I'm ready to be his completely.

The answer is yes. God, the answer is yes. But there's something that tells me he needs me to wait. To be certain. To come to him when there's no doubt left.

"Tomorrow," he says. "Dinner at my place. And if you still want this after . . ." He doesn't finish the sentence. He doesn't need to.

"I'll still want this."

"I hope so." He releases my wrist and takes a step back, putting space between us that feels like a wound. "Tonight, I need to know you're safe inside. Doors locked. Windows checked."

"Knox—"

"Please." The word comes out fractured, and I realize how much this is costing him. How much control it takes to walk away when every line of his body is screaming to stay. "Let me take the time it deserves."

"It's been a year—"

"Let me do this right."

I swallow hard and nod. "Okay. Tomorrow."

"Tomorrow."

He waits while I climb the steps, waits while I fumble with my keys, waits until I'm through the door and I hear the lock click behind me. Only then do his footsteps retreat down the stairs.

I lean against the door, heart pounding, body aching. Part of me wants to yank it open and drag him back. But he's right. Whatever this is between us, it deserves more than a frantic tumble born from weeks of tension. It deserves intention. It deserves certainty.

It deserves everything.

I cross to the window and pull aside the curtain, expecting to see Knox walking away into the night.

He's there, standing under the streetlamp, looking up at my building. Waiting to see my light come on. Making sure I'm safe.

But there's someone else, too.

Across the street. A figure, half-hidden in shadow between two parked cars. Tall. Lean. Perfectly still.

Not Knox. Knox is right there under the streetlamp.

This is someone else.

My blood goes cold. Knox's words from dinner echo in my head. *Like someone standing outside your apartment last night. Watching.*

I'd dismissed it. Laughed it off. Chalked it up to his overprotective instincts.

But he was right.

The figure doesn't move, doesn't shift, just stands there in the darkness, watching my building with the same patience Knox showed all those months he followed me. Except this doesn't feel protective. It feels . . .

And then, as if sensing my gaze, the figure turns. The streetlight catches his face for a moment—a flash of haunting features, dark eyes—before he melts back into the shadows and disappears.

My breathing stops.

Those eyes. That stance. Something sparks in my memory, a ghost of recall that I can't quite grasp.

I've seen that patience before. Five years ago. In a different life.

My phone buzzes, making me jump.

Safely inside?—Knox

I type back with trembling fingers: Yes. All locked up.

I watch him read the message, watch him look up at my window one more time, watch him finally turn and walk away into the snowy night. Part of me wants to call him back, to tell him what I saw.

But I don't.

Because if I'm right about who's standing in the shadows, this is something I need to handle myself.

I turn off the lights and stand in the dark, watching the empty street where that figure had been.

Just my imagination, I tell myself. Just paranoia.

But when I crawl into bed, I don't sleep.

Some ghosts don't stay buried.

Chapter Nine

KNOX

I don't want to leave her. Standing on the sidewalk outside her building, watching her window light up, I can still taste her on my lips. Still feel the press of her body against mine, the way she arched into me when I backed her against that building. Every nerve is screaming at me to go back up those stairs, to pound on her door and finish what we started.

But I told her tomorrow. Dinner at my place. I promised to do this right.

So I force myself to turn away, to start walking toward where I parked three blocks over. The cold air does nothing to cool the heat still thrumming under my skin. I keep seeing her face in the lamplight, lips swollen from kissing, eyes dark with want. The sound she made when I gripped her hip. The way she said *come upstairs* like it was a challenge and a plea wrapped together.

I wanted to. God, I wanted to.

I wanted to push her through that door and pin her against the wall. Wanted to fist my hand in her hair and pull until her throat was bared for my mouth. I've spent months imagining what she'd look like underneath me, what sounds she'd make if I bent her over and took what I wanted. Whether she'd fight back or melt. Whether she'd beg.

I'm betting she'd do all.

The fantasy is so vivid I almost miss him.

Almost.

A figure on the corner, half-hidden by a delivery van. I catch the movement in my peripheral vision and my training kicks in before my brain fully registers what I'm seeing. I stop walking. Turn my head just enough to get a better angle without telegraphing that I've spotted him.

He's watching her place. Same spot I saw him last night, give or take twenty feet.

This time I get more. The streetlight catches ink on his neck, dark lines crawling up past his collar toward his jaw. He's not wearing the hood tonight, but he's angled away from me, face in shadow. I can make out dark hair, a lean build. Wiry, like a distance runner, someone you'd underestimate right up until you couldn't. But the rest is just impression. If I passed him on the street tomorrow, I'm not sure I'd know him. All I've really got is the tattoos and the way he carries himself.

I take a step toward him.

He's already moving. Not running, not rushing, just gone. Around the corner and into the darkness like smoke dispersing.

By the time I reach the spot where he'd been standing, the street is empty. I scan doorways, parked cars, the gaps between buildings. Nothing. Whoever this guy is, he knows how to vanish when he needs to.

I stand there for a long moment, breathing hard, hands flexing at my sides. Close. I was so close.

The walk back to my car feels longer than it should. I drive home on autopilot, and by the time I'm sitting at my kitchen table with the leather notebook open in front of me, the want has curdled into darkness. Something that won't let me sleep.

I flip backward through the pages. Months of observations. Months of documenting every detail of her life like a man possessed.

October 3. She stayed late at the studio, left at 9:47. Stopped for Thai food on Smith Street. Nothing unusual.

October 17. Late night walk through the Village. Alone, no destination. Walked home alone. I followed from two blocks back.

November 2. She looked over her shoulder three times on her walk home. I thought she'd clocked me.

I pause on that entry. *Thought she'd clocked me.* I know better now. She told me tonight, standing in the snow with her fingers curled into my coat, that she's known for weeks. Maybe longer. She let me follow her. Wanted me to.

All those nights I congratulated myself on being invisible, she was playing me like a violin.

The thought should bother me more than it does. Instead, I find myself smiling in the dark of my kitchen, remembering the look on her face when she admitted it. No shame. No accusation. Just that spark in her eyes, like we'd been dancing this whole time and she was finally letting me know she'd been leading.

I keep flipping through the notebook, but now I'm looking for something else. Moments when her attention might have snagged on something other than me. Times when she seemed nervous, distracted, spooked by shadows I wasn't casting.

There. November 15. *She stopped at her mailbox and stood there for almost a minute, just staring at something in her hand. When she went inside, she left the lobby light on all night.*

And here. November 28. *She took a different route home. Doubled back twice. I thought she was testing me, but her shoulders were tight the whole walk. She looked over her shoulder six times in ten blocks.*

Something about it doesn't sit right. She knew I was there—she's told me as much. So why the tension? Why the doubling back? It wasn't for my benefit.

I close the notebook and open my laptop instead. When Hailey first started working for Sloane, I ran a background check. Clean record, solid employment history, good references. Nothing that raised flags.

But I only went back three years, and tonight I go further.

Five years ago, Hailey Parker appeared in New York. Got an apartment in Brooklyn. Started working freelance jewelry gigs, built a portfolio, climbed the ladder until she landed with Sloane. A clean trajectory that makes perfect sense on paper.

Before that? Nothing.

I've seen this before. Helped create it, back in my contractor days, for people who needed to disappear. It takes money and motivation and usually a very good reason to erase yourself so completely.

Hailey Parker is a ghost who became a person five years ago, and now there's a man with tattooed skin watching her apartment at night.

The roses bother me more now than they did before. I already knew they weren't from me—figured that out the first night I saw him standing across from her building. But back then I assumed it was just some random guy who'd fixated on her, someone harmless leaving flowers like a lovesick teenager. Now I'm not so sure.

Now I'm wondering if whoever's leaving those roses knew her before she became Hailey Parker. If he's part of whatever she erased five years ago when she built herself a new life from nothing.

She still thinks they're from me. Still has them hanging in her kitchen window, dried and preserved like love letters. I should have told her the truth that first night. Should have warned her.

But I didn't. And now I'm in too deep to explain why I kept it to myself.

The thought settles into my gut and stays there. This isn't random. This isn't some stranger who spotted her on the subway and decided to fixate. This is someone who was already looking. Someone who found her despite five years of careful anonymity.

I should tell her. Show her what I found, lay out my suspicions, let her decide how to handle whatever past is catching up with her.

But I don't know how to do that without revealing how deep I've dug. She knows I follow her. She's okay with that. But there's a difference between protective surveillance and excavating someone's buried history, and I've crossed into territory I'm not sure she'd forgive.

Morning comes too fast. I go to work, run through security protocols with Cole, approve the guest list for next week's gala. Meetings blur together while my mind keeps circling back to Hailey, to the tattooed stranger, to all the questions I don't know how to ask.

By 6 p.m. I'm parked outside her building again, an hour early because waiting in my apartment was making me crawl out of my skin.

I scan her window. The street. Every parked car, every passing figure, every shadow that might hide another watcher.

Nothing.

Just the usual evening traffic, neighbors walking dogs, the ordinary rhythm of a Brooklyn block settling into dusk. No stranger lurking on corners. No phantom in the dark.

I pull out my notebook and open to a fresh page.

Someone else is watching you now. I don't know who he is yet, but I will. Whatever secrets you're keeping, whoever this other guy is, I'm going to find out. Because I'm in too deep to walk away now.

I stare at the words until they blur. Threat or promise, I'm not sure there's a difference anymore.

Twenty minutes until I ring her buzzer. Twenty minutes to decide whether I tell her everything tonight or keep digging in silence, protecting her from a danger she doesn't know exists while I figure out exactly what we're dealing with.

Her silhouette passes the window. She's getting ready, probably putting on that dark lipstick, sliding those silver rings onto her fingers. Making herself beautiful for me while I sit in my car with a partial sketch and a growing list of questions.

I wanted simplicity. Dinners and conversations and the slow unwinding of two people learning each other. I wanted to earn her trust the honest way, to wait until she felt safe enough to tell me her secrets on her own terms.

Instead, I'm about to walk up those steps with lies of omission already forming on my tongue, wanting her so badly I can't think straight, already planning how to hunt down the man who believes he can watch her without consequences.

I will find out who he is. I will find out what Hailey's running from. And if he's a threat to her, I will end it.

Whatever it takes.

I get out of the car and head for her door.

Chapter Ten

HAILEY

I've been dreading tonight all day. Knox texted this morning about a work conflict, some security issue at one of Cole's properties that needed his attention, and my first thought wasn't disappointment. It was fear. Because a night without Knox means no one between me and Liam if he follows me again, and after last night, after I saw his face in the streetlight and felt my whole world crack down the middle, I don't know if I'm ready to face him.

I'm not ready to face him.

My present is finally worth something. I have friends and a career and a man who looks at me like I'm the best thing that ever happened to him. I spent five years building this life from nothing, and I'm not ready to watch it crumble because my past decided to show up on a snowy Brooklyn sidewalk.

But I can't hide in the studio forever, so I bundle into my coat and start the long walk home, scanning every shadow and doorway like the paranoid ex-criminal I apparently still am underneath all this legitimate jewelry designer polish.

He's there within two blocks. I feel him before I see him, that familiar prickle at the back of my neck that used to mean safety and now just means trouble. My old training kicks in without permission, instincts I thought I'd buried rising to the surface like bodies in a thaw. I catch his reflection in a storefront window as I pretend to examine a display of vintage ornaments. Half a block back, dark coat, hands in pockets, watching me with that patient focus I used to find so attractive.

I could turn around right now. March up to him and demand to know what he wants, why he's here, what happened to our agreement. We were supposed to wait ten years before we touched the diamond. Ten years for the heat to die down completely, for the man we stole from to stop looking, for the world to forget that the Snowflake Diamond ever existed. That was the plan. That was our retirement fund, our insurance policy, our ticket to whatever life we wanted once enough time had passed.

Five years isn't ten. Five years is too soon.

But I don't turn around, because I'm not ready for that conversation. I'm not ready to look into Liam Calloway's eyes and figure out whether he's here for the diamond or for me or for something worse. I'm not ready to explain where I've been and who I've become and why I never reached out, not once, in all the years since I disappeared.

So I keep walking, and he keeps following, and we maintain this careful distance like two magnets that know better than to get too close.

The smart thing would be to lose him. I know this neighborhood well enough to shake a tail, could duck through the bodega on the corner and out the back entrance, cut through the alley behind the laundromat, disappear into the subway and resurface somewhere he'd never think to look. I've done it before, back when losing a tail meant the difference between freedom and a prison cell.

But I don't want to run from Liam. I want to understand why he's here.

I just don't want to understand it tonight.

I turn on to my block and stop beneath a streetlight, letting the yellow glow pool around me. When I turn to face him, he's standing at the edge of the light with his hands in his pockets, watching me with those dark eyes that used to make me forget my own name.

God, he looks good. Liam Calloway was always unfairly beautiful, a man who could make you forget your own moral code just by walking into a room. His face has hardened since I last saw it, the boyish charm weathered into something more brutal, but it only makes him more magnetic. He stands there like a predator pretending to be tame, every line of his body radiating tension and quiet threat, and my body responds before my brain can stop it. Five years, and he still makes my pulse stutter like a rookie on her first job.

I remember what it felt like to have his hands on me. The way he used to fuck me like he was trying to crawl inside my skin, like he couldn't get close enough no matter how hard he tried. Liam never did anything halfway, and sex was no exception. He'd pin me against walls, bend me over tables, wake me up in the middle of the night because he couldn't stand having me next to him and not being inside me. I'd never felt so consumed by another person. So completely owned.

His hand closed around my throat in that hotel room in Vienna, not squeezing, just holding. Claiming. I was pinned beneath him, my back arching off the mattress, his cock buried so deep inside me I couldn't tell where I ended and he began.

"You're mine," he whispered against my mouth, his hips rolling slow and devastating. "Say it."

"I'm yours."

His grip tightened, just enough to make my head swim, and he smiled like I'd given him the world. "Every gorgeous inch of you. Every thought in that brilliant head. Every breath you take." He pulled out slowly, then slammed back in so hard I cried out. "I'm going to ruin you for anyone else, Hailey. And you're going to thank me for it."

He released my throat, his hand moving to grasp my hip, his fingers digging into my flesh as he ground against me. I could feel every ridge, every vein of him, as he slid in and out, his pace quickening. I wrapped my legs around his waist, pulling him deeper, my body meeting his thrusts eagerly.

His mouth left mine, trailing hot, open-mouthed kisses down my neck, pausing to suck at the pulse point. I could feel my heartbeat against his lips, my breath coming in short, sharp pants. His other hand cupped my breast, his thumb circling my nipple, sending jolts of pleasure straight to my core.

"Look at me," he commanded. I forced my eyes open, meeting his gaze. It was intense, possessive, and utterly consuming. "Who do you belong to?" he asked, his hips slamming against mine.

"You," I breathed, my body tensing, my inner muscles clenching around him. "Only you."

A satisfied growl rumbled from his chest, and he sat back, his hands gripping my thighs, his eyes never leaving mine. His pace quickened, his hips moving like a piston, driving me higher and higher. I could feel my orgasm building, my body coiling like a spring ready to release.

"Come for me, Hailey," he demanded. "Let me feel you come all over my cock."

I shattered, his name ripped from my throat like a confession. And when I could finally breathe again, I slid down his body and wrapped my lips around him, tasting myself on his skin as I took him deep, letting him fuck my mouth until his hands fisted in my hair and he spilled down my throat with my name on his lips.

That's the part that scares me most. Not that he found me, not that he's watching, but that some treacherous part of my body still responds to him like no time has passed at all. Like I'd let him back in if he asked. Like I'd forget everything I've built and everyone I've become just to feel that intensity again.

I can't let that happen. I won't.

We stare at each other across thirty feet of snowy pavement. I don't move toward him and he doesn't move toward me. Neither of us speaks. What would we even say?

He gives me that half-smile I used to love, the one that always meant he knew something I didn't. But there's no mischief behind it tonight. Just tired recognition, like he's been waiting a long time for this moment and now that it's here, he doesn't know what to do with it either.

Then he turns and walks away, disappearing around the corner like smoke.

I let out a long breath and my shoulders drop. My hands are shaking inside my coat pockets, and my heart is pounding so hard I can feel it in my throat.

That could have been a confrontation. That could have been answers.

Instead it was just two people acknowledging a shared history and agreeing, without words, that neither of them is ready to deal with it yet.

The walk up to my apartment takes forever. My legs feel like they're filled with sand, and my brain won't stop cycling through questions I don't have answers to. What does he want? Why now? What changed?

I'm supposed to be getting ready for dinner at Knox's place. I'm supposed to be putting on something that makes his jaw drop, maybe that black dress with the low back, definitely those silver earrings he bought me at the market. I've been thinking about tonight since he asked me last night, imagining being alone with him in his space, finally crossing the line we've been dancing around since the kiss.

But I can't do it. Not tonight. Not with Liam's face burned into my retinas and my past clawing at the edges of everything I've tried to build.

Knox will know something's wrong. He always knows. The man reads people like most humans read stop signs, automatically and without effort. One look at my face and he'll start asking questions, gentle at first and then more insistent, because that's who he is. He protects. He investigates. He doesn't let things go.

And what am I supposed to tell him? *Hey, funny story, before I was Sloane's assistant I was a professional jewel thief. My ex-boyfriend and I stole a twenty-million-dollar diamond from a Russian oligarch with connections to some very scary people, and we hid it in the Canadian wilderness as a retirement plan, and apparently my ex has decided that five years of radio silence is enough and now he's stalking me through Brooklyn. Also, I'm pretty sure I'm still attracted to him, which is super inconvenient given that I'm falling for you.*

Yeah. That conversation would go great.

I pull out my phone and stare at the screen for a long moment before I start typing.

I'm so sorry but I need to cancel tonight.
Not feeling well. Can we reschedule?

The reply comes almost instantly.

What's wrong?

I chew my lip, trying to figure out how much to say. Lying to Knox feels wrong in a way I can't quite articulate, like I'm betraying something precious before it even has a chance to grow. But the truth isn't an option either. Not yet. Not until I figure out what Liam wants and whether my past is about to detonate my present.

Just a headache. Long day. I
think I need to sleep it off.

Three dots appear. Disappear. Appear again.

Do you need anything? I can bring soup.
Or medicine. Or just sit with you.

God, this man. This ridiculous, overprotective, impossibly sweet man is offering to bring me soup because I have a fake headache. Meanwhile I'm lying through my teeth about who I really am.

No, I'll be okay. Just need rest.
I'm sorry to bail on you.

A pause. Then:

Get some rest. I'm not far if you need me.

He's not asking permission. He's just letting me know. And I should probably find that invasive, but all I feel is relief. If Knox is nearby, Liam will keep his distance. Whatever conversation we need to have, whatever reckoning is coming, it won't happen while I have a six-foot-three former Marine watching over me. I'm not ready to face my past yet, and Knox's obsessive protectiveness might be the only thing keeping it at bay.

Thank you. For understanding.

Always. Feel better, Hailey.

I set the phone down and move through the apartment on autopilot, checking windows, testing locks, yanking curtains closed like they'll protect me from whatever's coming.

The dried roses catch my eye when I pass through the kitchen. Still hanging in the window where I put them weeks ago, preserved because I thought they were romantic. Because I assumed Knox had left them and I wanted to hold on to that gesture.

A single red rose. Every time.

My stomach drops so fast I have to grab the counter.

Liam always brought me one rose. Never a dozen, never a bouquet. Just one perfect stem, because he said I wasn't the kind of woman who needed to be buried in flowers to feel special. It was our thing, our signature, our private language. On the pillow after our first night together. Waiting on my seat before a job. Tucked into my suitcase when I wasn't looking so I'd find it later and think of him.

One rose. Every single time.

And I've been drying them in my window like love letters from someone else.

How did I miss this? How did I not recognize his signature on every single stem?

Because I didn't want to. Because it was easier to believe that Liam had moved on, found some other partner, some other life, some other woman to bring single roses to. I told myself he wouldn't come looking because the alternative was too terrifying to consider. Liam can find anyone. I've watched him track down a forger in witness protection once, just for fun, just to prove he could do it. If he wanted to find me, nothing I did would stop him.

I just assumed he didn't want to.

Turns out I was the idiot who thought disappearing meant being forgotten. He's been here for weeks, maybe months, leaving his calling card on my doorstep again and again, and I was so caught up in Knox and my shiny new life that I couldn't see what was right in front of my face.

The roses weren't romantic. They were a message.

I found you. I've always known exactly where you are.

I sink onto the couch and press my palms against my eyes until colors bloom in the darkness.

What does Liam want?

The diamond. It has to be. Twenty million dollars in flawless perfection, hidden somewhere in the Northwest Territories that only I know about. Liam trusted me to stash it, and I never told him where. Insurance for both of us, he said. But really, it was insurance for me. A secret I've kept for five years, the one piece of leverage I have if everything goes sideways.

Something must have changed. Some pressure I don't know about, something that made him decide breaking our agreement was worth the risk. Or maybe Kedrov got close enough to spook him. That man doesn't forget, and he doesn't forgive. We always knew he'd keep looking.

But I'm not ready to go back to that life. I'm not sure I'll ever be ready. But if Liam is back, trouble is coming with him. It always does. And whatever brought him out of hiding is going to land on my doorstep whether I'm ready for it or not.

I watch the streetlight paint stripes across my ceiling through the blinds. Somewhere out there, Knox is probably parked in his car, watching my building. Protecting me from threats he doesn't even know exist. And somewhere else, Liam is doing the same thing, watching from whatever shadow he's found to hide in, waiting for me to be ready to face him.

Two men watching me. Two different versions of obsession.

One represents everything I want to become. The other represents everything I'm trying to leave behind.

Chapter Eleven

HAILEY

The envelope is waiting for me when I open my door the next morning, propped against the doorframe. No postmark. No return address. Just my name in handwriting I'd recognize anywhere, those confident loops and slashes that used to leave notes on my pillow, sign forged documents, scrawl love letters on hotel stationery across three continents.

My hands are trembling before I even get it open.

Inside, there's a photograph. Eight by ten, glossy, professionally printed. Twenty million dollars staring back at me from a piece of paper.

The Snowflake Diamond.

I sink onto the hallway floor right there, my back against the doorframe, unable to make my legs carry me any farther. God, I'd almost forgotten how beautiful it is. Twenty-three carats of perfect clarity, cut in that distinctive pattern that earned its name, each facet catching light like frozen starlight. In the photo, it's displayed on black velvet under museum lighting, probably the insurance company's documentation shot before we liberated it from Kedrov's private collection.

No note accompanies the image. Liam doesn't need one. The message is clear enough.

I know you saw me last night. I know you recognized me. And now we need to talk about the one thing that still binds us together.

I stare at the diamond for a long time. The last time I saw it in person, I was shoving it into a waterproof case and burying it in frozen ground while my fingers went numb and my breath fogged in the arctic air. I thought I was being smart. Careful. I thought I was buying us time.

I fold the photograph and tuck it into my coat pocket, then force myself to stand up and walk to work like a normal person having a normal day. The December air bites at my cheeks. Christmas shoppers crowd the sidewalks. Somewhere, "Silver Bells" is playing from a storefront speaker.

Merry fucking Christmas to me.

The studio doesn't help. Usually this space calms me down, the familiar smell of metal and flux, the orderly rows of tools, the soft natural light that Sloane insisted on when she designed the layout. But today I can't settle. I keep glancing at the door, at the windows, at my own reflection in the polished silver I'm supposed to be working on. Every footstep in the hallway makes my shoulders tense. Every notification ping from my phone sends my heart into my throat. I've built a life here. A real one, with health insurance and tax returns and a 401k that I actually contribute to. Hailey Parker, jewelry designer's assistant, law-abiding citizen, person who definitely does not have a twenty-million-dollar diamond buried in the Canadian wilderness.

Sloane notices around eleven.

"You okay?" She looks up from the commission piece she's been wrestling with all morning. "You seem jumpy."

"Just tired. Didn't sleep well." I force a smile that probably looks as convincing as a three-dollar bill. "Too much coffee, not enough food. You know how it goes."

She doesn't look convinced, but she lets it go. That's one of the things I love about Sloane. She knows when to push and when to give space.

"Speaking of which," she says, setting down her pliers, "I'm closing the studio for the holidays. Starting the twentieth."

I blink at her. "You're what?"

"Closing. The studio." She says it slowly, like I might be having a stroke. "That thing where we lock the doors and don't come to work? I've heard other businesses do it. Apparently it's very popular."

"Sloane, I've seen you answer client emails at midnight on a Saturday."

"That was the old me. The new me has the man I love, and he's going to have an actual vacation if I have to tie him to a beach chair myself." She grins. "I'm making Cole give everyone at Asher Industries two weeks paid time off. The twentieth through New Year's. Mandatory."

"You're making Cole Asher, workaholic billionaire, shut down his company for two weeks?"

"I'm very persuasive." The grin turns wicked. "Also, I told him if he doesn't, I'm hiding his laptop and all his devices in a location he'll never find. He knows I'm good at hiding things."

I snort. "And he agreed to this?"

"He grumbled about quarterly reports for approximately four minutes, and then I reminded him that he literally owns the company and the quarterly reports will still be there in January." She waves a hand. "Anyway, the point is, you're off too. Two full weeks, paid. No arguments. I don't want to see your face until after New Year's." She pauses, eyes gleaming. "Knox will have the time off too, by the way. Just in case you were wondering. Hint . . . hint . . . hint."

"Sloane—"

"Paid time off, Hailey. Those are three of the most beautiful words in the English language. The correct response is, 'Thank you, Sloane, you're a generous goddess and I don't deserve you.'"

Despite everything—the photograph in my pocket, the ghost from my past, the slow unraveling of my carefully constructed life—I feel my mouth twitch. "Thank you, Sloane. You're a generous goddess and I don't deserve you."

"Damn right." She picks up her pliers again. "Now stop looking like someone killed your puppy and go fix those earring backs. We've got to wrap everything up before I kick us both out of here."

I turn back to my workbench and pick up where I left off, but my hands won't cooperate. The tiny clasps blur in front of me. I'm on my third attempt at the same piece—at this rate, Sloane's going to demote me to coffee duty—when the buzz of the security door makes me drop my pliers.

Knox fills the doorway, broad shoulders blocking most of the light from the hall. He's wearing that charcoal suit that fits him like it was sewn directly onto his body, his hair slightly disheveled from the wind outside. Those gray eyes find me immediately, and my stomach seizes.

My pliers are on the floor. I'm on my hands and knees retrieving them like a very cool, very composed person. Fantastic.

"Security check," he announces, nodding at Sloane. But he's already crossing the room toward my workstation, his focus locked on me.

I used to find that flattering. Right now, it just sets my teeth on edge. Hard to enjoy being the center of someone's attention when you're busy having a small breakdown about your criminal past.

"Hey." I manage to sound almost normal. "Everything okay?"

"You tell me." He stops beside my bench, close enough that I can smell his cologne. Clean and expensive, with something warm underneath. "You canceled last night. Said you had a headache."

"I did have a headache."

"Mmm." He doesn't blink. "And now you look like you haven't slept, you're jumping at shadows, and you've got that tight thing happening around your eyes that you get when you're stressed."

Damn him and his observation skills. "Maybe I just don't like being interrogated before lunch."

"This isn't an interrogation." His voice softens. "This is me being worried about you."

I set down my tools because my hands aren't steady enough to hold them anyway. Knox is watching me like he wants to wrap me in bubble wrap and hide me somewhere no one can find me. And I want to tell him everything. The diamond, the theft, the five years of looking over my shoulder. The ex-boyfriend who just showed up like a ghost from a past I've tried so hard to bury.

But Knox isn't just a security expert with a protective streak. He's former military, law enforcement adjacent, a man who has spent his career on the right side of the law. If he finds out what I used to be, what I used to do, he won't just be disappointed. He might feel obligated to do something about it.

Would he still look at me like this if he knew? Would he still want to bring me soup when I'm sick, still park outside my building at night?

"I'm fine," I say. "Really. Just a rough night."

He studies me for another long moment. Knox isn't stupid. He knows I'm holding something back.

But instead of pushing, he just nods. "Okay. But you know where to find me if that changes."

"I know."

He glances around the studio, doing an actual security sweep now, checking windows and exits and blind spots. Professional Knox, doing his job. When he finishes, he pauses by the door.

"Dinner," he says. His eyes hold mine, steel-gray and absolutely certain. "Tonight. My place, like we planned."

"Knox—"

"Whatever's going on with you, you don't have to face it alone." His shoulders square. "Let me in, Hailey. Even if you can't tell me everything, let me be there."

I look at him standing in the doorway. This man who's been watching over me for months. Who tracked me through Bryant Park and never once made me feel afraid. Who bought me earrings at a Christmas market and kissed me on my front steps and offered to bring me soup for a fake headache. He's offering me everything I thought I wanted. A partner. Someone to lean on. A future that doesn't involve running.

This man equals stability.

Protection.

Someone who doesn't run away, but instead does the opposite. He'll charge full speed toward me. I know this. My gut knows this.

"Okay," I whisper. "Tonight."

His shoulders drop, just slightly. Like he'd been bracing for rejection.

"Seven o'clock. I'll text you the address."

Then he's gone, and I'm left staring at the door, too aware of the photograph in my pocket.

The next few hours pass in a blur of busywork. I fix the earring backs. I polish a set of silver bangles. I organize the supply closet, which doesn't need to be organized, but it gives me something to do with my hands that isn't checking my phone every thirty seconds. Sloane shoots me a few concerned looks but doesn't push, probably assuming my weirdness is Knox-related. She's not entirely wrong.

By mid-afternoon, I've almost convinced myself that the photograph was a fluke. A one-time message. Maybe Liam just wanted me to know he was in the city. Maybe he'll drop it now that he's made his point, let me go the way I let him go five years ago, and I can go back to pretending none of it ever happened.

I should know better than to hope for easy.

The courier arrives just after three.

Sloane's stepped out to grab us coffee from the place around the corner, which means I'm alone when the guy in the branded polo appears at the security door with a clipboard and a padded envelope. I sign for it with a fake smile and wait until he's gone before I tear it open.

A burner phone slides into my palm. Black, cheap, the kind you buy at a bodega with cash. Underneath it, a folded note in that same familiar handwriting.

We need to talk. Alone. The diamond isn't safe. Neither are you.
—L

The phone starts ringing before I've finished reading.

I glance toward the door. Still empty. Sloane won't be back for at least ten minutes. I slip into the hallway, pressing my back against the wall beside the fire exit, and answer.

"Liam."

"Hails." Five years, and he still says my name like that. Like we're mid-conversation, like no time has passed at all, like I didn't leave him with hollow words on paper and never look back. "It's good to hear you."

I want to scream at him. I want to demand to know why he's here, why now, why he couldn't just let me have this new life I've built from the ashes of the old one. But Sloane could come back any second, and the hallway isn't exactly soundproof. I keep it low, controlled.

"Why are you here?"

"Because someone's hunting us." No preamble. No charm. Just flat, serious Liam, which scares me more than any threat could. "Someone who knows about the diamond. They found me in Boston three weeks ago. Threats first, then surveillance. Then a break-in at my apartment while I was out." He pauses. "They tossed the place, Hailey. Took it apart like they were looking for something specific. I barely got out before they came back."

My fingers tighten on the phone. "How do you know it's connected to the diamond?"

"Because they left a message. A photograph, just like the one I left you. Kedrov's insurance documentation. They know what we took, and they want it back." I hear him exhale, rough and tired. "I tracked the threat back here. To New York. To you. Whoever's looking, they're going to find you next. If they haven't already."

The hallway feels colder than it did a minute ago.

"So what's your plan?" I keep it vague on purpose—I'm not saying a single word I wouldn't want Sloane to overhear.

"I have one. But not over a phone, Hailey. I need to see you."

I close my eyes and lean my head back against the wall. Somewhere down the hall, an elevator dings. Footsteps approach and then recede. Normal people, living normal lives, completely unaware that there's a former jewel thief having a crisis ten feet away.

"Tonight," I hear myself say. "We'll meet. Where?"

"I'll text you the address. Come alone."

He hangs up before I can respond.

I stand there for a long moment, staring at the burner phone in my hand. The photograph is still in my coat pocket. Two pieces of my past, pressing against me like weights.

Knox wants to have dinner at seven. Liam wants to meet in secret. And somewhere out there, someone is hunting for a diamond I buried in frozen Canadian soil five years ago, back when I thought I could outrun my own choices.

My past hasn't just caught up with me.

It's about to swallow me whole.

Chapter Twelve

HAILEY

The text to Knox takes four drafts to get right. I stand outside the subway station at Carroll Street, thumb hovering over send, watching my breath fog in the evening air while I debate the merits of honesty versus self-preservation.

Self-preservation wins. It always does with me.

> Running a little late. Having a quick holiday cocktail with Chloe first. I'll be there by 8. Save me some of whatever you're cooking.

His response comes in under thirty seconds. Take your time. I'm not going anywhere.

God. Of course he's not going anywhere. Knox Bishop has been not going anywhere for months now, stationed outside my life like a sentinel, and here I am lying to him before we've even had a chance to really begin. Guilt coils in my chest, hot and sour, but I pocket my phone and start walking anyway.

Red Hook in December looks like a postcard that got left out in the rain. The old brick warehouses hunker against the waterfront, strung with Christmas lights that somebody optimistic put up and nobody's bothered to take down since probably 2019. The wind off the harbor cuts right through my coat. I pass a coffee roaster, a distillery, a furniture shop selling reclaimed wood tables for prices that could fund a small revolution. The neighborhood can't decide if it wants to be working-class Brooklyn or artisanal Brooklyn, so it's settled for being both, uneasily.

Liam picked the bar. He always was better at tradecraft than me.

Rusted Anchor sits wedged between a marine supply shop and what might be an abandoned cannery. The kind of place tourists never find and locals pretend doesn't exist. No sign on the door, just a ship's anchor bolted above the frame, orange with decades of salt air corrosion. I push inside and the smell hits me first: old wood, older beer, and something fried that's probably been sitting under a heat lamp since the Obama administration.

Christmas lights here too, but these are ironic. A sad strand of multicolored bulbs droops across the back of the bar, and someone's stuck a Santa hat on the moose head mounted above the liquor shelf. The bartender looks up when I enter, takes one look at my face, and goes back to polishing glasses.

Good. I'm not here to make friends.

I spot Liam in the back booth before he spots me.

Five years fall away in the space of a heartbeat.

He's older. Harder around the edges, the softness of his late twenties burned off somewhere in the years between then and now. His dark hair is shorter than he used to wear it, and there's a scar on his jawline that wasn't there before, a thin white line that catches the light when he turns his head. But what really stops me is the ink. When I knew him, Liam had a few tattoos scattered across his chest and shoulders, nothing you'd see unless he took off his shirt. Now the black lines crawl up his neck, disappearing into his hairline on one side and curling along his jaw on the other. Intricate mandala patterns, geometric and hypnotic. That much ink on the neck takes hours in a chair and a high pain tolerance. It's striking. It's incredibly hot.

I shove that thought down hard. I'm here for information, not to catalog my ex-boyfriend's body modifications.

Those eyes are the same, though. Brown so dark they're almost black, quick and clever and seeing everything.

He's always been handsome in that rakish, slightly dangerous way that makes mothers lock up their daughters and daughters climb out their windows. I used to find it irresistible. I used to find a lot of things about Liam irresistible, which is how I ended up hiding stolen diamonds in the Canadian wilderness instead of finishing my art history degree.

He sees me. His mouth curves into that familiar half-smile, the one that used to make my stomach flip and my common sense evaporate.

"Hails."

"Don't call me that." I slide into the booth across from him, putting the table between us like it'll help. "That person doesn't exist anymore."

"Fair." He doesn't argue. Just accepts it the way Liam accepts everything, like water finding the path of least resistance. "You look good. Really good."

"I look exhausted because someone's been leaving cryptic photographs on my doorstep." I flag down the waitress, a woman in her sixties with forearms like a dock worker, and order a whiskey. When she leaves, I turn back to him. "You could have just knocked, you know. Instead of the whole mysterious stalker routine."

"Would you have answered?"

Probably not. I don't give him the satisfaction of admitting it.

He tilts his head, studying me. "You changed your hair."

"You got a face tattoo."

"Neck tattoo."

"Is there really a difference?"

"About three inches and significantly more career limitations." His grin is quick, disarming. The same grin that used to get us into VIP rooms and out of tight spots. "But you're deflecting. Your hair used to be longer."

"People change their hair, Liam."

He leans back in the booth, infuriatingly relaxed. "You're also wearing less black than you used to. More color. That green is new."

I hate that he notices. I hate more that some small, traitorous part of me is pleased.

"Did you drag me to a dive bar in Red Hook to critique my wardrobe, or is there an actual point to this reunion?"

"Can't it be both?" But his smile fades, and something more serious settles in.

"So," I say instead, keeping my voice low. "You really think returning the diamond is going to make this go away? That whoever's hunting you is just going to shrug and move on?"

"I think it's better than the alternative." He takes a drink from whatever's in his rocks glass. "Running didn't work. Hiding didn't work. The only leverage we have is the thing they want."

"And if they decide we're loose ends once they have it?"

"Then we make sure the handoff is clean. Anonymous, untraceable. They get what they want, we disappear, everybody walks away happy." He sets the glass down. "It's not perfect. But it's a plan."

The whiskey arrives. I wrap my fingers around the glass and don't drink yet, needing something to hold on to.

"Your plans used to involve more contingencies," I say. "Remember the Beaumont job? You had backup plans for our backup plans. Flow charts. Color coding."

"I didn't have flow charts."

"You had a laminated card."

"That was a quick reference guide." But he's fighting a smile now, and god help me, I almost smile back. "And the Beaumont job went perfectly."

"We had to leave through a window."

"A planned window exit."

"We were on the third floor."

"And we stuck the landing." He raises his glass to me. "Admit it. We were good together."

Changing the subject and not wanting to admit just how "good" he was at everything, I say, "So you need me. You can't find it without me."

"The agreement we made." His eyes hold mine. "Only you would know the location. Even if you told me now, described every landmark, I'd never find it. Remote Canada, unmarked terrain, five years of weather changing everything. I need you to take me there."

I think about that frozen ground. The weight of the waterproof case in my hands. The way my fingers went numb as I buried twenty million dollars in a place no one would ever think to look.

"When?" I ask.

"Tomorrow. I've already arranged transport and gear. We fly into Yellowknife and drive from there." He pulls out a phone—not the burner—and glances at the screen. "How much time can you get away?"

"My boss is closing the studio for the holidays. Two weeks off starting the twentieth."

"Perfect timing."

I laugh, but there's nothing funny about it. "Yeah. Perfect."

He's watching me again, cataloging every micro-expression the way he used to watch marks. Which is why he notices when I check my phone for the third time in five minutes.

"You're seeing someone."

I don't bother denying it.

"Knox." The name feels strange on my tongue in this context, like I'm introducing two worlds that should never touch. "He's . . ."

How do you explain Knox Bishop? Former Marine, head of security, a man who followed me through Christmas markets for months because he couldn't help himself? A man who looks at me like I'm something precious and breakable and doesn't know that I've been lying to him since the day we met?

Liam saves me from having to finish the sentence. "The security guy who's been following you around?"

I blink. "You've been watching him too?"

"Hard to miss a six-foot-three stalker when you're already doing surveillance on the same target." His smile is wry, almost amused. "You always did like the dangerous ones."

"Says the professional thief."

"Former professional thief." He tilts his glass toward me in a mock toast. "I went straight too, believe it or not. Got a legitimate job, paid my taxes, tried to pretend the last decade of my life didn't happen. But someone's dragging us back in whether we want it or not." He sets the glass down. "Come with me to Canada. Help me end this. Then we can both actually move on."

"And what's your legitimate job?" I ask, because I can't help myself. "Accountant? Insurance adjuster? Beekeeping?"

"Private security consulting." He has the grace to look slightly sheepish. "Helping companies find vulnerabilities in their systems."

"So you get paid to case buildings now."

"Legally. With a contract and everything. I even have business cards."

Despite everything, I feel my mouth twitch. This is the problem with Liam. He's too easy to talk to, too easy to fall back into rhythm with. Five years of silence and within twenty minutes we're bantering like nothing ever happened, like I didn't walk out on him in the middle of the night with nothing but a note on the pillow and twenty million dollars buried in frozen ground.

I look at him across the table, this man I used to love, used to run with, used to trust with my life when we were doing things that could have gotten us killed. We were good together once. A team. The kind of partners who could communicate in glances and finish each other's sentences during a job. Somewhere along the way, we became more than partners, and then somehow, we became nothing at all.

He still doesn't know why I left. I'm not sure I could explain it even now—just that one morning I woke up next to him and knew that if I didn't go, I never would. That the life we were living would become the only life I'd ever have. So I wrote three lines on hotel stationery, took nothing but my go bag, and disappeared. And he didn't come looking. I don't know if that made it better or worse. I took the heartbreak I'd caused myself and I used it to build a new life, one that didn't involve Liam or diamonds or looking over my shoulder every time I walked down the street.

Except now the past is sitting across from me in a dive bar in Red Hook, asking me to dig up twenty million dollars from frozen ground.

"He doesn't know," I hear myself say. "About any of it. Who I was, what I did. He thinks I'm just Sloane's assistant."

"And you want to keep it that way."

It's not really a question either.

"I don't know what I want." The admission feels like pulling a tooth. "I want to be the person he thinks I am. I want to deserve the way he looks at me. I want to pretend for just a little longer that I can have a normal life with a normal future."

"But you can't." Liam's voice is gentler than I expect. "Not with this hanging over you. Not with someone hunting for a diamond that can bring your whole new life crashing down. That could get you killed."

He's right. I hate that he's right.

I finish my whiskey in one long swallow and set the glass down harder than I mean to. The sound makes the bartender glance over, then look away.

"When do we leave?"

Something morphs across Liam's face. Relief, maybe. Or gratitude. Or something more complicated that I don't have the energy to unpack right now.

"In a couple of days," he says. "I'll send the details to the burner. Pack for cold—we're talking negative thirty, maybe worse."

"And Knox?"

"Tell him you're going somewhere for Christmas. Family emergency, old college friend, whatever story works."

"And if he wants to come with me?"

"Then don't let him." Liam's eyes are steady on mine. "This has to stay between us. The fewer people who know, the safer everyone is. Including him."

I nod, already calculating the lies I'm going to have to tell. The excuses. The misdirection. Knox will want to come. Knox will want to protect me, because that's who he is, and I'm going to have to push him away to keep him safe from a past he doesn't even know exists.

Merry fucking Christmas indeed.

"I should go." I slide out of the booth. "He's expecting me for dinner."

Liam stands too, and for a moment we're close enough that I can smell his cologne. Different than it used to be, something warmer and less sharp, but still somehow essentially him. My body remembers things my brain is trying to forget.

"Hailey." He catches my wrist as I turn away. His thumb presses against my pulse point, feeling my heart pitter patter. "For what it's worth, I'm sorry. For not giving you everything you deserved. For everything."

"Don't." I pull my hand back. "You don't get to apologize for five years of silence in a bar booth. Not tonight."

He lets me go. Liam's never been one to push when pushing won't get him anywhere.

"For what it's worth," he says quietly, "whoever this Knox guy is—he's lucky. I hope he knows that."

Something in my chest cracks, just a little.

"Tomorrow," he says.

I walk out into the December cold without looking back.

The whole subway ride to Knox's place, I rehearse the lies. Traffic. Chloe had a crisis. My phone died. Anything to explain why I'm showing up forty-five minutes late with guilt written all over my face and whiskey on my breath.

But when Knox opens his door, all my careful excuses evaporate.

He's wearing a soft gray henley pushed up at the sleeves, and there's a dish towel thrown over his shoulder like he forgot it was there. His apartment is warm behind him, golden with lamplight, and the smell of rosemary and butter drifts from the kitchen. He looks comfortable. Domestic. Like a home I didn't know I was missing.

"Hey." His face changes when he sees me—that instant softening, tender and open. "You made it."

"I made it."

He reaches for me, and I let him pull me inside, out of the cold, into the heat of his apartment and the smell of something incredible cooking. The door closes behind us and suddenly we're in our own little world, the city locked out, and he's cupping my face in both hands like I'm something fragile.

"You're freezing." His thumbs trace along my cheekbones, warming the skin there. "And you have snowflakes in your hair."

"It started coming down on the walk from the subway."

He doesn't respond right away. Just brushes the melting flakes from my hair with gentle fingers, tucking a strand behind my ear, his eyes searching my face like he's reading a map. Looking for something. I don't know if he finds it.

"Everything okay?" His voice is soft. "You look . . ."

I don't know how to finish that sentence for him. Guilty? Terrified? Like I'm about to destroy everything?

"Just tired," I manage. "Long week."

He keeps looking at me, those pale blue-gray eyes seeing too much, the way they always do. For a second I'm sure he knows. He has to know. You can't look at someone like that and not see the lies written all over them.

But then his thumb brushes the corner of my mouth, and he leans down and kisses me.

Not rushed. Not demanding. Just slow and thorough, his lips moving against mine like we have all the time in the world. One hand slides into my hair, cradling the back of my head, and the other settles at my waist, pulling me closer until there's no space left between us. He tastes like red wine and something sweet, and he kisses me like I'm the only thing that matters, like everything outside this apartment has simply ceased to exist.

I melt into him. I can't help it. My hands find his chest, feeling the solid warmth of him through the soft cotton, and I let myself get lost in this for a moment. In being wanted. In being held like I'm precious instead of a problem.

When he pulls back, his forehead rests against mine. His breath mingles with mine in the warm space between us. He kisses my forehead, soft and lingering, then takes my hand and leads me toward the kitchen.

"How was Chloe?" he asks over his shoulder, and the question lands like a knife between my ribs.

"Good," I lie. "She's good."

He doesn't push. He just squeezes my hand and tells me dinner's almost ready, and I follow him like the coward I am.

The guilt sits heavy in my stomach, right next to the whiskey.

Tomorrow. I have until tomorrow to figure out how to say goodbye.

Chapter Thirteen

KNOX

She shows up at 8:47, flushed from the cold and smelling faintly of whiskey.

Not wine. Whiskey.

I notice because I notice everything about her, and because during every meal we've shared, every bar, every late night at the studio, I've never once seen Hailey order whiskey. Another crack in the story Hailey texted me an hour ago, another piece of evidence I'm filing away without knowing what to do with it yet.

I take her coat, hang it by the door. "Wine?"

"God, yes."

I pour while she drifts toward the kitchen, her eyes skating over the set table, the candles I lit and then felt stupid about, the risotto I've reheated twice now. She's performing casual, but I've spent months studying this woman. I know what relaxed looks like on her, and this isn't it.

"Something smells incredible." She accepts the glass with fingers that aren't quite steady. "What did you make?"

"Mushroom risotto. Roasted vegetables."

"Knox Bishop, secret gourmet." She manages a smile that doesn't reach her eyes. "Should I be worried?"

"The Marines taught me to make MREs tolerable. The risotto I learned from YouTube."

She laughs, and some of the tension in my shoulders eases. This is familiar territory. This is us, trading quips and dancing around whatever's really going on. I can work with this. I can give her space, let her settle, wait for the right moment.

We sit at the small table by the window. The city spreads out beyond the glass, all those Christmas lights blurring together in the cold December air. For a few minutes we just eat. She makes appreciative sounds about the chanterelles. I refill her wine. We talk about nothing—whether Cole actually reads the security briefs I send him or just signs off, the client who wanted Sloane to design a collar for her Pomeranian, how long it would take me to tackle someone who broke into this apartment from where I'm sitting.

But she's not here. Not really.

I watch her push a Brussels sprout around her plate, watch the way her gaze keeps drifting toward the window like she's expecting to see someone looking back. Whatever happened tonight, wherever she actually was, it's sitting on her chest like a weight she can't shift.

"Where were you tonight?"

The words come out rougher than I intend. Her fork freezes halfway to her mouth.

"I told you. Drinks with Chloe."

"Hailey."

She sets the fork down. Swallows hard.

"How did you know?"

"Called Sloane earlier. About something else." I keep my voice level even though something hot is churning in my gut. "Chloe was with her. You weren't."

I watch her cycle through options, watch the calculation behind her eyes. She's good at this. Better than I gave her credit for. That realization lands somewhere uncomfortable.

"Knox—"

"Who is he?"

Her head snaps up. The color drains from her face.

"The man who's been watching your building." I lean forward, unable to stop now that I've started. "I've seen him. More than once. Dark hair, tattoos on his neck. Knows how to disappear when someone gets too close." I hold her gaze. "You went to meet him tonight. So I'll ask again. Who is he?"

She could lie. I see her consider it, see the practiced way she weighs her options. I've seen that look before, but never on anyone who wasn't trained for it.

Then something changes. Surrender, maybe. Or just exhaustion.

"Someone I used to know. Someone who's in trouble."

"What kind of trouble?"

"The kind I can't explain." Her eyes find mine, pleading. "Not yet."

I search her face, cataloging every tell. The pulse jumping in her throat. The slight tremor at the corner of her mouth. Whatever this is, it's real, and it's got her scared in a way I've never seen before.

"Are you in danger?"

She hesitates. That pause tells me more than words could.

"Maybe."

Something cold settles in my chest. I've faced worse situations than whatever this is, at least in terms of direct threat. But I've never cared about someone at risk the way I care about her. The stakes feel different when it's personal.

"Then we handle it. Together." I hold her gaze, making sure she understands I mean every word. "I don't care what you've done. I don't care what he is to you. If someone's threatening you, I will eliminate the threat."

"Knox—"

"I mean it, Hailey." I reach across the table and take her hand. Her fingers are ice cold. "I'm not going anywhere."

"You don't know what you're saying." She bites her lip hard enough that I want to smooth the damage with my thumb. "I've done things. Bad things. The kind that don't just go away."

"Everyone's done things."

"Not like this."

"I was a Marine for eight years." I squeeze her hand. "I've done things that still keep me awake. Things I can't take back. Whatever your past is, it's not going to scare me off."

She stares at me like I've said something impossible. Like no one has ever offered her this before.

I stand and move around the table to her side. She tips her head back to look up at me, and I cup her face in my hands, feeling the fine bones of her jaw beneath my palms.

"Let me help."

For a moment I think she's going to argue, going to insist on handling this alone. That's who she is. Self-sufficient to a fault.

Then she crumbles.

Not dramatically. She just leans forward until her forehead presses against my stomach, her shoulders shaking once, twice. Her hands fist in my shirt like she's anchoring herself against a current.

I thread my fingers through her hair and hold her, understanding for the first time how frightened she really is. This woman who's been performing calm all evening while her world comes apart at the seams.

I don't know what her past looks like. I don't know what kind of trouble she's in or who the tattooed stranger is.

But I know I'll kill anyone who tries to hurt her.

"Stay tonight," I say into her hair. "Please."

She nods against my stomach without looking up.

We don't finish dinner. I clear the plates while she curls on the couch, knees tucked up, wine glass cradled in her hands. When I come back, she makes room for me, and I sink down beside her, pulling her against my side.

"I'm sorry I lied," she says eventually, her voice muffled against my chest. "About Chloe."

"I know."

"I was going to tell you. I just didn't know how."

"You don't have to explain everything tonight." I press a kiss to the top of her head. "When you're ready."

She tilts her face up, and I see gratitude there. Relief. Something warmer underneath.

"Knox." Her hand flattens against my chest, right over my heart. "Thank you."

"For what?"

"For not pushing. For making me feel safe even when I'm not sure I deserve it."

I kiss her instead of answering.

It starts soft. Gentle. Just reassurance. But she makes this sound in the back of her throat, something between a sigh and a plea, and suddenly I'm pulling her into my lap, her thighs bracketing my hips.

Her fingers thread through my hair. My hands slide beneath her sweater, spreading across her shoulder blades. She arches into my touch, rolls her hips in a way that makes me growl against her mouth.

"We should stop." The words cost me. "You're upset. This isn't—"

"Don't." She kisses me harder, teeth catching my bottom lip. "Don't tell me what I'm feeling."

"Hailey."

"I want this." She pulls back just enough to meet my eyes. "I want you. Whatever happens tomorrow, I want tonight."

I should argue. I should be responsible.

But she's looking at me like I'm the only solid thing in her world, and I can't deny her anything.

"Okay." I cup the back of her neck. "But we're not rushing this."

She smiles for the first time since she walked through my door. A real smile. "Getting bossy already?"

"Getting protective."

I carry her to the bedroom, her legs wrapped around my waist. Set her down on the edge of my bed and kneel in front of her, working the hem of her sweater up while she watches me with dark eyes. When I pull it over her head, she's wearing a simple black bra underneath, nothing fancy, and my mouth goes dry anyway.

"Your turn," she says, reaching for my shirt.

I let her undress me. Let her push the fabric up my chest and over my head, let her fingers trace the lines of ink across my pecs and down my ribs. She's mapping me, I realize. Learning the terrain. Her touch is light but thorough, trailing over old scars and newer tattoos with equal curiosity.

"These are beautiful." Her fingertip follows a line of script along my collarbone. "What do they mean?"

"Later." I catch her hand, press a kiss to her palm. "Right now I just want to feel you."

I unbutton her jeans slowly, giving her time to change her mind, to pull back, to tell me this is too fast. She lifts her hips instead, helping me slide the denim down her legs. Black cotton underneath, matching the bra. Simple and devastating.

She reaches for my belt, and I let her unbuckle it, let her work my jeans open with fingers that tremble just slightly. When she pushes them down my hips, I'm already hard, straining against my boxer briefs in a way I can't hide. Her gaze drops, and I watch her throat move as she swallows.

"Knox."

"We're not rushing," I remind her. Remind myself. "We don't have to do anything you're not ready for."

"I know." She looks up at me, and every wall she keeps up is just—gone. Unshielded in a way I haven't seen before. "I just want to be close to you. Is that okay?"

"Yeah." My voice comes out rougher than I intend. "That's okay."

I ease her back onto the mattress and stretch out beside her, one hand sliding up her rib cage while I kiss her slow and deep. She presses against me, her leg hooking over my hip, and the friction makes us both groan into each other's mouths.

We stay like that for a long time. Kissing until my lips feel bruised, until I know the taste of her better than my own name. My hands roam her body, mapping the dip of her waist, the flare of her hips, the soft skin of her inner thighs. Every time I brush too close to where she's hot and aching, she shivers against me, and I pull back before I lose my resolve.

"You're killing me," she breathes against my jaw. Her hips rock forward, pressing against my thigh, seeking friction I'm not giving her. "Knox, please."

"Please what?"

"Touch me. Really touch me."

I slide my hand up her stomach, over her ribs, until I'm cupping her breast through the thin cotton of her bra. She arches into my palm, and I can feel her nipple hardening against my hand, straining toward me. I rub my thumb across it and she gasps, her whole body jolting like I've hit a live wire.

"Like that?" I do it again, harder this time. "Or like this?"

"Both. Either. God, I don't care, just don't stop."

I reach behind her and unhook the clasp with one hand, pulling the straps down her shoulders until she's bare beneath me. For a moment I just look at her, drinking in the sight. Small, perfect breasts with pink nipples already peaked in the cool air. The rapid rise and fall of her chest as she watches me watching her.

"Beautiful," I say, because she is. Because I need her to know.

I lower my mouth to her breast and close my lips around her nipple, sucking gently while my hand palms the other. She cries out, her fingers tangling in my hair, pulling me closer. I work her with my tongue, tracing circles around the sensitive flesh, then scraping my teeth across it just hard enough to make her hips buck off the bed.

"Knox." Her voice is ragged now, breaking around my name. "I need—I want—"

"I know." I kiss my way across her chest, giving her other breast the same treatment while she writhes beneath me. "I've got you."

I trail kisses down her stomach, pausing to taste the salt on her skin, to feel the way her abs clench with anticipation. When I reach the waistband of her underwear, I look up at her. Her eyes are dark, glazed, her lips swollen from kissing.

"Yes or no?"

"Yes. God, yes."

I hook my fingers under the elastic and drag the cotton down her legs. She's bare now, completely bare, spread out on my sheets like something I conjured from a fantasy. I can see how wet she is, glistening in the low light, and my cock throbs painfully against my briefs.

"You're so fucking perfect." I run my hands up her thighs, pushing them apart, making room for myself between them. "I've thought about this. You have no idea how many nights I've thought about this."

She props herself up on her elbows, watching me with hooded eyes. "Show me."

I lower my head and press a kiss to her inner thigh, right where the skin goes soft and sensitive. She makes a sound caught somewhere between a laugh and a whimper. I do the same to the other thigh, then work my way higher, leaving wet kisses along the crease where her leg meets her hip. So close to where she wants me. Not quite there yet.

"Knox." There's warning in her voice now. Desperation. "Stop teasing."

"I thought you wanted to take it slow."

"I changed my mind."

I grin against her skin and finally, finally press my mouth to her center.

She cries out, her hips lifting off the bed, and I pin them down with one arm across her stomach. She's hot and slick against my tongue, her taste flooding my senses as I lick a long stripe from her entrance to her clit. I circle that swollen bundle of nerves, learning what pressure makes her gasp, what rhythm makes her thighs clench around my head.

"Oh god." Her fingers twist in the sheets, her whole body trembling. "Oh god, oh god, right there, don't stop—"

I don't stop. I seal my lips around her clit and suck gently while my tongue keeps working, and she shatters against my mouth with a broken cry that sounds like my name. I feel her pulse around nothing, clenching on emptiness, and I want so badly to give her something to hold on to. My fingers. My cock. Anything.

But I promised we wouldn't rush.

I ease her through the aftershocks, licking soft and slow until her trembling subsides. When I crawl back up her body, she pulls me down into a messy kiss, tasting herself on my tongue.

"Your turn," she says against my lips, her hand sliding down my stomach toward my waistband. "Let me—"

I catch her wrist before she can reach me. "Not tonight."

"Knox."

"If you touch me right now, I'm going to lose what's left of my self-control." I press my forehead to hers, breathing hard. "And I meant what I said. We're not rushing this."

"That's not fair."

"I know." I roll onto my side, pulling her with me until we're facing each other, legs tangled together. "Rain check?"

She laughs, a little breathless, a little incredulous. "You just went down on me and you're asking for a rain check?"

"I wanted to. That was for me as much as it was for you." I tuck a strand of hair behind her ear. "When we do this for real, when I'm inside you, I don't want it to be on a night when you've been scared and upset. I want you present. I want you here with me, not half in your head worrying about whatever's coming tomorrow."

She's quiet for a moment, studying my face. Then she leans forward and kisses me, softer than before, lingering like she doesn't want it to end.

"You're a frustrating man, Knox Bishop."

"I've been told."

She tucks herself against my chest, her head fitting perfectly in the hollow of my shoulder. I pull the covers up over us and wrap my arm around her waist, holding her close.

"For the record," she says into my skin, "when we do this for real? I expect the full Knox Bishop experience. No holding back."

My cock twitches at the promise in her voice. "Noted."

We lie there in the darkness, my heart still pounding, my body still aching with unspent need. She traces lazy patterns on my chest, her breathing slowly evening out. I can feel sleep pulling at her, the exhaustion of the evening catching up.

"Knox?"

"Yeah?"

"I'm glad I'm here." Her voice is soft, drowsy. "With you. Even with everything else."

"Me too."

She falls asleep like that, curled against me, her breath warm on my skin. I listen to the steady rhythm of it while I stare at the ceiling, too wired to follow her down.

The man outside her building.

I keep coming back to him, worrying at the memory like a loose tooth. The glimpses I've caught. The silhouette I can't quite place. There's something familiar about him, about the way he moves. Not just military training, though he has that. Something more specific.

Like someone I used to know.

I close my eyes and try to summon details. Neck tattoos crawling toward his jaw. Lean build. The way he vanishes, smooth and professional, the moment he's spotted.

Where do I know him from?

Afghanistan? Timing doesn't feel right. One of my contractor gigs? Possible, but I worked with hundreds of people. A training exercise? A bar on some base, years ago?

The answer hovers at the edge of memory, refusing to come into focus.

Hailey shifts in her sleep, saying something I can't make out. I tighten my arm around her and force myself to let it go. Tomorrow I'll figure it out. Tomorrow I'll dig deeper into whoever's threatening her. Tomorrow I'll make good on my promise.

But tonight I hold her while she sleeps, her secrets heavy between us, and tell myself that trust is something you build one brick at a time.

Even when you can't see the shape of what you're building.

Chapter Fourteen

HAILEY

I wake up alone in Knox's bed, the sheets beside me already cold. For a moment I just lie there, breathing in the smell of him on the pillows, letting myself pretend this is normal. That I'm a woman waking up in her boyfriend's apartment after a night of . . . whatever last night was. Not quite sex. Something more intimate, maybe. Something that felt like a promise.

Then reality crashes back in, and I remember everything.

Liam. The bar. The diamond. Someone hunting us.

I sit up too fast, head spinning. Pale winter light filters through the curtains, and the clock on his nightstand reads 7:42. There's a note on the pillow where his head should be, written in blocky handwriting that's somehow exactly what I'd expect from him.

Early meeting with Cole. Didn't want to wake you. Coffee's in the pot. Stay as long as you want.

We'll figure this out together. I meant that.

—K

I read it three times. Trace my finger over the word *together* like I can absorb his certainty through the ink.

He doesn't know what he's promising. He thinks this is something manageable, some ex-boyfriend drama or minor legal trouble from my past. He doesn't know about the Snowflake Diamond. About Viktor Kedrov, the oligarch we stole it from, a man with enough money and enough grudges to hunt us for the rest of our lives. About the fact that I'm not just a woman with secrets—I'm a federal crime waiting to be discovered.

If Knox knew the truth, would he still look at me the way he did last night? Would he still touch me like I was something precious?

Or would he see me the way I sometimes see myself: a liar wearing a good woman's life like a costume?

I get up and find my clothes scattered across his bedroom floor. Last night comes back in flashes as I dress. His mouth on my breast. His hands pinning my hips to the mattress. The way he looked at me when he pulled back, all that hunger held in check by sheer force of will.

When we do this for real, I want you present.

God. This man.

I pour a cup of the coffee he left me because it gives me something to do, and I stand at his kitchen window watching the city wake up below. Snow fell overnight, covering everything in fresh white, making even the ugly parts look clean. A metaphor I don't want to think too hard about.

The burner phone buzzes in my coat pocket.

I freeze with the mug halfway to my lips. Set it down carefully, like sudden movements might trigger something. Cross to where my coat hangs by the door and fish out the cheap Nokia Liam gave me at the bar.

One text.

> Timeline moved up. They're closer than I thought—I'll explain when I see you. We need to get to it before they do. Don't tell anyone.

My stomach drops.

Now. He wants to do this now. Not tomorrow, not next week—now, while I'm standing in Knox's kitchen wearing yesterday's clothes and still feeling the phantom press of his mouth between my thighs.

I don't fully trust it. I don't fully trust Liam. But if someone really is closing in on the diamond's location, and I'm the only one who knows where it is, then sitting in Knox's apartment waiting for trouble to find me isn't an option either.

I should tell Knox. The thought rises up immediate and obvious, because that's what you do when you're trying to build something real with someone. You tell them the truth, even when it's ugly. Especially when it's ugly.

But what would I even say?

Hey, so remember when I said I'd done bad things? Funny story. My ex-partner and I stole a twenty-million-dollar diamond from a Russian tech billionaire five years ago, and I buried it in the Canadian wilderness, and now someone's hunting us for it, so I need to fly to the Arctic with Liam to dig it up. Cool? Cool.

He'd stop me. Or worse, he'd insist on coming, and then I'd be dragging a man who works in private security into the middle of an international theft recovery. Knox is law enforcement adjacent. He has contacts, connections, a reputation to protect. If this goes sideways—and things with Liam have a way of going sideways—I'd be destroying his career along with my own.

I can't do that to him. Not after last night. Not after the way he held me like he never wanted to let go.

My fingers hover over the phone. I should call him. I should at least leave a note, something better than the lie I'm about to tell.

Instead, I type back: Where do I meet you?

The response comes instantly, like he's been waiting. JFK. Terminal for private charters. Two hours.

Two hours. That's barely enough time to get home, pack a bag, and make it to JFK. No time for second thoughts. No time for goodbyes.

Maybe that's the point.

I switch to my real phone and pull up Sloane's contact. My thumbs hover over the keyboard for too long before I type: Hey! Since we're closing the studio for the holidays, I decided to take a last-minute trip. Getting out of the city for a bit. I'll see you in the new year! Happy holidays xo

It's vague enough to be true. Specific enough to not raise alarm bells. She'll assume I'm visiting family I've never mentioned or taking some spontaneous solo vacation. She won't think to worry until it's too late to do anything about it.

I don't text Knox. I tell myself it's because I don't know what to say. The truth is I'm afraid that if I open that door, even a crack, I won't be able to walk out of his apartment.

I wash my coffee mug and leave it in the drying rack. Straighten the pillows on the couch. Small acts of domesticity that feel like penance for what I'm about to do.

At the door, I pause. Look back at his apartment one more time. The morning light makes everything look golden, warm, like a place I could belong if I were someone else.

Then I leave, and I don't let myself look back again.

❄

LIAM IS WAITING at the private charter terminal, a duffel bag at his feet and two cups of coffee in his hands.

"You came." He holds one out to me. "Wasn't sure you would."

"Neither was I." I take the coffee but don't drink it. "I'm still not sure. Convince me this isn't you dragging me back into something I can't get out of."

He doesn't answer right away. Instead, he pulls a manila envelope from the duffel and hands it to me.

Inside: photographs. My building, taken from across the street. Sloane's studio entrance. Me walking home last Tuesday in the green coat I bought at that place on Atlantic. And the last one—my apartment door, shot from the hallway. Close enough to read my unit number.

"The photos aren't mine," Liam says. "I pulled them off a guy who was surveilling your block. He had your schedule, Hailey. Your routes. He knew where you work, where you shop, what time you lock your door at night."

My hands are shaking. Not from the cold.

So Liam didn't lead them to me. They were already there.

"This is why I couldn't explain over a phone," he says quietly. "I needed you to see it."

I want to argue. I want to demand names, specifics, some kind of assurance. But the pilot is already leading us across the tarmac toward a small jet, and for the first time since Liam reappeared in my life, I'm not angry at him for showing up. I'm scared of what would have happened if he hadn't.

The jet is nicer than I expected. Leather seats, polished wood accents, a mini bar stocked with top-shelf liquor. I raise an eyebrow at Liam as we settle in across from each other.

"Saved up," he says before I can ask. "Figured if this is our last job together, might as well do it in style."

Our last job. The words land somewhere complicated in my chest. There was a time when I couldn't imagine doing anything without Liam. When he was my partner in every sense of the word, the only person who knew all my secrets and wanted me anyway. We were going to retire together. Buy a house somewhere warm, live off the diamond until we got bored, then find some new adventure to chase.

That was before I realized adventures with Liam always ended with my heart in pieces.

The plane takes off, and I watch New York shrink beneath us. Somewhere down there, Knox is in a meeting with Cole, probably checking his phone, wondering if I've texted. I should text him. Should tell him something, even if it's another lie.

I don't.

"You're thinking about him." Liam's voice cuts through my spiral. "The security guy. Military?"

"Marines."

"Makes sense." Liam stretches his legs out, crossing them at the ankle. "You always did have a thing for military men."

"You would know."

"I would." His smile doesn't quite reach his eyes. "Once a Marine, always a Marine, right? At least that's what they told me."

We don't talk about Knox after that. Don't talk about the past, either, about what we were to each other or why it fell apart. Just logistics. The diamond is hidden in an abandoned mining site about three hours by snowmobile from the nearest town. I chose the location specifically because it was remote, inaccessible, a place no one would stumble across by accident. Getting there in December won't be easy, but it won't be impossible either.

Getting back out might be another story.

"Weather looks rough," Liam says, scrolling through something on his phone. "Big storm coming in tomorrow night. We need to be in and out before it hits."

"And if we're not?"

"Then we hunker down and wait it out. Won't be comfortable, but survivable."

Survivable. That's a word I haven't had to think about in a long time. Five years of normal life, and I'd almost forgotten what it felt like to make decisions based on whether I might die.

Almost.

We land in Yellowknife to refuel and switch to a smaller plane that appears to have been built during the Cold War and hasn't been updated since. The pilot is a weathered man in his sixties who doesn't ask questions, just grunts at Liam's instructions and gets us in the air.

The landscape below is white. Endless, featureless white, broken only by dark patches of frozen lakes and the occasional cluster of evergreens. It's beautiful in a brutal way. It would kill you without hesitation if you made a wrong step.

By the time we touch down at a tiny airstrip carved out of the wilderness, the sun is already sinking toward the horizon. It's barely three in the afternoon, but this far north in December, that's all the daylight you get.

A black van is waiting on the tarmac, AURORA LODGE printed on the side in elegant gold script.

"You booked us a resort?" I stare at Liam as we grab our bags. "We're here to retrieve stolen property and you booked us a luxury resort?"

"We need a base of operations. Somewhere with heat and food and snowmobiles we can rent." He shrugs, heading for the van. "Besides, if this is the last time we work together, I wanted to do it right."

There's that phrase again. *The last time.* He keeps saying it like he's trying to convince himself.

The driver is a young woman with a bright smile and too many questions. Where are we from? What brings us to the Territories in December? Are we here for the northern lights? The aurora has been spectacular this week, she tells us. Best viewing in years.

I give vague answers while Liam stares out the window, one knee bouncing. He's nervous, I realize. More nervous than he's letting on. That sets off alarm bells I try to ignore.

The drive takes more than an hour, winding through frozen forest on a road that's more suggestion than infrastructure. By the time the lodge comes into view, I've almost convinced myself we're lost.

Then the trees part, and I forget how to breathe.

The Aurora Lodge rises from the snow in sharp angles of wood and glass, perched on the edge of a frozen lake that stretches to the horizon. The architecture is modern, angular, designed to frame the wilderness rather than compete with it. Even in the fading light, I can see the faint green shimmer of the northern lights beginning to form above the tree line.

It's stunning. It's also completely wrong.

"How much did this place cost?" I ask as we pull up to the entrance.

"Don't worry about it."

"Liam."

"I said don't worry about it." He's already climbing out of the van, already walking toward the glass doors, already shutting down the conversation the way he always does when he doesn't want to answer questions.

I follow him inside, my instincts prickling.

Fireplaces crackle at both ends of the lobby. Exposed beams, warm wood paneling, thick rugs underfoot. Wealth pretending to be cozy. A woman behind the reception desk greets us with a smile that's just a little too polished.

"Welcome to Aurora Lodge. Checking in?"

"Two rooms." Liam slides his ID across the counter. "Under Calloway."

"Of course." She types something into her computer, still smiling. "And will you be joining us for dinner in the restaurant this evening? Our chef has prepared a wonderful tasting menu featuring local cuisine."

"Sounds great."

"Excellent." More typing. More smiling. "And what brings you to the Territories? Business or pleasure?"

"Pleasure," Liam says smoothly. "We're hoping to catch the lights."

"You've picked the perfect week. The aurora has been putting on quite a show." She hands him two key cards. "You're in rooms fourteen and sixteen. Down the hall to your left. If you need anything at all, don't hesitate to call the front desk."

I take my key and head for my room without looking back at Liam. I need space. I need to think. I need to figure out why every nerve in my body is screaming that something is very, very wrong.

The room is gorgeous. King bed with a white duvet, floor-to-ceiling windows overlooking the frozen lake, a bathroom with a soaking tub and heated floors. Somewhere Knox might take me for a romantic weekend, if Knox knew anything about who I really was.

I unpack my bag and count the security cameras I noticed on the walk from the lobby. Four in the main area. Two in the hallway. At least one more covering the entrance.

That's a lot of surveillance for a remote luxury resort.

I shower and change and try to quiet the voice in my head that keeps whispering *trap, trap, this is a trap.* Liam wouldn't walk into something dangerous, I tell myself. He's too smart. Too careful. Whatever's making me nervous, there's probably a reasonable explanation.

I almost believe it.

Dinner is in the lodge restaurant, where tall windows frame the lake and the aurora is beginning to dance overhead. Liam is already at a table when I arrive, a glass of whiskey in front of him that he hasn't touched.

"You look nice," he says as I sit down.

"I look exhausted."

"That too." His eyes don't quite meet mine. He's scanning the room, cataloging exits and other diners and the waitstaff moving between tables. "The aurora's really something tonight."

"Liam." I keep my voice low. "What's going on?"

"Nothing."

"You've checked your phone six times since I sat down. You keep looking at the door like you're expecting someone. Talk to me."

He's quiet for a long moment. Then, "Weather forecast. Storm's coming in faster than they predicted. We need to leave at dawn if we're going to make it to the site and back before it hits."

"That's not what's bothering you."

"It should be." He meets my eyes, and there's something there I can't read. "The storm's going to be bad, Hailey. Whiteout conditions, temperatures dropping to forty below. If we don't get the diamond tomorrow, we might not get another chance for weeks. And if whoever's hunting us figures out where we are before then . . ."

He doesn't finish the sentence. He doesn't have to.

I look out at the aurora, green and purple ribbons of light rippling across the sky like something alive. It's the most beautiful thing I've ever seen, and I can barely appreciate it because my stomach won't stop churning.

"Snowmobiles are arranged," Liam continues. "I've got GPS coordinates loaded and emergency supplies packed. We leave at first light, we push hard, we get in and out before the weather turns."

"And then?"

"And then we hand off the diamond and this whole mess goes away. We go back to our lives. Pretend it never happened."

Go back to our lives. He makes it sound so simple. Like I can just walk back into my apartment, show up at Sloane's studio, pick up where I left off with Knox. Like none of this will follow me home.

"Fine," I say. "Dawn. We get the diamond and we get out."

Liam nods, but his eyes are already back on the door.

I eat without tasting the food. Local fish, some kind of arctic char prepared three different ways. It's probably delicious. I wouldn't know. My stomach is a knot of anxiety that leaves no room for hunger.

After dinner, I go back to my room and try to sleep.

It doesn't work.

I lie in the dark, listening to the wind howl outside, watching the aurora paint shifting colors across my ceiling. Every time I close my eyes, I see Knox's face. The way he looked at me when he said *let me help*. The way his hands felt on my skin, so careful, so controlled.

I should call him. It's not too late to tell him the truth, to give him some version of what's happening. At least then he'd know. At least then if something goes wrong—

But I don't call. I just lie there, trapped between the life I want and the past I can't escape, waiting for morning to come.

Around 2 a.m., I hear footsteps in the hallway.

At first I think it's nothing. Other guests heading to their rooms, maybe, or staff making late-night rounds. But the footsteps don't pass. They stop. Regroup. There are more of them now, moving together, too coordinated to be accidental.

I'm out of bed before I've fully processed what I'm hearing.

Bare feet on cold floor. I cross to the door and press my ear against it, pulse loud in my ears. Voices now, low and clipped. The creak of gear shifting, bodies adjusting positions.

I know that sound. I've heard it before, in a hotel in Monaco when everything went wrong. The sound of a team getting ready to move.

I crack the door open, just a sliver, just enough to see.

Men in tactical gear. Black from head to toe, faces covered, moving down the hallway in formation. Six of them, maybe more. They're heading for my room.

For a moment I'm frozen. Ice in my veins, static in my brain, every survival instinct I have screaming at me to run, hide, fight, do something—

I try to close the door.

A hand catches it before I can. Gloved fingers, impossibly strong, wrenching it open as I stumble backward. I open my mouth to scream and another hand clamps over it, leather and sweat and something chemical I can recognize even as my mind rejects what's happening.

Then I feel it. A sting in my neck. Small and quick, like a bee, like nothing at all.

The world tilts sideways.

My legs stop working. I'm falling, or maybe I'm being lowered—I can't tell anymore, can't feel the difference between up and down, can't do anything except watch as the room blurs and stretches around me.

Somewhere down the hall, a door crashes open. Shouting. The sound of a struggle, bodies hitting walls. I turn my head—it takes forever, my neck a column of wet sand—and see them dragging Liam out of his room.

He's fighting. Of course he's fighting. Liam never goes down easy. But there are two of them on him, three, and even he can't beat those odds.

His eyes find mine across the hallway.

Shock. Confusion.

He didn't know, I think, the realization floating through my dissolving mind. *He didn't know this was coming. This wasn't his play.*

Which means we were both set up.

Which means we're both fucked.

The drug pulls me under before I can finish the thought. The last thing I see is Liam's face, blood on his lip, still fighting as they drag him away.

Then nothing.

Chapter Fifteen

HAILEY

My head is splitting.

That's the first thing I notice. Not where I am or how I got here, just this vicious, throbbing pain behind my eyes that makes even blinking feel like punishment. I'm lying on something soft, which is wrong. The last thing I remember is the lodge, footsteps in the hallway, the door splintering open.

I force my eyes to focus.

Not the resort. Not anywhere I recognize.

I'm in a cabin. Wood and stone construction, high ceilings, massive windows showing nothing but snow-covered pines and white sky. A fire crackles in a stone fireplace that takes up most of one wall, and in front of it—

Liam.

He's on a leather couch facing the fireplace, slumped sideways with one arm dangling toward the floor. Not moving.

I'm off the bed before I've fully processed what I'm seeing, crossing the room on unsteady legs, the drug still making everything tilt. I drop to my knees beside him and press two fingers to his throat.

Pulse. Steady and strong. Okay. Okay, he's alive. Just out cold, the same way I must have been. His face is pale under the stubble, his breathing slow and even. Whatever they gave us, it hit him hard.

"Liam." I shake his shoulder. Nothing. "Liam, wake up."

He doesn't stir.

I can't do anything for him except wait. In the meantime, I need to figure out where we are and how we're getting out.

My heart is pounding harder than it should be. I make myself breathe. In through the nose, out through the mouth. Panic won't help. Panic has never helped, not once in my entire life, and I'm not about to start letting it run the show now.

I stand up and really look at this place.

One large open room. The bed where I woke up, king-size, positioned against the far wall with a view of those floor-to-ceiling windows. The sitting area where Liam is still unconscious—two leather chairs and the couch, arranged around the fireplace. Beside the fireplace, an entire wall of firewood. Large pieces on the bottom, medium in the middle, kindling arranged by size on top. Someone spent way too much time on that.

Past the sitting area, a kitchen that makes me stop and stare.

This isn't a cabin kitchen. This is something you'd find in a Manhattan penthouse. Wolf six-burner range with a red enamel finish. Sub-Zero refrigerator humming softly against the stone wall. Granite countertops in a deep gray that match the fireplace. Professional-grade cookware hangs from a copper pot rack, each piece gleaming like it's never been used. I open the refrigerator and find it fully stocked with ingredients you see in food magazines. High-end cheese. Fresh herbs. Beef wrapped in butcher paper with a label I can't read. A bottle of Dom Pérignon chilling on the top shelf.

None of this makes sense. People who kidnap you don't stock the fridge with champagne.

A bathroom connects to the main space through a doorless archway. Rainfall shower, heated floors if the warmth under my socks is any indication, thick towels monogrammed with initials I don't recognize. White marble and brushed nickel and more luxury than most hotels I've stayed in.

The door catches my eye next. Heavy, solid wood with iron hardware that looks almost decorative. From the inside, there's no lock mechanism at all. Just a handle that turns easily when I try it.

The door doesn't move.

I try again, putting my weight into it. Nothing. Whatever's holding it shut is on the other side. Reinforced, probably. Bolted from the outside. I could throw myself against it all day and accomplish nothing but a bruised shoulder.

I check the windows. Triple-paned glass, set deep into the stone walls. I could throw a chair at them and it would probably just bounce off. Even if I broke through, I'd be facing sub-zero temperatures in whatever I'm wearing. No coat. No boots. Nothing but the T-shirt and leggings I fell asleep in at the lodge. Bare feet on heated floors—a detail that would be luxurious if it weren't so clearly designed to keep us from running.

We're trapped.

Whoever took us didn't just grab us and throw us in a hole. They prepared. They thought about thread counts and kitchen appliances.

That scares me more than a hole would have.

I glance back at Liam. Still out. Still breathing. One bedroom, one bed, and he's on the couch. Whoever put us here made choices about the arrangement, and I don't like what those choices imply.

I'm running my fingers along the window seals, looking for any weakness I might have missed, when I hear him groan.

He's stirring now, one hand coming up to press against his temple.

"Hailey?" He pushes himself up on one elbow and squints at me like I might be a hallucination.

"Yeah, I'm here." I cross back to him, crouching beside the couch. "How's your head?"

"Feels like someone's mining for copper inside my skull." He sits up slowly, steadying himself on the arm of the couch, and looks around. Takes in the cabin, the windows, the fire. I watch him change from confusion to assessment to something harder. "Where are we?"

"I don't know. Somewhere remote, based on the view. We were drugged at the lodge and brought here while we were out." I gesture at our surroundings. "I've already checked the door and windows. We're not getting out that way."

He stands, a little unsteady, and moves to the door to see for himself. I don't blame him. I wouldn't take someone else's word for it either. He tries the handle, examines the frame, runs his hand along the hinges.

"Steel plate behind the wood," he says after a moment. "Hinges on the outside. This was built to hold people."

"I figured."

He turns back to the room, and I see him cataloguing details the way I did. The exits that aren't exits. The windows that won't break. The one bedroom with the one bed. His eyes hold on that last part a beat too long, but he doesn't comment on it. Neither do I. We have bigger problems.

"The kitchen is ridiculous," I tell him. "Whoever did this spent serious money making sure we'd be comfortable."

"Comfortable." He says the word like it tastes wrong. "That's not reassuring."

"I know."

He's quiet for a moment, still scanning. "No phones. No clocks. No way to tell what time it is or how long we've been out."

"Nothing. I already looked."

"So we're blind and deaf and locked in a box, but at least we have a nice stove." He laughs, but there's no humor in it. "This is wrong, Hailey. All of it. People don't go to this much trouble unless they want something specific, and they don't make the cage this pretty unless they plan to keep you in it for a while."

I want to argue with him. I want to say we'll find a way out, that someone will notice we're missing, that Knox—

But Knox doesn't know where I am. Knox doesn't even know I left. I couldn't figure out what to tell him, so I told him nothing. Just vanished after everything we'd started building together.

The thought opens a pit in my stomach that I force myself to ignore.

"We'll figure it out," I say, because I have to say something. "We've gotten out of worse."

"Have we?"

A sound cuts through the silence. A soft electronic chime, like a notification alert.

We both freeze.

Above the fireplace, a screen I hadn't noticed flickers to life. Large, flat, built into the stonework like it was always part of the design. For a moment there's only static, gray snow matching the real snow outside.

Then a face appears.

A woman in her fifties, maybe older. Silver hair swept back from a face that's aged well, with high cheekbones and skin that's seen good dermatologists. She's dressed in something dark and elegant, a silk blouse or a tailored jacket. Behind her, I can see what looks like a study or office, leather and mahogany and art on the walls.

For a moment she just looks at us. Drinking us in. Her lips part slightly, and I swear to God her eyes are glistening.

"Oh," she breathes. "Oh, it's really you. Both of you, right there, in the flesh." She presses a hand to her chest. "I'm sorry, I promised myself I wouldn't get emotional, but I've waited so long for this moment."

Liam and I exchange a look.

"I have to tell you," she continues, leaning toward the camera like she's sharing a secret, "I am your biggest fan. I mean that literally. There is no one on this earth who has studied your work more closely than I have. No one who appreciates what you accomplished the way I do."

"What the hell is this?" Liam says, but she keeps going like she didn't hear him.

"The Beaumont heist in 2018." She ticks it off on her finger, beaming. "The Artemis collection the following year. That absolutely *inspired* bit of misdirection with the courier swap in Monaco." Another finger. "I've analyzed every detail I could find. The planning, the execution, the way you two moved together like a single organism. It was—" She stops, searching for the word. "Exquisite. Truly exquisite."

I feel like I've stepped into some alternate reality where nothing works the way it should.

"The Garrett Museum alone," she gushes on, practically glowing now. "Do you have any idea how sophisticated their security system was? I donated three million dollars to that museum. I know exactly what you went through. And you moved through it like it wasn't even there." She shakes her head slowly, reverently. "I've stayed up so many nights trying to reverse-engineer your methodology. So many diagrams. So many scenarios. You two are artists. Real artists."

"Who are you?" The question comes out steadier than I feel. I keep my face neutral. Don't let them see you scared. Another one of Liam's lessons.

"Oh, forgive me!" She actually laughs at herself. "Here I am gushing like a schoolgirl and I haven't even introduced myself. My name is Marlena Kade." She inclines her head, almost a little bow. "And I cannot tell you what an honor it is to finally meet the people responsible for some of the most elegant work of the past decade."

"So you drugged us and dragged us to the middle of nowhere because you liked our résumé?" Liam's moving closer to the screen, like he might be able to reach through it and grab her. "That's your explanation?"

"Well, that and you have something I want." Her smile doesn't waver. "But yes. When I learned you were coming to retrieve the Snowflake, I couldn't pass up the opportunity. The diamond is lovely, certainly. But meeting you? The actual architects of those beautiful jobs?" She puts both hands over her heart. "That's the real treasure."

I've been threatened before. Interrogated before. Held at gunpoint twice. I've never had a kidnapper look at me like I'm a celebrity she cornered at a cocktail party.

"The cabin," Marlena continues, gesturing at something offscreen. "I had it designed with you in mind. The kitchen because I've done my homework on you, Mr. Calloway. A girl doesn't spend five years researching someone without learning what makes him tick. You're a cook—a serious one, from what I can tell. I thought you'd appreciate having the right tools." She looks directly at the camera, at me. "The linens are Frette, Ms. Parker. When you run a media business with the kind of data access I have, people's preferences become very transparent. You like nice sheets." She shrugs, unapologetic. "I remembered. And the firewood—" She pauses, almost shy. "This is silly, but the firewood is organized the way the Garrett Museum's security logs were organized. By category and size. A small homage. I wasn't sure you'd notice, but I hoped."

"You organized our firewood as a tribute," Liam says flatly.

"I know it's a lot." She has the grace to look slightly embarrassed. "I can be intense about things I care about. But I wanted you to be comfortable here. I wanted you to know that whoever took you, it wasn't some thug who doesn't understand what you are. It was someone who appreciates you. Who sees you."

Sees us. Like we're specimens in a collection. Like we're art she acquired.

My skin crawls.

"Here's the thing, though." The shift happens so fast I almost miss it. One second she's gushing, and the next her eyes have gone flat and cold without her smile moving at all. "I want the Snowflake Diamond. You're going to tell me where it is. In exchange, you'll be free to go. I'll provide transportation back to civilization, money for your trouble, glowing references if you ever need them." She pauses. "But I should be honest with you, because I feel like we've established a rapport. If you refuse, or if you lie to me, I will hurt you. I'll hate doing it. It'll feel like vandalizing a Vermeer. But I will."

"So much for being our biggest fan," I say.

"I am your biggest fan. That hasn't changed." She spreads her hands. "But I'm also a collector, and the Snowflake has been on my list for five years. At a certain point, admiration has to become secondary to acquisition." Her smile softens again, almost tender. "I really would prefer not to damage either of you. Please don't make me."

She glances at something off-screen, then back to the camera. "I'll be in touch soon with more details about how this is going to work. In the meantime—" And just like that, her whole demeanor flips again, warm and bright like a hostess at a dinner party. "Make yourselves at home! There's fresh coffee in the kitchen and the shower pressure is divine. Bye for now!"

The screen goes dark.

Liam and I stand there in silence, staring at the fireplace where Marlena's face was a moment ago.

"What," Liam says, "the fuck."

"She organized the firewood like a museum security system."

"She knows what sheets you like."

"She told us to make ourselves at home."

"After threatening to hurt us."

"And then said the shower pressure is divine."

Liam turns to look at me, and for the first time since I've known him, he seems genuinely at a loss. "I've dealt with a lot of criminals in my life, Hailey. Mobsters. Oligarchs. A guy in Monaco who collected human teeth. But this?" He gestures at the blank screen. "This is new."

"She's going to kill us if we don't give her what she wants."

"Yeah." He runs a hand through his hair. "That part I understood."

I look around the cabin. The crackling fire. The gourmet kitchen. The one bed. Our insane captor who just told us to enjoy the shower.

"So," I say. "What now?"

Chapter Sixteen

KNOX

She didn't even tell me she was leaving.

That's what I keep coming back to as I push through the doors of the Aurora Lodge, Hailey's photo pulled up on my phone. She spent the night in my bed, let me hold her, let me promise we'd figure things out together. And then she vanished without a word. Not a text. Not a note. Just a cold pillow and a coffee mug in the drying rack and silence where she should have been.

I noticed within hours. I texted her, called her, got nothing back but dead air.

A year. I've been watching this woman for a year, and I still can't predict when she's going to slip through my fingers.

The first time I saw her, she was laughing at something Sloane said in the studio, her head thrown back, those silver rings catching the light as she gestured. Something in my chest just . . . stopped. Rearranged itself. I'd been walking through my life like a soldier on patrol, checking boxes, completing objectives, and then Hailey Parker looked up and met my eyes and I forgot what the objective even was.

I told myself it was temporary. A distraction. An inconvenient attraction that would fade once I got to know her.

Instead, I learned that she takes her coffee black but steals sips of other people's lattes when she thinks no one's looking. That she hums off-key when she's concentrating. That she bites her thumbnail when she's nervous and cracks her knuckles when she's bored. That she talks to herself when she thinks no one can hear, little running commentaries on whatever she's working on.

I notice everything.

Twelve months of noticing, and the obsession hasn't faded. It's metastasized. Spread into every corner of my life until there's no part of me that isn't thinking about her.

So I checked the tracker.

Yeah. The tracker. The one I hid in the sole of her Doc Martens three months ago, back when I was still telling myself that following her home every night was "protective" and not "deeply unhinged." In my defense, I'd planned to tell her about it eventually. In my defense, she always wears those boots, and I needed to know she was safe, and I wasn't thinking clearly because—

There is no defense. I know that. I put a GPS tracker in a woman's shoes without her knowledge or consent. That's not romantic. That's not protective. That's behavior that gets you a restraining order and a spot on a true crime podcast.

But watching the little dot on my phone blink from JFK to Yellowknife to a remote location in the Northwest Territories that my map could barely render? I'm not feeling guilty. I'm feeling vindicated.

Something is wrong.

Hailey doesn't take spontaneous trips to the Canadian Arctic. Hailey doesn't vanish without telling anyone where she's going. And Hailey definitely doesn't go dark for twelve hours in the middle of nowhere while the tracker signal dies at a place called Aurora Lodge.

I was on a plane before I finished processing what any of it meant.

Before boarding, I texted Cole. Not the full truth, but not a lie either. Just enough to cover my absence without raising alarms.

> **KNOX:** Taking some time off. Businesses shutting down for the holiday anyway.

Three dots appeared. Disappeared. Appeared again.

COLE: Time off? You?

KNOX: It happens.

COLE: In the five years I've known you, you've taken exactly zero vacation days.

KNOX: Seems like a good time to start.

A pause. I could practically hear Cole's skepticism through the screen.

COLE: This have anything to do with Hailey?

I stared at that message for a long moment. Cole knows me too well.

KNOX: Just need a few days.

COLE: That's not a no.

KNOX: It's not a yes either.

Another pause. Then:

COLE: Sloane's going to ask where you went.

That was the real issue. Not Cole's curiosity, but Sloane's. I didn't want her worrying, and I didn't want to put Cole in a position where he'd have to choose between being honest with her and keeping my business private.

KNOX: Tell her the truth. I'm taking a trip. You don't know the details because I didn't give you any.

COLE: So I'm not lying, I'm just underinformed.

KNOX: Exactly.

COLE: Convenient for you.

KNOX: I'm not asking you to keep secrets from her. I'm asking you not to dig for information I'm not ready to share.

The longest pause yet. Then:

COLE: Fine. But you owe me an explanation when you get back.

KNOX: Noted.

COLE: And Knox? Whatever's going on . . . be careful.

I pocketed the phone without responding. Careful wasn't really an option anymore. Not when it came to her.

The whole flight, I argued with myself. This is crazy. This is exactly the obsessive behavior you're supposed to be working on. She's allowed to take a trip without telling you. You've been on two dates. You don't own her.

But the tracker kept pinging from the same location. Stationary. For hours.

Either Hailey took off her boots and left them at a resort in the Northwest Territories—unlikely, given that she wears those things like they're welded to her feet—or something happened to her.

I wasn't willing to bet on option one.

The flight gave me too much time to think. Nearly nine hours, JFK to Toronto to Yellowknife, staring at seat backs and watching the clouds crawl past the window. Replaying every moment of the past year. The first time she smiled at me and I felt it in my spine. The way she looked at me in Washington Square Park, snowflakes catching in her dark hair, when I finally worked up the nerve to kiss her. How she tasted like coffee and something sweeter underneath. How I'd pulled back and she'd grabbed my collar and pulled me right back in.

I've never felt like this about anyone. Never wanted to crawl inside someone's life and make a home there. Never understood those love songs about obsession and need and losing yourself in another person.

Now I understand. Now I'm one of those idiots writing poetry in my head while chasing a woman to the Arctic because the thought of her being hurt, being scared, being anything other than safe in my arms—

I can't finish that thought. It goes somewhere too dark.

Now I'm here, and something about this place is wrong. It's too quiet, too polished, and the woman at the front desk is already watching me before I'm halfway across the lobby.

"Welcome to Aurora Lodge. How can I help you?"

I show her my phone. "I'm looking for this woman. Hailey Parker. She should have checked in yesterday."

The smile doesn't waver. "Ms. Parker checked out this morning. I believe she mentioned heading south?"

The tracker says her boots are still here, somewhere within a quarter mile of where I'm standing.

I smile back. "Must have gotten our wires crossed. Mind if I stretch my legs? Long flight."

"Of course, sir. The grounds are lovely this time of year."

I do a perimeter walk and count security cameras as I go. Twelve on the main building, six covering parking, motion sensors along the tree line. Armed guards run patrol routes that look casual but aren't.

That's too much infrastructure for a resort. Too much money spent on keeping people out—or keeping them in.

The creepy stalker tracking device I planted in Hailey's shoes is starting to look less like a character flaw and more like the only reason I have any chance of finding her.

Funny how that works.

I'm circling back toward the main entrance when three men intercept me near the equipment shed. They're wearing staff uniforms, but they move like operators. The real kind, not weekend warriors. Two flank me with their hands positioned for quick draws while the leader stands in front, something heavier bulking out his parka.

"Sir. We need you to come with us."

I do the math. I could take one, maybe two, but not all three without knowing where Hailey is. Starting a fight I might lose won't help her.

"Lead the way."

They take me to a side building. I expect zip ties and harsh lighting and questions about why I'm asking about a woman who supposedly checked out this morning.

Instead, the leader steps behind me while the other two hold my attention.

Something presses against my neck. A hiss. Cold spreading outward from the injection site.

I spin and get one hand on his collar before my fingers stop working. The floor rushes up. I fight it—I've been drugged before, trained to push through—but whatever they gave me is industrial grade.

My last conscious thought is her face. The way she looked at me this morning when I woke up with her in my arms. Soft and unguarded and mine.

I'm coming, Hailey. Just hold on.

The last thing I hear is the leader's voice, pleasant and calm.

"Sleep tight, Mr. Bishop."

Chapter Seventeen

KNOX

Cold wakes me first. Wind cuts across my face, bitter and sharp. Then comes the vibration—motor underneath me, world bouncing and jostling. I'm on a snowmobile, slumped against someone's back, my wrists bound with zip ties. I keep my eyes closed and focus on steady breathing. Let them think I'm still out.

We're climbing. I can feel the angle of the terrain, the machine straining against the incline. Through barely open lids I catch glimpses of trees everywhere, dense forest, old growth—wilderness that swallows people and never spits them back out. We're heading away from the resort, deeper into nothing.

Twenty minutes pass. Twenty-five. I try to track direction but the sky is flat gray and gives me nothing useful. Even if I got free right now, I'd have no idea which way to run.

The machine slows and stops.

Hands haul me off and I go limp, making myself dead weight, forcing them to work for it. Two of them drag me through knee-deep snow until a door opens and warmth hits my face.

They shove me forward, slam the door, locking it behind them.

I catch myself on bound hands, already scanning as I stumble. Wood floors. Stone fireplace. Windows showing nothing but white.

And Hailey.

She spins from where she's standing by the windows, and for a second neither of us moves. She's alive. She's here, she's standing, she's looking at me with those dark eyes gone wide and her lips parted like she's forgotten how to speak.

Thank god. Thank god. Thank god.

"Knox?!"

She's crossing the room before I can get my feet under me, dropping to her knees beside me, her hands on my face, my shoulders, running over me like she's checking for damage. I'm doing the same thing—scanning her for injuries, for bruises, for any sign that someone's hurt her. She looks exhausted and scared but intact. Whole.

"You're okay," I manage. The words scrape out of me. "Jesus, Hailey, you're okay."

"What are you doing here? How did you—"

"Doesn't matter." I reach up with my bound hands and cup her face, just for a second, just to feel her skin under my palms and know this is real. "Are you hurt? Did they hurt you?"

"No, I'm fine, I'm— Knox, how did you find me?"

"Later." I pull myself up to sitting, and the room tilts. Whatever they gave me is still sludging through my bloodstream, making everything soft at the edges. "How long have you been here? Who took you?"

"There's a lot I need to tell you. There's—" She stops. "Hold on. Let me get those off you. There's a knife in the kitchen."

She's back in seconds, sawing through the zip tie. The plastic falls away and I rub my wrists, feeling blood flow return to my fingers.

"Knox, there's something you need to know." Her eyes flick to something behind me.

That's when I see him.

There's a man standing by the fireplace. Something about his posture tugs at the back of my brain—the way he holds himself, weight on one hip, like he's ready to move in any direction.

I blink. The drugs are still messing with my head, because for a second I think I'm looking at a ghost. Someone from another lifetime, someone who shouldn't be here, someone who—

No.

I blink again, harder, trying to clear the haze. But his face doesn't change. The jaw is the same. The eyes are the same, dark and quick and seeing everything. There are tattoos crawling up his neck now that weren't there before, but the rest of him—

The rest of him is exactly how I remember. How I've been trying not to remember.

"Liam?"

It comes out like a question because it can't be right. It can't be him. Liam Calloway is somewhere else, anywhere else, living some other life that doesn't intersect with mine. We haven't spoken in twelve years. He doesn't know Hailey. He has no reason to be standing in a cabin in the Canadian wilderness looking at me like—

Like he's not surprised to see me at all.

"Knox." He says my name the same way he used to, that low familiar warmth in his voice. "Been a while."

I'm still on my knees. I should get up, but my legs aren't cooperating, and my brain is moving too slow, trying to fit pieces together that don't make sense. Liam is here. Hailey is here. Liam and Hailey are both here, in the same room, looking at each other like—

And suddenly I know exactly why the man outside Hailey's apartment seemed so familiar. Why I couldn't place him no matter how many times I ran through old contacts in my head. I was looking in the wrong decade.

"You're the one who's been following her." My voice sounds strange in my own ears. "The one I kept seeing outside her building. That was you."

"Yes."

"You two know each other?" Hailey's gaze ping-pongs between us.

"We served together," Liam says.

"He was in my unit," I say at the same time.

The words are true but they don't begin to cover it. They don't explain the way Liam used to find excuses to sit next to me in the mess hall, or the night we got drunk and he told me things he said he'd never told anyone, or the moment in the motor pool when we were alone and he looked at me and I looked at him and neither of us moved because we both knew what would happen if we did.

His mouth had been three inches from mine. I could smell the whiskey on his breath, feel the heat coming off his body. One of us would have had to close that gap. Neither of us did.

We never talked about it. Not once. And then he was gone.

"Someone want to tell me what the hell is going on?" I finally get my feet under me and stand, ignoring the way the room sways. "Because I've been tracking Hailey for twelve hours trying to figure out why she disappeared, and now I'm in a cabin in the middle of nowhere with her and a guy I haven't seen since Afghanistan. So I'd really appreciate some context."

They exchange a glance that feels like shorthand.

"It's complicated," Hailey says.

"Then uncomplicate it."

She takes a breath. "Liam is my ex. We were together for three years, before I moved to New York. Before I started working for Sloane."

I look at Liam. He meets my stare with that lazy confidence I remember, like nothing ever rattled him. Liam Calloway always looks like he knows something you don't.

Right now, looking at him feels like pressing on a bruise I forgot I had.

"Small world," I say.

"Getting smaller all the time."

"That doesn't explain why you're both locked in a cabin in the middle of fucking nowhere. Or why armed men just drugged me and dragged me up a mountain." I hold up my wrists, the marks from the zip ties still visible. "Start talking."

Another look between them, something passing I'm not part of.

"I'm not who you think I am, Knox."

"What does that mean?"

"It means . . ." She stops. Starts again. "Before I was a jewelry designer, before Sloane, before any of the life you know—I was a thief. Liam and I both were. We stole things. Jewelry, art, anything valuable enough to be worth the risk. We were good at it."

I wait for the words to make sense. They don't. I'm looking at Hailey—the woman who hums while she works, who wears the same boots every day, who fell asleep in my arms—and I'm trying to reconcile her with what she's telling me.

"A thief."

"Yes."

"You."

"Yes."

I look at Liam. "And you."

"Also yes."

The Hailey I know makes jewelry. She drinks too much coffee and gets paint under her fingernails and blushes when I catch her staring. She's not a criminal. She can't be. Except she's standing here telling me she is, and there's no hesitation in her voice, no uncertainty. She's not lying now. She's been lying—to me, to Sloane, to everyone—but right now, in this moment, she's finally telling the truth.

"What did you steal?"

Hailey doesn't flinch. "A lot of things. But the one that matters right now is a diamond. The Snowflake Diamond. Twenty-three carats, flawless, worth about twenty million dollars. We took it from a Russian tech billionaire named Viktor Kedrov five years ago. I hid it. I'm the only one who knows where it is."

"And this Kedrov wants it back."

"He's been hunting us ever since we took it. That's why Liam contacted me. To warn me they were closing in."

Ice slides through my gut. "Contacted you how?"

"He showed up at my apartment," Hailey says. "A few days ago. Told me Kedrov's people had found me, that we needed to move fast. Get the diamond, return it anonymously, make the whole thing go away."

"And you just went with him." I'm not looking at her anymore. I'm looking at Liam. "He shows up after five years and says jump, and you book a flight to Canada."

"It wasn't like that—"

"So he dragged you here." The cold in my gut is turning hot, spreading through my chest. "Into the middle of nowhere. With a Russian billionaire hunting you. And now we're all locked in a cabin because his brilliant plan went sideways."

"Knox—"

"Who grabbed you? Kedrov's people?"

"No." Liam pushes off from the fireplace. "Marlena Kade. She's a collector. Art, jewelry, rare experiences. She's been tracking the Snowflake for years, and when she found out we were coming to retrieve it, she grabbed us. She wants the diamond for herself, and she's not letting us go until we tell her where it is."

"So not only did you drag Hailey into the path of a Russian billionaire, you also managed to get her grabbed by some psychotic collector." I take a step toward him. "That about cover it?"

Liam doesn't move, doesn't flinch, just watches me with those dark eyes that used to make me forget my own name. Right now they make me want to break his nose. "She was already in danger. Kedrov was coming for her whether I showed up or not. I gave her a chance to get ahead of it."

"Some chance." Another step. We're close now, close enough that I can see the flecks of gold in his brown eyes, the small scar on his chin that wasn't there before. "She had a life. A real life. She got out. And you showed up and burned it down."

"I saved her life."

"You put her in a cage."

"Knox." Hailey's hand is on my arm, but I shake it off.

"This is what you did after you got out?" The anger is pouring out now, hot and bitter. "After everything we went through over there? You came home and became a thief?"

"You don't know anything about what I did after."

"I know you took an oath. Same as me. I know we watched people die for something that was supposed to mean something. And you came back and decided to steal from people for a living."

"Spare me the lecture on honor, Knox. Not everyone got to come home and land a cushy security job."

"You son of a bitch."

I grab him by the collar of his shirt and shove him back against the wall. The impact rattles a picture frame. Liam's hands come up but he doesn't fight back, doesn't try to break my grip. He just looks at me, and there's anger in his face, yes, but that's not all. There's heat under it. Hunger.

"Feel better?" he asks, low enough that only I can hear.

"Not yet."

"Knox, stop!" Hailey wedges herself between us, both palms flat on my chest, pushing. "This isn't helping. Let him go."

I don't want to let him go. I want to knock his teeth out. I want to make him answer for every choice that led us here—Hailey scared and trapped, a twenty-million-dollar target on her back—all because he couldn't leave well enough alone.

I want to know if he ever thinks about that night in the motor pool. If he remembers what almost happened. If it kept him awake the way it kept me awake.

"Knox." Hailey's voice is softer now. "Please."

I let go. Step back. My hands are shaking and I ball them into fists to hide it.

Liam straightens his collar, and the bastard is almost smiling, which makes me want to hit him all over again. "That's the reunion I get?"

"You're lucky that's all you got."

"Am I?" He holds my gaze for a beat too long. "Felt like you were holding back."

The words land somewhere low in my stomach. I tell myself it's just adrenaline. Just the drugs still working through my system. It's not the way his voice dropped on that last sentence, or the way his eyes flicked to my mouth for half a second before he looked away.

"We're not doing this," I say.

"Doing what?"

"Whatever game you're playing. I'm here for Hailey. That's it."

Liam's smile widens, just slightly. "Sure, Knox. Whatever you say."

Hailey looks between us like she's trying to solve a puzzle with missing pieces. "Okay. Clearly there's some history here I don't know about."

"There's no history," I say.

"Absolutely none," Liam agrees, and the way he says it makes it sound like the opposite.

Hailey's eyes narrow, but she doesn't push. "Can we focus on getting out of here? You two can beat the hell out of each other later."

"Looking forward to it," Liam says.

"So am I," I tell him, and I mean it as a threat, but it comes out sounding like something else.

"The cabin's locked down tight," Liam says, breaking eye contact. "Steel-reinforced door, triple-pane windows. I've been over every inch, and we're not walking out without outside help or divine intervention."

"How long have you been here?"

"No way to tell. No clocks, no phones. We don't even know how long we were out from whatever they drugged us with."

I move to the window and look out at nothing but trees and snow and gray sky. "Security at the resort—I counted twelve on the perimeter before they grabbed me. Armed, coordinated, professional. There's serious money behind this operation."

"They brought you up by snowmobile?" Hailey asks.

"Twenty-five minutes from when I woke up, uphill most of the way, dense forest throughout." I turn back to them. "We're miles from anything."

No phones. No way to call for help. And a collector who's willing to hold us here indefinitely until she gets what she wants.

"Christ." I rub my face with my hands.

"How did you even find us?" Hailey asks, her voice careful, like she's bracing for the answer.

I hesitate. "You really want to know?"

"Knox."

"I put a tracker in your boots."

Nobody says anything for a long moment.

Liam lets out a low whistle. "Wow."

"Three months ago." Might as well get it all out. "In the sole. You never take them off, so I figured—"

"You put a tracker in my boots." Hailey's face is unreadable. "Three months ago."

"Yes."

"That's . . ."

"I know what it is. Believe me, I've had plenty of time to think about what kind of person does something like that." I hold her gaze. "But it's also the only reason I knew something was wrong. The only reason I'm standing here right now instead of back in New York wondering why you won't return my texts."

She stares at me for a long moment. Then, incredibly, she laughs. It's not a happy laugh—more like the sound you make when the universe has gotten so absurd that crying seems pointless.

"I can't decide if I should be furious or grateful."

"Can it be both?"

"It's definitely both." She shakes her head. "We're going to have a very long conversation about boundaries when we get out of here."

"Fair enough."

Liam watches us, jealousy plain on his face now and directed squarely at me. "So let me get this straight. You stalked her for months, put a tracking device in her shoes, and followed her to the Arctic. And she's . . . okay with this?"

"She's processing," Hailey says.

"It's a lot to process," I agree.

"You two are perfect for each other." He keeps his voice light. His jaw tells a different story. "Jesus Christ."

"Problem?" I ask.

"No problem." But his eyes say otherwise. His eyes say he remembers that night too, and he's not sure anymore which one of us he wanted.

Good. Let him wonder.

The three of us stand there in thick silence.

My ex-squadmate who I never let myself want. Hailey, who turns out to be an ex– jewel thief. And me, zip tie marks still fresh on my wrists, stuck in the middle of whatever the hell this is.

Liam catches my eye, and something passes between us—not friendship. Not anymore. Whatever this is, it's been sitting too long. Gone sour.

"Just like old times," he says.

"Not even close." But there's gravel in my voice, and from the way his lips curl, he notices.

I turn away before he can see anything else on my face. Because sitting around waiting for a psychotic collector to decide our fate isn't an option. And standing here trading loaded looks with Liam Calloway isn't getting us any closer to freedom.

"Okay," I say. "Tell me everything. From the beginning."

Hailey starts talking. Liam leans against the wall with his arms crossed, watching me watch her.

This is going to be a problem. He's going to be a problem.

And the worst part is, I'm almost glad he's here.

Chapter Eighteen

HAILEY

The screen above the fireplace comes to life, and Marlena actually squeals. "Oh my god, you're all together! Look at you!" She's clapping her hands like a kid at a birthday party. "I've been watching the feeds all afternoon and I just—I can't get over it. The three of you. In one room. This is even better than I imagined."

Knox stands rigid beside me. He's been pacing the cabin for the last hour, checking windows and door frames he's already checked twice, burning off the restless energy of a man who's used to solving problems and can't solve this one.

"Mr. Bishop." Marlena turns her attention to him, pressing both hands to her chest. "I have to say—I pulled your service record after my team brought you in, and wow. Just wow. Two Bronze Stars? That thing in Fallujah?" She fans herself dramatically. "I got a little flushed reading it, if I'm being honest. Very heroic. Very sexy."

"Get to the point," Knox says flatly.

"So direct! God, I love military men." She shivers theatrically. "That commanding energy. The discipline. You can just tell he'd be incredible in—" She stops herself, waving a hand. "Sorry, sorry. Staying focused. My therapist says I have attention regulation issues. We're working on it. She's a wonderful woman, Dr. Knight. Very nonjudgmental. She's been helping me with my impulse control, which, honestly, is the only reason I didn't have my team bring Knox directly to my bedroom." She winks at the camera. "Growth mindset."

I exchange a look with Liam. His expression says *what the actual fuck* more eloquently than words ever could.

"Anyway! Business." Marlena claps once, shifting gears. "I've given you time to settle in, process your feelings, maybe hash out some of that delicious tension I've been sensing. But now we need to discuss terms. You know I want the diamond—obviously—and here's the fun part. I'm giving you a deadline. Christmas Eve at midnight. Ten days." She holds up both hands, fingers spread. "I find deadlines really motivating. Dr. Knight says I'm very goal-oriented. It's one of my strengths. We mostly work on my attachment style and my tendency to become obsessive about things I want. She thinks I'm talking about handbags." She laughs. "I mean, I am also obsessive about handbags, but that's not really the core issue."

She settles back in her chair, legs crossed.

"So! Ten days. Tell me where the Snowflake is hidden, you go free. New identities, travel money, my personal guarantee Viktor never finds you. I'll even write you a letter of recommendation if you want to get back in the game. I know people. Very connected people."

"And if we refuse?" Knox asks.

"Then I kill one of you."

Her tone doesn't change. Same bubbly energy, same pleasant smile. Like she's explaining the specials at a restaurant.

"The other two can watch and reconsider. I'll give you a day to grieve—maybe two, I'm not a monster—and then we'll have this conversation again. Hopefully with better results."

The fire pops. Nobody speaks.

"I know, I know." Marlena holds up a hand. "You're thinking, 'Marlena, that seems harsh. Marlena, is murder really on-brand for you?' And honestly? It's not. It's really not. I don't want to hurt any of you. Killing one of you would be like—" She looks up at the ceiling, searching. "Like using a Picasso as a dartboard. Like making a smoothie out of a first-edition Hemingway. Just—" She shudders. "Senseless destruction of something irreplaceable. So you understand why I really, really don't want to damage any of you. Hurting you would hurt me." She places a hand over her heart. "It would set back my whole emotional wellness journey. I'd need extra sessions with Dr. Knight. I'd probably need to increase my Lexapro. It would be a whole thing."

She sighs heavily.

"I've been working on myself, you know? Learning to set boundaries, practicing self-care, asking for what I want instead of just taking it. Well. Mostly instead of just taking it. Baby steps. Personal growth looks different for everyone. The important thing is that I'm trying."

I'm losing my mind. I have to be. Because this woman just threatened to murder one of us and then talked about her emotional wellness journey in the same breath, and somehow both things seem equally sincere.

"Here's what I need you to understand." For just a second I see something cold underneath all that warmth. Something that makes my stomach drop. "I've been waiting five years for this diamond. Five years of dead ends and false leads and watching it slip away. I'm done waiting. So when I say I'll kill one of you?" The smile comes back, but it doesn't reach her eyes. "I mean it. I'll cry about it afterward. But I'll do it."

Then, like flipping a switch, she's bright again.

"But let's not dwell on the negative! Let's focus on the positives." She starts counting on her fingers. "Beautiful cabin. Gourmet food. Excellent wine selection—try the Malbec with the steaks, seriously, it's an incredible pairing. And company you clearly enjoy." Her smile turns knowing. "I've seen the way you three look at each other. Very charged."

My face goes hot.

"You're insane," Knox says.

"I'm enthusiastic. There's a difference. Dr. Knight and I have discussed this. She says my passion for my interests is actually a strength, as long as I channel it constructively." She beams. "Which, again—strengths."

Knox looks like he's trying to solve an equation that doesn't have an answer. Liam has his hand over his mouth, and I can't tell if he's horrified or trying not to laugh. I'm somewhere between both.

"I'll check in again soon," Marlena continues, glancing at something off-screen. "In the meantime, make yourselves at home. Eat, drink, get to know each other better." She waves a hand. "I'll be monitoring—but not constantly. I'm not some crazy voyeur sitting here watching you like a peeping Tom. God, can you imagine?" She wrinkles her nose. "That would be so invasive. So pathological. Dr. Knight would have a field day." She shudders. "What you three do with your *personal* time?" She mimes zipping her lips. "None of my business. I'm a collector, not a pervert."

She pauses, tilting her head like she's reconsidering.

"I mean, I might check in occasionally. To make sure you're all still alive and cooperating. But if things get . . . intimate?" She holds up both hands, laughing. "I am immediately muting and looking away. Promise. Boundaries are important. Dr. Knight says healthy relationships require privacy and trust, and I want us to have a healthy relationship. Even if it's, you know. Kidnapper and kidnappees."

She pauses again . . . something or someone is distracting her.

"Ten days!" She holds up her fingers again. "Christmas Eve at midnight. Use the time wisely." She blows a kiss at the camera. "Bye for now! Remember—try the Malbec!"

The screen goes dark.

For a long moment, nobody moves.

"She's fucking insane," Liam says.

I start laughing. I can't help it—it bubbles up from somewhere hysterical, and once it starts I can't make it stop. Liam stares at me, then his mouth twitches, and Knox makes a sound that's either a groan or a laugh, and suddenly we're all standing in our beautiful prison losing our minds.

"We're so fucked," I manage between breaths.

"Thoroughly," Liam agrees.

The laughter dies as quickly as it came. Reality settling back in, cold and heavy.

Knox is already moving. "She said she's watching. We need to find the cameras."

He starts with the bookshelf, running his fingers along the spines, checking behind frames. Liam takes the kitchen, opening cabinets, examining light fixtures. I scan the main room—the fireplace mantel, the decorative objects, anywhere a lens could hide.

We search for twenty minutes. Every corner, every surface, every piece of furniture that could conceal surveillance equipment.

Nothing.

"They're too well hidden," Knox says, frustration bleeding through his words. "Professional installation. Could be pinhole cameras, could be built into the walls. Without equipment, we're not going to find them."

"So we just assume she can see and hear everything," Liam says.

"We have to." Knox's jaw tightens. "Every conversation. Every plan we make. She'll know."

The weight of that settles over us. No privacy. No secrets. Ten days of being watched like animals in a cage.

"You should eat something," Knox says to me. "Keep your strength up."

I shake my head. "My stomach's still off from whatever they drugged us with."

"Same," Liam admits. "Feels like I swallowed battery acid."

Knox nods slowly. "Yeah. Me too."

None of us move toward the kitchen. The thought of food right now makes my insides twist.

"So." Knox turns to face us, all traces of humor gone. "Now what?"

Liam pushes off from the counter. "We give her what she wants. Tell her where the diamond is, take the deal, disappear."

"No," Knox says.

"Knox—"

"Think about it. She lied about Viktor. She had to have manipulated you into bringing Hailey here. That whole thing about you retrieving the Snowflake—how did she know about that unless she set it up?" His jaw tightens as the implication lands. "Everything out of her mouth could be bullshit, including the part where she lets us walk away."

"She's obsessed with us," Liam says. "You heard her. We're irreplaceable. She's not going to destroy something she spent five years trying to acquire."

"She threatened to destroy it thirty seconds ago," Knox counters. "With a smile on her face."

"That was a negotiating tactic."

"That was a woman telling us exactly what she's capable of." Knox takes a step toward him. "The second she has that diamond, we're loose ends. Three people who know what she did, who she is, what she's willing to do. You really think she lets us walk away with all that?"

"So what's your plan? Die on principle?" Liam says. "I'd rather take the chance she keeps her word than guarantee she kills one of us on Christmas Eve."

Knox goes still. But he doesn't soften.

"The deal is the trap," he says. "She doesn't need us alive after she gets what she wants. Right now the diamond is the only thing keeping us breathing."

"Or we find a way out before it comes to that," Liam argues. "Get out of here—with the diamond if we can, without it if we have to. But sitting here refusing to engage isn't a strategy, it's a death wish."

"I'm not refusing to engage. I'm refusing to hand her the one card we're holding."

"You're gambling with Hailey's life."

"You're gambling with all our lives by refusing to consider the obvious solution."

They're squaring off now, and I can feel the tension ratcheting up. Different from their fight earlier—less about old wounds, more about strategy—but just as volatile.

"Stop," I say, stepping between them with my hands up. "Both of you. She's watching us right now. This is exactly what she wants."

They don't back down, but they stop advancing.

"Ten days," I continue. "We have ten days. We use the time to figure out our options, look for weaknesses, come up with something better than 'give her what she wants and pray.'" I look at Knox. "And something better than 'refuse to cooperate and hope for a miracle.'"

Neither of them responds, but some of the fight drains out of their postures.

"Can we do that?" I ask. "Can we at least try to work together?"

Liam nods slowly. Knox doesn't, but he steps back, which I'll take as agreement.

"Fine," Knox says. "We assess. We plan. But I'm not agreeing to hand over the diamond until we've exhausted every other possibility."

"And if we come up empty?" Liam asks.

"Then we revisit."

It's not a yes, but it's not a flat no either.

❄

Outside the windows, the light is already fading. The days are short this far north, and the afternoon has bled into evening without any of us noticing. We've been talking in circles for hours, going over the same arguments, reaching the same dead ends.

The bed dominates one corner of the room. King-size, piled with pillows, dressed in white sheets that look obscenely inviting after everything we've been through today. The couch faces the fireplace. The floor stretches between them.

One bed. Three people. Cameras watching from somewhere we can't find.

Nobody mentions the obvious. If it were just Knox and me, we'd climb into that bed together without a second thought. We've already slept wrapped around each other. Already woken up tangled in sheets that smelled like both of us. But Liam is standing by the fireplace, and Knox is standing by the window, and suddenly the math doesn't work anymore.

Knox glances at the bed. Then at me. Then—just for a second—at Liam.

"I'll take the couch," he says.

The words land wrong. Too casual. Too quick. Like he'd rehearsed them.

"Knox," I start, but I don't know how to finish. What am I supposed to say? *Sleep with me anyway? Ignore the fact that my ex is three feet away? Pretend this isn't incredibly fucking weird?*

Liam saves me from having to figure it out. "I'll take the floor," he says, already grabbing blankets from the closet. "Done it plenty of times."

But there's something in his voice too. Something careful. He's not looking at either of us, focusing instead on arranging the blankets into a pallet near the fire.

The silence stretches. Knox still hasn't moved toward the couch.

"This is stupid," I say. "That bed is huge. We're adults. We can just—"

"It's fine," Knox cuts me off. His jaw is tight. "Get some sleep, Hailey."

He's not looking at me. He's looking at Liam. And Liam is very deliberately not looking back.

I'm not part of what's happening right now. Some unspoken negotiation I don't have the decoder ring for. Knox on the couch. Liam on the floor. Me alone in a bed big enough for three.

Nobody's happy about it. But nobody's willing to be the one who suggests the alternative.

Knox settles onto the couch with a grunt, trying to fold his frame into a space clearly not designed for someone his size. His feet hang off the armrest. He shifts, trying to find a position that works, and I can already tell he's going to wake up with a knotted back.

I want to tell him to stop being an idiot. I want to pull him into the bed and curl against his chest and let the warmth of him drown out everything else.

But Liam is right there. Watching. Pretending not to watch.

And Knox won't cross that line. Not with an audience. Not when everything between us is still so new and undefined.

I climb into the bed alone.

The sheets are obscenely soft. Cool against my skin at first, then warming. Too much space on either side of me, too many pillows. I grab two and toss them—one to Knox on the couch, one to Liam by the fire. Neither of them says thank you. Neither of them needed to be told. But the bed is still too big. Designed for bodies tangled together instead of one woman lying awake and staring at the ceiling.

From across the room, I can see Knox's silhouette on the couch. He's not sleeping. I can tell by the tension in his shoulders, the way he shifts every few minutes trying to find a position that doesn't hurt.

Liam is a dark shape near the fireplace, wrapped in his blanket. I can't tell if he's asleep or just pretending.

Three people in one room. Close enough to touch. Choosing not to.

I think about Knox following me across a border because he couldn't stand not knowing where I was. The tracker in my boot that should make me furious but mostly makes me feel . . . I don't know . . . The way he looked at me when I told him the truth about my past—not with disgust or judgment, but with what appeared to be relief.

I think about Liam, who showed up after five years and turned my life upside down. Who looked at me like no time had passed. Who's hiding something—I can feel it, even if I can't prove it—but who also looked genuinely terrified when they dragged him out of his room.

I think about the two of them together. Their history I don't fully understand, the tension that runs underneath everything they say to each other. Knox pinning Liam against the wall, and the heat that flared in both their eyes before they remembered I was watching.

Marlena sees it too. That's why she put us here. One bed, one room, nowhere to go. She wants to watch us circle each other, wants to see what happens when the pressure builds and something breaks.

I won't give her the satisfaction.

But lying here alone, listening to them breathe in the darkness, I can't stop thinking about what it would feel like to not be alone. Knox's body warm against my back. Liam's hand on my hip. Both of them here, with me, in this bed that's too big for one person.

I close my eyes and try to make my brain shut up.

From the couch, I hear Knox shift again. A soft exhale.

Then Liam's voice, barely audible. "You awake?"

A pause. "Yeah."

"Me too."

Silence. The fire pops, sending a brief flare of light across the ceiling.

"This is fucked," Liam says quietly.

"Yep," Knox agrees.

"You really think she'll do it? Kill one of us?"

Another pause. Longer this time.

"Yeah," Knox says. "I do."

More silence. I hold my breath, not wanting them to know I'm listening.

"Then maybe I'm right," Liam says. "Maybe we should just tell her."

"And maybe she kills us anyway once she has what she wants."

Knox doesn't say anything else. The quiet stretches out, filled only with the wind and my own heartbeat loud in my ears.

"Get some sleep," Knox says. "We'll figure it out tomorrow."

"Yeah," Liam says. "Tomorrow."

The cabin settles into silence.

I lie there in the dark, in my too-soft sheets, and think about ten days. About Christmas Eve and deadlines and a woman who's working on her impulse control.

About the two men across the room, awake like I am, carrying the same weight.

Tomorrow we'll plan. Tomorrow we'll strategize. Tomorrow we'll try to find a way out of this that doesn't end with one of us dead.

But tonight, all I can do is listen to them breathe and wish I wasn't alone.

Chapter Nineteen

HAILEY

Marlena Kade is a psychopath with impeccable taste in bedding. That's the first coherent thought I have when I wake up alone, wrapped in sheets I want to hate but can't.

Morning light streams through the floor-to-ceiling windows, making the snow outside glitter like crushed diamonds. I lie there for a moment, listening. Knox and Liam are already up, their low voices drifting from somewhere near the kitchen. The cabin is one big open space—living area flowing into kitchen flowing into the bedroom nook where I'm currently cocooned—so I can hear every word even if I can't make them out.

Whatever they're saying, it doesn't sound friendly.

I drag myself out of bed and find clothes laid out on the dresser. More of Marlena's handiwork.

No. No no no.

I hold up the sweater. It's *pink*. Not even a cool dusty rose or something I could pretend is ironic. It's the color of cotton candy. Of baby showers. Of everything I've spent my adult life avoiding.

The jeans are fine, I guess. Light wash, which is a crime, but at least they're not bedazzled. There's a cream-colored cardigan as backup, cashmere and delicate and absolutely not anything I would ever voluntarily put on my body.

I dig through the dresser drawers hoping for something—anything—in black. A T-shirt. Socks. A goddamn scrunchie.

Nothing. Every item is soft and pastel and makes me want to set something on fire. Marlena has curated an entire wardrobe of things specifically designed to make me look like I'm about to brunch in the Hamptons.

I pull on the pink sweater because the alternative is freezing, and it fits perfectly. Of course it does. The woman kidnapped us with personalized wardrobes.

When I pad toward the kitchen, Knox is at the counter, a steak knife in his hand. He's not cutting anything. He's working the blade into the window frame, trying to wedge it into the seal.

Liam sits on the arm of the couch, watching him with his arms crossed.

Knox glances up when I approach, and his mouth twitches.

"Nice sweater."

"Shut up."

"Very soft. Very . . ." He tilts his head. "Cute."

"I will stab you with that knife."

Liam's watching me now too, and there's a grin spreading across his face that I don't like at all. "Is that *pink*?"

"It's the only option. Everything in that dresser looks like it belongs to a sorority girl."

"You look like you're about to ask me if I want to join your book club." Liam's grin widens. "Maybe bake some muffins. Organize a charity fun run."

"I hate you both."

"The color really brings out your eyes," Knox adds, completely deadpan.

"I hope Marlena kills you first."

I grab a mug from the cabinet and pour myself coffee from the pot someone already made, trying to ignore the fact that I can see my reflection in the window and I look like a J.Crew catalog threw up on me.

"Any luck?" I ask Knox, nodding at the knife.

"The seal is some kind of industrial polymer. I've been at it for twenty minutes and haven't made a dent." He sets the knife down, frustration evident in the set of his shoulders. "The glass is shatter-resistant. I could work on it for a week and not get through."

"So we're stuck."

"For now."

Liam pushes off from the couch and walks toward the bathroom. Knox tracks his movement without turning his head. I can see the line of his jaw tighten when Liam passes behind him.

Ten days. We have ten days to survive this cabin without killing each other.

I take a long sip of coffee and wish it were whiskey.

The next hour passes in silence that gets progressively louder. Knox tries a different knife on a different window. Liam paces by the windows like a caged animal. I pretend to be interested in a book I grabbed from the shelf, but I haven't absorbed a single word. The pages might as well be blank.

Knox is working on the window near the kitchen when Liam walks past him to refill his coffee.

Their shoulders collide.

Not hard. Not even particularly aggressive. But the contact is like a match dropped in gasoline.

Knox turns. "Watch it."

"You're in the way." Liam doesn't stop walking. "Some of us are trying to move around."

"I'm trying to get us out of here. What are you doing? Oh, right. Nothing. Just like always."

Liam freezes mid-stride. When he turns around, his expression has gone flat in a way I recognize from our years working together. That's his dangerous face. The one he wears right before everything goes sideways.

"What's that supposed to mean?"

"It means you're good at showing up when you need something and disappearing when things get hard." Knox straightens to his full height, which is considerable. "Over a decade, Liam. Not even a message."

My coffee mug hovers halfway to my mouth. I should intervene. I should say something, do something, diffuse whatever this is before it detonates.

I don't move.

"I couldn't," Liam says. "You know why."

"Enlighten me."

"Afghanistan. The things we didn't say. I thought distance would be easier."

"Bullshit."

Knox moves closer, and there's something almost magnetic about it. Like he can't help himself. Like Liam is pulling him in even as they're pushing each other away.

"You just didn't care enough to deal with it. Easier to run."

Liam's hands curl into fists at his sides. "You don't know what you're talking about."

"I know you brought Hailey into a trap. I know you're pushing to hand over the diamond to a woman who's clearly unhinged. And I know there's something you're not telling us."

"Back off, Knox."

"Make me."

They're chest to chest now. Close enough to feel each other's breath. Close enough that whatever's crackling between them has nothing to do with the fight.

I've seen men fight before. I've seen the way violence builds, the way it broadcasts itself in squared shoulders and clenched jaws. This isn't that. This is something else.

Knox shoves Liam. Hard. Liam stumbles back a step, then comes forward and shoves back harder. Knox's fist cocks back, ready to swing, and his whole body is a loaded weapon, and Liam's not backing down, and they're about to tear into each other like animals, and—

"ENOUGH."

I'm between them before I've consciously decided to move. My hands hit their chests simultaneously, shoving them apart with all the force I can muster. They separate, barely, still vibrating with unspent violence.

"What the hell is wrong with you two?" I'm shouting now, and I don't care. "We're trapped in here for ten days and you're going to beat the shit out of each other on day one?"

Knox is breathing hard, his gaze still locked on Liam over my shoulder. "He's hiding something."

"So ask him instead of starting a fight!"

I whirl on Liam, keeping one hand planted firmly on Knox's chest. I can feel his heartbeat through the fabric. Rapid. Furious.

"And you." I jab a finger at Liam. "Stop deflecting every time he questions you. If you have nothing to hide, then act like it."

Something shutters behind Liam's eyes. "There's nothing to tell."

"Then stop acting guilty!"

I look between them, my own anger building to match theirs. Two grown men who can't be in the same room without combusting. Two soldiers who survived god knows what together and can't seem to survive each other.

"We have one chance to get through this," I say. "One. And it requires us working together. So whatever this is?" I gesture at the space between them. "Fix it."

Neither of them moves.

Knox's chest is still heaving under my palm. His eyes haven't left Liam's face. And Liam is staring right back, jaw set, his composure cracking open at the seams.

There's a look on Liam's face that snags my attention. I can't name it exactly, but I've known Liam for years. I know his moods, his tells, the way he holds himself differently around people who get under his skin. I saw it in Barcelona, in that club where he spent three hours watching a bartender before disappearing into the back room. I saw it in Prague, the way he couldn't stop glancing at the locksmith who helped us with that job. Liam's attraction to men was never a secret between us.

But that's Liam. And whatever this is between them feels more complicated than simple want. There's history here, from their military days, that neither of them has told me about. An old wound tearing open.

Knox catches me studying them and immediately shutters his expression. He's good at that. Walls up in an instant, every emotion filed away behind that disciplined exterior. Whatever just passed between him and Liam, it's already locked down.

"You two need to figure out how to coexist," I say, stepping back from both of them. "I don't care if you like each other. I don't care if you hate each other. But this?" I gesture at the wreckage of their almost-fight. "This can't happen again. Not if we want to survive ten days in this box."

Knox exhales hard through his nose. Liam shoves his hands in his pockets, looking anywhere but at either of us.

"I mean it," I say. "Whatever history you have? Whatever grudge you're carrying? Table it. We deal with Marlena first. Everything else comes second."

Silence. The fire pops in the grate. Outside, wind presses against the windows like it's testing for weakness.

"Fine," Knox says.

Liam lifts one shoulder in a shrug that barely qualifies. "Fine."

They don't look at each other when they say it.

I drop onto the couch. Part of me wants to scream. Part of me can't shake the feeling that I'm only seeing the surface of what's between these two. But I'm too tired and too furious to chase it right now.

Knox is the first to step back. He runs a hand through his hair, that tell of his that means he's trying to regain control. Liam mirrors the movement, putting distance between them, but the air has changed. Whatever wall was between them just came down.

I take a breath, forcing myself to calm down. Focus on what matters.

"Knox. What were you going to ask him? Before you started swinging?"

Knox's gaze slides to Liam. Holds there. "Afghanistan. He said he left because of things we didn't say. I want to know what that means."

Liam is very still. The defiance has drained out of him, leaving something more honest in its wake.

"For who?" Knox asks, quieter now. "You said distance would be easier. Easier for who?"

Liam's shoulders drop. When he speaks, the words come slow.

"For me." He swallows hard. "I couldn't be around you without wanting . . ."

He trails off.

"Without wanting what?"

Liam meets his eyes. Holds the contact this time, even though he looks like he'd rather be anywhere else.

"You know what."

The cabin feels smaller suddenly. The walls pressing in. Nobody moves. I'm holding my breath without meaning to, watching twelve years of silence finally break.

Knox takes a step forward. Not aggressive this time.

"Twelve years," he says. "Twelve years, and you never said anything."

"Neither did you."

"I didn't know how."

"Neither did I."

They're close again. Not fighting anymore, but not quite anything else either. Suspended somewhere in between, balanced on an edge neither of them seems willing to tip over.

I watch them from the couch, my heart beating in a rhythm that feels unfamiliar. There's jealousy there, maybe. A twinge of it. But underneath that, something stronger. Something that looks a lot like want.

Both of them. Together.

With me.

The thought lands before I can stop it. I push it down before it can fully form, but it leaves echoes in its wake. Warmth spreading through my chest. An ache between my thighs that has no business existing right now.

We have bigger problems. Marlena and her deadline. The diamond and its location. Survival, escape, all the things that should be occupying every corner of my brain.

But right now, watching Knox and Liam stop pretending, all I can think about is what it would feel like to be caught between them both.

"So." I break the silence before it can swallow us whole. "Now what?"

They both turn to look at me. Knox's gaze is dark, heated. Liam's gone feral in a way I remember from late nights in hotel rooms, when we'd finish a job and need somewhere to put all that adrenaline.

"Now we figure out how to survive the next ten days," Knox says. But he's not fooling anyone, and he's still standing too close to Liam, and nothing about this feels like it's actually about survival at all.

"Together?" Liam asks. The question has layers I don't think he intended.

Knox looks at me. Then at Liam. Back at me.

"Together."

None of us moves for a long moment. Then Knox clears his throat and turns toward the kitchen, and the spell fractures just enough for us to breathe again.

Evening comes slowly. We cook dinner together because there's nothing else to do and because the alternative is sitting in separate corners pretending we don't feel whatever is building between us. Marlena's gourmet kitchen is fully stocked. Steaks, vegetables, that Malbec she mentioned. Everything we need for a meal none of us is hungry for.

The kitchen area is barely big enough for one person, let alone three. Every movement brings contact. Liam's hip brushing mine as he reaches for a cutting board. Knox's hand grazing my lower back as he passes behind me. Liam and Knox colliding at the sink, their bodies pressing together for one moment before they separate.

Nobody apologizes. Nobody pulls away faster than necessary.

"You've got flour on your sweater," Liam says, nodding at my chest. "Your very pink sweater."

"I will poison your steak."

"I'm just saying, it's a good look on you. Very domestic."

"You're a dead man, Calloway."

Knox snorts, and when I glare at him, he holds up both hands. "I didn't say anything."

"You were thinking it."

"I was thinking you look beautiful." He turns back to the steaks, but not before I catch the smirk. "The pink really does bring out your eyes."

"I want it on record that I hate both of you."

"Noted," they say in unison, and something about the synchronicity makes my stomach flip.

I slice vegetables and try not to think about the way my skin tingles everywhere they've touched me. Knox seasons the steaks with methodical focus, his forearms flexing as he works. Liam opens the wine and pours three glasses, his fingers lingering on mine when he hands me a glass.

We eat at the small table near the windows. Three chairs, barely enough room to fit. Our knees knock together underneath. Knox's thigh presses against mine on one side, warm through the denim. Liam's foot brushes my ankle on the other.

The Malbec is incredible. Marlena was right about that, at least.

"So," Liam says, swirling his wine. "Our captor has good taste."

"In wine," I agree. "Also in victims, apparently."

Knox snorts. "She called me sexy."

"You are sexy," I say without thinking.

His eyes meet mine across the table. Want flares there, banked but unmistakable.

"So are you," he says quietly. Then his mouth curves. "Even in pink."

"Oh my god."

Liam is watching us both. Like he's on the outside looking in. He doesn't say anything. Just drains his wine and pours himself another glass.

Knox turns to look at him. Really look, the way he's been avoiding all day. The moment stretches. Almost imperceptible, but I notice. I notice everything right now, every visible emotion, every shift in body language. The three of us are orbiting each other, pulled together by something we can't seem to fight.

After dinner, we clean up without speaking. The silence isn't uncomfortable anymore. It's anticipatory, like the air before a storm breaks.

Knox washes dishes. Liam dries. I put things away, reaching past them both, my body sliding between theirs in the cramped space. Every brush of contact sends sparks up my spine.

When the last plate is put away, we stand there. Three people, no more tasks to hide behind.

"I should shower," I say, because someone has to break whatever this is before it breaks us.

Knox barely gets the words out. "Go ahead. We'll figure out sleeping arrangements."

Right. One bed. Three people. The social experiment Marlena is so excited about.

I lock myself in the bathroom, leaning against the door for a moment to catch my breath. My reflection in the mirror looks flushed. Wild-eyed. The pink sweater is ridiculous and I'm ridiculous and this whole situation is completely insane.

The hot water helps. Not much, but some. I stand under the spray and let it beat against my shoulders, trying to organize my thoughts into something coherent.

Liam and Knox. Knox and Liam. The two of them together, their history tangled up in silence and want. And me, caught between them, wanting things I shouldn't want, feeling things I can't name.

Ten days.

Ten days of this. Of their proximity, their bodies, their unresolved history bleeding into every interaction. Ten days of one bed and no privacy and Marlena watching everything, waiting to see if her hypothesis proves true.

I turn off the water and dry myself slowly, delaying the moment I have to go back out there and face whatever comes next.

When I emerge, wrapped in the softest robe I've ever worn—cream colored, because fuck my life—the cabin is quiet. Knox sits on the couch, staring into the fire. Liam stands by the window, watching snow fall against the glass.

They both look up when I step out. Both of them, at the same time, and for a second nobody seems to know where to look.

"Sleeping arrangements," Knox says. "We need to figure them out."

"One bed," Liam points out. "Not a lot of options."

"Someone takes the couch," I say. "We can rotate."

"Or." Liam pauses. "We could share."

Knox goes very still. I feel my heart rate spike.

"Share," Knox repeats.

"None of us slept last night. Whatever she drugged us with doesn't count." Liam leans against the window frame, arms crossed. "If we're going to figure out how to get out of here, we need to actually rest. That couch is five feet long. Neither of you is sleeping on it and being worth a damn tomorrow."

He's not wrong. I got the bed to myself last night and they didn't. I can't exactly claim it all to myself two nights in a row.

"Fine by me," I say, surprising myself. "If you two can manage to stay on your own sides."

The challenge hangs in the air between us. Knox looks at Liam. Liam looks at Knox.

"We can manage," Knox says.

But the way he says it makes me think managing is the last thing any of us is going to do.

We turn off the lights and climb into bed together. Me in the middle, Knox on my left, Liam on my right. The mattress dips under our combined weight. Sheets rustle as we each try to find comfortable positions that don't involve touching.

It's impossible. The bed is big, but not that big. Knox's shoulder presses against mine. Liam's leg brushes my calf. We're breathing in syncopated rhythm, none of us sleeping, all of us pretending.

I lie there in the dark, acutely aware of the warmth radiating from both of them. Knox, whom I've spent a year circling without ever closing the distance. Liam, whom I spent five years trying to forget. Both of them inches away, and the darkness making everything feel closer than it should.

The snow falls. I close my eyes and listen to them breathe, feeling their bodies against mine, and wonder how long any of us can hold out before something gives.

Chapter Twenty

KNOX

The dream starts the way it always does. Dust and heat and the high whine of something mechanical failing. Kandahar, maybe. Or Helmand. The geography stopped mattering years ago. What matters is the convoy, the sudden wrong silence before the world tears itself apart, and the face I see through the smoke when I turn my head.

Liam. Covered in blood. Reaching for me.

Then the convoy becomes the lodge. The smoke becomes the hallway. Men in tactical gear drag Liam away while I watch, paralyzed, unable to close the distance no matter how hard I try.

Then Hailey's there too. They're dragging her in the opposite direction, her mouth open in a scream I can't hear, and I'm standing between them unable to save either one and the explosion finally comes and—

"Knox. Knox, wake up."

Hands on my shoulders. Gentle pressure. A voice cutting through the static.

My eyes snap open and I'm already half-sitting, muscles coiled, pulse pounding in my ears. The cabin. Stone fireplace, floor-to-ceiling windows, white morning light spilling across the sheets. Not Afghanistan. Not the lodge.

Hailey's face swims into focus. She's propped on one elbow beside me, hair a mess, those dark eyes causing my chest to ache. She'd slept between us last night—a buffer zone, a no-man's-land—and sometime in the night she must have shifted closer to my side.

On her other side, Liam is awake too, sitting up against the headboard, watching us in a way I can't parse.

"You're okay," Hailey says. "You're safe."

The lie of it almost makes me laugh. None of us is safe. We're locked in a cage by a woman who talks about murder with the same inflection she uses to recommend wine pairings. But Hailey's touch is warm and steady, and for a moment I let myself believe her anyway.

"Bad dream," I manage. My voice comes out wrecked.

"I figured that out from the thrashing." Her thumb traces my jaw. "Want to talk about it?"

"Not particularly."

"Okay." She doesn't push. Doesn't pry. Just keeps up that slow, grounding pressure like she knows exactly what I need without me having to explain it.

From the other side of the bed, Liam shifts. "Afghanistan?" he asks quietly, and there's no judgment in it. Just understanding. He has his own version of these dreams. You don't spend years in combat zones without accumulating some ghosts.

"Yeah."

"Those never go away." His voice is rough with sleep. "They just get quieter."

Something in my chest loosens at his words. At the fact that he knows. That I don't have to explain.

"Coffee," Hailey announces, sitting up. "I'm making some. You two stay."

"You don't have to—" I start.

"I want to." She leans down and kisses my forehead—brief, almost sisterly, nothing like the way she looked at me yesterday. Then she slides out of bed, still in the oversize T-shirt she found in the dresser, and pads toward the kitchen.

Liam and I watch her go. Neither of us moves to fill the space she left.

"So," he says after a moment. "That was the worst night's sleep I've ever had."

"Worse than Kandahar?"

"Different kind of uncomfortable." He scrubs a hand over his face. "I pulled a muscle in my neck trying to stay on my edge of the mattress."

"You could have taken the floor again."

"And admit defeat? Never." He meets my eyes, and there's something almost vulnerable there. "Besides, Hailey would've dragged me back by the ankle."

I don't have a good response to that, so I don't try.

The coffee maker gurgles to life across the room. We can hear Hailey moving around the kitchen, the soft clink of mugs being pulled from cabinets. Domestic sounds. Normal sounds. Completely at odds with the fact that we're prisoners waiting for a madwoman to decide if we live or die.

"How bad was the dream?" Liam asks. "Scale of one to ten."

"Solid seven."

"Seven's rough."

"I've had worse."

"I know." He's quiet for a moment. "Remember Marjah? You didn't sleep for three days after that convoy hit."

"I slept."

"Sitting up with your eyes half-open doesn't count."

"I was resting my eyes."

"You were hallucinating from exhaustion. You called our CO 'Mom' during a briefing."

The laugh surprises me, rusty and genuine. "I called him 'ma'am.' Not *Mom*."

"Nah, we all heard *Mom*."

From the kitchen, Hailey calls out, "Are you two actually bonding, or is this some kind of trauma-off?"

"Bonding," Liam says. "Through shared suffering. It's a military thing."

"I'm winning the trauma-off, though," I add. "I jumped on a grenade."

"It was a dud."

"I didn't know that when I jumped on it."

Hailey crosses back to us, three mugs balanced precariously in her hands. "I'm sorry, you jumped on a grenade?"

"Like a golden retriever diving after a tennis ball," Liam says, taking his mug from her. "Very noble. Very idiotic. Very Knox."

"I saved three people."

"You got a concussion and cried when they gave you a medal."

"I did not cry."

"Your eyes were definitely wet."

"That was dust. From the explosion."

"The explosion from the dud grenade that didn't explode?"

I open my mouth to argue and realize I've been thoroughly outmaneuvered. Hailey is grinning, and Liam looks insufferably pleased with himself.

"You're both the worst," I say, taking my coffee.

"And yet here we are, trapped together." Hailey settles onto the bed cross-legged, somehow managing to position herself exactly between us without touching either one. The distance feels intentional. Careful. "So. Day two. What's the plan?"

The question lands like a weight. Day two. Eight more days until Marlena's deadline. Eight more days to figure out how to get out of here without handing over a twenty-million-dollar diamond or watching one of us die.

"We keep looking for weaknesses," I say. "Check the windows again, test the door hinges, look for anything we might have missed."

"We did that yesterday," Liam points out. "The windows are industrial-grade. The door might as well be a vault. Short of finding a blowtorch in one of these cabinets, we're not breaking out."

"Yesterday doesn't count. Yesterday we were half-drugged and at each other's throats before we'd even finished our first cup of coffee. Today the fog has lifted and we're not swinging at each other, which puts us ahead."

"Then we look harder."

"Or," Liam says, and there's something careful in his voice, "we consider the other option."

"No."

"Knox—"

"We're not giving her the diamond."

"I'm just saying we should discuss it. Weigh the pros and cons. She said she'd let us go if—"

"She said a lot of things." I set my mug down harder than I mean to. "She also said she'd kill one of us, without blinking. You really want to bet our lives on the word of someone who monologues about her emotional wellness journey while threatening murder?"

He opens his mouth like he's going to push harder, then seems to think better of it.

"Fine," he says, but the word sounds hollow. "We look harder."

Hailey's watching the exchange with sharp eyes, her gaze bouncing between us like she's trying to read something neither of us is saying out loud.

"What?" I demand.

"Nothing." She takes a long sip of her coffee. "We just think maybe you could take a breath. That's all."

"I'll take a breath when we're out of here."

"You'll give yourself a stroke before we're out of here if you don't calm down."

"I'm perfectly calm."

Liam snorts. "You've got a vein pulsing in your forehead."

"That's my thinking vein."

"That's your 'about to have an aneurysm' vein. I've seen it before. Usually right before you do something stupid and heroic."

"I don't do stupid."

"Grenade," they say in unison.

I throw a pillow at Liam's head. He catches it, laughing, and for a second everything feels almost normal. Almost okay.

Then the laughter fades.

"Okay," Hailey says. "New plan. Knox works out his anxiety with push-ups instead of giving himself an ulcer. Liam cooks something for breakfast. I pretend to read that book I've been failing to read since we got here. We revisit the escape plan at noon. Deal?"

"That's not a plan," I say. "That's just . . . killing time."

"Fine. So we need another way out."

Liam catches my eye. Tilts his head toward the ceiling. I follow his gaze to the smoke detector above the kitchen area, and he raises his eyebrows. Message received.

He stands, stretches like he's just working out the stiffness from sleeping on the floor, and wanders toward the kitchen. Casual. Bored. He runs water in the sink, opens a cabinet, lets it bang shut. Noise cover.

I move closer. He leans in, mouth near my ear.

"Cameras," he whispers. "Smoke detectors. I want to see what's in them."

I nod. Grab a chair and carry it to the kitchen, positioning it under the detector like I'm checking something mundane. Hailey watches us from the bed. She's sharp enough not to ask out loud.

I pop the casing. Inside, right where the sensor should be, there's a lens and a circuit board. I angle it so Liam can see. He leans in close, turning the board with his fingers, tracing the wires.

"No mic," he breathes against my shoulder. Barely a sound. "Video only." He pauses, eyes on the chip. "Wi-Fi. That's how she's getting the feed."

Something passes across his face. He doesn't say anything else, but I can tell he's turning it over.

I fit the casing back together. Leave it exactly where it was.

Liam moves to the one above the main living area. Same routine. Hailey's on her feet now, standing close, pretending to look out the window while she watches us work. Liam pops the second casing, checks it, mouths "same" at me.

The third is above the bed, built into the light fixture. Same deal. Lens, board, no microphone.

Three cameras. All visual. No audio.

Liam steps down and crosses to where Hailey and I are standing near the windows. We cluster close together, backs to the room, faces toward the glass. Anyone watching the feeds would see three people staring at the snow.

"She can see us," Liam says, low but no longer whispering. "She can't hear us. As long as we keep our faces away from the cameras, she can't even read our lips."

Hailey lets out a breath. "You're sure."

"Standard surveillance hardware. High-end, but off the shelf. No audio pickup on any of the three boards."

"Okay." Hailey's quiet for a moment, processing. "So we can actually talk."

"We can actually talk."

Something shifts between the three of us. The first crack in the cage.

"Before we get into any of that," I say, "we should go through this place. Everything in it. Not checking locks this time. I want to know what's here that we can use."

We spread out. It's one room, so there's no privacy to the search, but we're thorough. To anyone watching the feeds, it looks like three bored people killing time. Hailey opens kitchen cabinets like she's looking for a snack. I check the bathroom like I'm hunting for an extra towel. Liam browses the bookshelves, pulls open the junk drawer, pokes around under the bed.

Nobody takes anything out. Nobody lines anything up. We just look.

When we've all finished, we drift back to the windows. Stand close, faces to the glass, hands near our mouths like we're warming them against the cold.

"Kitchen," Hailey says behind her fingers. "Steak knives, real ones. WD-40. Duct tape. Sewing kit with scissors. Under the sink—bleach, ammonia, drain cleaner."

"Bathroom," I say. "Fire extinguisher under the sink. Still charged."

"Junk drawer," Liam adds. "Twine, matches, rubber bands. Nothing else useful on the shelves."

We're quiet for a moment, cataloging.

Liam tilts his head, thinking. "Fire extinguisher point-blank to the face buys you thirty seconds. Maybe more."

Hailey's still staring out at the snow. "Bleach and ammonia in a closed space would clear a room. As long as we're not in it."

Liam and I both glance at her.

"What? I read."

"Remind me never to piss you off," Liam says.

She almost smiles. "None of this matters without a plan. Get out? Wait for someone to find us? Play along until we see an opening?"

"Nobody knows we're here," I say. "Rescue isn't coming."

"Cole might figure it out," Hailey says. "Eventually."

"Eventually isn't a plan. But if we could find a way to get a message to him, that's different. He's got the resources to actually do something with it."

Liam pulls a chair into the corner by the fireplace and angles it so his back is to the nearest camera. Hailey and I do the same. Three people huddled in a dead zone, finally able to talk.

Yesterday we had nothing. Today we have knives, chemicals, blind spots, and silence.

It's a start.

Every instinct I have is screaming at me to do something, fix something, solve the problem before it solves us.

"I'll make breakfast," Liam says, and I catch myself watching the way his shoulders move under his T-shirt before I force my eyes away. "Eggs and toast. Maybe that fancy bacon I saw in the fridge."

Hailey grabs her coffee and heads for the couch.

The morning crawls.

I try to pass some time and chill the fuck out. I really do. Push-ups on the rug in front of the fireplace. Forty. Fifty. Sixty. The burn in my arms drowns out some of the noise in my head, but not enough. Not nearly enough.

Liam moves through the kitchen, cracking eggs, laying bacon in a pan. Every cabinet closes with more force than necessary. Every utensil hits the counter harder than it needs to. He's wound just as tight as I am—he's just better at hiding it.

Hailey curls up on the couch with her book, turning pages at a pace that tells me she's not absorbing a single word. Her eyes keep drifting toward the windows. Toward me. Toward Liam.

We're all pretending to be calm and fooling no one.

Seventy. Eighty.

I catch Hailey watching me over the top of her book. Her gaze traces down my back, lingers somewhere around my hips, then snaps away when she realizes I've noticed. Heat crawls up my neck.

Ninety. One hundred.

I switch to planks. Hold until my core trembles, until sweat drips off my forehead and darkens the rug beneath me. My body screams for relief and I refuse to give it, because pain I can control is better than everything I can't.

"You know," Liam says from the kitchen, "there's a fine line between working out and self-punishment."

I drop out of the plank and flip onto my back, staring at the ceiling while my heart rate slowly returns to normal. Exposed beams overhead. Wood and stone and glass. A prison designed to make prisoners comfortable.

"Feel better?" Liam asks.

"No."

"Shocking." He starts plating food. "Breakfast is ready."

We eat in near-silence. The eggs are good, the bacon is perfect, and I can barely taste any of it. My eyes keep finding Hailey across the table. The way she pushes food around her plate without eating. The way her fingers drum against her mug. The way she very carefully doesn't look at either of us for too long.

Liam notices too. I catch him watching her, and the look on his face isn't casual. When Hailey reaches for the salt, Liam hands it to her before she gets there. Their fingers brush. She pulls back fast, but not fast enough.

The last time we were alone, I cooked her dinner at my apartment. She kissed me in my kitchen and I could still feel it days later. Now she's sitting three feet away from the man she used to share a bed with, and I'm supposed to act like that doesn't gut me.

"More coffee?" Liam asks her.

"I'm good."

"You haven't eaten."

"I'm not hungry."

"You should eat."

"Liam." She gives him a look. "I'm fine."

He backs off, but the familiarity of it stings. He knows she doesn't eat when she's stressed. Knows when to push and when to stop. I'm learning those things about her in real time. He learned them years ago.

I stand up and take my plate to the sink. Wash it. Dry it. Put it away.

The afternoon is long. We go over the plan again in the blind spot, refining details, poking holes. Liam does pull-ups on the doorframe, counting under his breath. Hailey goes back to her book. I check the windows again because I can't help myself.

At one point, Hailey and I end up in the kitchen at the same time. She's making tea. I'm getting water. The space is small and we're close, and when she turns around she almost walks into my chest.

"Sorry." She steps back, but not far.

"You're fine."

We stand there. The kettle hisses behind her. Liam is across the room, doing something with the bookshelves, not looking at us. Or pretending not to.

Hailey's eyes come up to mine. I can see her trying to say something and not finding the words for it. Not here. Not with Liam ten feet away.

She opens her mouth. Closes it. Shakes her head like she's arguing with herself, then takes her tea and walks back to the couch without a word.

I stay in the kitchen longer than I need to.

By evening, the plan has been picked apart and put back together twice. We've run through every scenario we can think of and most of them end badly. The wine comes out again because there's nothing else to do with the hours between sundown and sleep.

But the ease of last night isn't there. Liam tries to tell another story and it dies halfway through. Hailey stares into her glass. I stare into the fire.

"I'm trying really hard to be positive. But I'm also afraid we're trapped here," she says, her voice quieter now. "For eight more days. Maybe the rest of our lives, if Marlena has her way."

The silence stretches. The fire sizzles. Outside, wind howls against the windows.

Liam looks at me. I look at Hailey. Hailey looks at both of us.

Nobody moves.

"I'm taking a shower," she says flatly.

She stalks toward the bathroom. The door clicks shut behind her.

Liam and I stare at each other. The fire pops between us. I can still feel where Hailey almost touched me in the kitchen, the ghost of a conversation we didn't have.

"She's struggling," Liam says. Not to me, exactly. More like he's thinking out loud. "She used to do this. Shut down when she couldn't fix things. Go quiet. I'd have to—"

"I know what she needs."

Liam stops mid-sentence. Looks at me.

"Do you." His eyes hold mine, and then something shifts in them. "You always did run toward things without thinking. Some things never change."

The barracks. The night before I shipped out. He's not talking about the grenade and we both know it.

I don't have an answer. I've never had an answer. That's the whole problem—I want things I don't know how to name, feel things I don't know how to express, and every time I get close to the edge I pull back because it's safer than falling.

But safety hasn't kept me alive. It's just kept me lonely.

The water runs behind the wall. The fire continues to hiss. Liam watches me like he's waiting, and the hell of it is I don't think he knows what for. I don't think either of us does. I think he's just here, the way he's always just been here, planted in my head even when he's been gone for years.

There are words. Actual, specific words sitting right behind my teeth. They'd crack this whole thing open, and part of me is desperate to let them out and part of me would rather walk into an active minefield.

The minefield would be simpler. The minefield has rules.

"I'm taking a shower," I say abruptly.

Liam blinks. "She's in there."

"I know."

He gets it. He gets exactly what I'm about to do, and for a second I think he's going to say something. Stop me. Stake his claim.

He doesn't. He picks up his wine and turns back to the fire.

Chapter Twenty-One

HAILEY

The water isn't cold. I'd meant for it to be. Cranked the handle all the way to the left, ready to punish myself with ice water for that little performance at breakfast. But Marlena's luxury prison apparently doesn't believe in discomfort, and even the cold setting runs lukewarm at worst.

So instead I stand here under a spray that's slowly warming, steam curling up around me.

I tip my head back, letting the water run over my face. My cheeks are hot—water temp or arousal, I can't tell anymore.

I'm reaching for the shampoo when I hear it—the soft click of the bathroom door opening.

My hand freezes. Steam billows thick around me, and I lean forward, peering around the shower curtain just enough to see a slice of the bathroom through the haze.

Knox is standing there.

"Door was locked," I manage.

"Was." He takes a step closer, his eyes raking over the sliver of me visible past the curtain.

He doesn't have to say another word. I know exactly why he's here.

I turn off the water and reach for the towel, wrapping it around me as I step out of the tub. Knox is leaning against the sink, his arms crossed over his broad chest. His eyes never leave mine as I approach him, drops of water trailing down my legs.

A smirk tugs at the corner of his mouth, and he reaches up, tucking a wet strand of hair behind my ear. His fingers linger, tracing the line of my jaw. I lean into his touch, my heart pounding against my ribs.

Knox's eyes flare, and before I can react, he's crushed his mouth to mine. It's a fierce, demanding kiss, one that leaves no room for doubt or hesitation. I kiss him back with equal fervor, my towel dropping to the floor as I wrap my arms around his neck.

He lifts me onto the sink, his hands gripping my bare, wet thighs. He kisses me like a starving man, his tongue plunging into my mouth, his teeth nipping at my lips. His grip tightens, fingers pressing into my skin as he presses his entire body against mine. I can feel the hard bulge in his pants against my inner thigh.

There's no turning back now. I don't want to.

His hands leave my thighs, sliding up to grasp my waist as he pulls me closer to the edge of the sink, grinding against me. I can feel his heart pounding against my chest, matching the rhythm of my own. His mouth leaves mine, trailing hot, hungry kisses down my neck, pausing to suck and nip at my collarbone. I gasp, my head falling back, giving him better access.

His hands slide up my waist, cupping my breasts, thumbs brushing against my hardened nipples. I moan softly, arching into his touch.

"Shh," he whispers as he places his fingertip against my lips.

Liam's on the other side of the door . . . and for a moment I pause. A thread of doubt . . .

I push the thought of Liam away, looking into Knox's dark, hungry eyes. He's all I see, all I want right now. His fingertip slowly trails along my lower lip until it presses past my teeth, a silent command to keep quiet. I suck on his finger, swirling my tongue around it, tasting the salt of his skin. Knox's eyes darken, his gaze locked onto my mouth. He growls low in his throat, a sound of pure, primal want.

I want so desperately to replace his finger with his cock.

He pulls his finger from my mouth, trailing it down my chin, my neck, between my breasts, and down to my navel. I squirm under his touch, my body aching for more.

"Please," I whisper.

He leans in, his breath hot on my ear. "I told you to be quiet," he murmurs in a low rumble. "Do I need to fill that mouth of yours to make sure it happens?"

I nod, my breath hitching as his hand moves lower, his fingers brushing against the sensitive spot between my thighs. I gasp, my hips jerking at the contact. He chuckles, a low, throaty sound that vibrates against my skin.

"That's what I thought," he says, his hand wrapping around my thigh, hiking it up to his hip. He grinds against me, his clothed erection pressing against my nakedness. I whimper, my head falling back against the mirror, my eyes fluttering closed. His mouth is on my neck again, his teeth grazing my skin, his tongue licking away the sting.

I fumble with his belt, my hands shaking with urgency. He helps me, his hands covering mine as we work together to free him. He springs out, hot and hard in my hand. I stroke him, my thumb circling the tip.

A sound catches in his throat as I touch him, his forehead resting against mine. "Lick it," he commands. I can feel his heartbeat pulsing through his cock, a steady, insistent rhythm that matches my own racing pulse.

He's so fucking hot. Every hard inch of him.

I slide off the sink, my body pressing against his as I lower myself to my knees. The tiles are warm but hard beneath me, but I barely notice, my focus entirely on the man in front of me. I look up at him—his eyes are dark with lust, his breath coming in gasps.

I run my tongue along my lips, wetting them before I take him into my mouth. His taste is salty and masculine, his skin soft and smooth. I swirl my tongue around his tip, feeling his body shudder in response. I take him deeper, my cheeks hollowing out as I suck, my hand wrapping around his base, stroking him in rhythm with my mouth.

His hands tangle in my wet hair, guiding my movements, his groans of pleasure echoing through the bathroom. I can feel his control fraying, his hips moving to meet my mouth. I relax my throat, taking him deeper, my nails digging into his thighs.

His grip tightens in my hair, a silent warning that he's close. I can feel it too, his cock pulsing in my mouth, his breath hitching in his chest. I redouble my efforts, wanting to push him over the edge, wanting to taste his release.

But suddenly, he pulls me back, his cock slipping out of my mouth with a pop. I look up at him, confused, my lips swollen and shiny. He reaches down, pulling me to my feet, his hands gripping my shoulders.

"Not like this," he growls, his voice hoarse with desire. "I want to be inside you when I come."

He spins me around, my back to his front, his hands on my hips. He guides me to the sink, bending me over, my hands bracing on the cool porcelain.

I watch him in the mirror as he reaches into the top drawer and pulls out a condom, his eyes locked onto mine as he slowly rolls it on. He's taken his shirt off, his muscles rippling under his tattooed skin.

Knox is so far from the clean-cut, perfect, golden boy I thought he was. He looks like a wild animal, savage and ready to devour me. I push back against him, wanting to feel him inside me.

His hands grip my hips tighter, his thumbs tracing circles on my lower back. I can see the muscles in his jaw flex as he controls his desire, drawing out this moment, making me wait. I wiggle my ass against him, trying to urge him on, but he just smirks, his eyes never leaving mine in the mirror.

"Knox," I whine, breathy and desperate. "Please."

He leans over me, his body covering mine, his mouth by my ear.

"Please what?" he murmurs, his voice a low rumble. "Tell me what you want, pretty girl."

I swallow hard, my mouth dry with desire. "I want you," I gasp out. "Inside me. Now."

He chuckles, a dark, throaty sound that vibrates against my back. "I like a woman who knows what she wants," he praises, his teeth nipping at my earlobe. I squirm under him, my body aching with need. "But I also like a good girl who knows how to beg."

I can feel his smirk against my skin, the bastard. He's enjoying this, drawing out my torment, making me beg for it. I buck my hips back against him, urging him to end this torture, but he just presses me firmer against the sink, his body heavy against mine.

"Knox, please," I beg in a mere whisper. "I need you."

That's all it takes. With a growl, he surges forward, filling me in one swift, powerful thrust. I bite my lip to stifle a cry, my body arching as he stretches me, the sensation bordering on too much but exactly what I crave. His hands clamp down on my hips, holding me steady as he pulls back slowly, only to drive in again, deeper this time.

I watch us in the mirror, my reflection a mess of flushed skin and wild eyes, his body towering behind me, every muscle tensed and gleaming with a sheen of sweat. He's relentless, setting a rhythm that's hard and unyielding, each thrust pushing me closer to the edge. My breaths come in short, ragged gasps, and I grip the sink tighter, my knuckles turning white.

"Fuck, your pussy is so tight," he hisses against my shoulder. One of his hands slides up my back, tangling in my hair, pulling my head back just enough to expose my neck. He bites down lightly, not enough to hurt but enough to make me whimper, the mix of pain and pleasure igniting something submissive inside me.

Knox knows exactly how to pull the good girl out of me.

I push back against him, meeting his movements, our bodies slick and synchronized in this heated dance. The steam from the shower still lingers in the air, making everything feel hazy and dreamlike, but the feel of him inside me is sharp, real, overwhelming. Pressure builds low in my belly, coiling tighter with every thrust, and I know I'm close, so damn close.

"Knox," I gasp in barely a whisper, afraid that if I speak any louder, Liam might hear through the door. But Knox doesn't slow down; if anything, he drives harder, his free hand slipping around to the front, fingers finding my clit. He circles it with expert skill, the added stimulation sending sparks shooting through me.

I bite down on my lower lip, hard enough to taste copper if that's what it takes to remain silent. My body trembles, caught in the delicious torment of his touch, his thrusts growing more urgent, more possessive. In the mirror, our eyes lock again, and I see the hunger in his gaze, mirrored by my own desperate need. Sweat beads on his forehead, trickling down his temple, and I want to lick it off, taste every part of him.

The coil inside me tightens unbearably, and I feel myself teetering on the brink. "I'm . . . I'm going to . . ." I manage to get out, but he silences me with a rough kiss over my shoulder, his mouth claiming mine awkwardly from behind, all teeth and tongue and heat.

"Come for me," he orders against my lips, his voice a gravelly command that pushes me right over. The orgasm crashes through me like a wave, my inner walls clenching around him, pulling him deeper as pleasure radiates from my core. I shudder violently, my knees weakening, but he holds me up, his strong arms wrapping around my waist to keep me from collapsing.

"That's my pretty girl. Milk my cock."

He doesn't stop, riding out my climax with a few more deep thrusts before his own release hits. A low groan escapes him, vibrating against my back, and I feel him pulse inside me, filling the condom as his body tenses and then relaxes against mine. We're both panting, the bathroom air thick with the scent of sex and steam, our reflections blurred in the mirror now.

For a moment, we stay like that, connected, his forehead resting on my shoulder, his breath hot on my skin. I reach back, threading my fingers through his hair, pulling him closer if that's even possible. The doubt from earlier tugs at me—Liam just outside, unknowing . . . or maybe he knows exactly what's happening—but right now, in this haze of afterglow, it feels distant, unimportant . . . my past.

Knox pulls out, disposing of the condom quickly before turning me around to face him. He cups my face in his hands, his thumbs brushing away the remnants of my tears—tears I didn't even realize I'd shed from the intensity. "You okay?" he asks, his voice softer now, almost tender.

I nod, my smile still a little dazed. "More than okay."

He kisses my forehead, a gesture so tender it almost undoes me more than the sex did. Then he hands me the towel from the floor, and we both take a moment to make ourselves presentable. As presentable as two people can look after fucking in a bathroom while a third person waited outside.

Knox opens the door first. I follow behind him, my wet hair dripping down my back, my skin still flushed.

Liam is sitting on the couch, a book open in his lap. He doesn't look up right away. Just lets us stand there for a moment, marinating in the silence.

Then his eyes lift. They move from Knox to me, taking in my damp hair, my swollen lips, the way Knox's shirt is buttoned wrong.

He doesn't say anything. Neither do we.

The fire pops. Somewhere in the cabin, a clock ticks.

Finally, Liam closes his book and sets it on the cushion beside him. "Shower's free, then?"

I choke on something between a laugh and a groan. Knox tenses, but I catch the ghost of a smirk before he kills it.

"All yours," I manage.

Liam nods slowly. "Good to know."

And that's it. That's all any of us say about it.

The rest of the day is the strangest strategy session I've ever been part of.

We spend the afternoon huddled in the blind spot by the fireplace, talking in low voices with our backs to the cameras. Whenever one of us needs to get up for water or food or to use the bathroom, we break apart and act normal. Bored captives killing time. Then we drift back together and pick up where we left off.

The first problem is communication. The cameras in the cabin we can work around, but if we ever get out of here, Marlena's people will be between us and anything resembling freedom.

"The cameras have Wi-Fi—that's how she's getting the feed." Liam says it casually, like he's mentioning the weather. "I pulled the kitchen board while you two were in the shower. It's behind the bookshelf."

Knox and I both stare at him.

"You—when did you even—" I start.

"Figured if Marlena was watching anything, it wasn't the kitchen ceiling." He doesn't look at me. "With that board, I can rig the Wi-Fi chip to push out a signal. Reach Cole, maybe. Or at least a distress ping."

"Could you actually do that?" Knox asks.

"Give me a few hours with it tonight and we'll find out."

I pull my knees up, resting my chin on them. "What about when the ten days are up? Say we can't get a message out. Say nobody's coming. What then?"

That's the bigger question. The one none of us wants to sit with.

"She has to move us eventually," Knox says. "The diamond isn't here. Whatever happens at the end of this, she needs you to lead her to it. That means transport. That means a window."

"A window where we're outnumbered and she controls the logistics," Liam says.

Knox looks at both of us. "A window where she expects us to be cooperative. If we play along. Give her what she wants to see. Hailey agrees to take her to the diamond, but on her terms—all three of us go, or she doesn't talk. That's leverage."

"And then what?" Liam asks.

"And then we use whatever we've got." Knox's eyes are steady. I can see him thinking about the fire extinguisher, the chemicals under the sink, the knives. "We're not walking into that blind. We bring what we can hide and we wait for the right moment."

It's not a great plan. It's barely a plan at all. But it's the skeleton of one, and for the first time since we woke up in this place, the helplessness loosens its grip just a fraction.

We go quiet after that. There's only so long you can talk about your own potential death before you need a drink.

By evening, Marlena's wine collection has become our only reliable source of comfort. We sit by the fire, each of us nursing a glass of something expensive and red, the silence thick but not entirely uncomfortable. It's the silence of people who have too much to say and no idea where to start.

Liam pulls the camera board out from behind the bookshelf. He just sets the board on his knee and turns to Knox.

"I need another pair of hands. You in?"

Knox moves to the floor without a word. They sit close, the board between them, and Liam starts pointing out the components he'll need to work with. Their voices drop low out of habit even though we know the cameras don't have audio.

I stay on the couch with my wine and watch.

Liam's hands move while he talks, tracing the circuit paths, tapping the Wi-Fi chip with the tip of a butter knife. Knox is still beside him, taking it in. At one point Liam reaches over to reposition the casing in Knox's hands, showing him how to pop it without cracking the housing. His fingers close over Knox's and stay there. Not long. But long enough.

Knox doesn't pull away.

I take a sip of wine and pretend I didn't notice. But I did. And from the way Liam's eyes cut to me for half a second, he knows I did too.

They keep going. Liam explaining, Knox asking questions that catch Liam off guard. I can see it each time—the half-second where

Liam has to rethink whatever assumption he'd made about the man sitting next to him. He came into this cabin thinking Knox was just muscle. He's revising.

Knox says something I can't hear and Liam laughs. Not the performative charm he usually puts on. An actual laugh, startled out of him. Knox's mouth curves and he looks away, almost embarrassed, and I feel a pull in my ribs that I wasn't expecting.

I've been so worried about what these two are to me. I haven't stopped to think about what they might be to each other. They served together. They haven't spoken in more than a decade. And yet sitting on that floor with a stolen circuit board between them, they look like two people who never lost the rhythm. Whatever happened between them—whatever drove them apart and kept them apart—it left a mark deeper than either of them is letting on.

There's more . . .

Outside, the storm has finally eased into something softer—snow falling in lazy spirals past the windows, the world beyond them white and endless.

I drain the last of my wine and set the glass on the side table. "I'm going to bed."

Both of them look at me. Knox gives me a small nod. Liam's mouth opens like he wants to say something, then closes again.

"Good night," Knox says.

"Sleep well, Hails," Liam adds, his voice softer than I expect.

I don't trust myself to say anything else, so I just walk to the bed and crawl under the covers, turning to face the wall.

Behind me, I can hear them still by the fire. The soft clink of a wine bottle against glass. The occasional shift of weight on the couch. And then, after a long moment, the low murmur of voices too quiet to make out.

I close my eyes, hyper-aware of them just across the room, and try to let sleep pull me under.

It doesn't come easy.

Chapter Twenty-Two

KNOX

Liam and I don't stop working.

The circuit board sits between us on the floor by the hearth, guts exposed. We've been at it for an hour, maybe more, hunched in the blind spot with our backs to the wall. Liam's got the butter knife in one hand and a bent fork in the other, stripping insulation off a wire with steady, careful strokes that make it hard to look anywhere else.

So I look at the board. At the wall. At my own hands.

"Hand me the corkscrew," he says.

I pass it over. Our fingers brush in the hand off. I pull back too fast and he catches it, and we both let it go.

"The Wi-Fi module's the key." He turns the board so I can see. "If I reroute power from the camera feed, I can get it to broadcast independently. Fifteen minutes, maybe, before the whole thing fries."

"Who's going to be listening all the way out here?"

"Honestly? Probably nobody." He pries at a connector with the knife tip. "Without knowing what network she's running, I have no idea what's in range. Could bounce off a cell tower if there's one within fifty miles. Could get picked up by a passing aircraft. Could go absolutely nowhere and we burn our one shot for nothing."

"So we're just screaming into the void and hoping."

"That's about the size of it, yeah." He glances up. "Best case, it pings some tower and gets flagged as an anomaly. Maybe somebody investigates, maybe they don't. Worst case, Marlena's network is completely isolated and the signal dies before it clears the tree line."

"And the realistic case?"

"The signal goes out, lands on some server nobody checks for weeks, and by then it doesn't matter." He shrugs. "But I'd rather send it than sit here doing nothing."

His knee presses against my thigh. Has been pressing, actually, for a while now. The board is small and the blind spot is smaller and there's only so much room on this patch of floor, but he could shift over. Create space.

"Hold this." He hands me the board and picks up a chip he freed earlier, no bigger than a fingernail. "I need to solder the bypass, and by solder I mean hold two wires together and pray."

"Inspiring confidence over here, Liam."

"Just hold the board and let me work."

I hold it. He leans in, lining up the connection. His breath is warm against my hands. I can see the individual lashes framing his eyes, the faint scar bisecting his left eyebrow that I never got the story on. New. From the years between us. All that time and not one phone call.

His hand covers mine to position the module, pressing my thumb down against the chip. The pad of his thumb settles on the inside of my wrist. Right over the vein.

"Don't let it slip," he says.

I am not in any danger of letting it slip. I am in danger of forgetting what we're doing entirely.

He bridges the wire. Holds it. His mouth is inches from my knuckles, and if he turned his head even slightly he'd be pressing his lips to my fingers. The thought lands before I can block it.

A green light blinks on the module. Once. Twice.

"We're live," Liam says. "For whatever that's worth."

"You really know how to sell a plan."

"I know how to be honest about our odds. That should count for more."

We sit there, holding the assembly together, his hands on mine, the green light beating between us. Wind pushes against the windows. From the bed, Hailey turns over and goes still again.

No response comes. No crackle, no ping. Just us and a tiny signal going out into the dark, and no way to know if it's reaching anything at all.

"Even if it lands somewhere, there's no telling how long before anyone acts on it," I say. More to fill the air than because it needs saying. "Could be hours. Could be days. Could be never."

"I know. But every option we've got right now is a long shot. At least this one doesn't involve fighting our way through a blizzard in borrowed socks."

He adjusts his grip on the wire and his forearm lines up against mine, wrist to elbow, skin on skin where his sleeve has ridden up. Too much contact for two people just solving a technical problem.

Five minutes. Ten. The module heats under my thumb. Liam's hand hasn't moved. There's no reason for it to still be there. The contacts are holding fine. But his thumb rests on the inside of my wrist and I can feel my own heartbeat against the pad of it, which means he can too.

I think about turning my hand over. Lacing my fingers through his. Letting whatever this is become the thing it keeps trying to become.

My teeth ache from how hard I'm clenching them.

"You're tense," he says.

"I'm fine."

"Your whole arm is locked up." His thumb moves. A slow circle against my skin. Once. Deliberate. "Relax. I've got it."

Every thought I have evaporates.

I breathe. Force my arm to soften. His thumb doesn't move again, but it stays where it is, and the green light blinks between us and the room shrinks and I am aware of every square inch where his body meets mine.

The light stutters. Blinks fast, three times, and dies.

"Module's cooked." Liam swallows. "That's it for tonight."

He lifts his hand. Cold air fills the gap.

I set the board down. Lean back against the wall. My wrist throbs where his thumb was, which is insane, because the touch barely qualified as anything. Barely anything, and I still feel it under my skin.

Liam leans back too. Space opens between us. He rolls his neck, cracks his knuckles one at a time. Easy, unhurried, like the last ten minutes didn't happen. Like his hands weren't on mine while we both pretended to care about surveillance equipment.

"Other cameras tomorrow," I say. "We pull another module, rig a longer broadcast. Maybe we can figure out enough about the network to aim the signal instead of just throwing it blind."

"That would help." He tips his head back against the stone. Eyes on the ceiling. His throat is bare and the low light catches the hollow at its base and I count to five before I make myself stop looking.

He's going to say it. Whatever's been building in this room all night. I can see it in his shoulders, in his hands gone still, in his breathing slowed down to a rhythm too controlled to be casual.

"Knox." Just my name. Nothing after it.

"We should get some sleep." I'm on my feet before I've decided to stand. My knee pops. "Long day tomorrow."

He looks up at me from the floor. I don't let myself read what's on his face. If I read it I'll sit back down, and if I sit back down I'm not getting up.

"Yeah," he says. Takes his time with it. "You're probably right."

He wraps the dead board in a towel. Slides it behind the cushion. Stretches as he stands, his shirt riding up across his stomach, and I find a very interesting knot in the wood paneling to stare at.

Hailey's claimed the center of the bed, starfished under the blankets. Liam takes the right side, moving carefully. I take the left. Her in the middle, the way it keeps ending up. A border made of a sleeping woman and everything we're not saying.

I face the wall. Behind me, Liam settles. The mattress dips. Hailey murmurs and presses her back against my spine.

On the other side of her, Liam is awake. I don't need to check. A hundred nights in the field teaches you what a man sounds like when he's actually sleeping versus when he's lying in the dark with his eyes open, counting the same minutes you are.

Tomorrow, we pull another module. Try again. Keep our hands on the equipment and our heads on the plan.

I lie between the wall and Hailey's warmth and listen to Liam not sleeping.

Chapter Twenty-Three

LIAM

Third day in this fucking cabin, and I still can't stop watching him.

Knox sits by the fireplace, stoking embers that don't need stoking, his shoulders tense beneath that black thermal. The storm outside has quieted to a low moan, snow piling against the windows like it's trying to bury us alive. Maybe it is. Maybe Marlena's counting on nature to do what she's been too busy monologuing to accomplish herself.

Hailey's still asleep in the bed, buried under a mound of blankets, her breathing slow and even. She crashed hard after yesterday—we all did, in different ways. But sleep won't come for me. Hasn't come for me in years when Knox Bishop is in the same room.

The logs shift and settle. Knox doesn't flinch.

I study him from my spot on the floor, back against the wall, knees drawn up. The firelight catches the angles of his face, sharpens them into something almost brutal. He's aged since Afghanistan. We both have. But on him, it looks good. Silver threading through the blond at his temples. Lines around his eyes that weren't there before. He's harder now, leaner, like the years stripped away everything that wasn't essential and left behind only muscle and memory.

I've replayed a lot of moments in my head over the past decade. Jobs gone wrong, close calls, people I've lost. But there's one moment I come back to more than any other. One night that's branded itself into my brain so deep I can still taste the dust on my tongue, still feel the heat of his body close to mine.

The silence stretches between us like a wire pulled taut.

"In Afghanistan." The words spill from my mouth. "The night before you shipped out. You remember?"

Knox's hand stills on the poker. He doesn't turn around, but I see his spine go rigid beneath his shirt. For a long moment, I think he won't answer. That he'll pretend he doesn't know what I'm talking about, that we'll keep dancing around this thing between us like we've been dancing for years.

Then: "I remember."

Two words, barely audible over the hiss and snap of burning wood. But they hit me like a gut punch anyway.

We'd been drunk that night. Not sloppy drunk, but loose enough that the walls came down. We'd ended up alone in the barracks, everyone else passed out or gone, and he'd looked at me the way he sometimes did when he thought I wasn't paying attention. I'd moved closer. He'd moved closer. Our mouths had been inches apart, breath mingling, and then—

Nothing.

We'd pulled back. Both of us. Too dangerous, too complicated, too much at stake. The next morning, he was gone, transferred to another unit, and I'd spent the next ten years telling myself I'd imagined the whole thing.

But I hadn't. I know I hadn't.

"I've thought about it every day since." I push off the wall, get to my feet. My body moves toward him without conscious thought, like he's got his own gravitational pull. "Every fucking day."

Knox finally turns. His eyes find mine across the dim room, and the look in them makes my chest tight. He's not surprised. He's not confused. He knows exactly what I'm talking about because he's been thinking about it too.

"Why didn't you ever say anything?" He keeps it quiet, careful. "All those years. You could've found me."

"Because you terrified me." The words come out jagged, broken. "What I felt. What I wanted. You weren't just some guy I could have hooked up with overseas. You were—" I stop, teeth clenched, fighting for control. "You made me feel things I wasn't ready to feel. Want things I wasn't supposed to want. So I ran. Buried it. Told myself it was a fluke."

I'm close now. Close enough to see the pulse jumping at the base of his throat, to smell woodsmoke and sweat and skin. Close enough that if either of us leaned forward, we'd be touching.

"And now?" His eyes drop to my mouth, then back up.

"I still want it." No point in lying anymore. No point in pretending. "I still want you."

Knox exhales, a sound that's almost a laugh but not quite. "We're trapped in a cabin, about to die. Probably not the best time."

"Probably the only time."

He stares at me for a long moment, and I watch the battle play out behind his eyes. Duty versus desire. Caution versus need. I've seen Knox face down enemy combatants without flinching, but right now, looking at me, he's the most uncertain I've ever seen him.

Then something in him gives.

He closes the distance between us in one step, his hand fisting in the front of my shirt, yanking me forward. His mouth crashes into mine—hard, demanding, unleashing years of pent-up want in a single devastating kiss.

I respond like I've been waiting forever. Because I have.

My hands find his waist, his back, anywhere I can touch him. He tastes like coffee and something more dangerous, and when his tongue sweeps against mine, I groan into his mouth, my whole body igniting. This is nothing like the careful almost-kiss from Afghanistan. This is a wildfire. This is everything we've been holding back finally breaking free.

We stumble backward, mouths still locked, hands grabbing and pulling. Knox shoves me against the wall near the hearth, the wood cold against my back but his body hot against my front, and I drag him closer, needing more, needing everything.

We both glance at Hailey—still asleep, still oblivious—and we make a silent agreement. We'll be quiet. We'll be careful.

But we're not stopping.

I wanted my cock buried in Knox Bishop the minute I first saw him. Us being Marines didn't calm the beast inside me one bit. Every drill, every grunt in the mud, I watched him. Those broad shoulders flexing under his fatigues, sweat dripping down his neck like a fucking invitation. He was all discipline on the outside, barking orders with that gravelly voice that hit me right in the gut. I also saw the fire in his eyes when our gazes locked.

But nothing happened back then. As much as I wanted it to, nothing.

But now . . .

Now is different.

We're out of the Corps, both of us, the weight of those uniforms long shed like old skin. The fire is the only sound on this snowy morning. He doesn't pull back, just holds my stare, lips curving into a smirk that says he knows exactly what I've been thinking all these years.

He looks over his shoulder at Hailey sleeping in the bed. "Can you suck my cock quietly? I don't want to wake her."

My cock throbs at the question, the beast inside roaring to life. I can tell he isn't being sneaky or keeping this from her . . . it comes from consideration instead.

I nod. "Yeah, I can be quiet. For her." My heart pounds as I drop to my knees in front of him, the wooden floor cold against my skin but nothing compared to the heat building between us. Knox shifts, unzipping his pants with a deliberate slowness that makes my mouth water. His cock springs free, thick and hard, veins pulsing like it's been waiting for this moment as long as I have.

I lean in, wrapping my hand around the base, feeling the warmth of him, the weight that's all power and promise. My lips brush the tip, tasting the salt of pre-cum, and I take him in slowly, inch by inch, savoring the way he fills my mouth. He lets out a soft groan, muffled, his fingers threading into my hair—not pulling, just holding, like he's anchoring himself.

The flames cast flickering shadows behind us, and I glance up at him through my lashes. His eyes are dark with want, those blue irises nearly swallowed by his pupils, that smirk burning off, his expression going open and hungry. I work him with my tongue, swirling and sucking, keeping it steady, silent except for the wet sounds I swallow down. Hailey stirs once in her sleep, a tiny murmur, and we both freeze for a heartbeat, but she settles, oblivious.

Knox's grip tightens, his hips twitching forward just enough to urge me on. The animal in me loves this—pleasing him, finally, after all that pent-up hunger. I pick up the pace, hollowing my cheeks, taking him deeper until my throat burns with the effort to stay quiet. His breath hitches, ragged but controlled, and I know he's close, the tension coiling in his body like a spring ready to snap.

I feel the first shudder run through him, his muscles tightening under my touch, and I double down, sucking harder, my hand pumping in rhythm with my mouth. The taste of him grows stronger, saltier, as he swells against my tongue, pushing me to the edge of what I can take without gagging. His fingers dig into my scalp now, not painful, just desperate, guiding me without words.

A low, barely audible rumble escapes his throat, and I glance up again, seeing his teeth clenched, eyes half-lidded in that fierce concentration I've known from the field. It's like we're back in the mud, synced in silence, but this is so much fucking better. My own cock aches, straining against my pants, but I ignore it—this is for him, this release I've craved.

Then it hits. He bucks once, twice, spilling hot and thick down my throat. I swallow every drop, milking him through it, my lips sealed tight to keep it all contained, no mess, no noise. His body goes rigid, then slumps, a deep exhale the only sound as he rides the aftershocks. I pull back slowly, licking him clean, savoring the last taste before tucking him away with careful hands.

He looks down at me, that smirk returning, softer now, laced with something like gratitude. "Fuck, that was . . ." he whispers, trailing off as he helps me to my feet. My knees protest from the hard floor, but the fire in my veins drowns it out. We both glance at Hailey again—she's still out, curled under the blankets, her breathing even and peaceful.

Knox pulls me close, his mouth crashing against mine in a kiss that's full of heat and possession, tasting himself on my tongue. It's quick, intense, and when we break apart his hand is already moving, palming me through my jeans. I hiss at the contact, hips jerking forward.

"Your turn," he murmurs against my mouth.

He doesn't wait for permission. His fingers work my zipper, tugging it down, and then his hand is inside, wrapping around my cock with a grip that's firm and sure. I bite down on my lip to keep from groaning, the effort almost painful.

Knox strokes me slow at first, torturously slow, his thumb swiping over the head on every upstroke, spreading the pre-cum that's already leaking. My hands grip his shoulders, nails digging in, trying to anchor myself as my knees threaten to buckle.

"Quiet," he reminds me, lips brushing my ear. "Remember?"

I nod, not trusting myself to speak. He picks up the pace, his fist tight and relentless, and I bury my face in his neck to muffle the sounds trying to escape. He smells like smoke and sex, and it's intoxicating. My hips thrust into his grip, fucking his hand, desperate and shameless.

His free hand grips the back of my neck, holding me steady, holding me close. "That's it," he breathes. "Give it to me."

The tension builds fast, coiling at the base of my spine, every nerve ending on fire. Knox twists his wrist on the next stroke, tightens his grip, and I shatter. I come hard, spilling over his fist, my whole body shuddering as I bite down on his shoulder to keep from crying out. He works me through it, stroking until I'm wrung dry and trembling against him.

We stand there for a long moment, foreheads pressed together, breathing ragged. Knox wipes his hand on his jeans, then cups my face, tilting it up to meet his eyes. Blue eyes that have haunted me for years.

"I never forgot you." Barely a whisper. "Not once. Not ever."

My throat tightens. "I never wanted you to."

He zips himself up, and I do the same, both of us trying to look like we didn't just change everything. Knox's hand lingers on my hip for a moment before he steps back, putting space between us. We both walk to the kitchen to get something to drink but I'm insatiable. I'm not sure I'll ever be full after being hungry for so long.

I grab Knox by the front of his shirt, yanking him toward me with a force that surprises even me, my lips brushing his ear as I whisper, "I'm not waiting any longer." His eyes widen for a split second, that smirk turning into a grin that's full of challenge and heat, like he's been waiting for me to unleash this side of myself.

We move silently across the cabin, away from the bed where Hailey sleeps, the fire's glow dimming as we slip into the shadowed corner by the window. Snowflakes dance outside, muffling the world, but inside, my pulse is a war drum. I spin him around, pressing his back against the wall, my body pinning him there. His breath hitches, warm against my neck, and I can feel his cock already stirring again through his pants—fuck, he's insatiable, just like me.

My hands are rough, urgent, shoving his pants down just enough, exposing that perfect ass I've fantasized about for years. He doesn't resist, just arches into me, his own hands bracing against the wood. I fumble with my zipper, freeing myself, my cock throbbing painfully hard, slick with need.

"Top shelf in the bathroom," he breathes out, reminding me of the condoms and lube waiting there.

I growl low in my throat, not wanting to break the moment, but I know he's right. I pull back just long enough to dart into the bathroom, the door creaking faintly as I grab the supplies from the top shelf, my hands shaking with the urgency of it all. Condom packet tears open with my teeth, lube slick in my palm, and I'm back before the cold air can even touch him, pressing against his heat again.

He glances over his shoulder, eyes gleaming in the low light, that grin still challenging me. I roll the condom on, coating myself generously, my fingers trembling as I prep him too, sliding one in slow, then two, feeling him clench and relax, his breath coming in quiet huffs. "Fuck, yes," he says, pushing back against my hand, urging me deeper.

I can't hold back anymore. I withdraw my fingers, lining myself up, the tip pressing against him, hot and insistent. He nods once, a silent go-ahead, and I push in slow at first, inch by torturous inch, feeling him open for me, tight and perfect. A groan tries to escape my lips, but I bite it down, remembering Hailey, the cabin's quiet fragility.

His body tenses, then yields, his back arching as I sink deeper, buried to the hilt. Fuck, it's everything I imagined and more—velvet heat gripping me like a vise, his muscles flexing around me. I pause there, savoring it, my hands gripping his hips hard enough to leave marks, but he doesn't complain; if anything, he leans into it, grinding back with a muffled hiss of approval.

I start moving, shallow thrusts building to something fiercer, our bodies syncing like old times in the field, wordless understanding. The wall creaks under his palms, but it's faint, drowned by the snow outside. His breath comes in sharp pants, matching mine, and I lean forward, my chest to his back, one hand sliding up his shirt to feel the hard planes of his abs contracting with every push. I can tell he's close—his whole frame trembling, pushing back against me in desperate sync. I angle just right, hitting that spot that makes him arch, a muffled moan escaping.

"Harder," he whispers, daring me, and I oblige, slamming in deeper, the slap of skin on skin barely audible over my pounding heart. Sweat beads on my forehead, trickling down, and I taste salt when I bite his shoulder to stifle a moan. He's pushing back now, meeting me thrust for thrust, that fire in him matching mine, turning this into a battle of wills and want.

The pressure builds inside me, a storm that's been brewing since those endless drills, and I drive into him with everything I have, our rhythm turning frantic, desperate. His fingers scrape against the wall, nails digging in for leverage, and I feel the tremor in his thighs, the way his body clenches around me, pulling me deeper like he owns this as much as I do. Every thrust sends sparks up my spine, my balls tightening, the edge creeping closer with each shared breath. I reach around, wrapping my hand around his cock, stroking in time with my hips, feeling him throb and swell again. He shudders, a low rumble in his chest, and I know he's close too, the way his body clamps down on me, pulling me under.

Outside, the wind howls, but in here, it's just us, this pure connection suddenly free. I pick up the pace, relentless, my free hand covering his mouth gently when a groan slips out too loud. His eyes meet mine over his shoulder, dark and wild, urging me on without words.

It hits me like a grenade—wave after wave crashing through, my vision blurring as I empty into him, hips jerking erratically. He follows seconds later, spilling over my fist, his body locking up, then going slack against the wall. I hold him there, both of us panting, slick with sweat, the afterglow humming in my veins like victory.

We stay like that for a moment, catching our breath, before I pull out carefully, disposing of the condom in the bathroom trash with quick, silent moves. When I return, he's straightened his clothes, that smirk back in place, but his eyes hold something deeper—satisfaction, maybe even a promise of more.

And then—

A soft sound from the bed. A shift of blankets.

We both freeze.

I look past Knox toward Hailey, expecting to see her still curled under the covers, still lost to sleep. But she's not asleep. Her eyes are open, watching us. Not anger. Not betrayal. Something closer to heat. To understanding.

She's been watching.

I don't know how long. Don't know how much she saw. But from the flush on her cheeks and the way she's biting her lower lip, it was enough.

Knox is already moving, retreating to his spot near the door, spine straight, face unreadable. I move back to my corner by the wall, putting distance between us even though every instinct screams at me to stay close.

None of us says anything.

Hailey turns away, burrowing back into the blankets. The logs shift in the grate. The storm moans. And everything's changed.

We've crossed a line we can't uncross. And somehow, impossibly, I think all three of us know it was never going to stay uncrossed forever.

Chapter Twenty-Four

HAILEY

Three days in captivity, and I'm losing my goddamn mind looking for something to do besides think about the two men I've been sleeping with.

Well. One man I've been sleeping with. One man I've been very carefully not sleeping with, despite five years of distance doing nothing to kill the want.

We have a plan. Not a great one. Not even a good one, if I'm being honest. But it's a plan, and having it settled between the three of us has taken some of the poison out of the air.

Or at least given us an excuse not to talk about Knox and Liam fucking each other this morning while they thought I was asleep.

Because I wasn't asleep. I watched the whole thing from the bed with my eyes half open and my blood running so hot I had to bite the inside of my cheek to keep quiet. And when it was done and all three of us were awake and nobody could pretend otherwise, we sat in the blind spot by the fireplace and acted like it hadn't happened. I pitched a plan. Gave us all somewhere safe to put our eyes and our energy, and they grabbed on to it like drowning men reaching for a rope. Knox went into tactical mode. Liam started running scenarios. And just like that, we were three people with a mission instead of three people who couldn't look at each other.

The idea is mine, because I'm the one with leverage and I'm the one who knows Marlena's type. Collectors are patient until they're not, and when they're not, they get sloppy. So we wait. We let the deadline get closer. We let her stew and monologue and watch us on her cameras looking defeated and scared. And then, right when she's convinced we've run out of fight, I break. I give her what she wants. Mostly.

The details of "mostly" I'm keeping to myself for now. The broad strokes are simple. I cooperate, I give Marlena enough to believe she's won, and I hold back just enough to keep us alive and breathing and necessary. A woman like Marlena doesn't destroy an asset she still needs.

The tricky part is timing. Cave too early and she won't trust it. Hold out too long and she starts cutting off fingers to make her point. We're aiming for the sweet spot between broken and believable.

In the meantime, we wait. On the plan. On the distress signal Liam rigged from the camera's Wi-Fi module last night, which went out into the dark and came back with nothing. No ping, no response, no way to know if it reached a tower or just died in the cold. Knox and Liam are talking about pulling a second module to try a longer broadcast, but even if they do, we won't know if anyone heard us until we know. Sitting with that uncertainty is its own kind of torture.

So. Day three. Waiting.

The afternoon light streams through the frost-edged windows, pale and winter-soft. Everything feels different since this morning. Knox and Liam are in the living room, arguing over what to watch on the ancient DVD player—because apparently Marlena stocked the cabin with technology from 2005. The collection she left us ranges from romantic comedies to action movies, all of them at least a decade old. Liam called it "retro charm." Knox called it "psychological torture."

But they're doing that thing where they look at each other now. Actually look. No more of that cagey tension from the first two days. Something happened between them—I don't know the details, but I've seen the way they move around each other now. Easier. More fluid. Whatever wall they'd built between themselves has come down.

I cross to the pantry closet, mostly just to have something to do with my hands. The first two shelves are stocked with gourmet pasta, artisanal olive oils, and enough canned goods to survive a nuclear winter. I push past the truffle salt and imported tomatoes, reaching toward the back where I spotted something earlier.

My fingers close around cardboard. I pull the box forward, shoving aside a bag of organic quinoa, and nearly drop it when I see what's inside.

"Oh, you have *got* to be kidding me."

String lights. A fake tree about two feet tall. Glass ornaments in red and silver and gold. Velvet garland in deep green.

Knox looks up from where he's crouched by the DVD player. "What'd you find?"

I hold up a strand of tiny lights, letting them dangle between my fingers. "Christmas decorations."

Liam abandons the stack of DVDs and crosses toward me. "No way."

"Way." I dig deeper, pulling out a velvet tree skirt embroidered with snowflakes. "She really went all out with the holiday hostage aesthetic."

Knox joins us, peering into the box with the same tactical assessment he'd give a supply cache. "Fake tree. Ornaments. Even hooks." He pulls out a smaller box. "Gourmet hot cocoa mix."

"Naturally it's gourmet," I mutter. "Why hold people prisoner without Swiss chocolate?"

Liam reaches past both of us and grabs the tree. It's already fluffed, the branches that perfect manufactured pine shape that real trees never achieve. "You know what? We should set this up."

I stare at him. "We're being held captive by a lunatic who wants to kill us in a week. And you want to *decorate*?"

"Christmas Eve is in seven days." Liam shrugs, but the shrug doesn't sell it. His voice is too tight. "If we're going to die, might as well do it festively."

Knox snorts. "That's dark."

"I'm a dark guy."

I look at the tree in Liam's hands, then at the box of ornaments, then at the two men watching me with expressions that are trying very hard not to look hopeful.

Fuck it.

"Give me the lights," I say.

What follows is the most surreal two hours of my life.

Knox takes charge of the lighting situation because that's who he is. He examines the windows like he's planning a tactical operation, measuring distances with his eyes and muttering about even distribution and optimal coverage. Liam holds the ladder—which materialized from a hallway closet—and offers a running commentary.

"Little to the left. No, other left."

"I know where left is."

"Do you? Because that's distinctly right."

"That's *your* left, asshole."

"Left is left. It doesn't change based on perspective."

"It literally does. That's how directions work."

I tune them out and focus on the tree, which I've set up on the small table by the fireplace. The ornaments are beautiful—hand-painted glass balls, delicate wooden snowflakes, little silver birds with real feather details. Nothing mass-produced. Marlena must have spent a fortune on this box, which tracks. Evil billionaires don't do anything halfway.

I hang a red ball, then a silver one. Step back. Adjust the red one three millimeters to the right. This is stupid. We're going to die, and I'm worrying about ornament placement.

But my hands keep moving anyway.

"Higher," Liam says behind me.

I turn. Knox is stretching up to secure lights around the top of the window frame, his sweater riding up to expose a strip of stomach and the sharp cut of his hip bone. I watch Liam watch him, and my stomach flips.

"That's what she said," I offer.

Knox nearly falls off the ladder. Liam catches it, steadying the base with both hands while Knox glares down at me.

"Very mature."

"Thank you. I try."

By the time we're done, the cabin looks like a Christmas catalog exploded in the best possible way. Lights frame every window, casting the room in warm gold. The little tree glows on its table, ornaments catching the firelight. We even draped garland along the mantel, because apparently we're *those* people now.

"It's ridiculous," Knox says, standing back to survey our work.

"Completely absurd," I agree.

"I love it," Liam says quietly.

We both look at him. He's staring at the tree with a look I haven't seen on his face in years. Open. Unguarded.

"I haven't celebrated Christmas in five years." He doesn't look away from the tree. "Not really. After we went our separate ways, I just . . . stopped. Didn't see the point."

My throat tightens. I know exactly what he means. Those years apart, I'd treated December like any other month. Takeout on Christmas Eve. Netflix on Christmas Day. Pretending the loneliness was solitude instead of naming it.

"Same," I admit. "My Christmases in New York were basically me and Thai food and too much wine."

"Sounds depressing as hell," Knox says, but his voice is gentle.

"It was fine."

"Hailey." He gives me a look. "You can't be fine about Christmas."

"Watch me."

But I'm smiling when I say it, and so is he.

Liam moves toward the kitchen, opening cabinets with purpose now. "If we're doing this, we're doing it right. I'm making dinner. A real one."

"You cook?" Knox sounds skeptical.

"I cook *well*." Liam pulls out a roasting pan. "Unlike some people who think protein powder counts as a meal."

"That was one time."

"It was three times. This week."

Knox doesn't deny it.

I drift toward the kitchen island, watching Liam assess the ingredients Marlena has stocked. He moves with confidence, pulling out a chicken, root vegetables, herbs I couldn't name if my life depended on it. His hands are sure and steady, and there's a focus in his eyes I recognize from our old jobs. The same precision he brought to bypassing security systems, now applied to seasoning meat.

"You learned this where, exactly?" I ask. "Our old life wasn't exactly conducive to home cooking."

"After." He's rubbing the chicken with butter and herbs, his movements practiced. "I had a lot of free time and a lot of YouTube tutorials. Cooking felt like the opposite of everything we did before. Creating instead of taking."

The words land somewhere I wasn't expecting. I've never thought about it that way, but he's right. Five years ago, we took. Stole. Acquired. Now I make jewelry—tiny beautiful things that didn't exist until I created them.

Maybe we both found our way to building instead of breaking.

"Can I help?" I ask.

Liam hands me a bag of potatoes. "Wash. Peel. Cut into chunks. Try not to take off a finger."

"I have excellent fine motor skills."

"You once accidentally superglued your hand to a wall safe."

"That was *intentional*."

"The superglue?"

"The wall safe. The superglue was . . . an improvisation."

Knox appears beside me, reaching for a knife. "I'll help."

"Do you know how to chop vegetables?" Liam asks.

"I was in the Marines. I can follow instructions."

"Debatable."

But Liam's grinning, and Knox is rolling his eyes without any real irritation, and I'm standing between them peeling potatoes in a kidnapper's cabin surrounded by Christmas lights.

This shouldn't feel as normal as it does. It absolutely shouldn't.

It does anyway.

We argue over garlic. Knox thinks Liam's using too much; Liam thinks Knox wouldn't know good seasoning if it hit him in his pretty face. I nearly burn the rolls because I get distracted watching them bicker, but I rescue them in time, only slightly singed.

The kitchen fills with the smell of roasting chicken and herbs, and Liam makes us taste the gravy three times to confirm it's perfect. It is. I tell him it needs more salt just to watch his eye twitch.

"You're messing with me."

"Maybe." I steal another taste. "Maybe I just have a refined palate."

"Your palate thinks Flamin' Hot Cheetos are a food group."

"They *are* a food group. It's called joy."

Knox laughs, a real laugh, and Liam's outrage melts into warmth.

We set the table like civilized people. There's a tablecloth in one of the drawers—white linen—and we lay out cloth napkins and the nice dishes and even light candles. The flames flicker alongside the fairy lights, and the whole scene looks like a magazine spread about holiday entertaining.

And that's exactly the point.

Because Marlena is watching. We know she's watching. And the best thing three captives with a plan can do is look like three captives without one. So we give her a show. Happy prisoners enjoying their gilded cage, grateful for the gourmet kitchen and the fancy linens, too comfortable and too broken to cause any trouble. Every laugh is real, but it's also a performance. Every candle we light is us saying, *Look how tame we are.* Look how we've accepted this. Don't worry about us at all.

If she's buying it, good. If she's not, at least we're eating well while the clock runs down.

"Should we say grace?" Knox asks, completely deadpan.

Liam folds his hands, equally serious. "Blessed be this meal we're about to eat in our luxury prison. May our captor choke on her caviar. Amen."

I snort wine up my nose, which hurts like hell and is completely worth it.

Dinner is incredible. The chicken is perfectly crispy on the outside, tender and juicy inside. The vegetables are caramelized and sweet. The gravy is rich and savory and I want to bathe in it. We eat until we're stuffed, then eat more because it's that good.

And we talk. Really talk. Not about the diamond or Marlena or the countdown clock ticking toward whatever nightmare she has planned. We talk about other things. Normal things. Things three people who aren't being held hostage might discuss over dinner.

"Worst first date. Go." Liam points his fork at Knox.

Knox considers. "High school. Took a girl to a nice restaurant, ordered oysters to be sophisticated. Turns out I'm allergic. My face swelled up like a balloon, and I spent the rest of the night in the ER. She never spoke to me again."

"Oh my god." I'm crying with laughter. "Please tell me there are pictures."

"Absolutely not."

"I will find them."

"You will fail."

"I've broken into bank vaults. Your high school yearbook archive is nothing."

Liam raises his glass. "I've seen the pictures. They're magnificent."

Knox's head whips toward him. "How?"

"Remember Porter? From Kandahar?"

"That son of a bitch."

"He keeps a folder. Labeled 'Knox's Oyster Incident.' Very organized."

Knox drops his head into his hands, and Liam and I laugh until our stomachs hurt.

My turn. I tell them about the date who took me to an escape room and got so competitive he started screaming at the teenage employees for hints. Liam confesses to accidentally setting a girl's hair on fire with a candle at a fancy restaurant. "The waiter threw water on her head, it was a whole thing." Knox admits he once forgot a date's name and called her "sport" for three hours until she called him on it.

"Sport?" I wheeze. "You called a grown woman *sport*?"

"I panicked!"

"What happened after she called you out?"

"I pretended I had food poisoning and Ubered home."

"Knox Bishop, you absolute disaster."

"I was twenty-two. We all did stupid things at twenty-two."

"At twenty-two, I was stealing diamonds," Liam says thoughtfully. "Still less embarrassing than *sport*."

We move through topics like we have all the time in the world. Favorite movies—Knox loves action, Liam loves documentaries, I have a weakness for horror that makes them both question my sanity. Places we want to travel—Liam wants to see Japan, Knox wants to go back to Scotland, I want somewhere warm with no extradition treaty, which makes them both give me looks.

Knox tells a story about a mission in Kandahar that went sideways, but the way he tells it turns disaster into comedy. The interpreter who accidentally propositioned a village elder. The goat that ate their radio. The sergeant who got lost despite having GPS and a map and three people giving him directions.

"He walked in a circle for forty-five minutes," Knox says. "We could see him from the ridge. Just . . . circling. One of the guys started taking bets on how long before he figured it out."

"Did he figure it out?"

"No. The goat found him."

"The same goat that ate the radio?"

"Different goat. This one was angrier."

Liam does impressions of their old commanding officer, a colonel with a thick Boston accent. Knox nearly chokes on his wine. I've never seen him this relaxed, this unguarded. The vigilance softened by food and wine and company.

I tell them about my grandmother. The woman who raised me after my parents split, who taught me to pick locks for fun on rainy

Sundays, who always said rules were just suggestions for people without imagination. She would have loved this, I think. Drinking wine in a decorated cabin with two beautiful men, making the best of a bad situation with style and humor.

"She sounds incredible," Liam says.

"She was." I trace the rim of my glass. "She would have liked you both. She had a thing for charming men with questionable morals."

"I have excellent morals," Knox protests.

"You stalked me for three months."

". . . Situationally excellent morals."

After dinner, we migrate to the floor by the fireplace. Someone brings out the chocolate—the fancy stuff Marlena stocked—and we break off pieces and let them melt on our tongues. Outside, snow drifts past the windows. The lights cast everything in gold.

I end up with my legs across Liam's lap, my shoulder pressed against Knox's, some part of me touching both of them. It happens without thinking, natural as breathing. Knox's hand rests on my knee, his thumb tracing absent patterns. Liam's palm is warm against my ankle, fingers curled loosely around the bone.

"This is the strangest date I've ever been on," Knox says.

Liam hums. "Is this a date?"

I consider the question. The cooking together, the talking, the way we've arranged ourselves like we've been doing this for years instead of days. "I think it might be. Our first real one."

"First dates don't usually involve armed guards and potential death."

"Ours does. We're unique."

Knox's hand tightens on my knee. Just a little. Just enough.

"We might die in seven days," he says quietly.

"Yeah." Liam's voice is equally soft. "We might."

They both look at me. The firelight catches their eyes—Knox's gray-blue, Liam's warm brown—and I see the same thing reflected in both. Want. Fear. Hope. The desperate need to hold on to something real before it's ripped away.

"So we should probably make the most of it," I say.

The playfulness falls away. What's left is just want, bare and obvious. This has been building since the first day we arrived. Since before that. Since Knox started following me through Bryant Park. Since Liam sent that first message after five years of silence. Since the moment I realized I'd been running toward them both my whole life and never knew it.

I lean forward and kiss Liam. He tastes like chocolate and wine, and his mouth opens under mine immediately, welcoming me in. His hand slides from my ankle to my calf, pulling me closer. It's been five years since I've kissed him, and my body remembers everything—the way he tilts his head, the soft sound he makes when I bite his lower lip, the heat of his palm through my jeans.

When I break away, Knox is watching us. Not jealous. Wanting.

I turn and kiss him too. Different but just as right. Knox kisses like he does everything else—thorough, intense, completely focused. His hand comes up to cradle the back of my head, tilting me exactly where he wants me.

Then I'm pulling back, and they're looking at each other, and I hold my breath.

Knox reaches for Liam. Liam meets him halfway.

Watching them kiss feels like witnessing something inevitable. The tension between them, all those years of wanting and not having, finally given permission to exist. Liam makes a sound against Knox's mouth—relief, desire, everything in between—and Knox's hand fists in his shirt like he's afraid Liam might disappear if he lets go.

When they separate, we're all breathing hard.

"Bed?" I ask.

They both answer at once.

Chapter Twenty-Five

LIAM

We're a mess of hands and mouths as we move toward the mattress. Knox lifts Hailey like she weighs nothing, her legs wrapping around his waist, and I follow close behind, my palm sliding up her spine, unable to stop touching her. They tumble onto the bed and I'm right there with them, pulling at clothes, finding warm skin beneath.

Knox has her pinned beneath him, his mouth on her throat, and she's arching into it, one hand fisted in his hair, the other reaching back for me. I catch her fingers, kiss her knuckles, then let go so I can yank my shirt over my head.

She turns her head, finds me watching. "Get over here."

I don't need to be told twice.

I watch for a beat before joining them, slipping in on her other side. My fingers trail up her thigh, under the blanket, feeling the warmth of her skin, the way she arches instinctively into my touch. She breaks the kiss with Knox, turning to me, surprise melting into a sly smile.

I chuckle softly, my hand sliding higher, finding her already damp, ready. "This is a fucking dream," I whisper, nipping at her earlobe. "Both of you at once." Knox's laugh rumbles beside us, his hands working her shirt up, exposing her breasts to the cool air. She gasps, but it's not from the chill—it's from the way his tongue swirls over a nipple while I dip my fingers between her legs, stroking slow circles that make her hips buck.

She's responsive, fuck, so alive under our hands, her breaths coming faster as we work in tandem. I can feel Knox's gaze on me over her body, that same fire from before, like this is the mission we've both been waiting for.

Hailey moans into my mouth as I kiss her, her tongue tangling with mine while my fingers delve deeper, curling inside her wetness, feeling her walls pulse around me. She's drenched, slick from whatever thoughts she was having, and now we're turning them real. Knox shifts, his mouth moving to her other breast, sucking hard enough to make her back bow off the bed, her hand fisting in my hair as she pulls me closer.

"Fuck, you guys," she whispers, voice breathy and broken, her hips grinding against my hand like she's chasing the edge already. I add a third finger, stretching her, thumb circling her clit in firm strokes that have her whimpering, the sound muffled against my lips.

"I have to stretch this pussy of yours, baby. Make room for both of us," I warn.

She gasps at my words, her eyes widening with a mix of shock and excitement, body clenching around my fingers like she's already imagining it. Knox pulls back from her breast, his grin wicked as he meets my gaze over her shoulder, nodding once in silent agreement. We've always been on the same wavelength, and this? This is no different.

I keep working her, thrusting my fingers deeper, scissoring them to open her up, feeling her wet heat coat my hand. Her moans grow louder, but I shush her with another kiss, swallowing the sounds while Knox's hands roam her body, pinching and teasing her nipples until they're hard peaks. She's writhing between us now, legs spreading wider, inviting more, her nails digging into my arm as she rides my hand.

"Fuck, you're soaking," I moan against her lips, pulling my fingers out just enough to add pressure with my thumb on her clit, circling faster. She bucks, a whimper escaping, and Knox chuckles low, his voice vibrating against her skin. "Easy, pretty girl. We've got you."

Hailey's response is a shuddering gasp, her body arching like a bowstring pulled taut, and I can feel her getting closer, her inner muscles fluttering around my fingers with every thrust.

Knox watches us, his eyes hungry, then he leans in, his breath hot against my ear. "Let me help you stretch her," he murmurs, and before I can respond, his hand joins mine between her thighs, his fingers sliding in alongside mine, thick and insistent. The sensation of us both inside her—our knuckles brushing, working together to fill her up—sends a jolt through me, my cock twitching in need against her hip.

She cries out, the sound tender and desperate, her head thrown back against the pillow as we pump in unison, our rhythms syncing like we've done this a hundred times. "Oh god, yes," she pants, her voice breaking on the words, hands clutching at the sheets, at my shoulder, at anything to anchor her. I can smell her arousal, thick in the air, mixing with the faint smoke from the fire, and it's intoxicating, making my head spin.

I capture her mouth again, kissing her hard while our fingers drive deeper, faster, stretching her limits. Knox's free hand finds my thigh, squeezing in silent encouragement, and I know he's feeling it too—this electric pull between all three of us, turning the room into a haze of heat and need. Her climax builds like a storm, her breaths coming in short, sharp bursts, and when she shatters, it's with a muffled scream against my lips, her body convulsing, clenching down on us so tight it almost hurts.

We don't stop, though, riding her through it, drawing out every last tremor until she's boneless and gasping, her eyes glazed with pleasure. Knox pulls his fingers free first, wet and shining, and brings them to his mouth, tasting her with a low groan that makes my gut tighten. I follow suit, sucking her essence from my skin, the flavor salty-sweet and addictive.

"Think she's ready?" Knox asks, gaze locked on mine as he positions himself behind her, his hardness pressing against her ass. I nod, shifting to face her, my own erection throbbing with anticipation. Hailey looks between us, cheeks flushed, lips parted in a mix of exhaustion and eager want, and whispers, "Please."

"As much as I want to drive myself into this ass of yours," Knox says, "it's far from ready to take me."

"We've got all night to prep her properly," I agree. My hand trails down her side, fingers ghosting over the curve of her ass, feeling the way she tenses and then relaxes under my touch, like she's already surrendering to the idea.

She whimpers softly, shifting between us, her body still humming from the aftershocks of her release. "You two are going to ruin me," she purrs, but there's no fear in it—just hungry anticipation that makes my cock ache harder against her thigh. I lean in, capturing her lips in a slow, deep kiss, tasting the remnants of her moans, while Knox's hands explore her from behind, kneading the soft flesh of her cheeks, spreading them gently as if testing the waters.

"Damn right we are," Knox growls, his breath hot on her neck, and I feel his fingers dip lower, circling that tight ring of muscle with deliberate care, not pushing in yet, just teasing, lubing her up with the slickness we've already drawn from her pussy. She gasps into my mouth, her hips rocking back instinctively, pressing against him, and I swallow the sound, my own hand joining his now, mirroring his movements to ease her open bit by bit.

It's surreal, feeling our fingers brush again, this time in a new territory, her body yielding slowly under the dual assault. I break the kiss to watch her face, the way her brows knit in concentration, lips parting on a shaky exhale. "Breathe, baby," I coach, my thumb stroking her clit to distract from any discomfort, reigniting that fire in her core. She nods, eyes locking onto mine, trust shining through the haze of lust, and it hits me how perfect this is—us three, tangled in this unfiltered need.

"Grab the lube and condoms from the bathroom," Knox directs, and I quickly comply.

"Got it," I say as I kneel back onto the bed, popping the cap and squeezing a generous amount onto my fingers. Knox mirrors me, coating his own, and we lock eyes again, that unspoken sync kicking in. Hailey watches us, her teeth sinking into her bottom lip, body quivering with a mix of nerves and desire as I settle in front of her, pulling her leg over my thigh to open her up more.

I start slow, my lubed fingers circling her entrance first, then trailing back to that tighter spot, pressing gently against the resistance. She inhales sharply, but I lean in to kiss her neck, groaning, "Relax for me, baby. We'll go easy." Knox's hand joins mine from the other side, his finger probing alongside, and I feel her tense, then melt as we work in tandem, easing in just the tip, stretching her with careful patience.

"Fuck, that's it," Knox rasps, his free arm wrapping around her waist to hold her steady while I keep up the distraction, my thumb finding her clit again, rubbing in lazy circles that make her moan and push back against us. Her heat envelops our fingers, pulling us deeper inch by inch, and I can't help the groan that escapes me, my cock throbbing painfully now, begging for attention.

She's panting, her hands gripping my shoulders, nails biting into my skin as we add more lube, thrusting shallowly to open her further. "You feel so good like this," I whisper against her ear, nipping the lobe, tasting the salt of her sweat. Knox chuckles darkly, his breath fanning over us both, and I catch the way his eyes flick to mine, hungry and approving, like this is sealing some pact we've always known was there.

Hailey's whimpers turn to pleas, her body rocking between us, chasing the fullness, and when we slide in deeper, coordinated and relentless, she cries out, the sound muffled as I claim her mouth again, swallowing her ecstasy. We're in rhythm now, fingers pumping steadily, preparing her for what's next.

"I'm ready," she pants. "So ready."

Knox and I exchange a glance, our fingers still buried inside her, feeling the way she clenches around us, hot and eager. "You heard her," he says, pulling out slowly before grabbing a condom, then slicking himself up generously. I do the same, coating my length until it glistens, my heart pounding as I position myself in front of her, guiding her leg higher over my hip.

She reaches for me, her fingers wrapping around my shaft, stroking once, twice, making me hiss through my teeth. "Take me first," she murmurs, eyes locked on mine, bold and breathless. I nod, lining up at her entrance, pushing in inch by inch, her pussy welcoming me with that tight, wet heat that nearly undoes me right then. She moans, long and low, her walls fluttering as I seat myself fully, holding still to let her adjust while Knox presses against her from behind.

I can feel him there, the pressure building as he starts to ease in, his tip breaching that stretched ring we've prepped so carefully. Hailey's breath catches, her nails digging into my back, but she doesn't pull away—she pushes back, taking him deeper, her body trembling between us like a live wire. "Oh fuck," I groan, the sensation of him sliding in alongside me, separated only by that thin barrier, sending sparks up my spine. It's intense, overwhelming, our cocks filling her completely, rubbing against each other through her.

Knox grunts, his hand gripping her hip, steadying us all as he bottoms out, and for a moment, we just stay like that, connected in this impossible way, breaths syncing in the dim light. She whimpers, shifting slightly, and that's all it takes—we start to move, slow at first, alternating thrusts that have her gasping, her head falling back against Knox's shoulder. I capture her mouth, kissing her fiercely, tasting her cries as I rock into her, feeling every inch of Knox's movements amplifying my own.

"God, you're so full," I whisper against her lips, my hand slipping between us to tease her clit, circling it in time with our rhythm. She shudders, clenching down hard, drawing groans from both of us, and Knox picks up the pace, his free hand finding my ass, squeezing in that rough, possessive way that blurs the lines even more. The friction builds, heat coiling low in my gut, and I know none of us will last long like this—it's too much, too perfect, her body milking us as we claim her together.

Her moans turn frantic, body arching, and when she comes, it's explosive, her inner muscles pulsing wildly, pulling us right over the edge with her. I spill deep inside, groaning her name, feeling Knox do the same, his thrusts erratic until we're all spent, collapsing in a tangle of limbs and heavy breaths, the fire crackling softly in the background like applause.

Chapter Twenty-Six

KNOX

A click.

Quiet enough that most people would sleep through it. I am not most people.

My eyes open before I'm fully conscious, every nerve firing alert. The cabin is dim, that gray pre-dawn light filtering through the windows. Hailey's head rests on my shoulder, her breath warm against my collarbone. Liam's arm is draped across us both, his forehead pressed to my spine.

We've been sleeping like this for two nights now. Piled together like survivors on a life raft. I've stopped pretending I don't like it.

But that sound—

I hold still, listening. The wind has died down. That's the first thing I register. The constant moan that's been shaking the walls for days has gone quiet. The silence feels wrong. Heavy.

Then I hear it again. A mechanical click from the direction of the door.

Slowly, carefully, I extract myself from the tangle of limbs. Hailey murmurs something in her sleep but doesn't wake. Liam's arm slides off me, his hand curling into the empty space where I was.

I cross the room barefoot, the floorboards cold enough to make my jaw tight. The door is right there. Same door that's been locked since they threw us in here. Same door I've tested a hundred times.

The handle turns.

It opens.

For one wild second, my heart slams against my ribs. Freedom. We can just walk out. We can—

Then I see what's waiting for us.

Snow. Everywhere. A wall of white that comes up past my thighs at the porch line. The storm that's been howling overhead for days finally spent itself, and it dumped everything it had right on top of us.

The forest beyond is unrecognizable. Trees bent low under the weight. No paths. No landmarks. Just endless wilderness in every direction, the kind of terrain that would swallow three people in city clothes and never give them back.

I step out onto the porch. The cold slams into me like a fist. Minus twenty at least, maybe colder. My lungs seize with the first breath. I'm wearing nothing but sleep pants and a T-shirt, and within seconds my feet are going numb on the frozen boards.

We'd be dead in an hour out there. Less, probably. No gear. No direction. No food. Just miles of mountain forest waiting to freeze us solid.

"Knox?"

I turn. Hailey's in the doorway, blanket wrapped around her shoulders, Liam a shadow behind her. Both of them staring past me at the white expanse.

"Door just unlocked," I say. "Heard it click a minute ago."

Liam pushes past Hailey to stand beside me, his jaw flexing as he takes in the view. His breath fogs in front of his face. "That's not the escape it looks like."

"No. It's not."

Marlena's little joke. Give us the illusion of freedom while the weather makes damn sure we can't use it. She's probably watching right now, that crazy smile on her face, waiting to see if we're stupid enough to try.

We're not.

But then I spot something off to the side of the cabin. A small structure half-buried in the drifts. The woodshed. And inside, just visible through the gap in the door—an axe propped against a chopping block.

"At least I can get us more firewood now." I nod toward the woodshed. "She probably noticed the pile was getting low. Might be why she unlocked the door."

"I need to go out there." Hailey's voice is steady. "Get my bearings. See what we're dealing with."

I frown. "It's dangerous."

"It's dangerous in here too." She's already turning, scanning the room for the warmest clothes. "Twenty minutes. That's all. I need to know what's around us. What our options are."

I want to argue. Every instinct I have screams to keep her inside, keep her safe, lock the door again and pretend this never happened. But she's right. We've been blind in here for four days. If there's any chance of getting out of this, we need intelligence.

"We do it together," I say. "Nobody goes alone."

We layer everything we can find. Sweaters under sweaters, socks doubled on our feet, scarves wrapped over our faces until only our eyes show. Liam finds a pair of work gloves in the closet, stiff with cold but better than nothing. Shoved in the back of the same closet, three pairs of snow boots in varying sizes. Because of course Marlena thought of boots. She thought of everything else. The fit isn't great—Hailey's swimming in hers and Liam's are a half size too tight—but they beat barefoot in a blizzard. We've been padding around this cabin in borrowed socks for four days, and I'd almost forgotten what real shoes felt like.

"I'm grabbing the axe first," I tell them. "Wait here."

I wade through the snow to the woodshed, thigh-deep with every step, and grab the axe from where it leans against the chopping block. By the time I make it back to the porch, I'm already breathing hard.

"Just in case," I say when Hailey raises an eyebrow.

The first step off the porch together sinks us all thigh-deep. The snow is loose and powdery, the kind that looks soft until you try to walk through it. Each step is a battle—lift your knee to your chest, plant, sink, repeat. Within minutes my legs are burning and sweat is trickling down my spine despite the cold.

Hailey struggles beside me, her smaller frame working twice as hard. Liam brings up the rear, his breath rasping through his scarf.

We circle the cabin. The slope of the mountain becomes clear almost immediately—we're perched on the side of it, tucked into a small clearing surrounded by dense forest. The trees crowd in close, branches heavy with snow. No roads. No power lines. Nothing but wilderness as far as I can see in any direction.

"There." I point to a set of tracks cutting through the snow near the tree line. Snowmobile tracks. Already half-filled from the storm, but still visible.

"That's how they brought us in." Liam crouches, studying them. His face is red from the cold. "But look—already covered. Another few hours and they'll be gone completely. We'd never find our way following these."

He's right. The tracks wind into the forest and disappear into shadow. No markers. No breadcrumbs. Just an endless maze of white and dark.

We push farther, mapping what we can. A small clearing behind the cabin. The woodshed, stocked with split logs. Beyond that, nothing. Just the mountain sloping down into more forest, more snow, more of the same in every direction.

The isolation is complete.

"Fifteen minutes." My teeth are chattering. The cold has worked its way through every layer, settled into my bones. Hailey's shaking beside me, her cheeks raw. "Inside. Now."

Nobody argues.

We stumble back through our own trail, following the broken path we've already cut. By the time we reach the porch, my fingers are clumsy clubs at the end of my arms and I can barely feel my feet.

The cabin's warmth hits us like a wall. For a moment we just stand there in the entryway, dripping, shivering, too cold to do anything but breathe.

"Fire," Liam says through chattering teeth.

I move on autopilot, grabbing logs from the pile by the hearth, adding them to the embers. My hands shake as I work. Ice crystals melt in my hair, sending cold water trickling down my neck.

Behind me, I hear them peeling off wet layers. Soaked sweaters hitting the floor. Waterlogged socks.

"My jeans are frozen stiff." Hailey's voice is muffled. "Actually frozen."

"Body heat," Liam says. "Come here."

I get the fire built up, watch it catch, wait until the flames are steady. Then I turn around.

They're huddled together near the bed, blankets pulled around their shoulders, Hailey pressed against Liam's chest for warmth. Her eyes are closed. His chin rests on top of her head.

Something twists in my chest. Not jealousy—or not only jealousy. Something older than that. The recognition that there's history between them I'm not part of. Conversations they haven't had. Things they need to say to each other that have nothing to do with me.

I pull off my own wet clothes, exchange them for dry ones from the pile we've been rotating through. Jeans. A flannel shirt. My boots are soaked through but they're the only shoes I've got.

"I'm going to split some more wood." I say it to the room, not looking at either of them. "We're going to need it."

Hailey lifts her head. "Knox—"

"I'll be right outside. Twenty feet from the door." I pull on as many dry layers as I can find. "You two should warm up. Talk."

The look that passes between them tells me I've read the situation right. There are things unsettled between them. Five years of silence that needs to be broken. Old wounds that need to be either reopened or finally closed.

I'm not the one who can help with that.

"Be careful." Hailey's voice is soft.

"Always am."

I grab the axe and head back out into the cold.

Chapter Twenty-Seven

HAILEY

The door closes behind Knox, and I hear the crunch of his boots through the snow. Then the thwack of the axe, steady and rhythmic. I'm still pressed against Liam's chest, his arms wrapped around me, both of us cocooned in blankets. My shivering has finally stopped. Warmth seeps back into my fingers, my toes, the tip of my nose that was numb ten minutes ago.

Neither of us moves.

His heartbeat is steady under my ear. That familiar rhythm I used to fall asleep to in cramped hotel rooms and safe houses across Europe. I'd forgotten how it felt to be held by him. How safe. How known.

"Your hair smells like woodsmoke," he murmurs against the top of my head.

"Everything smells like woodsmoke. We've been living in a chimney for five days."

His chest vibrates with a quiet laugh. His hand moves up my back, slow, tracing the line of my spine through my shirt. Not sexual. Just . . . present. Grounding.

"He knew," Liam says. "Knox. That we needed this."

"He's perceptive that way."

"He's in love with you."

I lift my head to look at him. His brown eyes are soft, no jealousy in them. Just observation.

"I know," I say.

"Are you in love with him?"

The question should feel loaded. It doesn't. Maybe because we're past the point where jealousy makes sense. Maybe because the three of us have already crossed every line there was to cross.

"Yes," I admit. "But that doesn't change how I feel about you."

Liam's hand cups my face. His thumb brushes my cheekbone, tracing down to the corner of my mouth. "Five years," he says quietly. "You ever going to tell me why?"

I turn my face into his palm, pressing a kiss there. His skin is warm now, no longer frozen.

"I was scared, Liam." My voice isn't steady and I don't try to make it. "I woke up that morning and I could see the rest of it. Another job, another city, another hotel room. And I loved you too much to watch it turn into something I resented. So I ran."

"A note. That's what I got."

"I know."

"You should have talked to me."

"You would have talked me out of it."

Silence. Outside, the steady rhythm of Knox splitting wood.

"Yeah," he says finally. "I would have."

His other hand comes up, cradling my face between both palms. He looks at me like he's memorizing every detail. Like I might disappear if he blinks.

"I never stopped," he says. "Wanting you. Thinking about you. Every job I took, every city I landed in, I'd see something and think, 'Hailey would love this' or 'Hailey would hate this' or just . . . 'Hailey.'"

My throat tightens. "Liam—"

"I looked for you. Eight months. Every alias, every contact, every city you ever mentioned wanting to see. You covered your tracks too well." His mouth twists. "I'd taught you too well."

All this time. All this time I thought he'd read that note and shrugged and moved on to the next job. That I was easy to let go of.

"I thought you let me go," I whisper.

"I know you did." His voice cracks on the words. "I know."

He takes my chin in his hand, tilts my face up, and nips at my lip. Soft. Almost a question.

"If I told you I'm staying," he says against my mouth. "That you can't get rid of me again . . ."

I pull back just enough to see his eyes. The sincerity there makes my chest ache.

"You'd have to mean it," I say. "Actually mean it. Not just until the job is done or until things get complicated."

His thumb traces my lower lip. "I mean it."

"You should hate me," I say. "For how I did it. Disappearing. You deserved more than that."

"I did." He says it flat, no softening. "But you were right about the life. I wouldn't have stopped. Not for you, not for anyone. Took me a long time to figure out that I wanted to."

I push up onto my elbow, looking down at him.

He doesn't meet my eyes. His hand is still on my hip, but his grip has loosened.

"Liam."

He looks at me. There's something in his face I've never seen before. Fear, maybe. Or shame.

"The diamond," he says slowly. "The Kedrov job. There were things I didn't tell you."

My stomach drops. "What things?"

"I can't—" He stops himself, pressing his lips into a thin line. "Not yet. But I will. I promise, Hailey, I'll tell you everything. Just . . . not today. Let me figure out how first."

I should push. Every instinct I have screams to demand answers right now, to force him to tell me whatever he's been hiding for five years. But there's something in his eyes—something desperate and pleading—that makes me hesitate.

We have five more days. Assuming Marlena doesn't decide to move up her timeline.

"Okay," I say. "But you're telling me. Soon."

"Soon," he agrees.

"And I'm not running again."

"You better not be."

I search his face for any trace of a lie. Find nothing but honesty and relief.

He pulls me down and kisses me. Not soft anymore. There's heat in it now, five years of longing finally given permission to exist. His arms tighten around me, pulling me closer until there's no space between us. The blankets slip off my shoulders but I don't care. His body is warm enough.

His mouth moves to my jaw, my neck, that spot below my ear that he always remembered. I gasp, my fingers fisting in his shirt.

"Liam . . ."

"I've got you." His lips brush my throat. "I've always got you."

We shift on the bed, his body rolling over mine, and the tenderness catches fire. His hands grow bolder, sliding under my shirt, finding skin. I arch into his touch, my own hands working at his clothes, needing to feel him.

He sits up just long enough to pull his shirt over his head. The sight of his chest—the bullet wound from Prague, the knife scar from Lisbon, every mark on his skin a story we share—makes my breath catch.

"I know these scars," I whisper, tracing them with my fingertips. "I know every one."

"You were there for most of them."

"I was."

He bends down, capturing my mouth again. The gentleness hasn't disappeared—it's just burning hotter now, transforming into something else. Something familiar.

He pulls me up, lifts me like I weigh nothing, and carries me toward the kitchen. My legs wrap around his waist. His mouth never leaves mine.

Then I'm on the table, the cool wood against my thighs, and Liam's eyes go dark with that familiar want. The one that used to make my pulse race back when it was just us against the world.

He pulls me in without a word, his mouth crashing against mine, rough and urgent. My arms wrap around his neck, pressing my body to his, feeling the heat of him through what little we're still wearing. His hands slide down my sides, gripping my hips, and a few empty mugs scatter to the floor.

I hope Knox doesn't hear that.

I can feel the cool edge of the table beneath my thighs, but everything else is heat and need. Liam's fingers tangle in my hair, pulling my head back to expose my throat, his mouth devouring mine. I can taste the desperation in his kiss, the longing that mirrors my own. My hands fumble with the button of his jeans, eager to get him free.

His hands find the hem of my shirt, pulling it over my head. Then his fingers hook into my underwear, dragging it down my thighs.

The cabin air bites at my bare skin, but Liam's touch burns it away. He traces a path up my thighs, his calloused hands rough against my smooth skin. I shiver, anticipation building in my core. This is what I've missed—the urgency, the need, the way Liam makes me feel so alive.

His mouth finds mine again, his tongue sweeping in as his fingers find my center. I gasp into his kiss, my body bowing off the table. He swallows my moans, his fingers curling inside me, stoking the fire that's been building since he first touched me.

I reach for his belt, my fingers clumsy. He helps me, his mouth never leaving mine, his body pressing me back onto the table. I can feel him, hard and ready, and I wrap my legs around his waist, pulling him to me.

"You fucked another man," he says, nipping at my lip.

"Yes."

His hand moves to my throat, squeezing. "And you liked it."

"Loved it," I gasp.

His grip tightens, not to hurt, but to claim. I can see it in his eyes—he wants to possess me, to remind me I'm his, even if I've been with someone else. His jealousy, his anger, his lust—it's all there, swirling together.

His fingers retreat, leaving me gasping and empty. That wicked curve appears on his lips, the one that promises both pleasure and punishment. He leans down, breath hot on my ear. "I fucked him too. And I loved it."

"I know," I moan as he thrusts his finger into my pussy as deep as he can.

His finger withdraws, then plunges back in, setting a rhythm that has my hips lifting to meet each thrust. The pressure builds, the coil of pleasure tightening in my core. Liam's mouth moves from my ear to my breast, his teeth grazing my nipple. I cry out, the sensation sending shockwaves through me.

"I told you this body was mine," he says.

His teeth bear down on my nipple, pain mixing with pleasure, driving me wild. I can't think, can't breathe, can't do anything but feel.

His mouth moves back to mine, his kiss bruising, possessive. "I'm taking back what's mine."

He flips me around, spanking my ass hard. I grit my teeth, absorbing the sting of his hand on my flesh. The pain spreads into warmth, mingling with the pleasure. His palm squeezes my ass, fingers digging into my soft skin. His other hand stays between my legs, fingers pumping in and out, his thumb circling my clit.

I press my forehead against the cool wood, my breath coming in ragged gasps. Liam's body is pressed against mine, his hard cock grinding against my hip—when did his jeans come off? His heat, his need, his desperation surrounds me, consumes me.

"Liam," I moan, his name a plea on my lips. I need more. I need him. I need us, like we used to be. Before the cabin. Before Knox.

Not instead of Knox. Just . . . before.

He kicks my legs farther apart, his body covering mine. His cock presses at my entrance, hard and insistent. He pushes in, just an inch, just enough to make me cry out. His hand is still on my ass, fingers digging into my flesh. He thrusts into me, a brutal, claiming stroke that has me screaming his name.

His body covers mine, chest pressing against my back. He wraps a hand in my hair, pulling my head back, his mouth finding my ear. "Is this what you wanted?" he growls. "You wanted me to fuck you like this? Like we used to?"

I can only nod, my words stolen by the sensation of him filling me, stretching me, completing me. He thrusts again, hips slapping against my ass. His hand is still in my hair, pulling my head back, his mouth on my neck, my shoulder, his teeth nipping at my skin.

The table groans beneath us, wood protesting our weight. But Liam doesn't stop. He fucks me like he's possessed, like he's trying to exorcise his demons. And maybe he is. Maybe we both are.

His pace is relentless, his body demanding more from mine. Sweat slicks my skin, the slickness between us, the primal need driving us both. His hand leaves my hair, sliding down to grip my shoulder, fingers digging into my flesh for leverage. Each thrust sends shockwaves through me, the pleasure so intense it burns.

I reach out, grasping the edge of the table, holding on as if it's the only thing keeping me grounded. Liam's breath is hot on my back, his chest heaving against me. Our heartbeats pound together, wild and desperate. His hand slides from my shoulder, down my spine, coming to rest on my hip. He grips me tight, his fingers bruising as he changes the angle, driving deeper. I cry out, the sound raw and guttural, torn from my throat. The pleasure is too much, too intense. The coil in my core tightens, pressure building. I'm close. So close.

Liam seems to sense it, his body moving faster, harder. His hand slides from my hip, fingers finding my clit, circling it in time with his thrusts.

"Come for me," he demands. "Let me feel you come apart."

His words are my undoing. The coil snaps, pleasure exploding through me. I scream his name, my body convulsing around him. He lets out a low groan, his body tensing as he finds his own release. We stay like that for a moment, bodies still joined, breaths ragged. Then we collapse forward onto the tabletop, Liam's body covering mine.

He pulls out slowly, then rolls us both off the table. We end up on the floor, lying side by side, our faces inches apart. The tile is cold against my overheated skin. I don't care.

I can see the sweat on his brow, the flush in his cheeks, the satisfaction in his eyes.

"I never stopped loving you," Liam says into my hair. "Even after you left. Even when I was sure you were gone for good."

I close my eyes. Let the words wash over me.

"I know," I whisper back. "That's what made it hurt so much."

We lie there until the axe falls silent. Until footsteps crunch through the cold outside, heading toward the door. Until reality comes knocking in the form of Knox Bishop, who's about to walk in on us, naked on the kitchen floor.

I should probably move.

I don't.

Chapter Twenty-Eight

HAILEY

Days six and seven blur together in a haze of domesticity I've stopped questioning. We've found a rhythm, the three of us. Cooking together, bumping elbows in the tiny kitchen while Liam and Knox argue about whether pasta should be al dente. Talking for hours about nothing and everything. Touching constantly—hands finding hands, fingers tracing bare skin whenever we pass each other, like we need the physical confirmation that the others are still here, still real.

The physical intimacy has opened up something emotional. We tell stories, share secrets. Knox talks about his time in the Marines, the real version—what he saw, what he did, the friends he lost in Helmand. Liam talks about growing up in foster care, about learning to build things and take them apart in the one house that almost kept him. And I tell them about Mrs. Bilby, my neighbor who brings me soup every Sunday because she's convinced I'm too skinny. I bring her lockpick tutorials on YouTube because she keeps locking herself out, and neither of us has ever questioned this arrangement. How she would have loved this—drinking wine in a cabin with two beautiful men, making the best of a bad situation with style.

The sex has changed too. Not less intense, but more varied. Sometimes it's dark and demanding—Knox pressing me into the mattress while Liam watches and tells him exactly where to touch me. Sometimes it's slow and devastating, the three of us tangled together, taking turns. Sometimes it's just holding each other, touching, being close. The bed is too small for three people but we make it work. I fall asleep listening to two different heartbeats and wake up with hands I can't immediately identify sliding across my skin. It's domestic in a way that feels stolen. Playing house in our prison, making memories we might not live to keep.

On the sixth night, Liam finds the record player.

He's been poking around the cabin's built-in shelves, the ones tucked beside the chimney that I assumed just held dusty books and dead batteries. But there's a cabinet door at the bottom I never noticed, and when he opens it, his face lights up.

"Look at this."

He pulls out an ancient turntable, the kind with fold-out speakers and wood veneer finish. Underneath it, a stack of vinyl albums so old they probably predate my grandmother.

"That thing still work?" Knox asks from where he's stretched out on the couch.

"One way to find out." Liam plugs it in, and miracle of miracles, the power light turns on. He flips through the albums, holding up covers for us to see. Andy Williams. Nat King Cole. Dean Martin. And then he grins, holding up a Bing Crosby record. "White Christmas."

"Seriously?" Knox says.

But when Liam slides the vinyl out of its sleeve and sets it on the turntable, even Knox doesn't object. The needle drops with a soft crackle. Then that voice fills the cabin, warm and crooning, all dreams of a white Christmas and cards he's writing.

I'm standing by the Christmas tree we decorated days ago, the one with Marlena's hand-painted glass balls and delicate wooden snowflakes and little silver birds with real feather details. The lights twinkle against the dark windows. It's almost perfect. Almost normal.

"Dance with me," I say to Liam.

He doesn't hesitate. He crosses the room and takes my hand, pulling me close. His other hand settles on my waist, warm through my sweater. We sway together, not really dancing, just moving to the music in that way people do when they don't care if they look stupid.

His chin rests on top of my head. I can feel his heartbeat against my cheek.

Knox watches from the couch. I can't read his expression in the dim light, but there's something soft about the way he's looking at us.

The song ends. Another begins, strings swelling into something slower.

"Your turn," I say, reaching for Knox.

"I don't dance."

"Liar." I tug at his hand, pulling him up from the couch. He resists for half a second before letting me drag him to his feet. "You move too well to not know how to dance."

"Moving well in general isn't the same thing."

"It's all just rhythm and body awareness. Stop overthinking it."

He's stiff at first, holding me like I'm made of glass. But gradually, he relaxes. His grip loosens. His movements become less robotic. By the second verse, we're actually swaying together, his cheek brushing my temple.

"See?" I whisper. "Not so hard."

He doesn't answer, but he's almost smiling.

The song changes again, something upbeat and jaunty. Liam appears at my elbow. "My turn."

Knox releases me without argument. I step back and watch as Liam moves into his space. For a moment, neither of them moves. They're just looking at each other. Then Liam holds out his hand, and Knox takes it.

They don't dance the way Knox danced with me. It's different, more tentative. Liam's hand on Knox's shoulder, Knox's hand hovering somewhere around Liam's ribs like he can't decide where to put it. But they're moving together, careful and intimate, and a part of my chest cracks open watching them.

This is real. Whatever they're building between them, it's not just for me, not just because I wanted it. This is something that belongs to them.

I sink onto the couch and let myself just watch. The tree lights blink in the corner. Bing Crosby croons about chestnuts and open fires. And two men I'm pretty sure I love sway together in the middle of our temporary prison, finding something soft in all this hardness.

Later, we exchange gifts. It started as a joke—Liam found a roll of ribbon in the junk drawer and suggested Secret Santa, cabin edition. No actual presents allowed, just stuff found around here, points for creativity.

Knox gives me the ornament. One of the hand-painted glass balls from the tree, deep crimson with gold detailing.

"For good luck," he says, pressing it into my palm.

"Knox." My throat tightens. "This was on the tree."

"Tree has plenty. It won't miss one."

He then gives Liam an ornament and tells him it's for luck as well, but he seems a tinge uncomfortable with the exchange.

I close my fingers around the smooth glass. It's warm from where he's been holding it.

Liam goes next. He hands Knox a small object wrapped in a scrap of fabric torn from one of the dishtowels. Knox unwraps it slowly, revealing a wooden snowflake about three inches across. The edges are uneven, clearly carved by hand, but the pattern is intricate—six points, each one detailed with smaller branches radiating outward.

"Made it with a kitchen knife," Liam says, trying for casual. "When you two were sleeping."

"How did you even . . ." Knox turns the snowflake over in his hands, examining each carved line.

"I told you. I'm good with my hands."

The look that passes between them makes my stomach flip.

Liam hands me a carved snowflake that is slightly different, but means just the same.

I hand them both their bracelets. Simple things, just braided string in three colors—red, green, and white. I found the string in a craft box under the bathroom sink and spent yesterday afternoon weaving while the boys argued about escape routes.

"So we match," I explain, holding up my wrist where I'm already wearing mine.

Liam puts his on immediately. Knox stares at his for a long moment before sliding it over his hand.

"We look like we're at summer camp," he says.

"Sexy summer camp," Liam corrects.

"There's no such thing as sexy summer camp."

"Clearly you went to the wrong camps."

I laugh, and it comes out watery. This is ridiculous. We're locked in a cabin by a woman who's obsessed with a diamond I buried in frozen ground five years ago, and we're sitting here exchanging handmade Christmas presents like we're in some twisted Hallmark movie. But it doesn't feel ridiculous. It feels like the truest thing that's happened since we got here.

That night, after the record player has gone quiet and we've moved to the couch, Liam props himself up on one elbow.

"We need to talk about it," he says. "Christmas Eve. Marlena's deadline. What we're actually going to do."

I press my face into Knox's chest. "Tomorrow."

"Hailey—"

"One more night." I reach back, finding Liam's hand and lacing my fingers through his. "Give me one more night of this. Of pretending we're just three people who found each other. Tomorrow we have the hard conversation. Tomorrow we figure out how to survive. But tonight . . ." I squeeze his hand. "Please."

Silence. I can feel them communicating over my head, that wordless thing they've started doing.

"Tomorrow," Knox agrees.

Liam's body relaxes beside me. His arm comes around my waist, and I'm sandwiched between them, warm and safe and pretending that's enough.

Chapter Twenty-Nine

HAILEY

I lean back against the couch, letting my gaze linger on Liam's lips before shifting to Knox's intense stare. "Kiss me. Both of you. But make it count—no holding back."

Liam's eyes sparkle with mischief as he moves first, his finger trailing up from my collarbone to tilt my chin toward him. His mouth captures mine in a slow, teasing kiss that has me leaning into him before I even realize I'm doing it. My hand finds the back of his neck, pulling him closer.

Then Knox's grip on my thigh tightens, and he leans in, waiting until Liam pulls back just enough. His kiss is different—hungrier, more demanding, like he's been holding this in all night. I gasp against his lips, caught between them, the world narrowing to just the three of us and this heat building between us.

As Knox deepens the kiss, his hand slides higher up my thigh, fingers pressing into my skin with a possessiveness that makes something low in my belly tighten. I break away for a breath, only to find Liam watching us with that infuriating grin. He doesn't wait for an invitation; instead, he leans in again, this time brushing his lips against my neck while Knox claims my mouth once more. It's almost too much—Liam's gentle nips along my collarbone, Knox's tongue demanding everything I have.

I arch into them, my hands roaming freely now, one tangling in Liam's hair, the other gripping Knox's shoulder for stability. "More," I murmur between kisses, the word barely escaping before Liam captures my lips again, his free hand slipping under my shirt to trace the curve of my waist. The heat between us builds with every touch, every breath.

Knox pulls back slightly, his breath hot against my ear. "Tell us what you want next, Hailey," he whispers. I meet his gaze, then Liam's, feeling bold and more myself than I've ever been. "Everything," I say, pulling them both closer, ready to lose myself in whatever comes next.

Their hands are everywhere now, no hesitation left. Liam's fingers trail along my skin under my shirt, inching upward until they brush the lace of my bra, his touch light but insistent, drawing a soft moan from my throat. Knox, not one to be outdone, mirrors him on the other side, his palm sliding up my thigh to the hem of my shorts, teasing the edge as if testing my limits.

I shift against the couch, my body craving more contact. They're both naked, but I want more.

I reach out to pull Liam back in for a kiss while my other hand trails down Knox's chest, fingers mapping the hard muscle there. His skin is warm, slightly damp with sweat, and I love the way he shudders under my touch.

Liam breaks the kiss to trail his lips down my neck, across my collarbone, and lower still, until his mouth finds the swell of my breast. He teases the sensitive peak with his tongue, and I actually whimper—Knox mirrors him on the other side, their mouths working in tandem, and holy shit. My hands fist in their hair, holding them there, urging them on as I arch my back off the couch.

I'm drowning in it, a symphony of lips and tongues and hands that leaves me breathless. Knox's fingers dip lower, tracing patterns on my inner thigh before reaching where I ache for him most. He strokes me gently at first, then with more purpose, building something I can feel in my fucking teeth. Liam's hand joins in, exploring my curves, pinching and caressing in ways that make me moan louder, my hips bucking instinctively.

"I like seeing you boys share," I manage.

"We're just getting started," Liam says as his fingers hook under the waistband of my shorts, tugging them down slowly, inch by inch, exposing more of me to them.

Knox's eyes darken with approval, his strokes growing bolder, more insistent, as he watches Liam undress me. I gasp at the cool air on my heated skin, but it's quickly replaced by the warmth of their bodies pressing closer.

Once my shorts are gone, tossed aside with my panties, I'm fully exposed to them, vulnerable yet empowered by the way their eyes take me in. Liam's mouth returns to my breast, sucking gently while his hand slides between my legs, joining Knox's in a rhythm that has me losing my mind. Their fingers work together to tease my clit, circling and pressing in perfect harmony, building the pressure inside me until I'm panting, my nails digging into their shoulders.

Oh my god, is this really happening? Is this—

All thought disappears as their fingers push deeper, Knox's thick digits sliding inside me while Liam's thumb circles my clit.

I moan their names, the sounds blending into a desperate plea, my hips rocking to meet their rhythm. The couch creaks beneath us, but I barely notice, too far gone to care.

Liam lifts his head from my breast, his lips glistening as he captures my mouth again, swallowing my cries. His free hand cups my face, thumb brushing my cheek in a surprisingly tender contrast to the intensity below. Knox groans against my skin, his mouth moving to my earlobe, nipping it lightly before whispering, "You're so wet for us, Hailey. Let go."

I do, surrendering completely as my orgasm tears through me. My muscles clench around Knox's fingers, and I'm gone, crying out as the pleasure wrecks me. They don't stop, drawing it out, prolonging it until I'm trembling, boneless against the cushions.

As the aftershocks fade, I open my eyes to find them both watching me, satisfaction mixing with something hungrier on their faces.

"Kiss," I command on a pant. I want to see them kiss inches from me. For me.

Liam leans in first, his breath still ragged from our shared heat, and Knox meets him halfway, their faces inches from mine. I watch, mesmerized, as their lips brush tentatively at first, then crash together with an intensity that makes my spent body clench. It's beautiful—Liam's playful energy yielding to Knox's dominance, their mouths moving in a fierce, open-mouthed kiss that echoes the hunger they've just unleashed on me. I can feel the vibration of their low groans against my skin, so close that their stubbled cheeks graze my nose, my lips, pulling me into the moment like I'm part of it.

My hands slide up their necks, fingers weaving into their hair to hold them there, guiding the kiss as if it's my own creation. Knox's tongue claims Liam's, and Liam responds with a soft moan that sends renewed heat through me. They're doing this for me, because I asked, and the power of that is a rush all its own. I lean in closer, my lips brushing the corner where their mouths meet, tasting the salt of their skin mingled together. The kiss intensifies, their breaths mingling with mine as I dart my tongue out to join them, turning it into a messy, shared tangle of lips and heat.

"I want to watch you two fuck."

Liam hesitates for a split second, his eyes flicking to Knox, but there's a spark of intrigue there, mixed with the lingering heat from our kiss. Knox doesn't waver; his gaze locks on to Liam's, and he nods like this is just another layer of the game we've all plunged into.

"All right," Knox says, shifting his body to face Liam more fully. I'm still sandwiched between them on the couch, my skin buzzing from the afterglow, but now want coils tight in my belly as I watch them. Knox reaches out, his hand cupping the back of Liam's neck, pulling him in with that same possessive grip he used on me earlier. Their lips meet again, but this time it's so much more than just a kiss.

I scoot back a little to give them space, my breath catching as Knox's other hand trails down Liam's chest, fingers splaying over his abs before dipping lower. Liam groans into the kiss, his body arching toward Knox, and I can see how hard he is, straining. It's mesmerizing, the way Knox takes control, guiding Liam onto his back against the cushions, their bodies aligning in a tangle of limbs.

Knox breaks the kiss to glance at me, his eyes hooded. "This what you want to see?" he asks, but it's not really a question—more like confirmation as he positions himself between Liam's legs, his hand wrapping around Liam's cock with a firm stroke that makes Liam's hips buck.

"Yes," I whisper, pulse pounding as I lean in closer, not wanting to miss a single detail. Knox's grip tightens, stroking Liam with maddening slowness that draws out a low, throaty moan from him, his head falling back against the couch, eyes half-closed in bliss. The sight of them like this—Knox's powerful frame hovering over Liam's leaner one, their skin flushed and glistening—does something to me, a thrill that makes my thighs clench.

Knox stands from the couch, walks to the bathroom, and is back with a condom and lube before I can even steady my breathing.

I watch, my pulse still erratic from the climax they gave me, as Knox tears open the condom packet with his teeth, rolling it on with a practiced ease that shouldn't be as hot as it is. Liam props himself up on his elbows, eyes locked on Knox, a mix of nerves and excitement flickering across his face that I can practically feel radiating off him.

Knox kneels back on the couch, squeezing lube into his palm and warming it before reaching down to prepare Liam, his fingers gentle but insistent. Liam hisses at the contact, his body tensing then relaxing as Knox works him open, saying something low that I can't quite catch—maybe encouragement, maybe a tease. I shift closer, my hand trailing idly over my own thigh, unable to look away. It's intimate, and I love the sound Liam makes, how his fingers grip the cushions.

"Ready?" Knox asks, and Liam nods, pulling Knox down for a quick, fierce kiss before guiding him into position. I hold my breath as Knox presses forward, slow and careful, their bodies joining in a way that makes Liam gasp, his eyes squeezing shut for a moment before fluttering open to meet mine. There's something charged between all of us, Knox's hips rocking in a steady rhythm that builds, his hand braced on Liam's shoulder for leverage.

I lean in, my fingers brushing Liam's arm, feeling the tremor there as he moans, the sound going straight through me. Knox picks up the pace, thrusting deeper, and Liam arches up to meet him, their skin slapping together in a hypnotic cadence. It's beautiful and intense, Knox's muscles flexing with each movement, Liam's face lost in pleasure that's almost too much to watch without touching myself. So I do, my hand slipping between my legs to match their rhythm, circling my still-sensitive clit as I drink in every detail—the sweat beading on Knox's brow, the way Liam's toes curl against the couch.

"Fuck, Hailey," Liam pants, reaching out to grab my hand, pulling it to his chest. "This is . . . because of you." His words dissolve into another groan as Knox hits just the right spot, and I squeeze his hand, my own arousal spiking, the three of us linked in this wild, unspoken pact.

I take hold of Liam's cock as Knox is buried in his ass.

My fingers wrap around him, feeling the heat and the throb against my palm, syncing with the rhythm Knox sets as he drives into Liam again and again. Liam's eyes lock onto mine, wide and glassy with the overload of sensations, and he bucks up into my hand, a desperate whine escaping his lips that makes my core clench in response. I stroke him firmly, matching Knox's thrusts, twisting my wrist at the tip just to hear that sound again, to see his body tense and arch like he's chasing every bit of pleasure we can give him.

Knox glances down at me, fierce and approving, sweat trickling down his temple as he snaps his hips forward harder, the force of it jolting through Liam and into my touch. Liam's cock pulses in my hand, slick with pre-cum, and I speed up, loving the way he writhes between us, caught in this.

I can't resist dipping my head to taste him, my tongue flicking out to swirl around the head while my hand keeps pumping. Liam curses under his breath, his fingers tangling in my hair, holding me there as Knox groans above us.

Knox reaches down, his hand covering mine on Liam's cock, guiding my strokes with his own, our fingers interlocking in a messy, shared grip that amps everything up. "Come for us," Knox growls, and Liam does, breaking apart with a cry that echoes through the room. His release spills hot over our joined hands, his body convulsing as Knox follows him seconds later, thrusting deep one last time with a groan that shudders through all of us.

We collapse in a heap, limbs entangled, breaths ragged and syncing as the haze settles. I press lazy kisses to Liam's shoulder, then Knox's arm, savoring the aftertaste of our last night of peace.

Chapter Thirty

HAILEY

The morning of December twenty-third arrives with weak winter light and a silence that presses against my eardrums.

We're sitting around the small table—Knox on my left, Liam on my right, our knees not quite making contact underneath. The food is untouched. Eggs going cold, toast hardening. Marlena's stocked kitchen has been generous, but none of us have an appetite anymore.

Tomorrow is Christmas Eve. Tomorrow at midnight, Marlena's deadline hits.

Knox is staring at his coffee, turning the mug in slow circles on the table. Liam is pushing scrambled eggs around his plate. And I'm sitting here wondering how we went from mind-blowing sex to this funeral parlor atmosphere in twelve hours.

"So," I begin, "it's time we talk about it.

"The deadline," I add when neither of them responds.

Knox speaks first. "We find another way out."

"The door's unlocked." Liam sets his fork down. "And outside is miles of frozen wilderness that would kill us in an hour. No gear, no supplies, no idea which direction leads anywhere."

"There has to be something—"

"There isn't. Sometimes there just isn't, Knox."

"So we hand over the diamond and hope Marlena keeps her word?"

"I don't see you coming up with alternatives."

"Enough." I press my palms flat against the table. "Both of you."

They fall silent.

"Look," Liam says, his tone shifting. Softer. More careful. "Maybe there's a middle ground."

He turns to me with that earnest expression I remember from our years working together. The face he made when he was trying to talk me into something risky.

"Hailey. Tell us where it is."

I stare at him.

"The diamond. Where you hid it." He reaches for my hand. "Maybe if we know, we can figure out a way to get it ourselves. Get ahead of Marlena."

I pull my hand back and glance at the ceiling. At the corners of the room. At all the places we searched for cameras and found nothing—which doesn't mean they're not there.

"She could be listening right now, Liam."

"She said she's not watching constantly—"

"She said a lot of things. She also said she'd kill one of us without blinking."

My gut clenches. That old warning bell, the one that's kept me alive through jobs that should have gotten me killed.

I've been ignoring it since we got here.

"How did she know?" I blurt.

Liam blinks. "What?"

"Marlena. How did she know we were coming to retrieve the diamond?"

"She's been tracking it for years. She has resources—"

"We flew private." I'm watching his face now. "When we landed, she had teams waiting. Armed guards. Sedatives. This cabin stocked and ready. That's not tracking. That's advance notice."

Knox straightens in his chair.

Liam's appearance doesn't change. But I've known him longer than anyone, and I catch the sweat beading at his temple.

"Maybe she got lucky," he says.

"Nobody gets that lucky."

I think about the lodge. The way Liam kept checking his phone at dinner. The way he seemed nervous but kept deflecting. The way everything went wrong so fast, so smoothly.

"What was the original plan?" I ask. "When you showed up at my apartment after five years. What was supposed to happen?"

"Kedrov was closing in. We needed to—"

"You said there were complications. Things you didn't tell me about the job." My pulse is pounding. "You promised you'd explain."

"Hailey—"

"What was the plan, Liam?"

He doesn't answer. It's so quiet that I can hear the wind outside.

And I know. I've known since they threw us in here, if I'm honest. That whisper in the back of my mind that something was wrong, that the timing was too convenient.

I just didn't want to believe it.

"You told her." The words come out flat. "You told Marlena we were coming."

"It's not—"

"This whole thing. The resort. Getting grabbed." I'm on my feet, chair scraping back. "You planned this."

"It wasn't supposed to go this way."

Knox shoves back from the table.

"Explain," he says. "Now."

Liam runs both hands through his hair. "The kidnapping at the lodge was supposed to be it. Marlena's people grab you, scare you, demand the location. You tell them—under duress, which is important—and then she retrieves it herself. Done."

"And then she lets us go?"

"Yes. That was the deal. She gets the diamond, we walk away, and when Kedrov comes looking—"

"He'd still be furious we stole it in the first place."

"Yeah, but Kedrov's been hunting us for the location. That's why we're valuable to him—we're the only ones who know where it is. If someone else forces it out of us? We're useless. He'd have to go after Marlena to get the diamond back, not us. We'd be off his radar."

"You really believe that?"

"Revenge is expensive. Kedrov's a businessman. He's not going to waste resources tracking down two people who can't give him anything anymore when he could focus on actually getting his diamond back."

The logic is cold. Calculated. And so perfectly Liam that my throat tightens.

"So that was the plan," I say slowly. "Get us kidnapped. Let Marlena scare the location out of me. And then we're free because we're no longer worth hunting."

"Yes."

"And were you going to profit? Selling the diamond with Marlena?"

He flinches. "I . . . I don't know. Maybe. She kept implying there might be something in it for me, but the details weren't—"

"Weren't worked out yet."

"I was trying to protect you. Get you out from under Kedrov for good."

Knox moves so fast I barely see it. One second he's seated, the next he's got Liam by the collar, slamming him against the counter hard enough to rattle the pots overhead.

"You son of a bitch."

"I didn't know about the cabin." Liam's hands come up, not fighting. "The timeline, the death threats—none of that was the plan. She was supposed to let us go after a day. Two at most."

"And instead?"

"She played me." His voice cracks. "I thought I had leverage, but she was working her own angle. The second she had us both, she cut me out."

Knox cocks his fist back.

It connects with Liam's jaw faster than I can move. The crack of knuckles on bone echoes through the cabin.

But Liam doesn't crumple. He surges forward, driving his shoulder into Knox's chest, sending them both crashing into the table. My coffee cup shatters on the floor.

"You self-righteous asshole—" Liam gets a fist into Knox's ribs. "You want to play judge and jury?"

Knox grunts, twists, gets Liam in a headlock. "You sold her out—"

"And what did you do?" Liam wrenches free, blood on his lip. "You followed her for months. Memorized her schedule. Learned her routes. Put a fucking tracker in her boot like she was a package you were shipping."

Knox's next punch goes wide. Liam catches his arm, uses his momentum to slam him against the refrigerator.

"You're not her protector, Knox. You're her stalker. The only difference between us is I had the balls to show up at her door instead of jerking off to fantasies about her every night."

Knox roars and charges. They hit the floor hard, rolling, fists flying. The coffee table skids sideways. A lamp crashes.

"I did it to keep her safe—" Knox lands a blow to Liam's stomach.

Liam wheezes but doesn't stop. "So did I! That's literally what I just said—"

"Bullshit. You did it to save your own ass—"

"I did it so Kedrov would stop hunting her!" Liam catches Knox's wrist, twists. "You think I wanted to make a deal with that psychopath? I was out of options!"

"You had options. You could have told the truth—"

"Like you told her the truth? About the tracker? About watching her for months like some lovesick creep?"

Knox hesitates. Just a second. Liam uses it to flip their positions, pinning Knox's shoulders to the hardwood.

"We're the same," Liam spits. "The only difference is you lie to yourself about it."

"I never put her in danger—"

"You think obsessing over someone from the shadows is protection? That's not keeping her safe. That's making yourself feel better about wanting something you were too chickenshit to ask for."

I grab the cast iron skillet from the counter.

I slam it against the stovetop so hard the clang reverberates through my teeth.

Both men freeze.

"Get. Up."

They untangle slowly, breathing hard. Knox's lip is split. Liam's eye is already swelling.

"You." I point the skillet at Knox. "Followed me for months. Tracked my movements. Learned everything about my life without ever saying a word. All to 'protect' me."

I swing the skillet toward Liam. "And you. Made deals behind my back. Got us kidnapped. Lied to my face. Also to 'protect' me."

I set the skillet down with a clatter that makes them both flinch.

"Here's what you two need to get through your thick skulls. I don't need protecting. I'm not some damsel waiting to be rescued. I survived ten years in this life before either of you decided to make me your pet project. I've outrun cops, outmaneuvered mob bosses, and stolen from people who would have skinned me alive if they'd caught me."

I step closer, making sure they're both looking at me.

"I can take care of myself. I've been doing it since I was seventeen. So the next time either of you decides to 'protect' me by lying, manipulating, or tracking me like a goddamn FedEx package—don't."

Knox wipes blood from his mouth. He doesn't argue.

Liam touches his swelling eye. "Hailey—"

"I'm not finished." I take a breath. "Tomorrow is the deadline. And now I wonder if I can trust either of you to keep me alive. Fucking barbaric cavemen."

"Hailey—"

"Don't. I need to think. *I* need to figure a way out of this."

I grab a new cup of coffee and move to the couch.

The three of us. Trapped together. One day left.

And if Marlena's been watching this whole time? She's gotten one hell of a show.

Chapter Thirty-One

HAILEY

I wake to the sound of static.

The television screen flashes to life, and Marlena's face appears before I've even fully opened my eyes. She looks like she's been waiting for this moment, like Christmas morning came early and she's about to unwrap her favorite gift.

"Merry Christmas Eve." Her smile is a wound. "Have you made your decision?"

I scramble upright. The guys are already awake—Knox on his feet, Liam sitting on the edge of the couch, his face unreadable in the gray morning light. We fell asleep scattered across the living room after the fight, after the revelations, after everything. My back aches from sleeping on the floor. My heart aches from everything else.

Knox steps toward the screen. "You're early. We have until midnight."

"You've had ten days. I'm impatient." She adjusts something off-camera, nails clicking. "Besides, I wanted to give you ample time to say your goodbyes if necessary."

"Then you'll have to kill us." Knox's voice doesn't waver. "Because we're not telling you anything."

Marlena's smile widens. There's something wrong about it. Something that makes my stomach drop.

"How noble. But I don't think you understand the stakes."

The cabin door unlocks.

I didn't even hear anyone approach. No crunch of footsteps, no engine. But the door swings open and two guards step inside—

different ones than before, bigger, armed with weapons I don't recognize. Their faces are covered. Their movements are synchronized.

They go straight for Liam.

He fights. Of course he fights. Liam has never gone down without a struggle in his life, and he's not about to start now. He gets an elbow into one guard's throat, twists away from the other's grip, nearly makes it to his feet—

A third guard appears in the doorway. He has a gun pressed to my temple before I can even process that he's moved.

"No!" Knox freezes mid-step, hands going up. His eyes are wild, darting between me and Liam and the barrel against my skull. "Don't. Don't hurt her."

Liam stops fighting.

The guards drag him backward toward the door. The split on his lip has reopened, blood fresh on his chin. He's breathing hard, his eyes locked on mine.

"Let's try this differently." Marlena's voice cuts through the chaos, calm as ever. "Mr. Calloway comes with me. You two have until midnight tonight. Tell me where the diamond is, or I kill him." She pauses, letting it land. "Your choice."

The door slams shut.

The lock engages.

And then it's just me and Knox, standing in the middle of a cabin that suddenly feels impossibly empty.

The screen goes dark.

"She won't really kill him." Knox's words come out rough, like he doesn't quite believe them. He's pacing now, that restless energy he gets when there's nothing to hit. "This is pressure. Psychological warfare. She wants us scared."

"It's working."

"Hailey—"

"She's been hunting us for five years, Knox. Five years of resources and obsession and dead ends. You think she's bluffing?" I sink onto the couch, suddenly exhausted. "She absolutely will kill him if we don't give her what she wants."

"But if we do, she kills all three of us anyway. We know her face. We know her operation. We're loose ends."

He's right. I know he's right. There's no scenario where Marlena lets us walk away from this, not really. The moment she has the diamond, we become liabilities. Problems to be solved.

And yet.

"It could still be part of his plan," Knox says. He's stopped pacing, standing by the window now, staring at nothing. "Liam. He set this up once. Maybe he's got another angle. Maybe he's working Marlena from the inside—"

"No."

The word comes out harder than I intend. Knox turns to look at me.

"I know Liam," I say. "Better than anyone. He's a con man and a thief and apparently willing to sell me out to get us both off Kedrov's radar, but the look on his face when they grabbed him? That wasn't part of a plan. That was fear. Real fear."

Knox doesn't argue. Maybe because he saw it too.

"So what do we do?" he asks.

"We stick to the plan."

Knox stares at me. "Liam's gone, Hailey. She took him. The plan was built for three people."

"The plan was built around me having information Marlena needs. That hasn't changed." I'm already pacing, which is what I do when my brain is running faster than my mouth. Old habit from job days. Liam used to call it my scheming walk. "She took Liam to force my hand. Fine. Let her think it worked."

"What do you mean?"

"I mean when she comes back on that screen, I break. I give her the location. Every detail, every landmark, every turn in the trail. I make it so thorough she'll have no reason to doubt me." I stop pacing and look at him. "And I leave out the safe code."

Knox is quiet for a beat, processing. "She'll verify the location first. Send a team."

"Good. That takes time. A day, maybe more. And when her team finds the safe and can't open it, she needs me again. She needs me alive, and she needs me cooperative. Which means she needs you and Liam alive too, because she's smart enough to know I won't give her a damn thing if either of you are dead."

"And then what? She drags us out there to open it?"

"That's exactly what she does. And that's when we're outside this cabin for the first time in ten days." I let that land. "We've got the fire extinguisher. We've got the bleach and ammonia. Knox, we talked about this. Transport is our opening."

He runs a hand over his face. I can see him turning it over, testing it for holes, doing that tactical calculation he does where he weighs every variable against every risk.

"She'll have armed guards."

"She will."

"Multiple vehicles, probably. Maybe air transport."

"Probably."

"The odds are garbage."

"The odds have been garbage since day one. But out there we've got space to move, weapons she doesn't know about, and a woman too busy drooling over a twenty-million-dollar diamond to watch our hands. I'll take that over sitting in this cabin waiting to die."

He's quiet again. "We need to figure out what we can smuggle out of here without the cameras catching it."

"See, this is why I keep you around."

We spend the next hour going through it. Quiet, methodical, backs to the cameras whenever we need to discuss details. The fire extinguisher is too big to hide, but Knox thinks he can rig a smaller container with the ammonia and bleach that would fit inside a coat pocket. The steak knives are obvious but effective. We talk about positioning, about how many guards she's likely to bring, about what terrain we might be dealing with around the mine.

There are holes. Plenty of them. But standing around cataloging reasons it won't work hasn't kept anyone alive, and I didn't survive five years on the run by waiting for a sure thing.

Knox sits across from me at the table, his lip still swollen from yesterday's fight with Liam, a bruise darkening along his jaw. He looks like he's been through a war.

I probably look worse.

"I'm sorry," he says.

I blink. "For what?"

"For not seeing who you really are." He shakes his head. "I kept following you around, watching over you, like you couldn't handle yourself. But you can. You've been handling yourself since long before I came along."

"Knox—"

"You don't need a bodyguard, Hailey. You never did. I just couldn't get out of my own head long enough to realize it."

"You were both right," I say eventually. "You and Liam. About each other. He made deals behind my back and got us kidnapped. You tracked my movements like I was a target instead of a person. You both made choices for me without ever asking what I wanted."

Knox tenses, but he doesn't look away.

"But I also made choices." I gesture around the cabin, at the mess we've made of everything. "I came here. I stayed. I . . ."

I think about the past ten days. The fighting. The fucking. The way we fell into each other like it was inevitable, like gravity had been pulling us together since the beginning.

"This," I finish.

"Do you regret it?"

"No."

The word surprises me with how easily it comes out. But it's true. Despite everything—the danger, the betrayal, the fact that we might all die before midnight—I don't regret any of it. Not Knox. Not Liam. Not the complicated, messy, impossible thing the three of us have become.

"I don't regret you," I say. "Either of you. Even if we all went about it the wrong way."

Knox crosses the space between us. His hand cups my face, rough and gentle at the same time. He doesn't kiss me. He just holds me there, forehead pressed to mine, breathing the same air.

I close my eyes. "I love him too, you know. Liam. Flaws and all."

"I know." His thumb traces my cheekbone. "So do I."

His arms come around me, and I let myself be held. Let myself pretend, for a moment, that this is enough. That love is enough to keep us alive. Thirty seconds. That's what I give myself. Thirty seconds of this before I go back to being the woman with the plan.

Outside, the sun moves across the sky.

We don't let go.

By evening, I'm ready.

I've been here before. Not the captivity part, but the hours before a job, when the fear gets put in a drawer and the only thing left is what comes next. My body knows this rhythm even if the stakes have never been this high.

Marlena is going to come back on that screen. She's going to threaten Liam's life. And I'm going to give her exactly what she wants, minus the one piece she can't get without me standing in front of that safe.

Knox and I go over it one more time. What we're bringing. Where we'll hide it. What signals we'll use when we can't talk. He's good at this, better than me in some ways. The military trained him to plan for chaos. I was trained to plan for greed. Between us, we've got enough covered to be dangerous and not enough to be comfortable, which is pretty much how every job I've ever pulled has started.

The screen pops back on.

Marlena appears with Liam beside her, his hands bound in front of him. He looks roughed up—there's dried blood at his hairline, bruises I didn't see before—but he's alive. He's breathing. His eyes find mine through the camera, and I let every bit of fear I've been holding back flood my face. Let Marlena see a woman at the end of her rope.

It's not hard. The fear is real. I'm just choosing when to show it.

"Midnight approaches." Marlena checks her watch. "What's it going to be?"

Knox's grip on my hand tightens.

I look at the clock on the wall. 11:45. Fifteen minutes.

"I'll tell you where it is."

"Hailey—" Knox starts. And God bless him, the shock on his face looks genuine. We didn't rehearse that part.

"But you let them both go." I stare directly into the camera, at Marlena's perfectly composed face. "That's the deal. I give you the location, you release both of them. Unharmed."

Marlena considers. Her head tilts, bird-like.

"Acceptable. Tell me."

I take a breath.

"Northwest Territories. About two hundred kilometers northeast of Yellowknife. There's an abandoned tungsten mine—they shut it down in the eighties. The main shaft is collapsed, but there's a secondary access point on the eastern face of the mountain. You'll need climbing gear to reach it. Inside, about forty meters down, there's a natural cavern. The safe is hidden behind a false wall near the back. You're looking for a granite formation that looks like a fist."

Marlena is writing. I can hear her pen scratching.

"Thorough." She looks up. "I'll have my people verify. If you're lying, you die. If you're telling the truth . . ."

She pauses.

"We'll negotiate further terms."

The screen goes dark.

Knox stares at me. "Hailey—"

"I'm not watching her kill either of you."

Before he can respond, the door unlocks. Guards shove Liam inside, cutting his bonds before retreating. The lock clicks back into place.

He stumbles forward, catches himself on the back of a chair. His eyes are wrong somehow. Dull. Distant. He won't look at either of us.

"Liam?" I move toward him. "What did she do?"

"Nothing." His voice is flat. "I'm fine."

"You're not fine. You're—"

"I said I'm fine." He looks at me, and there's something broken there. "I just should have never put you two in this position."

Knox reaches for him, but Liam flinches away.

We spend the next few hours trying to get him to talk. Asking questions he won't answer. Offering comfort he won't accept. He sits in the corner by the tree, knees drawn up, staring at the ornaments like they hold the secrets of the universe.

Whatever happened while Marlena had him, he's not ready to share it.

Eventually, exhaustion wins.

We don't make it to the bed. We just collapse together on the floor in front of the cold hearth, Knox close, and Liam still keeping his distance. It feels like the last breath before drowning.

I fall asleep listening to their heartbeats.

I dream of diamonds and snow and a woman's laughter echoing through a mine shaft.

The screen wakes us.

Morning light streams through the windows. Christmas Day. I'd almost forgotten.

Marlena looks pleased with herself. Triumphant, even.

"Merry Christmas." She pauses for effect. "My team has verified the location. Well done, Ms. Parker. Your directions were remarkably precise."

Something cold settles in my stomach. Because I know that tone. I know what comes after it.

"However." Her smile turns vicious. "My people found the safe. And discovered you failed to mention one crucial detail."

I keep my face blank. Scared. Caught. Inside, my blood is singing.

"There's a code. A six-digit code to open it."

Knox's hand finds mine. He squeezes once. I squeeze back.

"So here's what's going to happen." Marlena leans forward, her face filling the screen. "You're coming with me to retrieve it. And I'm bringing your boyfriends along. If you want to continue withholding information . . ."

She lets the threat hang.

"Well. Let's just say fingers are easier to remove than you'd think. We'll start with theirs and work our way to yours. How does that sound?"

My throat closes. The threat is real even if the game is rigged.

"Consider it a family outing." She straightens, smoothing her collar. "Get ready. We leave in an hour."

The screen goes dark.

For a long moment, none of us move.

Then Knox turns to me, and I see the same thing on his face that I'm feeling in my chest. This is it. The plan we built in whispers with our backs to the cameras. The opening we banked everything on.

"One hour," he says.

"One hour." I'm already running through the checklist. Knives. The ammonia rig Knox built inside the coat lining. Positioning. Signals. "We need to get everything in place before they come through that door."

Liam is watching us. He looks like hell, bruised and hollow, but his eyes are tracking the conversation. Reading the room the way he always could.

"You planned for this," he says.

"We planned for this," Knox says. And there's weight in the *we* that has nothing to do with tactics.

Liam nods once, slow. "Tell me what you need me to do."

I look at him. The man who sold us out. The man who got beaten for it. The man I'm still furious with and still in love with and still need if we're going to walk out of this alive.

"Can you still fight?"

"Try and stop me."

"Then here's what's going to happen." I pull them both close, foreheads nearly touching, voices low. The cameras can see us but they can't hear us, and Marlena's too busy gloating to care what three beaten captives are whispering about. "When we get to the mine, I open the safe. That's when she stops watching us and starts watching the diamond. Knox, that's your window. Liam, you're on the guards closest to the exit. I'll handle Marlena."

Knox raises an eyebrow. "You'll handle Marlena."

"I've been handling women like Marlena since I was nineteen. She thinks she's smarter than me. That's the biggest advantage I've got. One hour," I say again. "Let's get ready. Whatever happens next, we face it together."

Liam looks at me. Then at Knox. Forgiveness, not yet, but something close. An understanding.

"Together," Liam echoes.

Knox nods once.

The clock on the wall ticks toward something new.

Chapter Thirty-Two

KNOX

They zip-tie our hands in front of us, which tells me something. Behind the back would be more secure, but front ties let you sit in a helicopter without dislocating your shoulders. These guys are professionals. They're planning for a long flight.

Front ties also mean I can reach the knife taped flat against my ribs under two layers of sweater. They didn't pat us down thoroughly enough. Marlena's people are disciplined but they're overconfident, which is exactly what Hailey predicted.

Hailey stands between me and Liam as we're marched out of the cabin for the first time in ten days. The cold is immediate and vicious, the kind that makes your nose hairs freeze on the first inhale. The wilderness stretches in every direction, white and flat and utterly devoid of anything resembling civilization.

The helicopter waits in a small clearing about fifty yards from the cabin, rotors already spinning. It's a Bell 412, civilian model but modified. I clock the reinforced skids, the extra fuel tanks. This thing has range. Whoever Marlena is, she's got serious money behind her operation.

Four guards flank us. I've been studying them since last night, cataloging details the way I used to catalog insurgent movements in Kandahar. Two Americans, one Canadian, one I can't place. All former military based on how they move, how they hold their weapons. Disciplined. No wasted motion.

The pilot makes five.

I catch Hailey's eye. She gives me the smallest shake of her head. Not yet. Too many guns, too tight a space. We wait for the mine.

She's right. We stick to the plan.

Bad odds. But we knew they'd be bad. The whole point was never to out-fight them head-on. The point is the moment Marlena opens that safe and forgets we exist.

Marlena is already inside when we climb aboard, settled into a leather seat that has no business being in a helicopter. She's wearing a cream-colored parka trimmed with silver fox fur, sunglasses pushed up on her head, gloved fingers wrapped around a travel mug of coffee. Steam curls from the lid.

She sips it as we're strapped in across from her. Takes her time with it.

"Good morning, kiddos!" She beams at us like a summer camp counselor about to announce the day's activities. "I hope everyone's ready for an adventure. I brought snacks." She gestures to a small cooler at her feet. "Trail mix, protein bars, those little cheese wheels with the red wax. Road trip essentials."

Nobody responds.

"Tough crowd." She shrugs and takes another sip of coffee. "Your loss. The cheese wheels are imported."

The guards take their positions. Two next to Marlena, two behind us. The doors close with a heavy thunk and the pitch of the rotors changes, noise filling the cabin until conversation becomes impossible without headsets.

Marlena has one. She doesn't offer us the same courtesy.

I watch the landscape tilt and fall away as we lift off. The cabin shrinks to a dark speck against the white, then disappears entirely. Nothing but wilderness in every direction. Mountains in the distance, their peaks lost in low clouds. Frozen lakes scattered below us, flat and gray.

No roads. No buildings. Nothing.

I catch Hailey's eye. She's watching the terrain too, and I can see her mind working. Calculating distances, memorizing landmarks. Probably building a map in her head the way I am. Old habits.

Liam sits on Hailey's other side, staring out the window. He's quiet and carrying bruises from his time with Marlena and guilt that runs deeper than the bruises, but his eyes are tracking the guards, the exits, the positioning of weapons. He's in the game. Hurting, but in.

I feel the knife against my ribs every time I breathe. Hailey's coat has the ammonia rig sewn into the lining. Liam has the second steak knife, passed to him in the huddle while Hailey blocked the camera's sightline with her body.

I want to hate him. Part of me does. He sold us out, made deals behind our backs, got us into this mess in the first place. But watching him now, zip-tied and silent, the bruises on his face from our fight still dark against his skin, I can't muster the energy.

We're past blame. We're in survival mode now.

The flight stretches on. One hour, then two. Marlena makes small talk through hand gestures and exaggerated lip movements, pointing out landmarks like an overeager flight attendant. That mountain. This lake. She mimes antlers at one point, then shrugs theatrically when we don't react.

Eventually she pulls out a laminated card and holds it up for us to read: THE TERRITORIES ARE BEAUTIFUL THIS TIME OF YEAR. HARSH BUT BEAUTIFUL. PERFECT FOR HIDING THINGS YOU DON'T WANT FOUND.

She flips to another card: I HAD THESE MADE SPECIALLY.

Then another: BECAUSE I KNEW YOU WOULDN'T TALK TO ME.

And another: IT'S FINE. I TALK ENOUGH FOR EVERYONE.

She winks at Hailey.

The helicopter begins descending around the two-hour mark. Below us, a makeshift airstrip emerges from the white. Just a cleared field, the snow packed down and marked with orange flags. A cluster of buildings sits at one end, low wooden structures with caved-in roofs. Old mining camp. Abandoned for decades by the look of it.

We touch down hard enough to rattle my teeth. The pilot cuts the engine and the rotors begin their slow wind-down, the noise fading enough that I can hear again.

"From here, we snowmobile." Marlena stands, adjusting her parka. "Which, full disclosure, is my favorite part. I had a whole PowerPoint presentation about the route but Kenny said it was 'too much.'" She air-quotes with her fingers, then gestures at one of the guards. "Kenny is no fun. Don't be like Kenny."

Kenny's demeanor doesn't change.

She claps her hands together. "Okay! Let's go find my diamond!"

The cold outside is brutal even with the winter gear they've provided. My fingers go numb in minutes despite the gloves. The guards load us onto snowmobiles without wasted movement. Me with one, Liam with another, Hailey riding behind Marlena.

I memorize the configuration as we pull out. Guard in front, guard behind, the rest flanking. Military convoy formation. Standard protection detail with standard weaknesses.

If I can find an opening.

The convoy heads into the wilderness.

I watch for opportunities as we ride, scanning the terrain through the face shield of my helmet. Frozen forest. Rocky outcrops. Ice-covered creeks that we cross without slowing. The terrain is rough, the snowmobiles bouncing over hidden obstacles, but our captors handle them like veterans.

They probably are. This isn't some amateur treasure hunt.

My hands are still bound. My muscles are cramped from sitting in the helicopter. I'm surrounded by armed guards on unfamiliar terrain in subzero temperatures with nothing resembling an exit strategy.

I've been in worse situations.

I'm having trouble remembering when.

We ride for what feels like forever. Ninety minutes, maybe more. The cold works its way through every layer until I stop feeling my feet. The landscape blurs into sameness, white and gray and white again, broken only by the occasional rocky outcrop.

Then the convoy slows. Stops.

We're at the base of a cliff face, massive boulders tumbled at its feet. It looks like every other rock formation we've passed, but Marlena's driver cuts the engine with the confidence of someone who's arrived exactly where he meant to.

Marlena bounces off her snowmobile. "Oh my god. Oh my god, this is happening." She grabs one of her guards by the arm. "Derek, are you seeing this? Five years. Five years, Derek."

Derek nods once.

"You could show a little enthusiasm. This is a momentous occasion." She releases him and waves at the other guards. "Clear it. Clear it, clear it, let's go."

Her team moves with efficiency. Two stay with us, weapons ready. The other two head for a gap between the boulders, clearing snow to reveal timber supports, old and weathered but still intact. A mine shaft entrance, descending into darkness.

They've been here before. Scouted it, probably. Mapped the tunnels. They just couldn't get past the safe.

That's what Hailey's for.

Someone produces industrial lights, the kind you'd use on a construction site. Generators hum to life. The darkness retreats, revealing rough-hewn walls and timber bracing and a tunnel that slopes gently downward.

"This is very Indiana Jones." Marlena peers into the entrance, delighted. "I keep hoping for booby traps, but my advance team was very disappointing on that front. Not a single giant rolling boulder."

She pulls out her phone and snaps a selfie in front of the mine entrance. Checks it, frowns, takes another one.

"Lighting's terrible," she mutters. "Derek, hold the light higher."

We descend into the mountain.

The temperature rises once we're underground, the earth providing insulation the open air couldn't. The tunnel is narrow at first, barely wide enough for two people side by side. Ice coats the walls, glittering in the industrial lights.

The guards move with the confidence of men who've walked this route before. They don't hesitate at the forks, don't consult maps. Marlena's been thorough.

But she couldn't crack the safe. Five years of resources and obsession, and she still needs Hailey for the final step.

The tunnel branches again and again. A maze. One wrong turn and you'd wander these passages until you froze or starved. I understand now why Hailey chose this place.

"Almost there," Marlena announces, checking her phone. "My team clocked it at fifteen minutes from the entrance. We're at twelve."

Three minutes later, the tunnel opens into a chamber. Natural cave formation, the ceiling arching overhead, stalactites hanging down in frozen curtains. The industrial lights throw strange shadows across the walls.

And there, set into the rock at the back of the chamber, is a safe.

Industrial grade. Serious hardware. The kind of thing you'd find in a bank vault, not buried in a forgotten mine. It's covered in frost but otherwise intact, the dial and handle still visible beneath the ice.

Marlena walks toward it slowly. For once, she's not talking. She reaches out and brushes frost from the metal surface, her movements almost reverent.

"Five years," she whispers. Then, louder. "Five years I've been looking for this. Do you know how many private investigators I've hired? How many psychics? *Psychics*, Ms. Parker. That's how desperate I was. One of them told me the diamond was 'somewhere cold.' I paid her four hundred dollars for 'somewhere cold.'"

She turns to face us, backlit by the industrial lights.

"But here we are. I guess she was right." Her composure snaps back into place, that manic brightness returning. "Now. The code, Ms. Parker." She pulls out her phone again. "And smile—I want to document this moment for posterity."

Chapter Thirty-Three

HAILEY

Six digits stand between us and whatever comes next.

The safe squats against the cave wall, frost crusted across its face. Five years since I programmed that code. Five years since I walked away from everything I was.

Marlena's staring at it like she's found God. Her crew has us positioned in a loose semicircle, guns ready. Eight of us crammed into this frozen chamber, plus her. I can feel Knox's shoulder against mine, both our wrists still bound.

"The code," Marlena says. Her breath fogs between us. "Now, Ms. Parker."

I don't move.

A guard grabs Knox from behind, forcing him down. His knees hit the stone floor hard. The guard presses a Glock to the back of his head.

"Now," Marlena repeats. No more camp counselor cheer. This is what lives underneath.

My throat closes. "Let me think—"

"One."

Knox finds my eyes. Even kneeling with a gun to his skull, he's calm. His left hand shifts against his thigh. One finger extended. We're on.

"Two."

I let the panic show on my face. There's a gun to his head and every part of me wants to scream. But the decision was made days ago in a blind spot by a fireplace, and this is me following through.

"Three."

I make my voice crack. "Three. Seven. Nine. Two. Five. Eight."

Marlena watches me for a long moment, looking for the lie. I give her nothing but a woman broken by a countdown. She must like what she sees, because her smile returns. She crosses to the safe, gloved fingers hovering over the dial. Each click sounds like a gunshot in the silence.

The door swings open.

Inside, cradled in foam I installed five years ago, sits the Snowflake Diamond. Twenty million dollars of crystallized carbon, smaller than people expect. About the size of a walnut. But the clarity is insane, flawless, throwing fractured light across the frozen walls.

Marlena lifts it like she's handling a holy relic. "Beautiful." Her voice drops to a whisper. "Worth every tedious moment." She tucks the diamond into her parka.

Liam steps forward. "Take me. Give me to Kedrov, tell him whatever story you want. But let them go. They're not part of this anymore."

Marlena laughs. "Oh, I'm absolutely giving you to the Russian. That was always the plan." A wave of her hand toward me. "But nowhere in our arrangement does it say I have to deliver you alive. Or her. You know how I feel about loose ends."

Liam goes white. "No. You said—"

"I lied." Her smile could freeze blood. "Did you really think I'd let you all live?"

The air in the chamber shifts. I feel it before I see it, that crackling tension before violence. Horror becoming calculation.

We planned for threats. Posturing. More negotiation. Not this. Not Marlena dropping every pretense with that smile on her face.

Liam recovers before I do.

He moves.

He grabs the nearest guard by the throat, wrenches the man's rifle free, slams the stock into his jaw. The guard crumples. Liam shoves his body into Marlena, sending her stumbling backward. She hits the cave wall hard, the impact knocking the wind out of her.

I'm already moving. In the chaos, with everyone's attention on Liam and the falling guard, I close the distance between me and Marlena. Her parka is still unzipped from when she tucked the diamond inside. My bound hands slip into the interior pocket, fingers closing around cold stone, and I pull it free in one smooth motion. The whole thing takes maybe two seconds. I shove the diamond into my own jacket and step back before she even catches her breath.

Five years out of the game, and my hands still remember.

Then the cave erupts.

Liam fires into the ceiling. The shots are so loud in the enclosed space that my ears ring instantly. Rock dust rains down. Guards scramble, their formation shattering.

Knox has his knife out. I don't see him cut the zip ties but his hands are free and he's pulling the ammonia rig from inside my coat—his hands are steadier than mine and we planned for this part. He cracks the seal and hurls it at the two guards nearest the entrance. The container splits on impact and the fumes hit them like a wall. They drop, choking, clawing at their faces.

I'm on my feet before I decide to move. The guard nearest me raises his weapon but I'm already there, my boot connecting with his kneecap. He goes down screaming. His gun clatters across ice.

"Knox!"

I grab for the weapon but my bound hands won't work the grip.

He's already scooping it up, pivoting, firing. Another guard drops. One left plus Marlena.

The chamber is chaos. Too many bodies, too close. Bullets whining off rock. Someone screams. Blood spraying across frost.

Liam's grappling with the last guard, using his rifle as a club. Marlena is pushing herself off the wall, one hand reaching into her pocket. Her face twists when she finds it empty.

Her eyes find mine.

I smile at her.

Knox tracks her with his weapon as she backs toward the tunnel. "Don't move!"

She stops. "You won't shoot me. You need me to get out of here. My people control the transport."

"Try me."

His finger tightens. I can see how badly he wants to pull the trigger.

But she's right. Even if we made it back to the airstrip, neither Knox nor Liam can fly a helicopter. We need her pilot, her vehicles, her way out. Killing her strands us here.

One of the guards recovers, tackling Knox from behind. The gun goes flying. They grapple, Knox trying to break free, the guard bigger, uninjured, not fighting with a handicap.

An elbow catches Knox's ribs. I hear the air leave him.

I scan the floor. My fingers close around a chunk of broken timber, rough and heavy.

The guard rears back for another hit and I swing with everything I have.

Wood meets skull with a wet crack.

He drops.

Knox rolls away, blood dripping from his split lip. His eyes find mine. Thanks. Relief. Something else.

"Ties," I say. "Off. Now."

Liam pulls the steak knife from his waistband and cuts my zip ties first, then his own, flexing his fingers to get blood back into them.

"Marlena." Liam nods toward the tunnel. "She's running."

Her silhouette is disappearing into the darkness.

Knox grabs his dropped weapon, sighting down the passage. The angle is bad. Too many curves. He lowers the gun. "We need to move."

I look at Liam. "Can we trust you?"

"I understand why you wouldn't." His gaze doesn't waver. "But I'm all you've got."

Knox meets my eyes. Nods once.

We run.

Marlena ripped the work lights off their stakes as she went. Smart. The tunnel is treacherous in the dark. I lead because the path is still burned into my memory. Left at the fork. Right at the rock that looks like a fist. Sideways through the narrow section where the walls close in.

Behind us, footsteps. The guards regrouping, coming fast and better equipped. It's only a matter of time.

Daylight hits us like a slap. Gray and blinding after the darkness. The cold seizes my lungs on the first breath.

Marlena is already outside, screaming orders. "Get the girl! Find her and bring her to me!" The snowmobiles wait in a loose row, but guards are taking defensive positions around them. Six more, at least.

"Outnumbered," I say.

"Outgunned," Liam adds, wiping blood from his eye.

Knox scans the terrain. "The snowmobiles. If we can reach them—"

"We'll be dead before we get close," Liam finishes.

A bullet sparks off the rock near Knox's head. We duck back into the tunnel entrance.

"Ideas?"

Liam's quiet for a beat. His eyes track upward, past the entrance, to the slope above us. Steep. Fresh powder piled heavy after the recent storm.

"The mountain," he says. "Look at it."

I follow his gaze. A massive cornice hangs near the top, overhanging and precarious.

Knox catches on. "You want to trigger an avalanche."

"It'll bury the entrance. Cut us off from pursuit."

"And trap us in the mountain."

"Not if we're already moving." Liam's voice is steady. "We trigger it, but we're on the snowmobiles first. Use the chaos."

I study the cornice. The way the snow hangs, ready to break. "How do we trigger it?"

"Gunfire. Enough shots in the right spot." He points. "That section. It's already cracking."

"Who's our best shot?"

Knox doesn't hesitate. "Me."

"Then you shoot."

It's insane. The kind of plan that kills people more often than it saves them.

Knox meets my eyes. "Go."

Liam and I burst from the tunnel, sprinting for the snowmobiles. Bullets kick up around our feet. I hear Liam grunt as one grazes his arm, but he doesn't slow.

We reach the machines. I throw myself onto the nearest one, hands shaking on the ignition. The engine catches. Liam's already slashing fuel lines on the others, gasoline spilling across the white ground.

The guards are closing in. Twenty yards. Fifteen.

I look back at Knox in the tunnel entrance, rifle raised, sighting on the cornice.

"Now!" Liam yells.

Knox fires. Once. Twice. Three times.

Silence.

Then a crack so loud it vibrates in my chest. The cornice breaks. A massive chunk of ice and snow separates from the slope.

And the whole mountain starts to move.

Knox runs.

The avalanche is faster. A wall of white roaring down behind him. I gun the engine, pulling around, reaching.

He launches himself onto the back of my snowmobile as the slide hits.

The world disappears. Snow in my eyes, my mouth, everywhere. We're racing ahead of it, barely staying in front. Liam beside us on the second machine. The roar drowns out everything.

We burst free and keep going.

Into the forest. Engines screaming. Trees closing in around us.

Five minutes. Ten. No sound of pursuit.

I finally stop. The engine idles, ticking. My hands won't stop shaking.

Liam pulls up beside us and cuts his motor. For a long moment, nobody speaks. Just breathing. Just being alive.

Knox's arms tighten around my waist from behind. "We need to keep moving. Get as much distance as possible before she regroups."

"She won't stop," Liam says. "Not after five years of hunting for that thing. She'll tear these mountains apart looking for us."

I reach into my jacket pocket. Cold metal. Crystallized carbon.

"She can look all she wants."

I pull the diamond out, holding it up. Even in the dim forest light, it throws rainbows.

Knox goes still behind me. "How?"

"When Liam tackled her, everyone was looking at him. Her coat was unzipped." I turn the diamond over in my palm, watching it catch the light. "Old habits. You can take the girl out of the game, but apparently you can't take the game out of the girl."

Liam stares at it. Then at me. Then he laughs, broken and exhausted and real.

"You magnificent thief."

Knox's breath warms my ear. "That's my girl."

I tuck the diamond back into my pocket.

"Let's go."

Chapter Thirty-Four

LIAM

We're stopped in a small clearing, surrounded by trees, miles from anywhere. The adrenaline that got us out of that mine is wearing off fast, leaving behind exhaustion and about six different flavors of guilt. I stand apart from Knox and Hailey because that's where I belong right now. On the outside. Watching them not look at me.

My ribs ache where one of Marlena's guards got a lucky elbow in. There's a graze along my left arm where a bullet caught the sleeve and kept going—shallow, barely bleeding, but it stings like hell in the cold. My wrists are raw from the zip ties. None of that hurts as much as the silence.

"I need to tell you both something," I say.

Knox crosses his arms. Hailey doesn't change, which is somehow worse.

Here goes nothing. Here goes everything.

"Marlena found me a few weeks ago. Not five years ago. Recently." I force myself to keep eye contact even though every instinct screams to look away. "She'd been hunting us since the theft, but it took her years to track me down. And when she finally did, she didn't just want the diamond. She wanted what she was owed.

"Marlena and Kedrov were married. Five years ago, when we pulled the job, they were already in the middle of a divorce. A vicious one. The Snowflake was listed as a joint asset—twenty million dollars that was supposed to be split between them in the settlement. But after we stole it, Kedrov reported it missing. On paper, the diamond ceased to exist. Which meant Marlena's share of it ceased to exist too."

Hailey's eyes narrow. I can see her running the math.

"It gets worse. Kedrov had already moved the diamond into her column during the asset division. He knew it was gone before the lawyers finalized everything, but he let it stay on her side of the ledger. So when the settlement went through, Marlena was credited with receiving a twenty-million-dollar diamond that no longer existed. She got less of everything else because of it. Less real estate. Less liquid cash. Less of his tech portfolio."

"He used our theft to cheat her in the divorce," Hailey says.

"She lost tens of millions because of a diamond she never held in her hands. A diamond we stole." I let that sit. "So when she tracked me down, this wasn't about collecting a pretty stone. This was five years of rage at her ex-husband, five years of being humiliated by a man she already hated, and the two thieves who handed him the ammunition."

The wind picks up, cutting through my jacket. Nobody speaks.

"I'm so fucking sorry." The words feel inadequate. They are inadequate. "I can't express it enough. To either of you."

Knox goes still. Hailey wraps her arms around herself, and I can't tell if it's the cold or if she's trying to hold herself together.

"Everything in the cabin—that was real." I need them to understand this part. "My feelings. The connection. All of it. I wasn't faking. I was trying to keep you alive while figuring out how to get us all out of this mess." A pause. "I know that doesn't make it better."

More silence. The trees creak around us. Somewhere in the distance, a bird calls out, oblivious to the disaster happening in this clearing.

"You should have told us." Hailey's voice is quiet but steady. "In the cabin. When we were alone. You should have trusted us."

"I know." I sit on the edge of my snowmobile because my legs don't feel entirely trustworthy right now. "I should have done a lot of things. I for sure should have done less. I fucked up. All of it." My hands hang between my knees. "But I'm here now. And we're alive. And Marlena doesn't have the diamond."

Knox exhales. For a long moment I think he's going to tell me exactly where I can shove my apology, and honestly, I'd deserve it.

"Well." He uncrosses his arms. "We're all guilty of fucking up. But right now we need to focus on survival." His gaze sweeps the clearing, the trees, the sky. "We're in the middle of nowhere, freezing, with no real plan and a deranged woman who wants her diamond back and us dead."

"Not quite square one." I pull out the items I grabbed from the emergency kit before we fled—maps, compass, emergency beacon. "I know where we are. And I know how to get us somewhere safe."

"Where?"

"There's a ranger station about forty miles northwest. It'll be manned, even in winter. We get there, we call for help, we get extracted."

Knox's eyebrows rise. "Forty miles on snowmobiles. In this cold. With no survival gear." He shakes his head. "That's nearly impossible."

"Nearly isn't never." I unfold the map, trace the route with my finger. "And it's our only shot."

"What about the helicopter?" Hailey asks.

"Neither of us can fly one," Knox says. "And even if we could, Marlena's pilot isn't going to hand over the keys."

"So. Ranger station."

We check supplies. One snowmobile has a partial emergency kit—some flares, a basic first aid kit, a survival blanket that looks like someone sat on it in 1987. Not enough, but something. The fuel gauges show half tanks, which should be enough for forty miles if we're careful and don't hit any obstacles.

The maps show the ranger station clearly—remote but accessible if we follow the frozen river system northwest.

"We need to move," Hailey says. Her jaw is set, her eyes clear. Whatever emotional reckoning is coming, she's filed it away for later. "Before Marlena's people regroup. Before this cold becomes a bigger problem."

We mount up—Hailey and Knox on one machine, me on the other. No one talks about what comes after. If we survive this. If we make it to safety. Then we'll deal with the question of whether this fractured thing between us can ever be put back together.

First, we have to not die.

I take point, navigating by compass and the position of the sun through the trees. The terrain is brutal. Steep slopes that make the snowmobiles whine in protest. Dense forest where we have to slow to a crawl to weave between trunks. Frozen lakes we cross holding our breath, listening for any crack in the ice beneath us.

Every mile feels like ten. The cold seeps into everything—through my jacket, through my gloves, into my bones. My face goes numb first, then my fingers. I flex them constantly on the handlebars just to confirm they still work.

Two hours in, and we're close. According to my calculations, maybe five or six miles from the station. Close enough that I can almost taste hot coffee and heated rooms and someone else being in charge of keeping us alive.

That's when I notice the sky changing.

Not darkening from sunset. Wrong direction for that. These are clouds rolling in from the west, thick and heavy, the kind that mean business.

Then the first flakes hit my visor.

Within minutes, it's not flakes anymore. It's a wall of white coming at us sideways.

"We need shelter!" I shout over the rising wind, but I'm not sure they can hear me. I signal frantically, pointing at the sky, at the chaos surrounding us.

Knox pulls up alongside me. His face is grim. "How far?"

"Five miles. Maybe six." The words taste like failure. "We can't push through this. We'd get turned around, drive off a cliff, freeze to death ten feet from safety without ever knowing it."

He stares into the whiteout, and I can see him doing the math. Weighing the risk. We're so goddamn close.

"We stop," he says. "Find shelter. Wait it out."

I scan the valley we've descended into, steep slopes on either side, forest dense enough to offer some protection but not enough to survive a full blizzard.

Then I spot it. A shape through the trees that doesn't belong to nature.

"There!" I point. "Old hunting cabin. This area used to have trappers, decades ago. Some of the cabins still stand."

We push toward it, visibility dropping by the second. By the time we reach the structure, I can barely see ten feet ahead.

The cabin is small and half destroyed. The roof has partially collapsed on one side, and one wall is more gap than wall. But three walls are intact, and through the doorway I can see a stone hearth.

It'll have to do.

We pull the snowmobiles close to the door, cutting the engines. The sudden silence is almost disorienting—except it's not really silence. The wind screams past us, driving ice and debris into every exposed inch of skin.

"Move!" Knox grabs the supplies. Hailey's already through the door. I follow, and the three of us crowd into the relatively sheltered space just as the storm becomes something biblical.

Inside is barely warmer than outside. The wind finds every crack, every hole, every gap where the structure has surrendered to time. The collapsed section of roof lets in a steady cascade of white that's already forming a drift in the corner.

But the hearth is intact. And intact means potential.

Knox takes command immediately, which is fine by me. He needs to be doing something, and I need to not be in charge of anything for a few minutes.

"Firewood. Anything burnable. Move."

We scavenge. There's old furniture in one corner—a broken chair, the remains of a table. Timbers from the collapsed section that are dry enough to catch. I start stacking it in the hearth while Hailey tears apart what's left of a wooden crate.

My hands are shaking. From cold, from exhaustion, from the adrenaline crashing out of my system. But I get the fire laid out, get the emergency matches from the kit, and on the third try, I get a flame to catch.

It grows. Slowly at first, then with more confidence. Heat. Finally, some goddamn heat.

We huddle around it, close enough that my cheeks sting from the temperature change. Knox goes through our supplies methodically. No food. The survival items from the snowmobile kit. The emergency blanket, crinkly silver mylar barely big enough for one person. The first aid kit. A handful of chemical heat packs that'll last maybe four hours at best.

Not great. But not nothing.

"We're going to have to share body heat," Knox says. His tone is matter-of-fact, clinical. None of us acknowledge what that actually means—pressed together all night, intimate whether we want to be or not.

But it's survival. And survival trumps awkward.

The storm rages. Hours blur together. We feed the hearth constantly, taking shifts to stay awake and maintain it. When the easy fuel runs out—the furniture, the dry timbers—I look at the remains of what we have and then at the door.

"I'll get more."

"Don't be stupid," Knox says.

"It's not stupid. The trees are right there. Dead branches. Won't take long."

Hailey grabs my arm. "You'll get lost. You won't be able to see anything."

"I'll tie myself to the doorframe. Old trick." I'm already pulling off my outer layer—too bulky for moving through dense brush. "I'll be fine."

I'm not fine.

The storm is worse than I expected. The wind nearly knocks me down the second I step outside, and visibility is measured in inches, not feet. But I tied a length of cord from the emergency kit to the doorframe, and I follow it out as far as it'll reach.

The trees are closer than I remembered. Small mercy. I break branches by feel more than sight, snapping anything that'll give, stuffing them inside my jacket because my arms are already shaking too hard to carry them properly.

By the time I follow the cord back to the cabin, I can't feel my hands at all. My face is a mask of ice. My legs move like they belong to someone else, stiff and uncoordinated.

The door opens. Hands grab me. Pull me inside.

"Jesus Christ." That's Knox. He's stripping my wet outer layer off before I can protest. Hailey wraps the emergency blanket around my shoulders, but it's not enough. Nothing feels like enough.

"You're hypothermic." Knox is checking my eyes, my reflexes. "Mild, but getting worse."

"I'm f-fine." My teeth are chattering so hard I can barely get the word out.

"You're not." He exchanges a look with Hailey over my head. Some silent communication passes between them. "We're all getting under that blanket. Right now."

We arrange ourselves on the floor near the hearth. Me in the middle—I'm too cold to argue about it. Knox presses against my left side, solid and warm. Hailey curves into my right, her body fitting against mine like we've done this a hundred times.

We have done this. Different circumstances. Different everything. But muscle memory doesn't care about context.

The emergency blanket barely stretches around all three of us, but we make it work. My shivers are violent at first, whole-body tremors that make my teeth clash together. Slowly, agonizingly slowly, the combined heat starts to seep in.

I feel Hailey's breath against my neck. Knox's arm is tight around both of us, anchoring us together. Neither of them speaks.

"This feels familiar," Hailey murmurs eventually.

Despite everything—the cold, the guilt, the absolute clusterfuck that brought us here—I feel Knox's body shift in what might be a suppressed laugh.

"Minus the king-size bed and gourmet kitchen," he says.

"And the psychotic billionaire watching our every move," I add.

We're quiet again. The storm screams outside. Our breaths sync up without anyone trying.

"I'm sorry. I know I keep saying it but . . ." The words come out before I can stop them. "I'll say it every single day, hour, minute, if it means you both will forgive me."

Knox is silent for a long moment. I can feel the tension in him, the war between anger and something else. He's been furious with me since the truth came out, and he has every right to be.

But we're pressed together in a collapsed cabin in the middle of a blizzard, and I nearly froze to death getting firewood to keep us all alive, and I don't know what any of that is worth except that it's what I have.

"I know," he says. "I'm still pissed. But I know."

"Me too," Hailey whispers. "And you don't need to ask for forgiveness. We've all done things that need forgiveness, but we also are who we are. I don't want to change you. I don't want to change Knox. And I sure as hell hope you both never want to change me."

Knox nods. "She's right. Fuck forgiveness. Let's just move on."

We stay like that. Conserving heat. Taking turns sleeping while one stays awake to keep the hearth fed. The storm howls through the gaps in the walls, relentless, like it's trying to claw its way in. But the three of us are a closed system now, sharing warmth, sharing breath, sharing this small pocket of survival we've carved out of the chaos.

My body slowly stops shaking. Knox's grip loosens slightly as he relaxes into sleep. Hailey's fingers find mine under the blanket, squeeze once, let go.

We're alive.

Together, for now.

And yeah . . . fuck forgiveness.

Chapter Thirty-Five

HAILEY

Dawn. The storm is gone, the sky a hard blue, everything buried under fresh powder.

We made it through the night.

I open my eyes between Knox and Liam, every muscle in my body screaming as I shift. The fire burned down to coals hours ago, and the cold has crept back in.

"Hey." Knox's voice is rough. "You okay?"

"I'm alive. I have all my fingers and toes." I force myself to sit up. "That's the bar we're working with."

Liam stirs beside me, his face still too pale but his eyes clear. "Storm's passed."

"Gold star for observation."

I push to my feet and stumble toward what's left of the doorway. The wilderness stretches out before us—mountains in the distance, trees heavy with white, everything pristine and deadly.

Knox appears at my shoulder. "How much daylight?"

Liam checks his watch. "Six hours. Maybe seven."

"And the ranger station?"

"Maybe six miles. If the snowmobiles work. If the fuel held."

A lot of ifs.

Knox moves first, wading through knee-deep powder toward where we parked the machines. They're half-buried now. He starts clearing snow while Liam works on the second one.

I watch them move in tandem. Something shifted between them during those long hours pressed together for warmth. I caught fragments of low conversations while drifting in and out of sleep. Walls coming down somewhere.

When they come back, Knox's hand lands on Liam's shoulder for a moment before dropping away.

"Both operational?" I ask.

"Both operational. Fuel's lower than I'd like, but we should make it."

We strip the cabin of anything useful, which amounts to almost nothing. Liam pockets his compass and maps, and we mount up—me behind Knox, Liam on the second machine.

The terrain has transformed overnight. What was rough before is now smoothed over, dangerous edges hidden under white. We move carefully, Liam in the lead, neither of us willing to rush when one wrong move could send us into something we can't see.

About an hour in, Liam signals and pulls over.

"What?" Knox cuts his engine.

Liam unfolds the map. "Lake ahead. Massive. We can go around—adds four hours we don't have with these fuel levels." He looks up. "Or we cross and cut our time in half. I'm pretty sure the ice is solid, but it is a large body of water so . . ."

Knox looks at me. "Your call."

"Why is it my call?"

"Because you're the one sitting on the back if we fall through."

Fair point. Four extra hours means running out of fuel in the middle of nowhere. Crossing means gambling on ice that might crack. Both options end in potential death.

"Cross," I say. "Fast."

The lake appears twenty minutes later—a frozen plain stretching to the horizon. Liam tests the edge first, walking out ten feet, stomping hard, listening. The ice groans but holds.

"Stay spread out," he says. "If one of us goes through, the other needs to be far enough away not to follow."

"Cheerful."

"I try."

We start across. The engines seem too loud against all that emptiness.

I hold my breath without meaning to, ears straining for any sound of cracking. The ice pops and settles beneath us—natural, but every noise makes my stomach drop.

Halfway. Three-quarters.

I let myself start to believe we're going to make it.

That's when I look back.

Shapes in the distance. A lot of them. Following the tracks we left in the fresh powder.

"Company," I say, tapping Knox's shoulder.

He looks. Goes rigid.

Liam's already noticed. I count the snowmobiles as they emerge from the tree line. Five. Six. Seven. All of them moving fast, fanning out in pursuit formation.

She brought everyone. Whatever forces she had left after the avalanche, she pulled them all together for this.

"How the hell did she find us?" Knox asks.

Liam doesn't answer. He reaches into his pocket and pulls out the emergency beacon he grabbed yesterday. A small red light blinks on it. Steady. Persistent.

His face goes white. "It's been transmitting. The whole time. I didn't check if it was already activated."

"You've been leading them right to us?"

"I didn't know."

No time to fight about it. Seven snowmobiles are closing the gap, and Marlena's people have fresh machines with full fuel tanks.

"Move." Knox guns the engine.

We race across the ice. The machines scream beneath us. Wind tears at my face. The pursuit is closing—I can hear their engines now, a swarm of angry hornets getting louder.

Three hundred yards from shore. Two hundred.

The ice cracks.

The sound is massive, a splintering that comes from everywhere at once. I feel the snowmobile drop, the surface sagging, and Knox swerves hard.

We hit solid ground as a section behind us collapses into dark water. Two of the pursuing snowmobiles veer wildly, one of them skidding sideways before the rider regains control. We don't stop to watch—we plunge into the forest, branches whipping past.

We slow down once I can't hear them anymore. Liam pulls up beside us, face ashen.

"How far?" Knox asks.

"Two miles. Maybe three." Liam looks back. "The ice bought us time, but not much. They'll find a way around."

"How many did we lose?"

"Maybe one went in. The rest will make it."

Six against three. And that's assuming Marlena doesn't have more people waiting somewhere.

"We need to be ready," Knox says.

The ranger station appears through the trees. Small building, Canadian flag, smoke from the chimney.

We skid to a stop and stumble off the machines.

The woman who opens the door stops me mid-panic.

She's not what I expected. Brown hair spills out from under a wool beanie in wild curls, framing a sun-freckled face with deep brown eyes. Late twenties, maybe, with the lean build of someone who spends her life outdoors. No makeup, no pretense—just clean skin and an easy confidence that makes me trust her immediately. The rifle in her hands looks as natural as an extension of her arm.

"Who the hell are you people?" Her voice is calm, curious even, like we're an interesting problem that wandered onto her doorstep.

We explain in fragments—kidnapped, hunted, armed people coming. She listens without interrupting, her head tilted slightly, those dark eyes moving between the three of us like she's cataloging everything we're not saying along with everything we are.

Halfway through, she holds up a hand. "Wait. Three people, held in a cabin, armed guards." She looks at Knox. "Did you rig something to send a signal? Some kind of W-Fi broadcast, maybe a week ago?"

The three of us go still.

"I picked up a ping on my equipment. Garbled, no coordinates, but it was repeating on a loop for about fifteen minutes before it cut out. Couldn't trace the source, but I flagged it with RCMP dispatch and started keeping an eye out." She looks us over. "That was you."

"That was us," Liam says. "We pulled a Wi-Fi module out of a surveillance camera and jury-rigged it to broadcast."

"Well, it worked. Sort of. Not enough to find you, but enough that when three people show up at my door looking like they crawled out of a war zone, I'm not starting from zero.

"How many?" she asks. "Coming after you."

"Six that we saw. Maybe more."

"Armed?"

"Serious hardware. Tactical weapons, body armor."

She nods slowly, like we just told her a storm was coming and she's calculating how much firewood she'll need. "Well. That's not ideal." She steps back from the door. "Get inside. I'll make coffee and call for extraction. Not necessarily in that order."

The station is warm. She moves through the small space with easy efficiency, one hand on the radio while the other sets a kettle on the stove. Her voice is steady as she coordinates with RCMP dispatch, rattling off coordinates and situation details like she's ordering supplies.

"Four to six hours," she says when she hangs up. "Nearest helicopter. Protocols and paperwork." She pulls three mugs down from a shelf. "Bureaucracy doesn't move fast even when people are trying to kill you. Cream and sugar?"

"Black," Knox says.

"Same," from Liam.

"Whatever you're having," I manage.

She pours with a steady hand, then doctors her own mug with enough honey to make my teeth ache just watching. "I'm Michelle, by the way. Since we're apparently going to be under siege together, seems like we should be on a first-name basis."

"Hailey. That's Knox, and Liam."

She looks the three of us over. "And there's more to this than you're telling me, but that's fine. People end up out here for all kinds of reasons. Most of them don't want to talk about it. I'm not going to ask questions."

"You're taking this very calmly," Knox says.

Michelle shrugs, those curls bouncing. "I've been doing this job for almost ten years. Started right out of high school—only thing I ever wanted to do. Three weeks ago I had to chase a wolverine out of my storage shed with a broom. Last summer a guy showed up convinced he was being hunted by the CIA. Turned out he'd eaten some bad mushrooms, but I didn't know that for the first six hours." She takes a sip of her coffee. "Armed mercenaries are new, I'll admit. But panicking never helped anyone."

Something about her steadiness is infectious. I feel my shoulders drop slightly, the tension easing just a fraction.

"The station," Knox says. "How defensible is it?"

"Built to handle the worst this territory can throw at it. Walls are reinforced—we get grizzlies up here, and they're persistent when they're hungry. Windows are small, good sight lines. I've got ammunition, supplies, and a backup generator." She meets his eyes. "I'm not saying we can hold off an army. But six people? We can make them work for it."

"You don't have to do this," Liam says. "We can lead them away from here, draw them off—"

"Stop." Michelle holds up a hand. "You showed up at my station asking for help. That means you're under my protection until the RCMP gets here. That's how this works." Her jaw sets. "I don't hand people over to be killed. Not ever. So drink your coffee and let's figure out how we're going to keep everyone alive."

I decide I like her.

Knox and Michelle move through the station together, checking sight lines, counting ammunition, discussing approaches and choke points. She knows the terrain, knows where attackers would likely position, knows the weaknesses and how to compensate for them.

Liam works the radio equipment, boosting the signal to reach a bar in a nearby town.

"Armed hostiles incoming," he tells whoever answers. "Anyone with a gun, we'll pay whatever you ask. Get here fast."

"Long shot," Michelle says when he hangs up. "But people up here help each other. Bill at the Rusted Moose knows everyone within fifty miles. If anyone's coming, he'll send them."

We wait. We fortify.

I help Michelle gather anything useful—flares, gasoline, kitchen knives. She moves through her supplies with practiced efficiency, handing me things without needing to explain what they're for.

"You've done this before," I say. "Not the mercenary thing. But the survival thing."

"Grew up out here." She pulls a box of ammunition from a high shelf. "My dad was a trapper. Mom was a bush pilot. I learned to shoot before I learned to drive." A quick smile that transforms her whole face. "City people think the wilderness is peaceful. It's not. It's constantly trying to kill you in creative ways. You either learn to handle that or you don't last long."

"Why stay?"

She pauses, considering. "Because it's honest. The wilderness doesn't pretend to be anything it's not. It'll kill you, sure, but it won't lie to you first."

She opens a gun cabinet and pulls out a second rifle, checks it, hands it to me. "You know how to shoot?"

"Yeah." I take the rifle, feel its weight, check the safety out of habit.

"Good. It's a bolt-action, so take your time between shots. Make them count." She hands me a box of rounds. "We don't have unlimited ammo."

The weight of it feels good in my hands. Solid. Useful. I'm done being the person who hides and waits.

Michelle spots them first. She's at the window, coffee mug still in hand, when her whole body goes still.

"Incoming. Six machines." A pause. "No, seven. There's another one hanging back."

Marlena. Of course she'd stay out of the initial line of fire.

She dismounts and walks forward until I can see her face. We've cost her time, resources, reputation. She's done playing.

"Ms. Parker. Mr. Bishop. Mr. Calloway." Her voice carries clearly. "Come out. Return what's mine. I'll make your deaths quick."

Michelle sets her coffee down and picks up her rifle. "That her?"

"That's her."

"She always this dramatic?"

"You have no idea."

Michelle moves to the window. "Not happening," she calls out. "These people are under my protection. Turn around and leave, or things are going to get ugly."

Marlena laughs. "How charming. The park ranger thinks she's in a Western." She gestures at her people. "Twelve professionals against four? I admire the spirit, but let's be realistic."

"Five minutes," Michelle says calmly. "Then I start shooting. Your choice how this goes."

She steps back and checks her ammunition. "She's going to attack. People like that don't back down."

"You sure about this?" Knox asks.

Michelle's eyes are steady. "I told you. I don't hand people over. Not ever." She moves to her position. "Besides, I don't like her. The dramatics are annoying."

Despite everything, I almost laugh.

Knox takes the main window. Liam takes the side. Michelle guards the back. I position myself at the smaller window near the door, rifle braced against my shoulder.

Five minutes pass.

Marlena signals.

Her people open fire.

Bullets punch through the boarded windows and thud into walls. I duck below the sill, then rise just enough to sight down the barrel.

A figure is moving between trees, trying to get closer. I track him, steady my breathing, and squeeze the trigger.

He drops.

"Nice," Michelle calls from across the room.

Knox returns fire with measured precision—no panic, just methodical targeting. Liam covers his angle.

"Two o'clock, behind the big spruce," Michelle calls out. "He keeps poking his head up."

Knox adjusts, fires. The man crumples.

Glass shatters. Boards splinter. I work the bolt, chamber another round, and wait for my next opening.

"They're flanking left!" Liam shouts.

"I see them." Knox shifts, fires twice. One of them drops.

"Nice shot," Michelle says. "The one behind him is mine."

Her rifle cracks. He goes down.

Movement at my window. Two of them now, using the chaos as cover. I sight on the one in front, fire, work the bolt, swing to the second. He sees me aiming and tries to dive behind a snowbank. Too slow. I squeeze the trigger and he collapses into the snow.

My ears are ringing. My hands are steady. Funny how that works—I'm calmer now than I've been in days. Something to do, finally. Something I can control.

The siege stretches on. Marlena's people try to advance, get driven back. They flank again, find every approach covered. But Knox is rationing shots now, his jaw tighter every time he pulls the trigger.

An hour in, two hours, ammunition running low.

"We need those townspeople," Liam says during a brief lull. "Where the hell are they?"

"Takes time to mobilize." Michelle's changing position, covering a gap. "Bill has to call around, people have to gear up, drive out here. Could be another hour."

"We might not have another hour."

"Then we make it stretch."

I check my rounds. Six left.

Engines. New ones. Coming from the north.

Everyone freezes.

Knox risks a look and his whole body relaxes. "It's them. Dozen machines, maybe more."

I scramble to see. A convoy of snowmobiles is roaring in from the tree line, rough-looking men and women with hunting rifles and the kind of expressions that say they're not here to negotiate.

"Bill came through," Michelle says. There's satisfaction in her voice. "Told you. People help each other up here."

The locals don't ask questions. They see attackers shooting at the ranger station and they open fire. Marlena's crew gets caught in a crossfire, outgunned and outflanked.

Three of her people go down. The others break and run, engines roaring as they disappear into the forest.

Marlena stands her ground.

Even with everything falling apart around her, she doesn't move. She's staring at the window where I'm visible through a gap.

Our eyes meet.

I see rage. Calculation. She's already planning her next move.

Then she turns and runs.

The gunfire stops.

Michelle heads outside to talk to the locals. Through the window I watch her move among them, shaking hands, clapping shoulders, her curls bright against all the dark winter gear. They clearly know her, respect her. One grizzled old guy actually picks her up in a bear hug that makes her laugh.

Knox, Liam, and I stay inside.

I set the rifle down carefully—my hands are shaking now that it's over—and lean against the wall. Slide down until I'm sitting. Liam sits beside me. Knox follows.

"She's still out there," Liam says.

"I know."

"She's not going to stop."

"I know."

I pull the Snowflake Diamond from my pocket and hold it up. Even here, it catches the light.

"So what do we do with this?"

Knox looks at it. At me. At Liam.

"Later," he says. "Right now I just want to sit here and be alive."

I lean my head against his shoulder. Liam's hand finds mine.

The door opens and Michelle steps back in, stomping snow off her boots. "RCMP's twenty minutes out now. Locals are going to stick around until they get here, make sure your friend doesn't circle back." She looks at the three of us on the floor. "You did good. All of you."

"We didn't do anything," I say. "You and your neighbors saved us."

"You survived long enough to get here. That counts." She picks up her coffee mug, finds it empty, and sighs. "I'm making more. Anyone want some?"

We all nod.

She moves to the kettle, humming something under her breath, and I watch her for a moment. Untamed curls, steady hands, easy confidence.

"Hey, Michelle?"

She looks over her shoulder. "Yeah?"

"Thanks. For everything."

She smiles, and it reaches her brown eyes. "That's what neighbors are for."

Outside, I can hear helicopter rotors approaching. Help coming. Statements and paperwork and eventually, maybe, home.

But Marlena is still out there.

This isn't over.

Chapter Thirty-Six

KNOX

The authorities finally arrive—RCMP in helicopters, taking statements, securing the scene. But it's going to be a long process. Hours of questions, documentation. Michelle offers us a back room to rest while we wait our turn for interviews.

The room is small—cots, a space heater, nothing fancy. But it's private. Safe. I close the door, and for the first time since escaping the cabin, we're alone together.

The adrenaline is still coursing through me. Combat high, survival instinct, the need that comes after nearly dying. I can see it in Hailey and Liam too—the same wired energy.

"We lived," Hailey says to me, shaky. "We actually lived, Knox."

I pull her into my arms. She's trembling—delayed shock. I hold her tight, grounding her. Over her shoulder, I see Liam, standing apart, uncertain.

I make a decision. Extending my hand. "Get over here."

Liam hesitates. "Knox—"

"Now."

Liam moves into the embrace. The three of us together, arms around each other, breathing hard, alive. The touch shifts. Need. Want. The connection from the cabin, still there despite everything.

I tilt Hailey's face up, kissing her hard. She responds immediately. Then I'm turning to Liam, claiming his mouth too. Liam makes a sound—surprise, relief, desire—and kisses back.

I can feel Liam's stubble against my lips, the roughness a contrast to Hailey's softness. The room is warm, too warm, but it's not just the space heater. It's us, the heat between us, the desperation to feel alive after staring death in the face.

Hailey's hands are at my waist, gripping tightly, her breath hot on my neck. Liam's body is pressed against mine, his heart pounding in sync with ours. It's chaotic, messy, but there's a rhythm to it, a dance we all know the steps to.

I pull back slightly, just enough to see their faces. Hailey's eyes are wide, pupils dilated. Liam's gaze is intense, focused. There's a question there, a silent conversation. We've crossed a line, but there's no going back. Not after everything we've been through.

Hailey reaches up, her hand cupping my cheek. She turns my head to face her, her lips brushing against mine softly this time. It's a stark contrast to the earlier desperation, but it's no less intense. Liam's hand is at the small of my back, supporting me.

The sound of voices outside the door brings us back to reality. We should pull apart—but fuck that. I need them now.

I lean forward, kissing Hailey again, and she melts into me. Liam's hand lifts to my neck, tugging gently until I turn and his mouth finds mine. He tastes of blood and winter, and there's a rawness in both of us that makes it urgent, almost violent. Hailey bites my lower lip, just shy of pain, and when I gasp she laughs, breathy and reckless.

We tumble onto one of the cots. The scratchy wool bites my skin, but I don't care. Everything is about sensation: the slide of Hailey's hands under my shirt, the way Liam's fingers move from my hair to my jaw, holding me firm. I kiss them both in turn, greedy, not willing to waste a single second of this borrowed peace.

When I press Hailey's body down, Liam follows, wrapping his arms around us both. We move together, a tangle of limbs and fevered mouths, until I'm dizzy with it. It's not about sex—at least not just that. It's about affirmation, hunger, the certainty that we made it out and are still here.

"Fuck me," I hear her say.

Liam looks as startled as I do, his eyes shooting to mine and then to Hailey, searching for confirmation. She repeats it, some dark smile playing at the corners of her mouth, and then pulls me in by the belt loops as if daring either of us to say no.

I kiss her, then Liam, until I can't tell whose hands are whose, whose lips, whose teeth. Hailey is the first to get her shirt off, tossing it aside before crawling into my lap and straddling me.

But the cot is too small for all three of us, and by the sound of the creaking, I'm not sure it will hold all our weight.

I push up from the cot, decision made before I even think it through. "Floor," I mutter, and we spill onto the cold linoleum, dragging blankets with us in a haphazard nest. It's not comfortable, but it's space, and that's what we need.

Hailey's on her back now, arching as I slide over her, my hands pinning her wrists above her head. She wriggles, testing my grip, her eyes gleaming with that same wild spark from the cabin. Liam's beside us, his shirt half-unbuttoned, fingers fumbling with the rest as he watches, breath coming fast.

I release one of Hailey's hands to help him, yanking the fabric open and off his shoulders. His skin is warm under my palm, marked with bruises from the fight, but he doesn't flinch. Instead, he leans in, capturing Hailey's mouth while I work on her pants, tugging them down her hips.

She kicks them free, laughing again—that sounds like a dare—and pulls Liam closer by his hair. I feel a surge of something possessive, but it's tangled with want, not jealousy. This is us, all of us, no room for anything else.

My own clothes come off in a blur—belt clinking against the floor, boots thudding as I shove them aside. Naked now, the air hits me, but Hailey's body heat draws me back like a magnet. I settle between her thighs, feeling her slick and ready, her nails digging into my shoulders as I push in slow.

She gasps into Liam's kiss, her body clenching around me, and it's everything—tight, hot, alive. Liam breaks away to watch, his hand trailing down my back, then lower, urging me on with a firm press.

I thrust deeper, finding a rhythm that matches the pounding of my heart, each movement pulling a moan from Hailey's lips. She's writhing beneath me, her free hand clutching at Liam's arm, drawing him in closer. He leans down, his mouth on her breast, sucking and teasing until she arches higher, her inner walls pulsing around me in response.

The floor is unforgiving against my knees, but the discomfort only sharpens the edge of it all, makes every sensation more vivid. I can feel Liam's hand sliding farther, fingers exploring the curve of my ass, pressing in a way that's both commanding and tentative, like he's testing boundaries we've already shattered.

"Knox," Hailey breathes, her voice breaking on my name, eyes locked on mine. There's a vulnerability there, mixed with the fire, and it hits me hard—how close we came to losing this, losing each other. I lean down to kiss her, swallowing her cries as I pick up the pace, driving into her with a need that's almost punishing.

Liam shifts, his body pressing against my side now, his erection hard against my thigh. I reach for him without thinking, wrapping my hand around his length, stroking in time with my thrusts. He groans, the sound low and guttural, his hips bucking into my grip. His free hand finds its way between Hailey and me, fingers circling her clit, making her buck wildly.

"I don't ever want this to end. Us," she moans.

His fingers don't let up on her, circling faster, and she shatters first—clenching around me in waves, her cry muffled as she buries her face in my neck, nails raking my back.

That pushes me over, the sensation too much, and I come hard inside her, groaning into her hair, hips jerking as everything whites out for a second. Liam's right there with us, his body shuddering as I stroke him through it, feeling him pulse and spill over my hand, warm and messy. He collapses against me, all three of us a heap on the blankets, breaths ragged in the dim light.

I lie there, sandwiched between them, my chest heaving as the world sharpens back into focus. Hailey's head rests on my shoulder, her fingers tracing lazy patterns on my chest, while Liam's arm drapes over my waist, heavy and possessive.

Chapter Thirty-Seven

LIAM

The interviews take forever. We tell our story three times each, to three different officers, in three different rooms that all smell like stale coffee and industrial cleaner. I stick to the edited version—kidnapped by Marlena Kade, held captive, escaped. I leave out certain details. The Snowflake Diamond currently tucked in Hailey's pocket, for instance. The fact that we stole it in the first place. Minor omissions.

The RCMP are skeptical at first. Can't blame them. A wealthy collector kidnapping three Americans in the Canadian wilderness sounds insane. Michelle backs us up with what she knows—the distress signal she flagged a week ago, three beaten strangers on her doorstep, armed mercenaries who followed them to her station and opened fire. She doesn't know the full story, but she doesn't need to. The avalanche site. The siege at her station. The bodies of Marlena's guards scattered across the snow.

They start taking it seriously after that.

"We'll issue warrants," the lead investigator tells us. She's a no-nonsense woman in her fifties with steel-gray hair and tired eyes. "But Ms. Kade has resources. Private jets, offshore accounts, properties in countries without extradition treaties. She could be anywhere by now."

True. Marlena's gone to ground, disappeared into whatever bolthole she prepared for exactly this scenario. A woman like her always has contingencies. I wonder if losing the diamond will eat at her, if she'll come back to finish what she started. Part of me hopes she does. Part of me knows better than to feel safe yet.

During a break between interviews, I step outside to clear my head. My phone—recovered from the cabin, miraculously still functional despite everything—buzzes in my pocket.

Unknown number.

I answer cautiously. "Yes?"

"Mr. Calloway." A man. Russian accent, soft but with an undercurrent that makes the hair on my neck stand up. "My name is Viktor Kedrov. But you already know that, don't you? I believe you owe me a diamond."

I freeze.

Viktor Kedrov. The original owner. The man we stole from five years ago. The reason Hailey and I have been running ever since.

"The Snowflake Diamond," he continues, almost conversational. "My diamond. I've been tracking it for five years, Mr. Calloway. When Marlena Kade began her hunt for you and Ms. Parker, my people took notice. I've been watching this entire situation unfold with great interest."

My mind races through the implications. He knows where we are. He knows what happened. He's probably known every step of the way, was just waiting for the right moment to make contact.

"Hold on," I say. "I'm putting you on speaker. My partners need to hear this."

I head back inside and find Knox and Hailey in the station's small cafeteria, sitting at a plastic table with cups of terrible coffee neither of them is drinking. Hailey looks up when I walk in, and something in my expression must tip her off because her whole body goes tense.

I set the phone on the table between us and tap the speaker icon. "Go ahead. They're listening."

"Excellent," Viktor says. "Then I won't have to repeat myself. I have a proposal for you. Give me back the diamond and I let the three of you live. But that's not all I want. Marlena Kade has become a thorn in my side for reasons that don't concern you. I want information. Tell me where she'll go, who she'll contact, how she'll try to move the pieces she's stolen. In exchange, I'll ensure your safety.

My people will deal with Ms. Kade, and you three will never hear from me again."

Knox stiffens. Hailey's gone very still.

"And if we refuse?" I ask.

His laugh is soft. Chilling. "Then I assume you're working with Marlena. Accomplices. And I treat you accordingly." A pause. "Mr. Calloway, I am not an unreasonable man. But I am also not a forgiving one. My diamond was stolen. I want it back. Other priceless items have been taken by Ms. Kade over the years—items that belonged to associates of mine. I want them back as well. Help me retrieve them all, and we part as . . . not friends, certainly. But not enemies either."

"How do we know you'll keep your word?" Knox cuts in.

"You don't," Viktor says. "But consider the alternative. Marlena has resources, but she cannot hide forever. Neither can you. Eventually, one of us will find you. I prefer we reach an accommodation now, while you still have something to offer."

"We need a minute," Hailey says.

"Five minutes," Viktor agrees. "I'll call again."

The line goes dead.

We stare at each other across the table.

"It's another trap," Knox says immediately. He's already positioning himself between me and the door.

"Maybe," I say. "But Viktor's different from Marlena. He's old school. Russian mob ties going back decades. Men like him operate on a code. If he says he'll let us go in exchange for information, he might actually mean it."

"Or he kills us the second we give him what he wants," Hailey says. She's turning her coffee cup in circles, not looking at either of us.

"That's the risk," I admit. "But think about it. We help Viktor track down Marlena, he gets whatever else she's stolen from his people, and we walk away clean. No more looking over our shoulders. No more wondering when the next attack is coming."

Knox is quiet, thinking. I can practically see him running tactical assessments in his head, weighing probabilities and outcomes. "What exactly would we have to do?"

"Give him the diamond. Tell him where Marlena's likely to try to fence what she has. Black market contacts, private collectors who don't ask questions. I know some from our old days." I glance at Hailey. "You probably know more."

She nods slowly, still not meeting my eyes.

"And if Marlena gets caught in the crossfire?" she asks.

"Then karma's a bitch." I don't feel even a twinge of guilt saying it. "She kidnapped us. Threatened to kill us. Sent armed mercenaries after us through an avalanche. I'm not losing sleep if Viktor catches up to her."

We discuss it for the remaining minutes, voices low so the officers passing through can't hear. The ethics of selling out another criminal to save ourselves. The risks of trusting a man like Viktor Kedrov. The potential reward of finally being free.

It's tempting. God, it's tempting. Not money this time, not a score. Just safety. Just the ability to live without fear, to sleep through the night without one eye open, to walk down a street without checking every reflection for someone following.

I watch Hailey's face as she thinks it through. Watch Knox's. We've been through hell together, the three of us. Survived things that should have killed us. Whatever we decide, we decide together.

Finally, Hailey looks up. Meets my eyes, then Knox's.

"Fuck her," she says quietly. "She made her choices. Now she gets to live with the consequences."

Knox nods once. "Agreed."

The phone rings exactly five minutes after Viktor hung up. I answer on the second ring and put it back on speaker.

"We'll do it."

"Excellent." Viktor sounds pleased but not surprised. He expected this outcome. "Tell me everything."

"Not yet," Hailey says.

I look at her. Knox looks at her. She's leaning forward with her elbows on the table, wearing the expression I remember from every job we ever pulled together. The one that means she's three moves ahead and everyone else is still playing the last turn.

"You want the diamond. We'll give it to you. But we both know that's not enough to keep you from coming after us once you have it. So here's what we're offering on top of it, and here's what we want in return."

Kedrov is quiet. Listening.

She looks at me. My cue. She doesn't know what I have. Neither does Knox. I never told them what happened when Marlena had me alone. But Hailey knows me well enough to know I walked out of that room with something.

"I spent six weeks in direct contact with Marlena before she grabbed us," I say. "I know how she communicates, who she uses as intermediaries, how she moves money. I know the channels she operates in because they're the same channels we used to work, and she recruited me through those networks."

Knox's eyebrows go up. This is new information for him too.

"She uses a broker in Zurich as her primary go-between. A woman named Adler. Everything flows through her. Acquisitions, payments, logistics. You find Adler, you find Marlena's entire supply chain.

"When she pulled me out of the cabin, she had me for hours. She talked. She couldn't help herself. She told me about properties she owns under shell companies, places she goes when things get hot." I can feel Hailey and Knox staring at me. I never shared any of this. I wasn't ready. But Kedrov doesn't need to know that. "I'll give you all of it."

Hailey recovers fast. "And during transport to the mine, we saw her operation firsthand. Helicopter model, airstrip coordinates, guard count, the mining camp she's been using as a base. Knox can give you every tactical detail down to the weapons her people carry."

"She also talked about the divorce," I add. "About how you listed the Snowflake as her asset after you already knew it was stolen. About how she lost tens of millions in the settlement because of a diamond that didn't exist anymore. She's not just hunting this stone because she wants it. She's hunting it because destroying you is the only thing she's thought about for five years. If you want to find her before she finds you, we can help. Nobody else is going to hand you that."

"And in return?" Kedrov asks.

"You leave us alone. Permanently. No surveillance, no contacts, no surprises. We disappear, you forget we exist."

"And if I choose not to honor that arrangement?"

Knox speaks up. "Then our friend Cole Asher gets involved. You may know the name. Tech billionaire, extensive private security, the kind of resources that make your operation look like a lemonade stand." He lets that sink in. "Cole knows where we are. He knows who we're talking to. And if anything happens to any of us, a car accident, a mugging, a gas leak, anything, he has instructions to make your life very expensive and very public. Every asset, every shell company, every connection you've spent decades building. He'll burn it all down and enjoy doing it."

Nobody speaks for long enough that I start to wonder if he's hung up.

"Mr. Asher," Kedrov says finally. "Yes. I know the name." Another pause. "You've thought this through."

"We've had ten days in a cabin with nothing to do but think," Hailey says.

"Very well. The diamond and the information, in exchange for my complete disinterest in your future existence. I accept these terms."

So we give him everything. My six weeks of direct contact with Marlena's network. The broker in Zurich. The shell companies and bolt-holes she mentioned while she had me alone. Knox walks Kedrov through the transport details: helicopter make and model, airstrip location, guard rotations, weapons, the mining camp layout.

I fill in what I remember from our days working the circuit. Fences she'd use to move stolen pieces, a German in Munich, a Frenchwoman in Lyon, an Italian family operation in Milan. Between the three of us, we hand Kedrov a map of Marlena's world he couldn't have assembled on his own.

"There's a private collector in Geneva," Knox adds. We both look at him. He shrugs. "Cole Asher's world. You hear things. Guy named Renaud, buys high-end pieces, doesn't ask where they come from."

Hailey nods and keeps going. Underground auction houses that operate in the shadows of the legitimate art world. How Marlena thinks, what drives her, the obsession with Kedrov that's eaten her alive for half a decade.

Viktor is thorough, asking clarifying questions, cross-referencing information. He knows more than I expected—testing us, probably, making sure we're not feeding him false leads.

When he's satisfied, there's a pause.

"You've been most helpful," Viktor says. "As agreed, you will not hear from me again. But Ms. Parker—a word of advice, if I may."

Hailey leans toward the phone. "I'm listening."

"If you choose to continue in this profession, choose your targets more carefully in the future. Stealing from someone like Marlena Kade?" He makes a dismissive sound. "Foolish but survivable. Stealing from me?" His tone goes cold, all pretense of pleasantry stripped away. "There would be no second chance. Do we understand each other?"

"Yes," Hailey says quietly. "We understand."

"Good." The warmth returns, artificial as a mask. "Then I wish you a happy new year. And a long, quiet life."

The call ends.

None of us speaks for a long moment.

"So that's it?" Knox asks. "We just . . . trust him?"

"We don't trust him," Hailey says. "We trust Cole. And Kedrov trusts that we're not bluffing about Cole." She picks up her coffee, looks at it, puts it back down. "That's not the same thing as trust. But it holds."

"And Marlena?"

I shrug. "Viktor's people will find her eventually. Either way, she's not our problem anymore."

It should feel like a victory. We survived. We're free. The threat that's been hanging over us has been neutralized, one way or another.

But sitting in this fluorescent-lit cafeteria with bad coffee going cold in front of us, all I feel is tired. Exhaustion that has nothing to do with the physical ordeal we've been through.

We finish with the RCMP another hour later. Sign statements, provide contact information, promise to make ourselves available if they have follow-up questions. The investigation will continue, but we're cleared to leave. Just victims caught up in something beyond our control.

Michelle meets us outside the station, her dark hair catching the late afternoon light. She's back in her ranger gear, looking more at home than she ever did holding a rifle during the siege.

"So you're really heading back to New York," she says. It's not quite a question.

"Yeah." Hailey pulls her into a hug. "Thank you. For everything. We'd be dead without you."

Michelle hugs her back, then steps away with that easy smile. "Just doing my job. Well, slightly outside my job description, but close enough."

Knox clears his throat. "About that." He pulls a business card from his wallet—I didn't even know he still had one on him after everything—and hands it to her. "If you ever want a change of scenery, look me up. Cole Asher runs Asher Industries in Manhattan. We could use someone with your skills. Security, crisis management, keeping idiots alive when they get in over their heads." He glances at Hailey and me. "We seem to attract a lot of that."

Michelle looks at the card, then back at Knox. A smile tugs at her lips. "I appreciate the offer. Really. But I belong out here." She gestures at the mountains rising behind us, the endless stretch of forest. "The woods are home."

"Fair enough," Knox says. "But the offer stands. Anytime.

"One more thing," Knox says. "My friend Cole, the one I work for. His company has been funding rural infrastructure projects for the last few years. Clean energy, satellite internet, equipment upgrades for communities that are off the grid. It's good PR for him and actual help for people who need it." He pauses. "I can make a call. See about getting some resources sent up here."

Michelle looks skeptical. "What kind of resources?"

"Start with a generator that doesn't sound like it's dying. Maybe a satellite uplink that doesn't cut out every time the wind changes. Go from there."

Michelle laughs, shaking her head. "I'm not going to say no to that."

Hailey grins. "You better watch out. You may end up liking being a city girl."

Michelle laughs and tucks the card into her pocket. "I'll keep that in mind. Now get out of here before another psychopath shows up and I have to save your asses again."

We catch a ride to the nearest town with an airport. Book flights back to New York. First class, because after everything we've been through, we deserve comfortable seats and free champagne.

Hailey and Knox take the two seats together. I'm across the aisle, close enough to see them but not touch. She falls asleep against his shoulder somewhere over Manitoba, and he pulls a blanket up over her without waking her. His hand rests on her knee, protective even in sleep.

I watch them for a moment before looking away. We've been tangled together for days—the three of us sharing warmth, sharing breath, sharing things I never expected to share with anyone again. And now there's an armrest and an aisle between us, and it feels like more.

Knox catches my eye across the gap. Holds my gaze for a long moment. Then he reaches across the aisle, palm up.

I take his hand. His grip is warm and solid, and I feel a sense of calm.

We stay like that as the plane crosses into American airspace. Knox's hand in mine, Hailey's head on his shoulder, the three of us connected even with the distance between us.

I should sleep. I'm running on fumes and adrenaline and whatever reserves I didn't know I had. But my mind won't stop spinning.

We made a deal with one devil to escape another. Sold out Marlena Kade to save ourselves. It was the right call—the only call, really. But I can't help wondering what it says about us that the choice came so easily.

Maybe nothing. Maybe survival is its own morality. Maybe when someone tries to kill you, all bets are off and you do whatever you have to do to make it out the other side.

Or maybe we're just not as good as we like to think we are.

I close my eyes and try not to think about it. Somewhere over the Great Lakes, I finally drift off, Knox's fingers still intertwined with mine.

Chapter Thirty-Eight

HAILEY

The brownstone looks exactly the same as when I left it.

Two weeks. I've been gone two weeks, and nothing about this building has changed. The same worn steps. The same brass knocker. The same crack in the second-floor window.

I dig my keys out and unlock the door. Knox and Liam follow me up.

My apartment smells stale. Closed-up. The heat must have kicked off at some point because it's barely warmer inside than out. I flip the light switch and there it is: my life, exactly as I left it. Bookshelves overflowing. Dark walls I painted myself. The dried roses hanging near the kitchen window, petals faded, stems brittle.

Knox moves past the threshold slowly. When he picked me up for our first date, he'd stood right there, too polite to come in without invitation. Now he walks through my space like he's finally been given permission.

Liam stops in front of the roses. His roses.

"You kept them," he says quietly.

"I kept all of them."

I watch them both taking in my space—Knox by the bookshelf now, running his finger along the spines, Liam still transfixed by the dried petals he left on my doorstep week after week. They've spent months learning me from the outside. My patterns, my habits, my secrets. They know if I've been bad or good. And they're still here.

I pull my phone from my bag—the RCMP returned our belongings from the lodge before we flew out. The phone's been dead since before the kidnapping. I'd meant to charge it that first night, but then the door splintered open and nothing else mattered.

The charger is where I always leave it. I connect the phone and wait.

The screen lights up. Then the notifications start.

Missed calls: forty-seven. Voicemails: twelve. Text messages: I stop counting after sixty.

Sloane's messages escalate from concerned to frantic. The most recent, sent this morning: I don't know what's happening but please just let me know you're alive. Please.

I'm alive, I type quickly. I'm so sorry. I'm back in the city. I'll explain everything, I promise. I just need a few days.

The response comes in seconds: OH THANK GOD. I've been losing my mind. What the hell happened? Are you okay? Do you need me to come over?

I'm okay. Really. And no, don't come over yet. I just need some time.

Time for WHAT? Hailey, you've been GONE for two weeks. TWO WEEKS with no word except that bullshit text about a "trip." I almost called your parents. Do you even have parents? I don't actually know because you never talk about your life before New York!

She's not wrong.

I know. I'm sorry. I'll tell you everything. Just . . . not yet. Please.

A long pause. Then: Fine. But you owe me the world's longest explanation and at least three bottles of wine.

Deal.

I send a similar message to Chloe, who responds with seventeen exclamation points and a promise to murder me if I ever scare her like that again.

"Cole's going to want answers," Knox says. "I told him family emergency, but he's not stupid."

"What are you going to tell him?"

"Haven't figured that out yet." He pulls out his phone, scrolls through his own wall of messages. "He can wait until after New Year's, and after we hand off the diamond to Viktor. I don't want Sloane and Cole anywhere near that when we do."

Liam reaches up and touches one of the dried petals. "This is strange," he says. "Being inside. Being here because you asked me to be."

"And now?"

"Now I don't know what to do with my hands."

Knox snorts. "Welcome to the club."

"We should order food," I say. "I've been craving Thai from that place on Smith Street for two weeks."

We get Thai. We eat on the bed because my kitchen table only fits one. Knox argues about peanuts in pad thai—he's wrong—while Liam systematically steals every dumpling when we're not looking.

Somewhere between the second bottle of wine and the last of the spring rolls, we start talking. Really talking. About what happens next. About Knox going back to work, about me going back to Sloane, about Liam staying.

"I don't know how to do this," he admits. "The staying part. I haven't had a real address in five years."

"You learn. You figure it out."

"And if I screw it up?"

"Then you have people who help you fix it."

He looks at me, then at Knox.

"I love you," I say. "Both of you. I need you to know that."

Knox goes still. Liam's breath catches.

"I love you too," Liam says quietly. "Both of you. I've been trying not to say it because I thought it would ruin things."

Knox reaches for us both, pulls us in. "I love you," he says, rough and low. "I'm shit at saying it. But I do."

We sit there tangled together, letting those words settle.

"You need your rest," Knox says, solidifying that even in safety the man is always going to be my protector.

I pull back slightly from Knox's embrace, meeting his gaze with a playful smirk. "Rest? With you two around? That's ambitious."

Liam stands up from the bed, stretching his arms overhead, his shirt riding up just enough to reveal a sliver of toned abdomen that makes my pulse quicken. "She's right. We're not exactly the lullaby type."

I don't even hesitate before I completely strip down to nothing.

"Fuuuuuck," Liam groans.

I stand there, exposed and unapologetic, feeling the cool draft from the window kiss my skin.

He steps closer, his hand reaching out to trace the curve of my hip, tentative at first, then bolder, his fingers warm against my chilled flesh.

Knox doesn't say a word; he just moves, closing the distance in one fluid motion, his mouth crashing onto mine. I arch into him, my hands fisting in his shirt, pulling him tighter as Liam presses in from behind, his lips brushing the nape of my neck.

Liam's kisses trail lower, his hands sliding around to cup my breasts, thumbs circling my nipples until they harden under his touch. I gasp into Knox's mouth, our tongues tangling in a heated dance that steals my breath, his grip on my waist firm and possessive. Outside the city hums with a million lives, but it's nothing compared to what's building between us, raw and urgent.

I reach back with one hand, finding Liam's thigh and digging my nails in, urging him closer. He grinds against me, his arousal evident through his jeans.

Knox breaks the kiss just long enough to yank his shirt over his head, revealing the hard planes of his chest, marked with faint scars that only make him sexier. I trace one with my fingertip, feeling his heart thud wildly beneath.

"God, you're fucking beautiful," Liam praises against my ear as he nips at the lobe. His fingers dip lower, teasing between my thighs, finding me already wet and ready.

"Get naked. Now," I order both of them.

They comply without a word, Knox's eyes darkening with hunger as he strips off his jeans, kicking them aside, his cock springing free, hard and ready. Liam follows suit, shedding his clothes in a hurried blur, his body lean and powerful, every inch of him screaming desire. I drink in the sight of them both, my heart pounding, fire erupting in my core.

Knox pulls me back into his arms, his bare skin hot against mine, while Liam circles around, sandwiching me between them. I feel Liam's erection pressing against my ass, insistent, as Knox claims my mouth again, deeper this time, his hands roaming down to grip my thighs and lift me slightly off the ground. I wrap my legs around his waist, moaning as the friction sends sparks through me.

"Take me," I whisper against Knox's lips. "Hurt me in the best way possible."

He lowers me onto the bed with slow intent, his body covering mine like a shield against the world, but there's no shielding from this heat. Liam slides in beside us, his hand trailing fire down my side, fingers digging into my hip as if to anchor me.

"You sure about that?" Knox asks as his lips brush my collarbone before he nips at the skin there, hard enough to sting but not break. I arch up, a whimper escaping me, loving the bite of pain that blooms into pleasure.

"More," I demand, my fingers tangling in his hair, pulling him down. He obliges, his mouth latching onto my breast, sucking and teasing with his teeth, while Liam's hand slips between my legs again, two fingers plunging inside me without warning. I cry out, my body clenching around him, the sudden fullness making my head spin.

The pleasure builds in waves, crashing over me as Liam's fingers curl inside, stroking that perfect spot that has me bucking against his hand. Knox's mouth moves to my other breast, his tongue swirling around the peak before he bites down just enough to send a jolt straight to my core. I gasp, my free hand reaching for Liam's hair, pulling him closer so his lips find my shoulder, where he sucks a mark into my skin.

"Knox," I breathe, my voice ragged, "I need you inside me. Now."

He lifts his head, eyes blazing with that wolfish intensity I crave, and positions himself between my thighs. Liam withdraws his fingers, leaving me aching and empty, but only for a moment. Knox thrusts in deep, filling me completely, and I cry out, my nails raking down his back as the stretch borders on too much, just the way I like it.

Liam shifts, kneeling beside us, his hand wrapping around his cock, stroking slowly as he watches. "That's it, take him like a good girl," he praises before leaning down to capture my lips in a bruising kiss. I moan into his mouth while Knox sets a punishing rhythm, each drive pushing me higher, the bed creaking under us.

Knox's hips slam against mine, his hands pinning my wrists above my head. I struggle against his hold, not to escape but to feel the restraint, the delicious burn of his grip. "Harder," I beg, and he complies, his teeth grazing my neck, leaving marks that will linger tomorrow.

Liam breaks the kiss, trailing his mouth down to join Knox's assault on my senses. He bites at my earlobe, then whispers, "You're ours," before sliding his hand between us to circle my clit, the added pressure making stars explode behind my eyelids. I arch off the bed, caught in their dual rhythm, pleasure coiling tight in my belly like a spring ready to snap.

"Don't stop," I gasp, my body trembling, on the edge of oblivion. Knox growls low in his throat, thrusting deeper, faster, while Liam's fingers work me relentlessly. The wave crests, and I shatter, screaming their names as ecstasy rips through me, my inner walls pulsing around Knox, pulling him over the edge with me.

He follows seconds later, burying his face in my neck with a guttural moan, his release hot and claiming. We collapse in a tangle of limbs, breaths heaving, but Liam's still hard against my side, his eyes dark with unspent need. I turn to him, a wicked smile curving my lips. "Your turn."

Knox rolls to the side, his chest still rising and falling rapidly, but he watches us with a satisfied smirk, one hand lazily stroking my thigh as if to remind me he's not done yet.

I push Liam back against the pillows, straddling his hips, feeling his cock twitch eagerly beneath me. "You've been so patient," I coo, grinding down just enough to tease, watching his jaw clench with restraint. My hands explore the ridges of his abs, nails scraping lightly, leaving faint red trails that make him hiss in approval.

"Patience has its rewards," he rasps, his fingers digging into my hips, guiding me as I position myself over him. I sink down slowly, savoring the way he fills me, inch by delicious inch, my body still sensitive from the first round. A low moan escapes me, and I rock my hips, setting a rhythm that's about drawing out his pleasure, making him beg for more.

Knox shifts closer, his lips brushing my shoulder, then trails kisses down my spine. "Ride him hard, pretty girl," he encourages. "Let him stretch that tight pussy of yours with his big dick." His hand slips between us, finding my clit again, rubbing in slow circles that match my movements. I gasp, leaning forward to brace myself on Liam's chest, my breasts brushing his skin as I pick up the pace.

Liam thrusts up to meet me, his hands roaming to squeeze my ass, pulling me down harder with each stroke. "Fuck, you feel incredible," he groans, his head tipping back, exposing the column of his throat. I lean in, nipping at it, sucking a mark that mirrors the ones they've left on me, claiming him right back.

The intensity builds again, faster this time, my body coiling tight around him. Knox's fingers don't let up, and he reaches around with his other hand to pinch my nipple, twisting just enough to send a spike of pain-laced pleasure straight to my core. I cry out, my movements turning frantic, chasing that peak once more.

Liam's control snaps, his hips bucking wildly beneath me, driving deep. "Come with me," he demands, his voice strained, and that's all it takes. The orgasm hits me like a thunderclap, ripping through every nerve, my vision blurring as I clench around him. He follows with a shout, spilling inside me, his body shuddering in release.

We collapse together, a sweaty, satisfied heap, with Knox wrapping his arms around us both. Outside, the city hums on. In here, our breaths sync in the quiet.

Later, tangled in sheets that need washing, Liam traces patterns on my hip.

"New Year's Eve," he says. "That's when we face everything?"

"That's when we start," Knox confirms.

Four more days. The three of us.

I close my eyes, pressed between two heartbeats. My apartment with its dried roses and dark walls.

It's not the cabin.

It's home.

Acknowledgments

I want to start off by thanking my husband for reading every single one of my books. Every single one and never said a negative word. To my daughters, who tolerate what it means to have an author as a mother and the grammar police overseeing every text message. It's because of you that I keep my dream alive. You are my inspiration. The three of you are the reason I spend countless hours writing these books.

I also wouldn't be here typing this book if it weren't for Laura and Katie. Laura . . . we make a damn good team. And Katie . . . you keep me sane. I reached *New York Times* because of you two, and that will never be forgotten.

And I also want to thank all my industry friends I have made along the way. I don't have a normal workday, ordinary coworkers, or your traditional water-cooler talk. But I wouldn't trade it in for anything. And Zoe . . . thank you for the daily.

And one last thank-you to the friends and family who often questioned if I had a real job. Well . . . if you are reading this, then I think you now know I do!

Thank you everyone. I'm living my dream.

Acknowledgments

About the Author

Alta Hensley is a *New York Times* and *USA Today* bestselling author of dark romance. Twisted, clever, and occasionally unhinged, her books deliver morally gray anti-heroes, sharp-tongued heroines, and happily ever afters that taste even sweeter after a little ruin. With a signature blend of grit, wit, and heat, Alta's stories prove one thing: Villains deserve love too. Alta lives on the foggy coast of Oregon with her husband, two daughters, and a pair of dogs who think they're in charge. When she's not writing redemption for the irredeemable, she's walking the coastline or sipping craft beer in eccentric little bars that feel like they belong in her books.